PRAISE FOR *THE GRAYS*

"A terrific read . . . A quantum leap back to the top of his fictional form, powered by his newer nonfiction obsessions."
—*Booklist*

"*The Grays* is the novel Whitley Strieber was born to write. It's more than just an alien-abduction novel. The aliens feel so authentic, and their collaborators—our own high-ranking government officials—are so unforgettable, they will forever change the way you view the world. When you put the book down in the wee, wee hours before dawn, you *will* believe. If you thought *Communion* chilled you to the bone, *The Grays* will freeze your marrow. As with all of Whitley's books, you are in for the ride of your life."   —Douglas Preston,
New York Times bestselling author of *Tyrannosaur Canyon*

"Strieber's aliens and their blood-curdling plot to comman-deer our very souls come shockingly alive in this utterly unique thriller. When I put it down, I was afraid to leave my house. His characters seem so real—especially the children—you start to believe we *are* under alien occupa-tion. I'll never laugh at alien-abduction stories again. Whit-ley Strieber crams more thrills and chills into a novel than any other writer I know."   —David Hagberg,
USA Today bestselling author of *Soldier of God*

"In *The Grays*, Whitley does for alien occupation what he and Art Bell did for global warming and planet-wide disas-ter in *The Coming Global Superstorm*. Whitley has written the definitive alien-occupation novel."   —William J. Birnes,
coauthor of the *New York Times* bestseller
The Day After Roswell

THE
GRAYS

WHITLEY STRIEBER

A TOM DOHERTY ASSOCIATES BOOK • NEW YORK

This is a work of fiction. All of the characters, organizations, and events portrayed in this novel are either products of the author's imagination or are used fictitiously.

THE GRAYS

A Forge Book
Published by Tom Doherty Associates, LLC
175 Fifth Avenue
New York, NY 10010

www.tor-forge.com

Forge® is a registered trademark of Tom Doherty Associates, LLC.

ISBN-13: 978-0-7653-5259-0
ISBN-10: 0-7653-5259-1

First Edition: August 2006
First Mass Market Edition: June 2007

Printed in the United States of America

0 9 8 7 6 5 4 3 2 1

This book is dedicated to those millions of people around the world who, like me, have faced the enigma of the grays and are also left with the certain knowledge that they represent a genuine and spectacularly provocative unknown. It is my hope that this work of fiction will penetrate into that unknown and draw its secrets into discovering light.

ACKNOWLEDGMENTS

THE GRAYS has been many years in the making. I have not the words to thank Anne Strieber for her patience, her great courage, and her willingness to travel with me on what must seem like a quixotic journey indeed, seeking to find in fiction the truth about the grays, which is too elusive to bring to genuinely sharp focus in factual narrative.

I would also like to thank my agent, Russell Galen, whose faith in this project kept it alive, Tom Doherty and Bob Gleason of Tor Books, who were willing to say yes and have provided me with such useful discipline and insight, Cary Brokaw and John Calley, whose enthusiastic support has been an inspiration, and Aaron Craig Geller, whose attention to detail and story sense so helpfully illuminated my efforts.

THE GRAYS

PART ONE
NIGHT FLYERS

Who's in the next room?—who?
  I seem to hear
Somebody muttering firm in a language new
  That chills the ear.
No: you catch not his tongue who has entered there.

—THOMAS HARDY
  "Who's in the Next Room?"

ONE

BECAUSE WE KNOW IT IS there, danger in an obvious place—on a battlefield, say—is often far less of a threat than it is on a quiet street in a small town. For example, on a street deep in America where three little boys rode interlocking figure eights on their bicycles, and on a sweet May evening, too, any danger would be a surprise. And a great and terrible danger—impossible.

Not all of the boys were in danger. In fact, two of them were as profoundly safe as anybody else in Madison, Wisconsin, on the scented evening of May 21, 1977. The third boy, however, was not so lucky. Not nearly.

Because of something buried deeply in his genes, he was of more than normal interest to someone that is supposed not to exist, but does exist—in fact, is master of this earth.

It was too bad for this child—in fact, tragic—because these creatures—if they could even be called that—caused phenomenal trauma, scarring trauma . . . to those of their victims who lived.

Play ended with the last of the sun, and lights glowed on the porches of Woody Lane, as one by one the boys of the lane retired.

Danny rode a little longer, and was watched by Burly, the dog of Mr. Ehmer. Soon Mr. Ehmer himself came across his lawn. His pipe glowed as he drew on it, and he said, "Say there, Danny, you want to come night fishin' with me and your Uncle Frank? We've been getting some good'uns all this week."

Danny was a lonely child, saddled with an alcoholic mother and a violent father, so he welcomed these chances to be away from the tensions of home. He could take his sleeping bag and unroll it in the bottom of the boat, and if his line jerked it would wake him up. But not tonight. "I got Scouts real early," he said, "gotta get up."

Mr. Ehmer leaned back on his heels. "You're turnin' down fishin'?"

"Gotta be at the park at nine. That means seven-thirty mass."

"Well, yes it does. It does at that." He drew on the pipe again. "We get a sturgeon, we'll name 'im for you." He laughed then, a gentle rustle in his throat, in the first gusts of the wind that rises with the moon. He left Danny to go down the dark of Woody Lane alone, pushing the pedals of his Raleigh as hard as he could, not wanting to look up at the darkening sky again, not daring to look behind him.

As he parked his bike and ran up to the lit back door, he was flooded with relief as he hopped on the doorstep and went into the lighted kitchen. He smelled the lingering odor of fried chicken, felt hungry but knew there was none left in the house. He went into the living room.

He didn't stay long. *Love Boat* was like a religion with Mom and Dad, and then came *Fantasy Island*. He'd rather be in his room with the *Batman* he'd bought from Ron Bloom for twenty cents.

At the same moment a few miles away, Katelyn Burns, who adored *Love Boat*, watched and received advice from her mother about painting her toenails. Very red, and use a polish that hardens slowly. They last longer, chip less, good on the toes. Next week school was out and she wanted—had—to paint her toenails for Beach Day.

A magnetism of whispers that Katelyn assumed were her own thoughts had drawn her to Madison, Wisconsin, and to this shabby apartment near the water. An easy place, Madison, the thoughts whispered to her, for a divorcée to find a man. An easy place, they most certainly did not tell her, from which to steal a child, carry her out and take her far, so that when her screams started, there would be none to hear her but the night wind. And so it would be this night, after the Love Boat sailed away and silence filled the house.

As Saturday evening ended, the moon rode over houses that, one by one, became dark. Madison slept in peace, then, as the hours wore past midnight.

Sometime after three, Danny Callaghan became aware of a change around him, enough of a change to draw him out of sleep. He opened his eyes—and saw nothing but stars. For a moment, he thought he'd gone night fishing after all. Then he realized he was still in bed and the stars were coming from his own home planetarium, bought from Edmund Scientific for nine dollars. It was a dark blue plastic sphere with a light in it. The plastic was dotted with pinholes in the pattern of the night sky, and when you turned out the lights and turned the planetarium on, magic happened: the heavens appeared all around you.

He hadn't turned the planetarium on, though, and that fact made the acid of fear rise in his throat. He opened his mouth to call for his dad, but there was no sound, just a puff of breath. As the stars crossed his face, twisting along his nose and across his eyes, his tears flowed in helpless silence.

The only sounds were the humming of the planetarium's motor and the breeze fluttering the front-yard oak. Dan sat up on the bedside. Like a man buttoning his coat for a journey, he buttoned his pajama top, until all four big buttons were neatly closed. A thought whispered to him, "Stand up, look out the window . . ." He clutched the bedsheets with both hands. The old oak shook its leaves at him, and the thoughts whispered, "Come on . . . come on."

Then he knew that his toes had touched the floor, and he was up in the flowing stars. Then he floated to the window. As he moved closer, he saw it sliding open. Then he went faster and moved through it. He tried to grab the sash as he passed, but missed. Then he was moving through the limbs of the oak that stood in their front yard, struggling and grabbing at them.

He got his arms around one, but his body turned upward until his feet were pointing at the sky. He held on with all his might, but the pull got stronger and stronger. "Dad," he yelled as he was dislodged and drawn into the sky.

He heard a dog raise a howl, and saw an owl below him, her wings glowing in the moonlight, her voice swept away by the wind.

He rose screaming and struggling, running in the air, clawing at emptiness. Far below him, moonlight danced on Lake Monona's baby waves. And then he was among the night clouds, and he flew in their canyons and soared across their hills, and heard their baby thunder muttering.

The wonder of it silenced his screams at last, but not the tears that poured down his face, or the trembling gasp that came when he slowly passed across the top of a cloud and saw, so very far below, the silver lake and the dots of light that were Madison. He closed his eyes and covered his face with his hands as he moved up toward what looked like a silver island in the sky.

The island had a round opening in it, dark and black.

Then Danny was through the round opening. He stopped in the air, then fell to a floor. Opening his eyes, he found himself in darkness, but not absolute darkness. Moonlight sifted in the opening. Far below, he could see the pinpricks of light that marked fishing boats on the lake's surface.

A cold sorrow enveloped him. Now, here, he remembered this from before. He did not want the little doctors to touch him ever again. He knew, also, that they would, and soon. He thought of jumping back out through the opening, but what would happen then? He went closer to it, leaned out as far as he dared. "MR. EHMER! UNCLE FRANK! HELP ME! PLEASE, UNCLE FRANK!"

A rustling sound. He cringed closer to the edge, wishing he dared jump through. A voice whispered, soft: "Hello?"

He backed away from the form. He could see white—a white face, loose white clothes.

"Help me," the form said.

It was a girl, he could see that now, could hear it in her voice. She was standing on the far side of the opening in

the floor, her face glowing in the faint moonlight that
slanted in.

"Are you from Madison?" she asked. Her voice trembled.

"Yeah. I'm Danny Callaghan."

"I'm Katelyn Burns. I never saw anybody else here
before."

"Me, neither."

"Where are we?"

"I'm not sure."

"'Cause when I come here I remember I was here before, but then when I go home I don't remember anymore."
She lowered her head. Her voice dropped to a hesitant murmur. "Do they take your clothes off, too?"

His face grew hot. He clutched his own shoulders.
"Uh-huh."

"They do stuff to me that's *weird*."

"Some kind of operations."

Her eyes flashed. "Yes, but this isn't a hospital!"

As the two children came together and held each other,
they were watched by cold and careful eyes.

The embrace between the children extended, the girl
in her nightgown, the boy in his pajamas stained with
yesterday's oatmeal. It had nothing to do with sex, they
were too young. They were like two little birds stolen
from the nest, trying to find some safety where there was
none.

"If we dive down to the lake, would that work? Instead
of just jumping?" Dan asked Katelyn.

"I don't know. Maybe not."

"I've got a diving merit badge. I'm going to try," he said.

She sighed, understood. The children moved along a
rickety catwalk, going closer to the opening they had been
drawn through. The ship wasn't high tech. It didn't even
have a way of closing its hatch. It was old and handmade,
but the materials involved were far in advance of our own. It
was constructed of sticks that would not break or burn, and
aluminum foil you could not penetrate even with a bullet.
There were no glowing control panels, nothing like *Star
Trek*. Just tinfoil and plywood, and a tin box full of an ex-

traordinary substance mined out of the Earth, that resisted the pull of gravity.

The creatures hiding near the children knew what they were thinking because they could see not only their fleshy bodies wrapped in their fluttering cloth covers, but also their electric bodies, a shimmering network of lines that coursed through them, the fiery nerves that carried sensation and love and memory, and blue fear racing from the heart.

They could see, in the heads, lines of gold and green changing to red and purple, and they knew that these were also the colors of fear.

Katelyn and Dan gazed down at the shimmering, wrinkled surface of the lake.

"You gonna?" Katelyn asked.

Danny could imagine Mr. Ehmer on the lake smoking his pipe and watching his line. He took a deep breath. What would Mr. Ehmer see, though—a boy falling out of the sky? Maybe, but probably not. Probably they'd think the splash was just a fish jumping.

Then he heard the fluttering sound in the dark that meant the *things* were on the move.

Katelyn drew close to him. But then the slowest trace of a smile flickered on her lips, and she raised her hand. In it was a match.

There was buzzing now, urgent, coming closer.

Katelyn shouted out the opening, "I live in Madison! I live in Madison, Wisconsin!" Her voice carried past the thin walls, echoing loudly, but only the clouds heard it.

Cupping his hands around his mouth, Dan shouted, "Uncle Frank, help us!"

"Who's that?"

"My uncle. He's down there fishing."

She struck the match, and in its flare something moved behind her. A green glow. As he watched, it resolved itself into the slanted shape of an insect eye, but huge. It was right behind her, just inches away. It glittered and disappeared into the shadows, and then the match burned out, and then something slid up under his shirt and slithered along his chest.

He heard Katelyn gasp, heard a scream explode out of her and screamed himself, screamed with all his voice and soul. Arms came around him, and a prick like fire penetrated his chest, went deep, made him gag and filled his mouth with a taste like a dead thing smells.

Now he could not move, could not make a sound. He felt himself being carried, felt his stomach twisting and knotting until gorge came up into his throat.

He could see nothing, hear nothing except Katelyn breathing in little, shocked cries.

There came a hand, extended into a faint light, as if it was meant for him to see, a long hand with fingers like naked branches, each tipped by a black, curving claw. In this hand was a kitchen knife with specks of rust on the blade.

The knife came down on his chest, pricking, then, as the tip of the blade ran along his abdomen, tickling. In the dark nearby, he heard a slicing sound, then a crack, and the bubbling of breath being sucked through liquid. Then a coldness came that extended from his neck down to his groin, and he saw the handle of the knife, which was being used like a saw. As it rose and fell, a coldness grew in his chest. Then, with a sucking sound, two great white things were lifted away from him. He raised his head, looking down at himself. What he saw was so bizarrely unexpected that he just stared. He saw what looked like a wet hamster curled up in the center of his chest, shivering furiously. It lay in a pool of ooze. On either side of it, things like big rubber bladders were expanding and contracting, and hissing as they did so.

Freezing cold and deadly weak, he fell back, his head hitting the hard iron of the bedstead upon which he had been laid.

Then stars came, millions of tiny stars all gold and green and speeding like sparks on a windy night. They surrounded the children, swirling around their bodies. They moved with the grace of a vast school of fish, swarming through the body of one child and then into the air, then through the body of the other. Again it happened, and again, and each time the stars invaded the profound nakedness of their open bodies, the veins and organs glowed. Light poured from their screaming mouths, blasted out of their ears and eyes.

The children struggled but could not rise, screamed but were ignored. The torture, terrible, somehow beautiful, went on.

HALFWAY ACROSS THE CONTINENT IN Colorado, a young officer picked up a phone and called Washington. "Sir, we have a glowboy hovering over Madison, Wisconsin."

"How long?" came the tired voice of Lieutenant Colonel Michael Wilkes.

"Twenty-two minutes, sir. Shows no sign of moving."

Wilkes glanced at his watch. Pushing four in the morning. "You were right to inform me, uh—"

"Lieutenant Langford, sir."

"Yes. Thank you." He put down the phone. The spruce-sounding young lieutenant would order a jet up if the glowboy stayed very much longer. Couldn't have one of the damned things lingering over a major metro area after sunrise. Mike wondered what deviltry it was up to, sighed at his own helplessness, then tossed a pill out of a bottle, knocked it back with a glass of water he kept at his bedside, and hit the sack again.

He might request Eamon Glass to ask Bob about the stationary glowboy, but probably not. Bob was one of the two living grays they had acquired during an extraordinary incident in the New Mexico desert when one of the grays' craft had crashed after it had moved into the range of powerful new radars being tested at White Sands. They had not expected these radars to be there, and their ship's ability to stay aloft had been affected.

The Air Force had raced to the site of the crash and recovered two grays alive, one dead. Three were a triad, the equivalent of a single human being. Without their third partner to complete their decision-making process, the two that remained alive had been relatively helpless, and the capture had been a brilliant success . . . unless, of course, it was, instead, an even more brilliant deception on the part of the grays.

You communicated with Bob and Adam via thought— or rather, Eamon, who was the only person they'd ever found who could manage it, communicated with them.

Somehow, the man used his mind to exchange pictures with them. It was a very strange business, and nobody was sure if it was even really working, but it was all they had, and some of the technological information Eamon had gotten from the creatures was making valuable scientific sense, so there had to be something in it.

But they could not find out what the grays *did* with people. It was awful, though, that was certain. Awful and it came from the sky and the Air Force couldn't do a damn thing about it. So it was secret, and would remain secret.

He groaned, turned over, waited miserably for the pill to work.

IN THE SILVER VEHICLE, THE children struggled, twisting and turning in their captivity. Dan saw something white. He looked at it, trying to resolve its meaning in the haze that still obscured his vision. It was very dark, but he could still see this thing. It dangled as if it was hanging on a clothesline, and he thought it might be a big sheet, wet, because it was dripping, the drops pinging on metal somewhere below.

It was a very strange sort of a sheet, though, because it had a kind of face, a mouth gaping like that of a big lake bass, with two distorted black sockets above it. Were they eye sockets? He thought they must be, because there was also a darkness above them that looked like it might be hair. Then he saw a curliness to it, and a lightness and he knew that it was blond hair—and he had seen blond hair on Katelyn when she lit the match.

He tried to say her name, but there was only a gusty whisper. He wanted his mother, he wanted his dad, he wanted Uncle Frank, who was damn tough, to come up here and *help them*!

Drip, drip, drip.

Then he saw that there was another one, and it had short brown hair and its face was all wobbled like a mirror in the Crazy House at Madison Playland.

When he stared at it, though, he knew: it was his skin. But if it was up there and he was down here, then—

His stomach churned, his heart began raging in his chest, and his throat became so dry it felt as if it had been stuffed with ashes. He wanted to scream, he wanted to beg God for help, but he couldn't make a sound.

Off in the dark, a buzzing sound started. The things in the dark were coming. He looked, but he knew he would not see them, he never had.

Then his skin flew up and out, and spread like a huge cloud above him, a cloud with a gaping mouth and holes for eyes, and it came down on him as gently as dew falls when you are camping under the stars, and enclosed him in the deepest warmth he had ever felt in his life.

He uttered a long, delicious groan of raw human pleasure and profound relief. Beside him, Katelyn groaned, too, and he knew that she had, as well, been covered once again in her own skin.

Instantly, without them going out through a door or anything, the silver ship was rushing away overhead, turning into a dot. Wind screamed around them, their hair blew, and Dan thought they'd been pushed out and were going to die in the lake.

Below, Mr. Ehmer saw beams of light playing out of the summer clouds. "What the hell," he said. Then Frank said, "Ho, got a strike goin' here." They brought up another bass.

DAN WOKE UP SCREAMING. HE was upside down and the covers were all over the room. He got out of bed, immediately felt incredibly thirsty, and went into the bathroom and drank and drank. His mother heard him and came in behind him. "You okay, Dan?"

Then he cried, clutching her with all his might, burying his face in her nightgown that smelled of cigarettes and gin.

"Hey, hey there—"

"Mom, I had a dream. It was real bad, Mom."

She went into his room with him and sat at his bedside.

"It was these Indians, they got us, and they skinned us alive."

"Skinned who alive?"

"Me! Me and—her. I don't know. Me and this girl."

A cool hand touched his forehead. "You dreamed you were naked with a girl, and that's a little scary, isn't it?"

"The stars," he said, "the stars . . ." But what about the stars he could not recall. He closed his eyes, and his mother's hand on his brow comforted him, but deep inside him, down where screams begin, there was a part of him that remembered every terrible moment, and would never forget.

His mother, drunk though she was, sad though she was, sat a while longer with her child, then went back down to the kitchen and resumed her mechanical and relentless assault on a bottle of cheap gin.

Katelyn found herself on the floor naked and covered with sweat. Not understanding how she had gotten there, she scrambled to her feet—and found that she was afraid to look in the mirror—terribly, agonizingly afraid. She stood, her head bowed, holding onto the sink and crying bitter, bitter tears.

Her mind could not seem to make sense of what had just happened. Why was she naked? What was she doing on the floor? Who was that boy, and why did she remember a boy at all?

She returned to her room, found her nightgown, and put it on. She went to her window seat and sat down, and watched the moon ride low over the lake, and smelled honeysuckle on the air.

Then she was sick, and ran into the bathroom and threw up. She washed her face, brushed her teeth, and finally saw in the mirror her own haggard face. As if she was seeing a miracle, she touched the glass. Tears beaded in her eyes and rolled down her cheeks. She went to her bed, then, and lay down, and slept the dismal and uneasy sleep of a captured soul.

TWO

ON A SOUR OCTOBER FORENOON in 2003, Lieutenant Lauren Glass watched her father's coffin being lowered. She was now alone, given that her mother had abandoned them when she was twelve, returned to Scotland, and no longer communicated.

Also at the graveside were four men, none of whom she knew. They were, she assumed, members of whatever unit he was involved in. She did not know its name, what it did, or anything about it at all.

The wind worried the flowers she had brought, the chaplain completed his prayers, and she threw a clod of earth and said inside herself, *You will not, you will not* and then she cried.

He had died on duty, somehow. She had not been told how, she had not been allowed to see his body. The coffin was sealed with federal seals warning that it was a crime to open it. Lead solder filled the crack beneath its lid. She had wanted to at least be alone with it for a short while, but not even that had been allowed. There had been no obituary, nothing to mark all he had done in this world, what she believed must have been a heroic life.

She had been given a five-thousand-dollar death benefit, and he had been listed as killed in action.

Killed how? In what action? He'd left home as usual that morning, then driven to his work, she assumed. They lived on Wright-Pat in Dayton, but he commuted to Indianapolis on the days he worked, which were sporadic.

As the ceremony concluded, to her amazement a missing-man formation flew overhead, wheeling majestically away toward the gray horizon. Then, down at the end of the field, an honor guard she had no idea would be there fired twenty-one times. The highest salute. Taps were sounded.

He was being buried with the highest of honors, and she felt bitter because she did not know why.

The four men were walking away from the grave when she caught up with them. "Can you tell me anything?"

Nobody answered.

"Please, I'm his daughter. Tell me, at least, did he suffer?"

One of the men, tall, so blond that he might have been albino, dropped back. "Should I say no?"

"You know how he died?"

"I know, Lauren."

He knew her name. But who was this man in his superbly tailored civilian suit, as gray as the autumn clouds, with his dusting of white hair and his eyes so pale that they were almost white as well?

"Who are you? Can you tell me what my dad did?"

"I want you to come to an office. Can you do that?"

"Now? Is this an order?"

"I'm so sorry. Are you up to it?"

This walk across this graveyard was the saddest thing she had ever done. She did not understand grief, it was a new landscape for her. Could you go to an office in grief? Talk there in grief? In grief, could you learn secrets? "I want to be at home," she said.

He gave her an address on base. "You think about it, and I want you to bear in mind that we wouldn't be asking this if—"

"I know it's urgent. Obviously it's urgent."

"I'm Lewis Crew," he said. "If you don't mind, please do not mention the appointment to anybody, or my name."

"Okay," she said. "Will you tell me what happened to my dad?"

He gave her a long look, long enough to be disquieting. He was evaluating her. But why? She had no clearance, she was a lowly procurement officer, she had not cared to follow her dad into Air Force Intelligence.

"Will you?" she asked again.

"I'm so sorry to have to ask you to come in on a day like this."

"So am I." She walked away from him then, passing among the neat lines of identical military graves into which the Air Force had poured so many lives, in so many steel coffins, most of them too young, too innocent, too good to die the sorts of improbable and terrible deaths the Air Force had to offer.

It was duty that had taken them. Duty, always, her dad's breath and blood. "The oath, Lauren, never forget the oath. It might take you to your death, and if it does, that's where you have to go."

She'd thought, *If some stupid president sends me to some dumb country where we shouldn't even be, is it my duty to die there?*

She'd known the answer.

Had Dad died a useless death? She hoped not, she hoped that the missing-man formation was more than just a passing honor.

Her life with her dad had not been perfect. Eamon Glass could be demanding, and he had not been happy with the way her career was unfolding. "You need to push yourself, Lauren, Air-Force style. Be ready when it matters, be willing when it counts."

Boy, was he out of it. He was part of another Air Force, as far as she was concerned. In her Air Force, the main issues were things like padded bills and missing laptops, not duty and dying amid huts and palm trees.

"Who were you, Dad? Why did this happen?"

Dad had nightmares. God, did he have nightmares, screaming cyclones of terror from which he could not awaken. And you couldn't get near him. He'd belt you and then in the morning be so upset by what he had done that he'd be in a funk for days.

Often, he would ask if he'd said anything in his sleep. It worried him, obviously, worried him a lot.

She'd listened for some meaning in the screams, but never found any.

She got in her car and started it, eager for the heater to drive out the deep Canadian cold that was sweeping down the vast plains from the north, shivering the naked trees and the stubble-filled fields.

She drove home across the great, gray base to their apartment. She stood in the living room thinking how anonymous it all seemed, the inevitable landscape on the wall, the not-too-challenging books on the shelves, the oldish TV. And his chair, big and comfortable, and beside it the magazine rack filled with *Time* and the *National Review* and *National Geographic*.

All so ordinary, and yet so filled with him that every step deeper into the place was a step through more memory and greater loneliness.

She made coffee, and was drinking it when she realized that it was Dad's mug in her hand. That did it: she cried again. These, she knew, were the anguished tears of the bereaved, that belong both to grief and defeat.

She had a last confession of love that must remain frozen in her forever. Most importantly, there was the conversation that had been their life together, that could never now be brought to rest.

A whole career, and there had only been five people at his funeral. But it hadn't been announced in any way. So his unit was not large, obviously. A colonel, looked about fifty, with the name tag Wilkes. A younger one, Lieutenant Colonel Langford. Maybe thirty-eight. Then a civilian, dumpy, wearing an ill-fitting suit. He'd cried, the civilian had, silent tears that he had flicked away as if they had been gnats landing on his face. And then Mr. Crew, tall, no way to tell the age, looking a little like the Swedish actor Max von Sydow. Great suit, and those eyes. White-gray. Unique.

Dad's people. His coworkers. She shook her head, considering the little collection of silent men.

She went into her bedroom and lay down, closing her eyes and contemplating what the voyage of her life would be like now.

Dad had had one of those stealth tempers that would boil up out of nowhere and, for a few minutes, rock the world. He had been bitter about never making general. "It's the damn work I do, nobody else can do it and it's not a general's job." He had hated it and loved it. He would drink at the kitchen table, lifting shots of vodka, and then he would be poetic, which was beautiful and awesome and scary, because he had such a huge memory for quotations, and because when he was like that, being with him was like looking into the darkest room in the world.

"When in disgrace with fortune and men's eyes," she could hear him reciting, "I all alone beweep my outcast state . . ." and then looking at her and adding, "pardon my bathos."

"Oh, hell," she said, "I'm going to miss you! I am going to *miss you!*"

How could he be dead? How in God's name do you get KIAed in Indianapolis?

Well, hell. As far as he was concerned, the day she received her commission, she had been on her way to general. He would manage her career. "You can't fly combat, so you need to get on a hot staff."

He had stared at her orders to report to the supplies depot for a long time. Stood there and stared, so still she thought he might have gone to sleep on his feet. He put them down far too carefully, on the back of the couch. Then he had marched off into his office. She'd heard him yelling, and gone to his door, which was not right, she knew, but she was involved, for God's sake. She'd only heard one thing, but it had been repeated a number of times, "put her on ice." And he'd cursed the person at the other end of the line with a venom that was far beyond his worst tantrums, that had frightened her because it had implied that the hidden thing in his life somehow also involved her.

Thinking back, she closed her eyes for a moment. Fortune and men's eyes . . .

There had also been another thing between her and Dad, that would come at moments of silence and his strange sorrow, a kind of bond that would seem to enter the air between them, almost as if they could somehow link their minds. Or so she imagined.

The phone rang. She looked at the incoming number. Base call. Could it be the guy from Dad's funeral? Could he actually be pressing her this hard, on this day? She didn't believe it.

"Hello?"

"Lieutenant—"

"Look, mister, are you somewhere in the chain of command, because if you aren't, very frankly, I am here trying to deal with the death of my father and really my only friend, and I am just not doing this."

There was a silence. It extended. "I am in the chain of command," he said at last. "My orders are legal."

Could this be real? Could this guy really, actually be on the phone pushing her around like this now?

"I'd like to do this tomorrow."

"You have your orders, Lieutenant."

She hung up the phone and wanted, very badly, to do something hurtful to this man. But that was military life, wasn't it? You weren't here to grieve.

She reported to an impressive but sterile office suite that had all the anonymous earmarks of being some kind of official visitor's lair. She was called in immediately.

With Mr. Crew was the younger of the two colonels, Langford. She was just as glad—the older one had exuded something that had made her uneasy, Wilkes or whatever his name was.

The office was large and the furniture real wood, but there wasn't a single citation on the walls, nor a photograph, nor anything that might identify him further. Obviously, a spook, but not Air Force or he'd be in uniform.

She saluted the colonel. He returned. "At ease, Lieutenant," he said, smiling and shaking his head slightly.

"Please take a seat," Crew said.

"I want to extend my sympathies, too," Langford added. "Your father was a great man and a national hero. You should know that he's going to receive the Intelligence Medal." He paused. "And also the Medal of Honor."

She knew that her mouth had dropped open, because she had to snap it closed. "The Congressional Medal of Honor?"

Crew nodded.

She was stunned silent. In awe. In sorrow that he had not been able to share what terrors must have beset him in his work, and had killed him.

"Do you remember the tests you took at Lackland?"

What in the world did that have to do with anything? "I took a lot of tests during basic."

"One of them involved a page of numbers, and you were supposed to draw lines between them."

"Sure, I remember it," she said. The test had been tucked in among the standard battery of aptitude tests she'd taken as a recruit. "Sort of connect-the-dots type thing." She'd sort of doodled it, as she recalled. "I messed it up."

The two men stared at her, saying nothing. They looked, she thought, like people must look to an ape from inside his cage. "What on earth does it matter now?"

"I have another test for you," he said.

"Another test? That's what this is about? Because—"

"Lieutenant, it's terribly important."

Langford's voice had an edge that told her to listen and keep her mouth shut.

"You need to fill out a consent."

"I thought you were going to let me know something about my dad."

"I am."

She took the form he handed her, and was very surprised, as she read it, to see that it was no ordinary medical consent.

She looked at Langford. His face was bland. A dentist's face—that is to say, a mask. She read aloud, "Any commentary or discussion or unauthorized record of any subject or meeting or action carried out within the context of the project is prohibited conduct and subject to prosecution under provisions of the National Security Act of 1947 as amended." She tried to laugh. They remained silent. "This is very heavy stuff." Still nothing. "Excuse me, but this is a very serious document, here." She pushed the paper back toward Crew's side of the desk.

"We can't bargain with you," Langford said, "and we can't talk until you sign."

"Volunteer or be shot, in other words."

Langford pushed the paper back toward her. "Don't miss this," he said. "You're first in line, Lieutenant Glass, but there is a line."

"If I sign and don't like what I hear, can I walk away?"

Langford turned toward Crew, who didn't so much as blink. "I'm sorry, but the agreement is binding," Langford said.

"It commits me to something I can't learn about until I'm in it? And then I can't get out?"

"I know it sounds unreasonable."

"Unreasonable? It's downright scary. More than scary. I mean, the Air Force doesn't handle things this way." She wondered if that was actually true.

"Sign it. It would be very helpful."

Maybe her dad was looking down on her right now. Probably was, assuming there was anything left of him, any sort of a soul.

She picked up a pen off the desk . . . and had the odd feeling that these two guys were waiting, but in a funny way . . . like they were hungry, almost, and she was lunch.

"So, I don't think I need to do this," she said. "No." And she was more than a little ashamed. *Sorry, Dad, but this does not feel right.*

Crew unfolded his long legs and leaned forward. She expected him to speak. But he did not speak. He just looked at her. It wasn't a special expression, not at all. But it moved her. It did, definitely. A very serious, very important moment.

"I can't very well jump off a cliff without knowing what's at the bottom, can I?"

Crew sighed. Was it anger? Suppressed impatience? Boy, she could not read this guy. You thought saint, then you thought—well, something else.

"We want you to continue your father's work," Crew said. "If you pass this small test."

"It's urgent," Langford added. "You'll need to start this afternoon."

Crew pushed the agreement back at her.

"But . . . what did he do?"

"Please help us," Crew said. His voice was still as soft as ever, but the desperation in it was somehow terrifying.

"What if I . . . can't?"

He smiled then, very slightly.

Suddenly she knew that she would not walk away from this. She could not live the rest of her life in ignorance of what her dad had done, knowing that she had passed up this chance.

He had been killed, though.

She grabbed the paper, signed, then thrust it back.

Colonel Langford took it, folded it once, and slipped it into a manila envelope. "You'll get a copy countersigned by the Secretary of Defense," he said.

"You're kidding."

"Lauren, you have a very unique ability," the big man said, "inherited, we believe. That first test you took, you passed. You were the only person to have done so in the forty years it has been administered, in one form or another, to every military recruit in the United States, Canada, Great Britain, New Zealand, and Australia. The only one who even came close. But we weren't surprised, given who your father is."

That sort of sounded . . . whoa. "Did you say, uh—what's that?"

"You are one in many millions, Lauren. You have inherited an absolutely unique skill from your dad."

What in the world could this be? "I have to tell you honestly, I have no unusual skills."

"I want to warn you, you're going to have a very extraordinary experience. I want you to understand that it will not be in any way pleasant or easy. I won't pretend that there is no danger, because it must be obvious to you that there is great danger. What's more, we're not going to be able to help you. You have to do it on your own. And you are on your own."

"But, uh, you said there was a list, Colonel Langford.

And you were going to . . . you were going to the next person if I didn't sign."

"I lied. And you will, too, many times. It will be a big part of your job."

"If I'd said no—despite Dad, absolutely and finally no—what then?"

Crew said, "We would have had to say something dramatic, like the survival of the human race might depend on you."

The words hung in the air. Unbelievable. Crazy, even. She didn't know whether she should be scared or what. Finally, the whole idea just seemed so overblown that she burst out laughing—and it was the only sound in the room, and it stayed the only sound in the room. She looked from one deadly serious face to the other. They actually were not in any way kidding.

But she was a girl, she was twenty-two, and, while she liked being both things, neither suggested that she had any sort of amazing mission in life. "This is too weird," she said slowly. "I mean, are you telling me I'm some kind of outrageous, like, freak?"

Langford cleared his throat. "You know nothing about your father's work?"

She shook her head.

"You're what we call an empath. You can hear thought and you can transmit it to others who can hear it."

"Yeah, Dad used to say that. He read science fiction, too. Arthur C. Clarke kind of thing."

Crew handed her a yellow pad. "Write down the first thing that comes to mind."

She took the pad, thought for a moment, then scrawled the first word that came to mind. "The name of my dad's barber," she said. "Adam."

Now Langford pulled an envelope out of his pocket. "The person you will be working with cannot speak. His brain is so entirely different that, without a person like you, we can only exchange the most rudimentary ideas. At present he is terribly upset, but we have succeeded in getting him to transmit the name we call him to you."

He handed her the envelope.

In it was a note scrawled on a piece of paper that smelled oddly of what she thought might be Lysol. The single word written there was "Adam."

She looked at it. She looked back up at the two men. "Who . . . who is this guy, anyway?"

"That's part of what we've been trying to understand, Lieutenant Glass. What your father spent his career working on."

"His name is Adam but you don't understand . . . what?"

"They don't have a naming convention in their culture. Adam and Bob are really just our labels."

"Bob?"

"Died."

Another death. She noted that. But who in the world would communicate via thought and not use names?

"Our next step will be to send you to meet the head of your part of the project. He operates a very small unit and runs a very, very tight ship," Colonel Langford said. "You have to understand, you are never to speak to him about your background, about your meeting with us, about anything that you do not absolutely need to talk to him about in order to do your work. Do you understand that?"

This was sounding crazier and crazier. "So I just walk up to the guy—my commanding officer—and I say—what?"

The colonel handed her an envelope. "You don't say anything. You give him this. He'll take it from there."

She recognized the envelope, of course: it carried orders. She started to open it.

"No."

"No? I don't open my own orders?" She shook her head. "Why am I not surprised?"

He gave her a card with an address in Indianapolis on it. "You'll drive to your new assignment. Colonel Michael Wilkes will be expecting you. You saw Mike at the funeral. You will receive further orders from him verbally." He paused for a moment. "Lauren," he continued, "I want you to understand that there is an extremely good reason for all this secrecy. In time, you'll come to know this reason, and you will find yourself in the same position we are—it's a secret that you won't hesitate to defend with your life."

She found herself walking toward the parking lot with this weird verbal order to report to an address in University Heights in Indianapolis, and to be there by six this evening. Not impossible, given that it was a little over a hundred miles and she had five hours. Typical of the Air Force, though, she'd been sitting in procurement for two years and then, with barely time to go back to the apartment and grab her toothbrush, she was on the move to, of all places, Indianapolis, and not even a USAF facility as far as she could tell.

"You just get your belongings out of your billet and go," Langford had said. "No good-byes, no e-mails, no cell calls."

She had friends, a life, at least something of a life. No, hell, there was Molly at the office who was going to wonder, there was Charlie Fellowes who was getting to be more than just a friend, but he was out on a refueling mission and wouldn't be back for forty-eight hours—so he was just going to find her apartment empty, her cell phone disconnected, and her e-mail bouncing everything back.

She worried that she'd run into a familiar face on her way home, but all was quiet. She knew the Air Force: her current commanding officer, General Winters, would have been duly informed of her transfer, etc., but nothing would run smoothly. Undoubtedly, the next thing she'd get from her current unit would be a notice that she was AWOL.

She spent three quarters of an hour packing. At the last, she put their small photo album in a suitcase. Her and Dad through the years. She staggered down to the parking lot under her bags, and got the Focus pretty much stuffed to the roof liner.

Then she was gone, outta here, no looking back.

It was not until she was sailing west on 70 and WTUE was rocking into her past that she began to think again about Dad's dreams.

As a little girl, she'd covered her head with her pillow and begged God to help him. Later, she'd gone into his bedroom to try to provide him with whatever support a daughter could. She would find him with his eyes wide open, screaming and shaking his head from side to side, and you could not wake him up.

He'd said it was 'Nam coming back to haunt him. He'd flown Hueys in 'Nam, and he had two Hearts for his trouble. Also a scar down his back where he'd been wounded. His story was that a lot of guys had burned alive in a hospital tent that had been torched by the V.C. Helpless guys, guys with no faces, guys with no legs. He'd had a broken arm and a bad infection, but he could run, at least.

There was, of course, a problem with this. It was that, as she knew, her father had not served in Vietnam. She'd seen his duty book, and he just had never served there.

In fact, her father had served at White Sands, then at an army base in Arizona called Fort Huachuca. Her earliest memories were of the wonderful rocks around Fort Huachuca. After that, they'd come to Wright-Pat, where he'd been connected with the Air Materiel Command. She knew that because his unit was attached to the Behavioral Research Directorate, which was a division of AMC. She knew that behavioral research was about understanding things like pilot alertness and endurance. Also, muddier stuff, nonlethal weapons and such.

It was a nice drive, once you got out of Dayton traffic—which was, truth be told, pretty minor.

Farms, midsummer corn, a different way of life out here. She'd like to run tractors and combines and things. She liked big machines.

She'd been around the Midwest for a while now, so Indy was no stranger to her. Back before Mom moved home to Glasgow, they'd gone to the 500 here practically every year. Mom was into fast cars—or rather, the drivers, the mechanics, and just about anybody connected with racing. Actually, just about anybody else at all, as long as it wasn't Dad.

She was expecting an office building at least, or maybe some kind of lab facility tucked away next to the university. But this was pure residential around here. Wide streets, big old houses, quiet in the late afternoon.

She drove past 101 Hamilton and was, frankly, confused. It was a house. Looked like it had been built around 1910 in the Craftsman style. Beautiful place, for sure. But a *house*? An Air Force facility was in a house in a neighborhood?

Okay, so be it. She pulled into the driveway behind a

very sweet-looking SLK convertible, that was, no, not your usual Air Force colonel's automobile. It was possible, of course, that the car belonged to somebody else, but she'd been told that the chilly Colonel Wilkes ran the place and this car was in a special little chunk of tarmac all its own. Commanding officer's privilege, for sure; she knew her Air Force.

There was only one other vehicle there, though, and the garage was padlocked. The other car was an Acura, not too young. So there was Colonel Wilkes with a fast car and a flunkie to be named later. Not the lowest of the low, they'd be in your Focus or your Echo like her, trying to make ends meet on just enough money to make that impossible.

As she mounted the stairs to the porch she noticed, of all things, a pair of longhorns over the front door. She stood looking at this incredibly improbable choice of decoration for Indianapolis, Indiana.

The front door had one of those old-fashioned bells on it that you twisted. She turned it and was rewarded by a dry crunching sound, not loud. In fact, hardly audible. So she did it again, a couple of times.

She was still doing it when the door swept open and Colonel Wilkes, looking shockingly older than this morning, stood there staring at her out of bloodshot eyes. "Please come in," he said, stepping aside.

His voice sounded sad, and she had the odd impression that he might have actually been crying. She noticed that there were boxes against the wall.

"They're yours," Wilkes said. "Eamon's things."

"Colonel, nobody has told me yet what happened to my dad. I've been ordered to come to this place and I have no idea why, beyond reasons that sound like some sort of science fiction crap to me, and I have to tell you that this is not being done right. Couldn't someone have at least warned me that I'd come here and see Dad's stuff in damn boxes!"

"Who sent you here?"

She could not believe that he actually didn't know. "I've been ordered not to tell you."

He nodded, as if that was the most natural thing in the

world. She followed him into an office that had clearly been carved out of what was once the master bedroom.

"This place was built in 1908 by Indy's only cattle baron," he said as he dropped down behind his desk.

There had been no exchange of salutes. But he was her superior officer, so she brought her hand to her forehead and said, "Lieutenant Lauren Glass reporting as ordered, sir."

He looked up at her. "Obviously. Please go to the scrub room and get prepped."

"Excuse me?"

"The scrub room. You'll find it at the base of the shaft."

"Sir, I have to explain to you, I have no idea what's going on here. I would like a little more information, sir."

"You'll get the hang of it."

"Uh, look, what is this scrub room? What do I have to scrub for?"

"Listen, I know you don't understand any of this. We were planning to bring you along as your dad reached retirement. Nobody thought it would be like this. But we have a desperate situation, Lauren."

She found a chair. "Sir, I'm sorry to disabuse you, but I have not been on any training program in any way, shape, or form. I am not prepared for whatever this is. I basically have no idea what you're doing here at all, but whatever it is, it killed—" She had to stop. Her grief, appearing suddenly, had choked her on her own words.

"Lauren, I knew your dad for a long time. So you'll know that what I'm about to say is not meant to be hard or callous. It is what your dad would say to you if he could talk right now. Your dad would say to you, 'Soldier, you have a duty. Do your duty.'"

"Sir, respectfully, you tell me in one breath that my predecessor is a KIA, then you tell me to proceed into whatever situation he was in with no training or prep whatsoever. Sir, I would like to understand this order a little better. I know that I am dealing with somebody called Adam, and my father dealt with him and with somebody called Bob, and my father died as a result. That is the extent of my knowledge."

He stood up so suddenly that she did, too. He turned his

back on her and strode to the window. "There is no training, and there is no time. I want you down there now, because we have a situation, Lieutenant, and I believe—no, I
know—that you are the only person remotely available to
us who might be able to help."

When he attempted to smile at her, she saw that coldness
again, this time more clearly than she had at the grave. This
was a driven man, she thought, a fanatic. And she wondered, should she trust a fanatic?

Well, Dad had. This was his commanding officer, this
frosty man with his carefully decorated office and his fabulous car.

He showed her to a small elevator that opened under the
front stairs. "There's a very skilled man at the other end
who will be there to help you."

She stepped into the dim interior and descended. It felt
as if it was moving fast, and continued for more than a
minute. When the doors opened, she found a chunky young
man in a white sterile suit waiting for her . . . and saw that
he had been the fourth man at the funeral.

"I'm Andy Morgan," he said. "Welcome to the facility."

"This place is *deep*."

"We're two hundred and eighty feet down. Deep in the
bedrock." He tapped a foot on the floor. "Basalt."

Faintly, she could hear another voice. It was groaning
and sounded tired. Also angry. She looked around but saw
nobody.

"Who is that?"

Andy Morgan shook his head. "You're good," he said.

"Who's moaning? What's going on in here?"

"Lauren, listen to me. You're going to meet him in a moment. Sort of meet him. What you're hearing is coming
through a six-foot-thick tempered steel wall that is further
protected by a high-intensity electromagnetic field."

"Then how can we possibly be hearing it? Because it's
perfectly clear. And the man is in agony."

"I can't hear it."

"But that's crazy. Listen to him, he's wailing!"

"The fact that you can hear his thoughts is why you're
here."

"What thoughts? He's crying!"

"You need to go in there," Andy Morgan said. The same tone, she thought, that he might have used if he had told her it was time for her to do her wingwalk, or perhaps go over Niagara Falls in a barrel.

Behind him was a steel door, armored and locked with great, gleaming bolts. Why in the world would anybody be that locked up? What did they have in there, some kind of deranged superman? She tried to conceal her total and complete mystification, not to say her fear, and to concentrate on what she needed to know, here, on a practical basis. "Now, is this person going to be violent?"

"Baby, he is *flyin'* in there! He's been bouncing off the walls ever since the colonel bought it. Excuse me! Since your dad passed away."

"Before I go in there, I think you'd better tell me exactly what happened to him."

He lowered his head. "Nobody told you?"

"They did not."

"Okay. Your dad got a scratch."

"A *scratch*?"

"That caused an allergic reaction so intense that he bled out."

She did not need to think very long about that. She sat down in one of the two chairs that stood before the control panel. "I'm not doing this."

He was a gentle-looking guy, more than a little overweight, with sad, sad eyes. "They sent you all the way down here without telling you a damn thing, didn't they?"

"That would be correct."

"Okay, I'm going to level with you. Have you ever heard of aliens?"

"Yeah. No green card."

"The other kind."

"Oh, that stuff. I have no interest in that stuff."

"Perhaps you had better see your dad's office."

"God, I'd love that."

Across the small room was a door. The nameplate holder was empty. He unlocked the door and she saw a small, windowless space that had a steel desk, a couple of chairs, and a cot. There was a bookcase, also, and it was filled with books on electromagnetism and, of all things, UFOs. She read the titles, *Intruders, Communion, UFO Condition Red, UFOs and the National Security State,* and dozens more.

"You can pick what you'd like to keep. We'll ditch the others." He lifted a picture that was lying facedown on the desk. "I knew you'd want this."

It filled her heart and her eyes, the picture of the two of them taken when she was twelve. They were at Cape May, New Jersey, she was wearing her new bathing suit, and her Boston terrier, Prissy, was still alive. For a moment she smelled the salt in the air, remembered a radio playing down the beach, and heard the breeze fluttering in their cabana.

He took the picture and set it on the desk. "This is your office, now."

"There's an alien down here."

"And your father was his empath, and you will be his empath."

"Meaning?"

"You are going to find that you can see pictures he makes in his mind, and describe what you see to us."

Her father had kept quite a secret. "I should have been trained."

"Your dad wanted to wait until you'd had a little more Air Force. You know, you sign up and you wear a uniform, but really becoming part of this crazy organization takes time. Your dad wanted you to have that time."

"I'm an Air Force brat down to my toes."

"He knew that. He respected that. But duty is something different. I mean, our kind of duty. Keeping a secret so big that it is a kind of agony. Above all, knowing every time you go in that room over there, that you might die. Every time. But doing it like your dad did, on behalf of the Air Force, the country, and future of man." He took the picture from her, looked at it. "We need you to get in there and calm Adam down. If we can't get him to pull himself together, he's going to literally be busted apart by knocking into those walls in there. Considering that he's been doing this since your dad passed, we're desperate, Lieutenant."

Either she took up her dad's sword or she let it lie, and let the meaning of his life lie with him in his grave.

There was no real choice here. Never had been. She took a deep breath. "Okay, what do I do?"

He drew her through a steel door into a tiny dressing area. She stood naked in a shower with nozzles on the ceiling and walls, turning slowly as instructed with her hands raised over her head while green, chemical-stinking liquid sluiced over her.

Still wet, she donned an orange isolation suit and what felt like asphalt gloves, they were so thick. "He's electro-magnetically active," Andy explained. "If you touch him, he'll extend into your nervous system and take over your body. You don't want that."

"No."

"Cover your face with Vaseline. And here's an epinephrine injector. If you get the least feeling of even so much as a tickle in your throat, press it against your leg and get out of there."

As she dug into the Vaseline container, she reflected that her father's hand was probably the last one to do this. She could almost feel him beside her right now, telling her not to be scared, to remember her duty, that he was with her every step of the way.

Then something changed. The room, the guy—everything around her disappeared. She was suddenly and vividly in another room. It had stainless-steel walls, a black floor, and a fluorescent ceiling. There was a man on a table, naked, surrounded by people in full protective gear, sterile suits, faceplates down, the works. The man was purple, his chest was heaving, and blood was oozing out of his eyes, out of his nose, down his cheeks like tears.

The hallucination, or whatever it was, was so vivid that she might as well have actually been standing in the place. She could even hear the air-conditioning hissing, and the muffled voices of the doctors behind the masks, who were trying to save the man on the table.

He gasped, gasped again as they set up an IV. A nurse intoned, "BP 280 over 200, heart rate 160, basal BP rising, glucose 320 rising, we have another infarction—"

There was a high-pitched whine and blood began spraying out of his skin, spraying their face masks and their white sterile suits, beading and running down to the floor as he bled from every pore, a haze of blood pink and fine, like it was being sprayed from a thousand tiny high-pressure nozzles affixed to his body.

Then his head turned and she saw his face, and an ice cold spike stabbed her straight in the heart.

In that instant, the vision of her dad's death ended.

She realized that she was still in the basement room she had entered in the first place, and Andy was supporting her under her arms.

"Sorry," she managed to mutter, regaining her footing and stepping away from him, "I—uh—I think it's the . . . depth."

"If you say so." He put an arm around her.

"Back off!"

"Hey, okay! Okay. I'm just trying to help, here."

She blew out breath, then shook her head. That had been vivid. That had been real vivid.

Andy watched her. "You sure you're okay?"

"I'm not okay. No."

"Uh, was that a seizure, because—"

"It's my business, okay!"

"Okay! Sorry." He paused, then, and when she said nothing more, continued. "I'm going to open up the cage itself. When you enter, you'll see a chair and a table. Sit in the chair."

"That's it? That's all I get to know?"

"It's all any of us know. Frankly, what your dad did, and what we know you can do, is not understood. You just have to do it."

"And what if I can't?"

"You've passed the test." He went to a small keyboard and keyed in a combination. "I'll be in the control room. You'll be able to see and hear me, and vice versa. If you get into trouble, I'll pull you out. But obviously things can happen fast in there."

He left the dressing room, closing the heavy outer door behind him. A moment later, his voice returned, tinny, coming out of a ceiling speaker. "You reading me?"

"Yeah."

"Okay, the door's opening now."

There was a loud click, then a whirring sound, and the wall of the little chamber slid back. She saw before her a room lit by what appeared to be ultraviolet light. It reminded her of the Animals of the Night exhibit at the Cleveland Zoo, where the vampire bats and things were deceived into thinking it was dark during the day. "Are there any lights?"

"Don't worry about seeing him. You won't. If you get so much as a glimpse, count yourself lucky. Pay attention to the corners of your eyes."

"The corners of my eyes . . . you mean use my peripheral vision?"

Then the air hit her. It was dry—*real* dry. She could feel her face shriveling, it was so dry, feel her lips starting to crack. The function of the Vaseline was now clear, and she grabbed another handful of it right in the glove and slathered it on.

The room open before her was not large, maybe twenty by twenty. It looked like it had rubber walls. There was a window on the far side, and Andy could be seen sitting there at a control panel. His face glowed green from the instruments before him.

Suddenly something shot past so fast she lurched back waving her hands. It felt like nothing so much as being buzzed by a fly—but not a small fly, no. More like the size, say, of a buzzard.

There was also a voice: groaning, howling, wailing, and it was the strangest voice she had ever heard, because of the way it echoed in her ears and her mind at the same time, as if she was hearing both sounds and thoughts that were the same as the sounds.

A thud, bzzzt, thud, bzzzt, thud, bzzzt, shot around the room, and with it the wailing, mourning voice, its howl thin and pitiful now.

She saw something—a flash of something that gleamed black. It was big, the size of a hand, and slanted. It was also brilliantly alive—a big, gleaming eye. A sound came out of her that she knew, objectively, was a scream. Sharp, intense, made of pure fear.

The wailing at once increased. Now it was desolated, like he'd been instantly aware of her revulsion and her fright and it was making him feel really, really miserable.

"Hold on," she said. Dimly, she was conscious that Wilkes was now standing beside the tech at the control panel.

Suddenly, the buzzing stopped. There was no sound now but the hissing of the powerful air-conditioning.

"Sit down in the chair," Wilkes said over the intercom.

"Where is he?"

"He moves with your eyes, so he appears totally still. The eye doesn't see anything that's totally still."

"Yeah, like a rock or a mountain."

"No," Wilkes explained, "when you look at anything at all, *you're* in motion, so you see it. Since Adam is constantly making micromovements to match your eyes' own natural flickering, he doesn't register in the optic nerve at all."

"What in hell is this *about*?"

"Tell you what. If you want to see him, make a very sudden move. As you do that, concentrate on the corners of your eyes, not your central vision. You'll see him."

She sat, took a deep breath, tried to concentrate on her peripheral vision, and leaped to her feet.

Not a foot away, there was a shadow. Then it was gone again.

"He's right here! He's right on top of me!"

Then he started wailing again, and she could feel him whizzing around the room. More and more, he was racing past her face at the distance of what felt like about an inch. Dad had gotten scratched. She sat frozen, terrified.

"Stay with it. You're doing marvelously."

She could see Wilkes nodding and smiling at her. "This is one hell of a sucker play," she yelled. "False damn pretenses!" She got to her feet. Adam whizzed past so close she was forced to sit back down. She jumped up again. Same thing happened.

"He likes you, Lauren," Wilkes said.

It felt a lot like getting a bat in her hair or something. How had Dad ever stood this, it was just way, way too weird.

"So what are we doing with an alien?" she screeched. "How in the world did we capture an alien?"

"We got two of them in a crash in New Mexico. They may have been given to us, we're not sure."

Bzzzt! Whooosh!

"Get away!"

"He wants to touch you. Let him touch you."

She began waving her arms around her head. "No way, I'll bleed out!"

"Remember, that was an accident. He's in an agony of grief, that's why he's like this. Now you settle down, young woman, and follow your orders."

Pictures of Dad kept flashing through her mind like photographs. With them came emotions of grief and the most acute regret. It was clear that they entered from the outside, although she could not say how she knew that. It was sort of like breathing a kind of emotional smoke.

"Shh," she whispered, "now, baby . . ." She looked toward the control room. "The buzzing stopped again."

Something brushed her cheek.

"I think he just touched me. I know you're sorry," she whispered, "I know . . ." She looked again toward the figures in the control room. "What am I supposed to do now?"

No response.

So she comforted him. She went through her mind, seeking for the words of some song from childhood, some sort of comforting song. Dad had not been a big singer. Mom had her Elvis, but this did not appear to be your basic Elvis moment.

Then a sort of hallucinatory flash took place. In it, the light in the room was deep red and there was a man at the table, sitting across from Adam. On the table, a bright green light like a laser that hopped up and down in the air. The man was her dad.

It was so real, it was so good to see him again, that the tears were immediate. And then she heard inside her head, *oohhhhh*, and she knew that Adam had realized who she was.

"Yeah," she said, "yeah, he was my dad."

Ohhhhhh! Ohhhhh!

"Oh, yeah," she managed through her own tears, "I miss him, too, I miss him bad."

She saw next a glowingly beautiful woman, her face surrounded by a halo of golden light. It was, she knew, herself as Adam saw her.

Empath. One who empathizes. Turned out it was in the blood. No training needed. Genetic thing, she supposed. Maybe their ancestors had been psychics or witches or something. Dad's grandfather had come from Ireland, that was about all she knew of their bloodline.

In the control room, Colonel Wilkes and Specialist Martin exchanged looks. "He's got her wrapped around his little finger," Wilkes said.

"For sure, sir."

"He knows how to handle 'em, the little bastard. That is one smart piece of work in there."

They said no more. Lauren Glass had been captured. She would not escape, never, not until she followed her father and his predecessor, both of whom Adam had killed with a scratch.

PART TWO

THE THREE THIEVES

They stole little Bridget
   For seven years long;
When she came down again
   Her friends were all gone.

—WILLIAM ALLINGHAM
   "The Fairies"

THREE

DAN CAME INTO THE KITCHEN while Katelyn was washing spinach and nuzzled her neck. She moved her head back, enjoying him. In their case, not even thirteen years of marriage had been enough of a honeymoon, and she was very far from being used to this guy of hers.

They had met here at Bell, two days after he arrived. Bizarrely, it turned out that they'd both grown up in Madison, Wisconsin, just a few blocks from each other. He'd been crossing the campus in that aimless way he had, looking here and there, smiling even though there was no reason to smile. He was a strikingly handsome man, the last person you'd pick for a professor, let alone a specialist in physiological psychology. But that's what he was, and he'd just snared a provisional professorship when they met. Now Bell had reached a point of no return with him. This was, at last, his tenure year, and in a few days, his career here—and their pleasantly settled life—would either continue or it would end.

"What's Conner up to?" she asked. "Is he downstairs?"

"He's in the living room."

"Too bad, he'd hear us if we went upstairs."

"Mmm." He continued nuzzling.

Their son was more than a genius. A well-constructed, handsome towhead, gentle of eye and so smart that he was a de facto freak. His IQ of 277 was, as far as anybody could determine, the highest presently on record.

Dan came up from nuzzling and said, "He's in a funk."

"Symptoms of said funk?"

"Staring miserably at the TV pretending not to stare miserably at the TV."

"He's eleven. Eleven has stuff." She arched her back, drew his head over her shoulder, and kissed the side of his lips.

"He's watching *2001*."

Which meant that it was a serious funk and he needed Mom. "Why didn't you say that in the first place?"

"In the first place, I wanted some love."

She went into the family room, stood for a moment looking at the back of her son's head. On the ridiculously huge TV Dan had unveiled at Christmas, the apes were howling at the monolith.

She sat down beside him. "Can I interest you in—" She glanced at her watch, picked up the *TV Guide*. "A *Mork and Mindy* rerun? *The McLaughlin Group*?"

"Invasion of my space, Mom."

"Point taken, backing off." But she didn't do that. She knew to stay right where she was.

"And just because I'm watching *2001* does not mean that I'm sad."

What could she say to the misery in that voice? "Conner, a genius does not an actor make."

"Mother, could you consider dropping that label? You say that all the time and it does not help."

"That you're not a good actor?"

"Okay, let's do this. Would you care to come out on the deck with me?"

"On the deck? It's twenty-six degrees."

But he'd already gotten to his feet and slid open the door. He gestured to her, and she saw the anger in it. She went out with him.

The air was sharp with smoke, the western sky deep orange beyond the black skeletons of the winter trees. One would have thought that a winter silence would prevail, but instead she heard the shrill voices of preteen boys.

When she looked down toward the Warners' house, she saw streaks of light racing around in the backyard.

"You're not invited?"

He went back in the house, sat down, and jammed the button on the remote. The bone sailed into the sky, the "Blue Danube" started.

Paulie and Conner had been friends effectively from birth—Conner's birth, that is. Paulie was a year and a half older.

"Conner, what happened?"

"Nothing."

"Something happened."

"Mom, I've asked for space."

"Honey, look, you've got one place you can go. Here. Two people who are one hundred percent on your team, me and Dad. And I want to know why you aren't at that party." And why, moreover, was it unfolding outside where Conner could watch from a distance? That was real hard, that was.

Conner was ten months younger than the youngest child in his class at Bell Attached, the school that served the children of Bell College's professional community. He was nowhere near puberty, in a class where half the boys were shaving at least occasionally.

"Conner, would it make you feel better if I told you that puberty turns boys into monsters?"

"Thank you for that little dose of sexism, Mother. Girls have trouble with puberty, too."

"But boys *really* do."

She could hardly believe that Maggie and Harley would allow Paulie to leave Conner out like this. "What's really wrong?"

"All right. Fine." He got up, crossed the room, and went downstairs.

She heard him shut the door to the basement that Dan had finished for him when he was five. It was boy heaven down there, with an Xbox and a TV/DVD combo and a hulking but powerful Dell computer, plus his dinosaur collection, all of them painted with the utmost realism, and his train set, HO-grade, which had lighted houses, streetlights lining the streets, and lighted trains. He would play trains in the dark down there by the hour, muttering to himself in

the voices of a hundred train men and townsfolk, all of
whom he had invented, all of whose lives evolved and
changed over the years. Katelyn thought of the train set as
a sort of ongoing novel, and that her boy was a word genius as much as he was a math genius.

The care he lavished on everything he modeled came
from his ability to concentrate. Even when he'd been little,
he hadn't been clumsy. When he was eight, she'd discovered while cleaning up one day that the tiny human figures
in his train set all had different-colored eyes, they had been
that carefully finished.

She had loved him so, then, looking down at a tiny
suited figure with a tie so small that you had to look under
a magnifying glass to see the design he'd painted on it. And
then you would hear him deep in the night talking to himself, and you would realize that he was reciting a book he'd
read, maybe even years ago, all from memory, just to enjoy
it again.

Conner and Dan had celebrated the completion of the
room by putting a plaque on the door: THE CONNER ZONE.

She and her husband had celebrated in quite a different
way, later that night. This was your garden-variety tract
house, as isolated as it and its three neighbors were, and the
walls were tract-house thin. They did not feel that this extremely sensitive child needed to overhear the sounds of
sex in the next room. And on that night, at last, they had
been able to use their bed the way a bed was meant to be
used, instead of being as still as possible, wincing at every
squeak, and keeping their cries to a whisper.

"Dan," she said, walking into the kitchen where he had
begun trimming ribs, "there's something kind of ugly going on. Paulie's having a party and Conner's not invited."

"Jesus."

"They're actually outside playing with flashlights, which
I kind of have the feeling is on purpose."

"Kids are cruel."

"Listen, incidentally, I had an e-mail from Marcie Cotton about you."

"Oh?"

"They've reached the point of asking general-faculty opinion."

"Oh, God."

"I gave you a great report."

"What a relief."

"Come on, what else would I do?"

"Tell the truth like everybody else. I'm dull as dishwater in the classroom."

"No, you're actually interesting. It's physiological psychology that's dull. In the hands of most profs, it causes birds to die in the trees outside their classrooms. At least yours just fly off."

"Dull is dull. I should've used puppets or worn costumes."

"I would have preferred almost any other referee, frankly."

"Yeah, you and me both. But I can handle her . . . maybe."

"Not too much."

Dan went to her, embraced her. "You're my girl."

There came a sound from below—a crash.

"He just kicked the wall," Katelyn said. "Like father, like son."

"Maybe a mano a mano would be good."

One of the most precious things about this Dan Callaghan whom her heart had whispered to her to marry was that he was a genuinely good father—not an easy thing to be for a boy as challenging as their son. But Conner's brilliance and demanding personality also made him fascinating, and she thought that the rewards for loving their boy were substantial. "Maybe a mano a mano would be very good," she said.

As he went downstairs, he noticed that the Conner Zone sign had been removed from the door, leaving some areas of peeled paint that would have to be repaired. But not right now. He started to open the door, thought better of it, and knocked.

A moment of silence was followed by a grudging, "Okay."

The room was dark and the trains were running. Conner

loomed over the board like some kind of leering godlet, an image that Dan found oddly creepy. In fact, he found Conner, in general, oddly creepy—a great kid, he was crazy about him . . . but there was something sort of fundamentally creepy about somebody who was probably smarter than Shakespeare, and certainly smarter than you—way smarter.

"Hey there, I see you've abolished the Conner Zone."

"It's stupid."

A streetcar, wonderfully modeled, shot around on the tracks, racing through intersections, wheeling out into the forest and then returning to the town, passing Andy's Garage and Sill's Millinery and Carter's Groceries, racing along as crossing guards whipped up and down and the figures inside sat as still as if frozen in terror.

"Isn't it going a little fast?"

"I'm exceeding the speed limit and maybe they're all going to die."

"It hurts, buddy. It's meant to. Only, we need to get in front of it. Figure out what we're doing wrong and not do that anymore. That way, we don't lose our friends."

Conner turned the transformer up a notch and the streetcar shot off the tracks, tumbled through the woods, and crashed to the floor. The roof broke off and half the figures came out. Conner leaped around the table, grabbed the remains of the car, and smashed it to pieces against the tiles.

"Hey. Hey! You're killing the floor, here." Dan went down to him, but he was up again and off across the room.

"I've gotta get rid of this whole kid setup," he said, his voice cracking. "I'm an asshole, Dan. I'm a *little boy*. In fact, I'm *the* little boy."

Dan went over to the bed where Conner had thrown himself. "Conner, your mom and I both felt you needed to skip grades. You were bored silly in third grade. You could do all the problems, you could read all the books."

"I can still do all the problems and read all the books. Only the difference now is, I'm the class freak, Dan. The *freak*!"

"You're not a freak. You just happen to be somewhat smarter than most people."

"You know who I really relate to? I really relate to Junior Hamner. Do you know who that is?"

Dan thought that the Hamners had a little boy with Down syndrome. "He's that mentally disabled child, isn't he?"

"Exactly. Another freak. We should be joined at the hip."

"Except that your mind—who knows what it might do one day? And Junior Hamner's always gonna be eleven years old."

"Actually, he's four. Mental age."

"Okay, let's get down to it. What, exactly, happened to cause you to get ditched?"

"I told you, I'm a little boy. Little boys aren't allowed."

Dan had, to be honest, been one of the bullies. He'd had a childhood full of nightmares, so many and so intense that he now speculated that he might have been an abuse victim. He'd often been taken night fishing by an old man who lived down the block. Most of the time, his uncle Frank had been with them, and Frank was to this day as straight an arrow as had ever been carved, but there had been times when he and Mr. Ehmer had been out there alone all night, and he wondered what had transpired then.

He remembered strange violence. Screaming. Being swarmed by flies. And maybe those were screen memories for things Mr. Ehmer had done, that should not have been done.

Dan had been angry and big, so he used to push the little kids around—whip their butts, take their money, you name it. So he could understand the ugly frustrations of Paulie Warner and the other boys as well as he could his own boy's hurt. He put his arm around Conner's shoulders, gave him a friendly squeeze. "This was not like this a week ago. Two days ago."

"Let me tell you what they've done. They have created a club called the Connerbusters. Clever name, do you get it? Everybody in the seventh grade is supposed to be a Connerbuster except me, of course—" He stopped, his voice cracking.

Dan looked over to see the young face twisted in pain. Agony.

"I'm sorry, Dan, here I go being a *little boy*."

"Look, I was a class bully. I would've been a Conner-buster. For sure. But I cried, too. And you can be sure that Paulie Warner and the rest of them are just as vulnerable. You're a little behind them physically, Conner, but mentally, you're on another planet. In another universe."

"Aye, and there's the rub. So listen, my friend, and you shall hear, of the careful humiliation of Conner the queer."

"You're not gay?"

"I have no idea, I'm prepubescent. And incidentally, without hurting her, you have got to tell Mom to stop bragging about me to the other mothers."

Now, that was a stunner. Katelyn was hardly your braggart mama. "That doesn't sound like her, somehow."

"She refers to me as a 'genius.' 'My son is a genius,' she says. And do you know that Mrs. Warner resents this? And Mrs. Taylor and Mrs. Fisk and probably every other faculty wife with a kid at B.A. Because they all *want* geniuses, Dan. This is a college! These are college people! And I really am a genius and they resent me. So you give a kid ammo like that—the parents can't stand some classmate with an unfortunate disability like mine—and that poor cripple is fair game."

Dan could certainly see, from Conner's standpoint, why he might view his intelligence as a deformity. It was ugly, though, to see him driven to feel that way about a gift so rare.

The thing about Katelyn was, if you were going to love her and you were going to be her husband, you were going to have to accept that Conner was the center of the universe for her. He was, indeed, a professor's dream child and she was, indeed, a professor. "She's always bragged, Conner."

"She's really messing me up."

At that moment, flashlights began appearing in their yard, swarming over from the Warners'. There were also voices making low howling sounds. "Great," Conner muttered as he turned out his bedside light.

For a few more seconds, Dan hoped that this was something nice, but when he heard them calling Conner's name, he knew that it was more cruelty, and he, perhaps unfortunately, got mad. He headed for the glass door that opened out onto the underdeck and the yard.

"Dan, please just go upstairs."

"Conner, those kids don't have any business in this yard."

"Dan, please!"

Dan opened the door. Behind him, Conner pulled his bedspread over his head. Then Dan heard cracking sounds. He realized that somebody was hitting the aboveground pool with what sounded like a board or even a hammer.

"All right, that's enough," he shouted as he strode up to the shape that was hacking away at the pool. It was a kid he didn't recognize, but when the boy saw him, he tried to run. Dan got him by the collar of his jacket.

The kid swung and managed to land a crooked blow on Dan's thigh. And the rest of them didn't run. He heard Paulie Warner say in an almost bored voice, "Let 'im go, Dan."

Dan carried him across to the fence and dumped him over. "Get out of here, all of you." He grabbed Paulie as he was leaving. "You oughta be ashamed of yourself."

Paulie snorted—laughter. Only a miracle from above prevented Dan from smacking him. Instead, he brushed past him and strode across the Warners' driveway. "Get off my property," Paulie shouted from behind him.

He hammered on the front door. A couple of seconds later, Maggie opened it. He was so furious that for a moment he was at a loss for words, and the two of them just stared at each other. Finally, he spoke. "Keep those vandals out of my yard, Maggie, or I'm calling the cops."

"Dan?"

"Paulie had his gang out there busting up our pool, damnit! It's not on, Maggie. If I have to, I'll see you guys in family court. Paulie might not like Conner anymore. That's his privilege. But when he starts vandalizing our stuff—that I am not going to allow."

She turned around, called into the house, "Paulie?" Then, *"Paulie!"*

He came, not looking afraid in the least, Dan noted. He was growing up, Paulie Warner was. The peach fuzz was getting dark, the eyes getting hard.

"Did you bust up their pool?"

"No."

"Yeah, you did—or your friend did. I think they have a little gang, Maggie. What's your little gang called, Paulie?"

"I don't have a gang."

Maggie shoved his shoulder. "Where's Conner, Paulie?"

"He couldn't come."

"They cut him out and the gang is called the Conner-busters, and they invaded our yard with the intention of vandalizing us, and I'm not gonna stand for it, Maggie."

"Okay! Hey!" Maggie called into the house. Boys began to appear, just young enough to be a bit wide-eyed with worry. "Party's over, fellas. Call your parents and tell 'em to pick you up. You can wait on the front porch, I don't want you in here anymore. I've already had a shelf busted in my fridge—"

"That was an accident, Mom!"

"—and now the neighbors are complaining and I've had it. You go up to your room, young man."

Paulie started to speak, but she cuffed him in the back of the head. "Learn how to choose your friends, dummy," she said.

He went upstairs, his face red, fighting tears.

As Dan left, the other boys filtered out behind him. They crowded together on the front porch, blowing on their hands and waiting for their rides. He walked across the yards, feeling the cold now through his cotton chinos and his light sweater. The kids sure were growing up, and it was sad. Last July, he supposed, had been the high summer of Conner's childhood. He remembered those days of his own life. He'd been like some kind of water creature, like all the kids who lived along the lakes of Madison.

He went over to the pool. The moon was rising, and in its light he could see that the little creep had done a fair job on the fiberglass.

As he was walking back to the house, something caught his eye—a flash, he thought, coming from somewhere to the west, in the direction of the town. An explosion? There was no following rumble, so he supposed not. Nothing ever happened around here, anyway . . . except for kid trouble. Kids were a problem in any college town. Bored, affluent, smart, faculty brats were a notorious irritant on every campus he'd ever worked.

He went in and gently explained to Conner what had happened. "Son, there will be no fallout from this. You'll see, Monday morning in school it'll be as if none of it ever happened."

"I'm so glad."

"Count on it. They went a step too far, that's all. They're testing, trying to figure out who they want to be—and they're not like you, they're much simpler, to be honest. So even though they're older, in many ways they're less mature."

"Dan, do you think you could find out about the Wilton public schools for me, since I really can't return to B.A.? I think the, uh, middle school—what's it called, Colonel Saunders Memorial or something—has a rather good reputation in shop. And, of course, the football team is the stuff of local legend. Who knows, maybe I can try out for back end."

Dan saw that there was nothing to be gained by arguing with him. He'd go up and report to Katelyn.

As he left, Conner said, "Promise me, Dan. Call Wilton."

"I'll call them first thing Monday."

"And that boot camp in Lockridge. I could commute, actually, on the Louisville bus. I wouldn't have to live in the barracks or anything."

"Yeah, that's a possibility, too." Dan turned to leave and, to his surprise, saw a boy standing just beyond the deck. His shape was clearly visible in the moonlight. He was not one of the gangling creeps from Paulie's party. This kid looked even smaller than Conner. Which was very strange, because Conner himself was the youngest child on Oak Road, not counting six-month-old Jillie Jeffers.

It was dark in the underdeck, but the child was in the light of the moon.

Something struck Dan, then, hit him like an axe blow between the eyes. He was in a loud, echoing space looking down through a round hole, and there was a surface far below glistening silver just like this, in moonlight just like this. He felt in that moment a longing so powerful that it seemed to stop his blood, to cripple him with a sense of loss that might actually be larger than he could contain. For a moment, he was disoriented, as if detached from the ground, and he fell forward.

Then next thing he knew, somebody was calling him. Far away.

"Dad! Oh my God. Mom! *Mom*!"

Then footsteps, then he was aware that he'd fallen, and his head—his head hurt. That was it, he'd hit his head on a beam. Katelyn and Conner were there, they were terrified.

No problem, had to calm them down. "Oops," he croaked.

"Dan, don't move."

He sat up. "I about knocked myself silly."

"What happened, honey?"

"I was—" He looked around the cold, dark space. "I hit my head. One of the beams. I thought those kids had come back."

"What kids?"

"Paulie and his buddies."

"What were they doing in our yard?"

"It's a long story, Mom. And there *was* somebody out there just now." He pointed. "Something, anyway. It was an owl, right over there. A barn owl standing beside the pool."

There was nothing in the backyard now except the pool itself, gray in the moonlight, and beyond it the strip of woods that separated all the houses from a cornfield that fronted on Wilton Road.

Nothing more was said about the incident. Katelyn spent some time, then, with her son. She already knew all that had happened. Maggie had called, full of apologies. The boys had overstepped. Paulie would resume the old friendship, she would make sure of that.

She left him listening to a Leonard Cohen CD, another of his private eccentricities. God forbid that any of the other children should ever find *those* CDs, or his audio books of things like James Joyce's fantastically obscure and prolix *Finnegans Wake,* from which he drew some sort of equally obscure comfort. Maybe he even understood it, who could know?

She took a bottle of wine and a couple of glasses up to their bedroom, and drank some wine with her husband. No more Conner until the morning. They lay together, then, with the light of the westering moon falling on their naked bodies, and the wine in them. Dan said, "You want to give it a try?"

"With no diaphragm?"

"Clean and clear."

She kissed him. "I do, I do."

"Oh, wow, hey—" He reached over, got his wineglass and raised it. "To the next genius Callaghan. If we make it."

"Okay, listen, you—I do want to, but this is not the right moment, Dan, and you know that."

"The tenure will come."

"The tenure may come. And when it does, we celebrate." She laughed a little. "By doing this incredibly profound thing of making another child. But, Dan, if you do not get it, then—"

"The tenure will come!"

"Marcie is a complex, difficult human being."

He threw himself back on the bed. She laid a hand on his head.

"You sure you're okay, Dan?"

"Absolutely."

"Well, you know there's no beam down there you could've hit your head on. So that's not what happened."

He knew it. He allowed himself to consider the possibility of a seizure. He'd had them as a child, he remembered them, they would start with an aura that involved seeing his planetarium lights, then progress to this bizarre, echoing room where there would be unspeakable things, human bodies with no skin, giant flies—and then it would be morning, and he'd wake up perfectly fine.

He had never told a soul about the seizures, and he didn't intend to tell Katelyn now. They were, perhaps, one of the reasons that he had become a physiological psychologist. His own suffering had led him to a fascination with the mechanics and abnormalities of the brain.

They slept then, joined to the sleeping world of man, a place that is different by night, that is not at all what it seems.

They did not sleep alone, though. They were watched, and carefully watched. Minds very different from our own, with objectives and needs completely beyond the imagining of the Callaghans, drew conclusions about what they saw, and acted on those conclusions.

Deep in the night, they acted, and Marcie Cotton became the latest victim of a great and intricate terror.

And then things went wrong. Very, very wrong.

FOUR

OAK ROAD WAS SO QUIET at 3 A.M. that you could hear the whispering fall of individual pine needles as they dropped in the woods that separated the houses from the farmer's field behind them. So when screams erupted, every human being and all the animals woke up instantly.

Marcie Cotton also heard the cries, and an expressionless voice repeating again and again, "What can we do to help you stop screaming?" Only when she felt herself suck breath, and realized that the narrow, black cot from which she could not rise was not her bed, did she connect with the fact that the screaming was coming from her. She thought: *nightmare*. And then she screamed again.

THERE WERE FOUR FAMILIES LIVING at the end of Oak Road, all Bell College faculty. The last house on the dead end was occupied by the Jefferses, Nancy and Chris, and their baby daughter. Beside them were the Callaghans, next the Warners, Harley and Maggie, Paulie and Amy. The house closest to the beginning of Oak Road belonged to the Keltons, two parents and two teenage sons.

At the Kelton house, Manrico, the family dog, sat up and snorted, then stood and commenced barking. The two teenagers leaped out of bed and started pulling on their pants.

Nancy Jeffers also screamed, and Chris, the youthful

head of the physics department, jumped up as if there was a snake in the bed. Out the bedroom window, he saw a glow through the woods. "Dear God there's a fire," he shouted, pulling on a pair of rubber overshoes and an overcoat.

THE TRIAD HAD BEEN COMMANDED to bring Marcie Cotton to Dan Callaghan. The collective wanted them to bond her to him, so that she would do anything to make sure his tenure bid succeeded. There must be no chance that the Callaghans would leave Wilton, where every street, alley, basement, attic, and mind was known to the collective. An attack on the Callaghans was inevitable, and the collective's plan to defend them had been constructed around their staying in the town.

Important work, certainly, but not all that they intended to do on this night. There was a reason this particular triad called themselves the Three Thieves . . . which was their imperfect ability to handle temptation. And Marcie was such very strong temptation.

PAULIE WARNER RAN INTO HIS parents' room, shouting that the Keltons' house was on fire. Harley Warner said to his wife, "My God, they might be trapped."

Maggie went to the window. "Is that a fire? It's very steady."

"Somebody's really screaming," Amy said, coming in behind her brother.

"Let's get over there," Paulie said.

Harley was pulling on his jeans. "Not you kids."

"Aw, *Dad*!"

"Paulie, not until I know what's going on out there." He did not want his children exposed to whatever might be happening over there, not given the agony he was hearing in those screams.

THE MORE MARCIE SCREAMED, THE more excited the Three Thieves became. They knew they were too low, they knew they should quiet her, they knew there was a dog nearby, and they could not control dogs. But they also knew that they could reach into her and taste of her emotions, and the taste would fill them with a delicious fire that their kind did not possess, the fire of strong feeling. Man might not be intelligent enough to save himself from the environmental imbalance overpopulation had caused on his planet, but his emotional genius was beyond compare.

They dug into her gushing terror like wolves digging into the flowing guts of a deer . . . and the collective at first reacted with surprise. Then it raged.

Conner thought the female voice was his mother screaming, and she thought that it was him. They met in the living room, and threw their arms around each other. Then Dan said, "There's a light in the field." From their perspective on their rear deck, it was clear that none of the houses were involved.

Conner and Katelyn stayed behind while Dan, wearing slippers and a robe, went out onto the deck and down into the backyard. He carried a flashlight.

Their scraggly yard was quiet. The toys of summer—the slide, the swing set, the empty aboveground pool—were sentinels in the stark light of the setting moon. He moved toward the glow, which was in the field beyond the end of the yard, past a stand of narrow third- or fourth-growth pines.

Katelyn and Conner came out on the deck.

"I think it's a fire in the field," he said.

"Are you serious?"

"Oh, God, somebody help me! Somebody help me!"

Katelyn clutched her son. "Conner, we're going back in."

Conner broke away from her and went racing down the deck stairs. "Look at that," he yelled.

As he and Dan crossed the yard, hurrying toward the thin woods, a huge light loomed up from below the tree line. They stopped, stunned by this second moon rising.

Katelyn arrived beside them. "Conner, put this on."

"Thanks, Mom!" He dug his arms into a jacket. "You know what that is?"

"No."

Dan walked closer to the edge of the woods. "Can we help you?" he shouted.

"Don't go too close, Dad."

The thing seemed to wobble, then rise.

"It's moving this way, Dan!"

It hung above the woods. Not a sound, now.

"I think it's a balloon," Katelyn said.

Then more screams whipped out, shrill to cracking.

"A balloon is on fire!" Katelyn shouted.

The three of them ran again, fumbling in the brush, guided by the light.

"Who in the world would be up in a hot-air balloon at night?" Conner asked. "And that's not fire, that's a piezo-electric effect of some kind. Look at it shimmer."

"It's a student," Katelyn said. "Something's gone wrong with some prank."

It wasn't anything to do with hazing, not in February, but it could indeed be a prank. Every house that backed onto the field was occupied by a Bell College professor.

THE THREE THIEVES LOOKED OUT across the electromagnetic haze that flowed off the wires with which humans surrounded their shelters. Sharp eyes watched Conner and Dan.

DAN PAUSED IN THE WOODS. "Maybe nothing's gone wrong. Maybe the screaming is the prank."

"I hope so," Katelyn said, calmer now, embracing this most reasonable of probabilities.

"Come on," Conner said.

Before them, as they left the woods, they saw people running toward the object from various directions, Harley Warner, but not Paulie or his mother or sister, Chris and Nancy Jeffers, and the entire Kelton family, robes flying, Manrico barking furiously, but hanging well back. Jimbo Kelton was using a video camera, and Nancy Jeffers held her cell phone out like some kind of shield, no doubt taking pictures with it.

Another scream pealed out.

Dan shouted, "DO YOU NEED HELP?" He hoped it was just a prank because Bell did not need adverse publicity, not with the sort of enrollment problems faced by a small college located at the burnt-out end of a bus line that only served what the college brochure gamely called "the sophisticated little city of Wilton." What sophistication there might be in a row of closed stores and a grain elevator was anybody's guess.

"Oh, God, God!"

The words seemed to ring in the trees, to leave their narrow trunks trembling.

"Can't you see that she's in real trouble?" Conner yelled. He took off toward the object.

THE ONE WATCHED CONNER, WHILE the Two and the Three regarded Marcie with the reverent cunning of boys in a candy store. The Two drew closer, now pressing his face into her churning aura. Angry static bounced around the tiny space—the collective was furious that they were not performing as directed.

Which made little difference. The thousand grays who were here were spread all over the planet, feeding in Brazil and Britain and China, mining gravitite in the iron deposits of New York, extracting Helium 3 fuel on the moon. They were linked to the great collective, yes, but it was moving toward Earth far more slowly than the lead group, so what could it actually do? Nothing, and they would carry out its orders . . . eventually.

The Three Thieves would have been more efficient with Marcie, but the luscious fears, the darting hopes, the bright, wet desires that filled her smooth flesh were just too much of a temptation. Dan Callaghan was awake anyway, so the whole expedition was a waste. They might as well make of it whatever they could.

The Two, as the negative pole of the triad, showed her a long needle. Her eyes widened as she saw the silver of it appearing out of the dark that surrounded her. She could not see the Thieves, of course, they were too careful for that.

He plunged the needle into her forehead and she shrieked and they gobbled her agony . . . for the moments that it lasted feeling as alive as their distant ancestors must have, before they had enhanced themselves with machine intelligence, and lost contact with the only thing that mattered, in the end, which was feeling.

Without it, life was ongoing death, and to find it again, crossing a galaxy was as nothing, not even if the journey took fifty generations, not even if it took a thousand.

From a billion times a billion miles away, they had seen Earth glowing with emotion. It had drawn them like excited moths to its mystery, first in hundreds, then in thousands, and soon the billions would come to drink the healing waters of the human soul . . . if all went well.

THE KELTONS WENT CLOSE, RUNNING low like actors on a movie battlefield. It occurred to Dan that Jimbo Kelton might be recording the prank for the later amusement of fellow perpetrators.

All the people in the neighborhood were not only known to each other, they counted one another as friends. Nancy and Chris were dear friends of Katelyn and Dan. Kelton was a historian, working at the far end of the campus from the Hall of Science, but still a member of the cozy little Oak Road crowd. The Warners and the Callaghans were very close—or had been.

Nancy clutched her cell phone to her ear. Dan felt for his, miraculously found it in a pocket of his jacket. He punched in 9-1-1. "This is Dr. Daniel Callaghan, one-oh-three Oak Road. There's a fire in the field behind our house that borders Wilton Road. Somebody's trapped in it."

The screams lost form, became a continuous roar of pain.

Dan closed his cell phone while the dispatcher was still talking. He was now convinced that this was serious. Those screams were real. He took off after Conner, going flat-out.

"Don't let him near it," Katelyn howled, passing him in her pursuit of her son.

As Dan ran, he looked for the basket, for the burning student, but he could see only the fearsome glare, like looking into a thousand car headlights or a flashbulb that would not quit. He shielded his eyes and struggled closer. "Conner! Conner where are you?"

"I can't see him, Dan! CONNER! CONNER!"

Another scream came, trembling and high, desolate with agony, then the object wavered a little in the air. Far off, the thin wail of a siren could be heard, then more sirens, getting louder.

"Conner, oh thank God!"

He was with the Kelton boys, his small form hidden in the bulk of their teenage bodies.

"Come on, we're getting out of here," Katelyn said.

"Mom!"

"Come *on*!" She took him by the wrist, yanked him away, heading back toward their empty house.

"No!" He broke away.

And suddenly she was terribly afraid. Afraid for her son. He was vulnerable—to what, she did not know, but she knew that he was vulnerable.

"Conner, please, I am begging you. I am begging you right now to come back with me."

"Mom, I think I know what this is!"

"Conner, no. You have no idea. Nobody does. But it's not right and it's dangerous."

He threw his arms around her. "Mom, don't worry." In an instant, he had broken away and was running back into the light.

The Thieves were concerned now. Conner should not be here, and they could feel the fury and the fear of the whole collective. Of course everybody was scared: their survival depended on this child, who had been bred through fifty human generations.

Katelyn had the awful and frightening sense that the thing was somehow *watching* her son. She took off after him, her feet slamming into the winter-hard ground, and she tackled him and brought him down.

It made him cry out in astonishment. Katelyn had never disciplined him physically. Such a thing was unthinkable, to humiliate a brilliant child in that way—or any child, for that matter.

She got up on all fours, crying, trying to keep herself between him and the thing. She had the hideous feeling that it would somehow suck him into its fire, and he would join the poor woman who was screaming there.

He stood up. Glaring down at her, he turned away from the object and strode back toward the house. Thanking God in her heart, she followed her son home.

FIVE

THE YOUNG LIEUTENANT HANDED COLONEL Robert Langford a sheet of paper. "My God," he said as he read it.

"Sir?"

"This is under the blanket," he said. The young man, who was not cleared to hear what was about to be said, left the room.

The glowboy that had been snooping around Wilton, Kentucky, had just done something that Rob had never seen, and that he was quite sure no monitor had seen from the beginning of this mission, which dated back to 1942.

He pulled up a satellite view of Wilton. The glowboy was bright, its plasma fully deployed. The thing was ready to move out of there fast. He zoomed in on the image. Disbelieving, he zoomed in on it again. What in hell were people doing crowding around the thing? The grays considered their secrecy essential, and they had threatened dire consequences if it was ever compromised. But they themselves were breaking it.

And also breaking a fundamental policy of the United States of America, which was to keep their secret until and if something could be said to the public other than, "We know they're here, we know that they come into your bedrooms and kidnap you in the night, but we don't know why and we are helpless to stop them. And yes, some of you disappear, and some of you die."

He stared at the image, watching the figures move, trying to form some sort of a rational explanation of what might be happening.

Rob spent too much time in the Mountain, or so he'd been told by practically everybody who worked with him. Because the grays operated at night and tracking their movements was his duty, over the years he'd gradually become a night person.

Mike Wilkes had negotiated a treaty with the grays, using the interface between Bob and Adam and Eamon Glass. The agreement was that they would limit their abductions in number and region. In return, the United States had guaranteed to protect their secrecy.

It was Rob's job to keep track of the abductions, and, in the most extreme cases of treaty violation, to put up a show of force.

This was not to be done lightly. The grays would not stand to be fired upon. That had been tried back in the forties, and the reply had been horrifying. The grays had caused six hundred plane crashes in the year 1947. Shortly thereafter, President Truman had ordered that they were not to be interfered with in any way. Nobody cared to challenge the grays, but now was one of those dreadful moments when something had to be done.

Early on, there had been a fear that the Soviets would find out how the collective minds of the grays worked, and announce to the world something like, "We have seen the future and it is Communist." However, nobody except the United States Air Force possessed a gray. Therefore the rest of the world—including the remaining U.S. military, the intelligence community, and the government—was at best minimally informed. Within the Air Force, fewer than twenty people knew about this project.

He put his hand on the phone. There was nobody else in the world who could make this decision, or even offer advice. If he was wrong, there was just no way to tell what the grays would do.

Could he bring about the end of the world when he picked up that phone?

He lifted the receiver, punched in some numbers. "Jimmy, Rob. Do you have my glowboy coordinates?"

"Yes, sir. It's been ground bound for a while, sir."

"I need a scramble out of Alfred moving on it *instamente*."

"Yes, sir!"

He paused, then. Took a deep breath. "God be with us," he said into the phone. His next step was to inform Wilkes of what was happening, and that required setting up a listening device on the call. Mr. Crew expected all contacts with Wilkes to be logged, recorded, and sent to him.

Personally, Rob was convinced that Crew was right to be suspicious of Wilkes. He believed that the man was using the empaths to discover new technologies, and selling them to the private sector. Also, Wilkes's pathological hatred of the grays was inappropriate. He believed that they were bent on invasion. They scared him and that's why he hated them. But hate does not win wars, knowledge does, and that's what Wilkes's empath unit was supposed to be gaining from the one remaining gray in captivity. But damned little useful information came out of the new empath.

Rob did not understand the grays but he didn't hate them. In fact, he found them incredibly interesting. They'd been here for fifty years and they hadn't invaded yet, so that didn't seem to be a very real concern. What they did to people was weird, but you didn't see folks disappearing or being injured, at least not physically. Obviously, though, whatever the grays were doing to the people they abducted was damned important to them. Otherwise, there would not be threats. They were taking something from us, no question of that, but in the way a farmer takes milk, not meat.

The information flow, Rob believed, was being shunted to Wilkes's real buddies, the quiet companies who fed off the United States' one-hundred-and-twenty-billion-dollar annual black budget. In Rob's opinion, there was a pipeline that led, through Wilkes, from Adam right back to the industry. It would certainly explain why an Oklahoma orphan boy, who had nothing to live on but his soldier's pay, called a multimillion-dollar house in Georgetown home . . . and why an officer whose work was in a hole two hundred feet below Indianapolis, Indiana, even needed a presence inside the Beltway.

"Mike, it's Rob. Sorry about the late hour, but I have a

situation. There's a glowboy on the ground near Wilton, Kentucky. I know, it's very odd and very disturbing. What's even more of a concern is that there are civilians in the field around him. He's got his plasma deployed and he's ready to run, but he ain't running. There have gotta be video cameras down there, all kinds of trouble. I'm doing a scramble, I've got to get that guy out of there. Do you think you could get Glass in the hole with Adam? Let's reassure him that it's just a friendly warning that they might spill their own secret. And let's please find out what we can about what in sam hill they're up to."

He waited until he heard Wilkes's grunt of assent. The good colonel did not like to be dictated to, which is why Rob did just that whenever he had a chance.

ALFRED AIR FORCE BASE WAS a training facility. It was still up and running largely because Kentucky's senior senator was a member of the Armed Services Committee and powerful enough to hold onto his bases.

Whatever, Rob was damned relieved that the place was still operational. He widened the image on the overhead satellite, punched a couple of keys, and saw a white outline of the base superimposed over its location. The base was barely thirty miles from the unfolding incident.

IN THE FIELD IN KENTUCKY, they were standing in helpless amazement, watching the object. Nancy Jeffers had gone home, because she and her husband had no wish to leave their baby alone with something like this taking place. Katelyn and Conner were also gone, and Dan was just as glad. A child had no business out here, and he thought that Kelton was letting his boys get way too close with that camera of theirs.

Without warning, a clap of thunder hit. Dan cried out, they all did. Chris Jeffers covered his head with his hands. Dan saw a double star wheeling in the sky. Then he heard the shriek of a jet and realized that what he was looking at were afterburners. "It's the Air Force!" he shouted.

Its underside glowing in the light being given off by the object, the fighter howled past so low that a hot stench of burning jet fuel washed over them.

The object turned purple. It moved, wobbling, above the ground.

The voice in the thing cried out, "Help me, help me, oh God, no! *NO NO NO!*"

The light rose into the sky. It hung there, still wobbling slightly. The jet's glowing afterburners turned and started back.

"Stop it! Stop that!" came the voice. Then more screaming. *"Ah! Ah! Ah! Oh aaaaaa . . ."*

Maggie Warner screamed with her, crying into the agony of it.

In that instant, the object rose a hundred feet or so, then shot off to the north literally like a bullet. It went faster than Dan had ever seen anything go.

The jet passed over again, its engines screaming. It turned and followed the object. They watched the afterburners creep away into the sky.

Into the silence that followed, Chris said, "God help her."

"That was a UFO," young Jimbo Kelton announced.

Maggie asked, *"Was* that a UFO?"

"Dear heaven," Harley Warner said, "I think so."

Dan was looking at a small shadow in the field standing where the glow had been. "Folks," he said, "uh, I don't think we're alone here."

But when he shone his flashlight toward it, there was nothing there.

SIX

LAUREN GLASS WAS ENJOYING TEDDY Blaine's lovemaking, powerful and persistent from this sweet, rough guy. As a fellow Air Force officer, he was carefully disinterested in Lauren's classified work, and that made this particular affair very fun and very easy. As long as she was involved in heavily classified work, Lauren's plan was to keep the lovers moving through her life. Nobody deep, because it made it too hard to keep her secrets.

When Colonel Wilkes called her, she tried to ignore it. She pushed the chiming out of her mind, concentrated on the warmth under the covers, and the fabulous young man who was loving her.

The warble became a whine.

"Oh, Lauren," Teddy whispered, sinking down onto her, burying his face in her neck, kissing her now gently, pressing his prickled cheek against her soft one.

"My love," she said, and thought that she really did kind of mean it. Which meant—should she ditch him on the never-get-too-close theory?

The whine became a wail.

He jerked like he'd been stuck with a pin. "I don't believe this."

"My cert's up," she said, referring to the security certification system on her computer, which started automatically when she began receiving a classified message.

But why was he after her now, at—what—jeez, it was

3 A.M. She'd been in the cage for six hours yesterday waiting without result for Adam to at least take a breath, and
she was most certainly not ready to return to his dark,
claustrophobic hole.

Throwing off the covers, she went over and typed her
password. Code came up, four lines, which she sight read.
"They've got a virus," she muttered, striving not to reveal
to him her true horror. The message communicated extreme urgency. Something was wrong. *Real* wrong.

"Let somebody else fix it."

"I have to go," she said, going to her closet and starting
to dress.

"Miss Indispensable."

"Unfortunately." Zipping her jeans, she went over and
kissed him. "I'll be back, love," she said.

He drew her toward the bed. Briefly, she sat down. They
kissed. She looked into his eyes. She sighed. "You know
the rules." And she realized how much she hated what she
did—how deeply, profoundly twisted it felt . . . but she
loved the perks, and, quite frankly, she was also sort of
okay with Adam. The facility was a hole, but at the bottom
of that hole was a most extraordinary being.

The thought that Adam might not be well crossed her
mind. That made her hurry even more. She threw on a sky-
blue cashmere sweater and her black jacket. After a per-
functory brush of her hair, she strode across her large
living room and out the door.

She did not look back toward Ted. When she returned,
he might well be gone. Fine, she'd rustle up another roll in
the hay, maybe a civilian this time.

She had a lot for a girl of twenty-six. But she did a lot.
As far as anybody knew, there was only one person on this
earth who could do what she did. No doubt there were others, but how to find them? The Air Force had never been
able to succeed at that, which was fine by her, since it
meant that she could name her price, which had been pro-
motion to full colonel. So now Mike's orders were re-
quests . . . but this was one she would certainly meet.

In the elevator, she turned her mind to her work. What
could be wrong? She wished the elevator would go faster.

She arrived in the condo's garage, strode to her car, and sped off to the facility. It wasn't far. She couldn't live far from Adam.

She turned two corners onto Hamilton, and made her way down the tree-shaded street to the old house.

Wilkes met her at the door, which was unusual in the extreme. "A glowboy kiped a newbie in the forbidden zone and there were civilian witnesses," he said all in one breath. "I want you to query Adam on it."

"Why?"

"Because it's so extremely unusual, obviously."

"You understand, they don't have the concept of treaty. They don't know what that is. And they futz with newbies all the time. You just don't see them do it, because they stay in the approved zones."

"You know this?"

"What if I told you that they're a rambunctious, fun-loving bunch of extremely brilliant but weird people? How would that sit?"

"First, they are not people. Second, they are not only extremely brilliant, they are extremely sinister and they have no emotions."

"Adam showed grief when Dad got killed."

"He was faking it."

"Plus, he—I don't know how to put it, it's not human emotion, not at all, but he does care about me."

"You're projecting. End of story. Now, let's go down. We have work to do." As they waited for the elevator, he added, "We have a scramble running on the glowboy, incidentally."

"Oh, great, how do I explain that?"

"Communicate that it's a friendly warning. The civilians are liable to have cameras. There could be a security breach that's beyond our control."

"Wunderbar." She was annoyed when Wilkes got into the elevator with her. She did not like him around when she and Adam were together.

A few moments later, the doors opened onto the control room and, beyond it, the huge door that sealed Adam's space.

As Lauren stripped, Andy began opening a fresh prep kit.

She dropped her sweater to the floor and rubbed her temples. "So I need to find out why this triad is off-station?"

Lauren threw off her clothes in front of both men. Let them see. She was proud of what she was.

"Lauren, I need concrete information from you on this."

She let Andy cover her body with the emollients that would protect every inch of her skin. Over the years, she'd gotten drier and drier from the zero-humidity conditions in the cage. At twenty-six she had the skin of a forty-year-old. She caked her face in Vaseline.

Andy's hands felt only clinical to her, but she was aware that she did not feel clinical to him. She knew because of the way he would turn away when he was finished, his cheeks burning, poor guy.

She pulled on her orange coverall, zipped it, and wrapped the neck shield tightly. Andy fitted her cap. Then she rolled her heavy latex gloves onto her hands.

She faced the steel door.

Andy pushed up the sleeve of her coverall and injected her. "Sorry," he said, as always. He kissed her then, very quickly, on the place he'd just pricked.

She opened the door, stepped into the airlock, and waited. The inner door hissed and slid aside.

She entered her secret heaven and hell, the world of love and terror that she shared with Adam.

SEVEN

AS A SOCIAL SCIENTIST, KATELYN Callaghan understood the impulse to congregate after a tragedy, which was why the Jefferses had returned, baby in carrier, and now sat before the Callaghan fireplace. The Keltons had rushed home to study their video, the Warners to keep their excited kids from doing anything rash.

Hell's gate had opened for somebody tonight, and now there must be congregation—the ancient holy act that was intended by deepest human instinct to declaim the persistence of life.

Chris and Nancy sat with straight backs, methodically sipping wine. Six-month-old Jillie slept in her carrier between them, her little mouth open, her pacifier in her hand.

Katelyn wanted only to go downstairs to Conner. As irrational as it probably was, she was nevertheless experiencing an urge to guard him, and this urge was growing by the minute.

Nervously, she paced in front of the fireplace, drinking rather than sipping. She feared that Conner might go back out there on his own. That was why the Warners were staying home, to keep Paulie in. Conner could easily leave via the door that led from his basement room under the deck, and out into the yard.

She stepped onto the deck and looked out across the yard. No movement. Total silence.

It had seemed like half the campus police department,

the entire volunteer fire department, County Emergency Services, and the state police had come.

None of the official types had seen the light, but the Air Force jet had still been maneuvering around when they came, at least. Police Chief Dunst had called Alfred AFB, only to be told that there were no fighters in the air at that time. No planes at all, in fact. He'd closed his cell phone in disgust. "Guess that was a privately owned F-15 on afterburners," he'd muttered.

The emergency crews had combed the field with infrared detectors. It had all been very impressive, but it would have been more impressive if they had found something resembling human remains, or even a shard of debris of some sort.

"Well," Nancy said at last, "what do we think?"

"We think some damned kids are in big trouble. I mean, I saw the Air Force out there," Katelyn said.

"Dan. Danny Dan." Chris laughed silently.

"No, Chris," Nancy said.

"No? With regard to what?"

"With regard to the fact that you think it was a flying saucer."

"With an abductee aboard, yes, I do think that."

Now it was Nancy's turn to drink deep. She glared at her husband. "I don't want to hear this."

"It's true, though."

"Maybe and maybe not, but I do know one thing, we're here because of this UFO stuff! Shunted off into this backwater with barely enough of a salary to raise our baby— and it's because you side with the trailer trash instead of your fellow physicists. Excuse me, folks. Family stuff."

"No, it's true," Dan said, "everybody here is a failure somewhere else."

"They're real, they're here, and my colleagues are wrong. If that video—"

"Don't you dare go on TV about this, Chris. Don't you *dare*!"

Chris raised his hands defensively. "Be it far from me, unless—"

"Unless nothing! No more, Chris. I have gone from Cal-

Tech to U. Mass to this because of your damn UFOs. Below here, we are looking at the junior-college pit."

"I reserve judgement until I have seen the video. If it's as good as I think it's going to be, it might just get us back to CalTech."

"You are so fired, Chris. You will never, ever get back there. My God, you made a public idiot of yourself on national television."

"I told the truth!"

He had appeared on *Dateline* as an advocate for the reality of UFOs, and his status as a CalTech professor had been used to give him credibility. Within a year, he was out. At U. Mass, it had been an article in the *Boston Globe* that had quoted his *Dateline* statements. He lasted six months that time.

Dan told himself to keep out of it. But then he thought that the poor woman was just so vulnerable, with that little baby, and, as much as he liked Chris, he was way off base on this one. "Alien abduction is seizure-related folklore. Did I ever tell you that I suffered from waking nightmares when I was a child? Which is why I know what this is. I saw these little figures. Yeah, me, Chris. I'm an abductee, by your rather dubious—excuse me—standards. But because I also happen to possess a little professional knowledge of the brain, I know where the aliens come from—" He pointed to his own head. "The same place that ghosts and demons and—whatever—goblins come from. And not from some damn field on the outskirts of a one-horse town in Kentucky."

"Officially, I believe that Wilton is classified as a half-horse town."

"Whatever, we saw a prank, it was terrifying, and now the Air Force is involved, and there is likely to be hell to pay for these students and this institution, and that is a damn crying shame! Although they do deserve it. The students, not poor Bell."

"The Air Force said they weren't there."

"Dan," Nancy asked, "are you concerned about your tenure bid? You must be." She turned to her husband. "Because he won't involve you. That I will not let him do."

"All the witnesses—"

"Don't even start, Chris, my dear love. Dan and Katelyn did not see this. And Kelton, look at him, he's on thin ice as it is, the history department's a basket case. Don't involve them, Chris. Don't you dare." She looked at Dan. "How's it going, by the way?"

"Marcie is how it's going."

"Marcie is your referee? You've got to be kidding. She hasn't voted yes on a tenure since Clinton was in the White House."

Now Dan went for the bottle, poured a glass, sucked it dry. "This is pretty bad," he said, looking at the label.

"Six dollars at Kroger, don't knock it," Chris said. "Now, listen to me. I don't want to set you off again, but you do realize that this is a historical event. A large group of witnesses, armed in some cases with video equipment, have observed, and, I hope, recorded, a UFO on the ground up close. Exhibiting every evidence of the presence of an abductee inside. Which I intend to proclaim to the world."

"Chris, shut up!"

He looked at his mild-mannered wife in open astonishment. "Excuse me?"

"Just you shut up! Are you hard of hearing or something? Okay, look, you do this and you do it without me and Jillie, because we will be gone."

"Where?"

"Anywhere!"

"Nancy, this is proof!"

"Oh, Jesus. Junior college, here we come." She stood up. "I think I'm leaving." She picked up Jillie in her carrier.

What Katelyn feared was that there had been a murder out there, involving God only knew what sort of bizarre method. A murder, and, perhaps, if the shadow Dan had seen was really somebody, a murderer who was still nearby.

"If you get yourself fired," Nancy told Chris as she pulled on her coat, "expect divorce papers, mister."

"Let's approach it from the direction of each of our specialties," Chris suggested.

He seemed unbothered by his wife's outburst. And indeed, Nancy did not actually walk out the door. Katelyn thought, *It's a real marriage, then. They're long-haulers like us.* She knew where this kind of fight took you, in the end. It took you to bed. "Well, certainly," she said, attempting to move things to a somewhat calmer level, "from the standpoint of the sociologist, we witnessed a real, physical event that I fear was tragic. We all do, or we wouldn't be here huddled together in the back of the proverbial cave in the dead of the night."

Dan said, "I'm in agreement that it wasn't a hallucination. It was a prank and possibly somebody was injured. I agree there. Unless some genius actress has just recently emerged here at Bell, which I very much doubt."

"I thought *Death of a Salesman* was pretty good," Chris said.

Dan smiled. "*Death of a Salesman* is not working when you find yourself pulling for Willy Loman to commit suicide."

"What we didn't see was an alien spacecraft taking somebody on a rough ride," Nancy said. "I want that established, Chris. Admitted."

"So, what did we see?" Chris's question was softly put.

Silence fell.

Katelyn said, "My concern is the injury issue. And frankly, getting awakened in the middle of the night. It *is* the middle of the night. I am outraged and I am scared." She told herself it was mostly outrage. She knew that it was mostly fear. "I think somebody might be badly injured, hidden in some dorm basement right now, trying to tend her burns with Bactine or something."

"Don't say that," Nancy said, shivering

"What's the enrollment picture looking like, Nance?" Dan asked. He was well aware that the psychology department was overstaffed. If Bell had another bad enrollment season, he could not only be passed over for tenure, he could see his professorship dissolved. Obviously, a campus death would not be helpful.

"Iffier than last year, actually."

"Maybe the idea that we've had an alien visitation would actually help," Chris said.

"Excuse me, guys," Nancy asked, "but who's in the kitchen?"

"That would be nobody," Katelyn said. Except she had also heard a sound—a chair scraping against the kitchen tile floor. "Excuse me," she said, standing up. "Is that somebody there?" she asked as she headed across the dining room.

The kitchen was empty, but as she walked in, Katelyn thought she might have seen the back door closing. She called, "Dan, come in here."

Dan got up, sucking in breath as he did so. He came into the room. Nancy and Chris followed close behind.

"I don't want to alarm anybody," Katelyn said softly, "but I think someone just went out on the porch."

Dan opened the door. The tiny side yard was bright with moonlight, and clearly empty. He peered along the driveway, then stepped out and looked at the street. Cold, quiet, that was all.

"What gives?" Katelyn asked as he returned.

He shook his head. "All quiet on the Oak Road front."

"I heard the chair, and I thought—I don't know what I thought."

"It must have been the wind."

"There is no wind." She put her hand on a chair, dragged it. "It was somebody doing this."

"There's nobody," Dan said. He locked the back door. "At least, not anymore." He had the odd feeling, though, that this was not right. He shuddered. The room seemed somehow— what? It was clean enough, but it seemed—well, there was no way around it: the place felt . . . occupied. "Does it seem—" He shook his head. How could he explain what he felt? Watched, when there was obviously nobody else here.

Chris lunged suddenly, slapped the kitchen table with his open hand.

The sound silenced them all.

"I—uh—there was a fly."

"In February?" Nancy asked.

"No, there wasn't a fly. Something moved. I saw it out of the corner of my eye. A cat—maybe a cat . . . over there by the pantry. Could a cat have gotten in here?"

"Stranger things have happened," Dan said.

"Obviously," Katelyn said as she got a bottle of wine from the cabinet where they were kept, "just an hour ago." She looked at the bottle. "Will our five-dollar cabernet beat your six-dollar merlot?"

Dan checked the pantry. The familiar neat rows of canned goods stood untouched on the shelves, there if they ever got snowed in. He shook a box of cereal Conner had left open, re-rolled the wax paper inside, and closed it.

As he turned away, he felt something—like somebody's hand had brushed against his left ear. He fumbled for the light, turned it on.

There was nobody in here but him.

Then a pain like a blowtorch flashed through the ear. He gasped, cried out, stifled the cry.

Katelyn had the chair in her hand. He staggered toward it.

"Dan?"

"I'm okay!" He fell into the chair. He could do nothing else, he was in agony. "Jesus, Jesus," he said, trying not to gasp, trying not to seem to be in pain and failing utterly.

"What the hell?" Chris said.

"It's my ear," he breathed. "Oh, Jesus!"

Katelyn looked at it.

"Whoa, that smarts. Christ."

"It looks fine."

"Oh, man. It must be—" He tried to get up, failed. He was too dizzy. "Am I having a stroke? Does anybody know the symptoms?"

"Is it a headache, honey?"

"My God, it's my ear, it's killing me."

"Perhaps a visit to the health center," Nancy suggested.

"Dr. Hamner's on senility leave," Dan said. "Anyway, it's closed at night because people might need it then."

The pain began to get a little less. Dan managed to come to his feet. Still dizzy, he staggered a step. "Better," he said.

At that moment, everything in the room rattled, there was a loud whoosh, and the back door opened and slammed itself.

"The *wind*," Nancy shrilled, then knocked back a full glass of wine and poured another.

Katelyn did not tell them what she had just seen, which was a sort of light flickering along the back porch and into the yard, a light like a narrow searchlight beam from somewhere over the house.

In her most private self, in places inside herself where she almost never went, there were vague memories from childhood, memories that had drawn her to watch a TV documentary here and there about alien abduction, and to wonder. The memories were very unformed and very strange, but the fact remained that when she had first seen one of those big-eyed alien faces depicted on the cover of some stupid book, she had been transfixed, literally unable to move, and unable to stop the tears.

She would never tell Dan this, not with his childhood seizures. He needed to leave apparitions, demons, and all of that sort of thing behind him.

She could only think now of one thing: Conner, because, in her heart of hearts, she worried that he might be seizure-prone, too. Or worse, *what if it was true?* Even more than a criminal or idiot pranksters, if there were aliens out there right now, her place was with her little boy. She stepped back toward the living room.

"Katelyn?"

"Sorry, Dan, I thought I heard Conner."

"Help me, here." He went toward her.

She strode over to the freezer, rummaged for the blue cold pack, thrust it at him. He took it with thanks, pressed it against his head. "Better," he said. "Somewhat."

She went downstairs. On this night, she would sleep on the floor beside her son.

"Hi," he said as she came in.

"Not asleep yet?" She sat on the bed. "It's terribly late."

"Three twenty-eight. I guess that qualifies."

"Conner, I'm so sorry I knocked you down like that. I was just—oh, honey, I was so scared. I've never been that scared in my life!"

"You want to know a secret, Mom?"

"Sure."

"That you *swear* you will especially not tell any Warners?"

"Sworn on the old heart."

"I've never been that scared in my life, either. Mom, you know what I felt like? I felt like it was watching me."

She did not—dared not—tell him of her own feelings.

No matter all the elegantly dismissive conversation above, the dumping on Chris with his silly ideas, down here in the dark with Conner, she found a truth that she could not deny. Whatever had happened out in that field, it had nothing whatsoever to do with any pranks, and murder was even more far-fetched.

The truth was, it had everything to do with the night and the unknown.

She took Conner in her arms, and prayed to the good God that she be granted the right to never, ever let go of him again. Soon, his breathing grew soft and steady, and she, also, closed her eyes. With her boy safe beside her, Katelyn slept.

It was then that the shadows came, stealing in from the dark place under the deck where they had been hiding.

PART THREE
THE SECRET OF THE GRAYS

Late at night, when the demons come,
I want my pillow to push between them,
So they can't get on my skin.
I cry they rub my head I cry.

—SALLY, AGE 9, FROM HER STORY,
    "Beings Come to Our House"

EIGHT

ROB LANGFORD HAD NOT BEEN called by Lewis Crew in months, but he was not surprised to receive a summons on this night, when a glowboy had acted up like this. He had driven hard up from the Mountain, and now moved carefully along Lost Angel Road in the Boulder foothills, trying to find the address Crew had given him. He'd never met the owner of the house, Dr. Peter Simpson, but he'd heard Crew mention him often enough. In their field, need-to-know was so extremely strict that this kind of compartmentalization was normal. They all knew the reason, too. In fact, once you were told, it became the center of your life, the one thing you never forgot.

Back in 1954, long before the empath program existed, there had been a brief, fumbled meeting between President Eisenhower and a triad of grays at an air base in California. The president had come away shattered, saying that if we revealed that they were here, the aliens would destroy Earth completely.

This extraordinary threat had built the absolute wall of secrecy and inspired the intricate labyrinth of need-to-know that surrounded the reality of the grays.

Bob and Adam had never responded in a coherent manner to questions about it, either, which had made the threat seem more dire.

Rob found the house, set well back from the road, and turned in the driveway. As per regulations, he was in civilian clothes. Even the license plate on the car he was driving was registered to a civilian. He carried both false and real identification. The false ID, provided by AFOSI, would hold up under police scrutiny—say, if he got stopped for speeding.

Simpson's house was dark in front, but the door opened before he rang the bell. There stood the imposing Mr. Crew, looking a bit older, his white hair even more white.

As Rob entered the tiled foyer, a compact man appeared behind Lewis Crew. "Rob, this is Dr. Pete."

"It's a pleasure to meet a legend."

Simpson laughed a little. "I wish the circumstances could be more pleasant. Come on back."

They went along a hallway, then through a room cluttered with books. Surprisingly, Dr. Simpson read a great deal of poetry. He unlocked a door into a small office. There was some damaged equipment there. Rob asked what it was.

"A quantum communications device," Dr. Simpson said. "It passed signals between entangled particles, and thus was capable of instantaneous transmission across the entire universe. But no longer."

"Things have been at crisis for some time now," Crew said. "And we've reached a very serious point. A flash point, we believe."

Given the threat they were under and the absolute inability of the Air Force to offer any defense against the grays, those words made Rob feel a little sick. "What sort of a flash point?"

"We need to take you to another level, Colonel," Simpson said. "I've revised your job description and your need-to-know."

"You can do this?"

He laughed a little. "Colonel, you're talking to your boss—for the first time in your whole damned career. Isn't it the damnedest thing?"

Rob shook his head. "Maybe we're a little too bound up in need-to-know."

"I'm a Defense Intelligence Agency specialist and chairman of the Special Studies Sciences Committee." Special

Studies was the umbrella euphemism for all the scientific groups that worked on the problem of the grays.

The Sciences Committee, Rob knew, oversaw the whole operation, including his own Air Force mission. The poetry man was indeed his boss.

"How has my mission changed, sir?"

"We'll get there. First things first. I brought you here for the specific purpose of showing you this device, because you need to understand exactly what it did, why it's been destroyed, and by whom. Because you are about to be tested, Colonel, more rigorously than you have ever been tested before. I cannot stress this enough. In a few moments, I am going to ask you a question. Your answer will be crucial."

"If I answer wrong?"

Simpson gazed at him. The man's eyes were rat-careful. "This machine gave us communications access to Mr. Crew's species," he said. "Which we very much needed, because they were generating questions for Bob and Adam that were, frankly, a lot more subtle and a lot more effective than anything Michael Wilkes has ever come up with himself."

Rob realized that he'd just been told that his old friend Crew was an alien. He looked at him, pale in the dim light that filled the room. He appeared human enough. But then again, Rob had read enough UFO folklore to know the stories of a tall, blond race from a planet somewhere in the direction of the Pleiades. "You're what the UFOnauts call a Nordic."

"Ours is a very stable agricultural world with as much land mass as Earth, but barely a million people."

"But you look so much like us. What are the odds of that?"

"We've done DNA studies," Dr. Simpson said. "We and Crew's line split from one another about a hundred and fifty thousand years ago."

"But we—we're the same species? On two different planets?"

"So it would seem," Simpson said. "The most bizarre part is that the DNA trail is quite clear. We are not their colony, Crew's people are our colony."

"But in the past, uh, weren't we pretty damn primitive? How could we possibly have colonized another planet? We couldn't do that now, couldn't begin to."

"The past is a greater mystery than we allow ourselves to believe," Crew said.

Rob's mind raced. "All of those ruins that nobody can understand, things like the pyramids and the fortress at Sacsayhuaman in the Andes and that impossibly huge stone platform at Baalbek in Lebanon—all of those ancient engineering impossibilities . . . does this explain them?"

"The remains of our lost civilization, or so we believe."

"The legends of the fall . . . Atlantis, that sort of thing, the war in space narrated in the Vedas—"

"Distorted memories of a world that was lost in a ferocious war that plunged Earth back into savagery and caused you to lose contact with us altogether. The Book of Ezekiel in the bible is a confused account of a failed mission on our part to rescue you, when we built the Great Pyramid at Giza. We had to come physically, and that is extremely slow. The journey took thousands of years on a multigenerational starship."

"The Great Pyramid is dated. We know who built it."

"You know that Khefu put his mark on it. We returned in force about thirty-five hundred years ago. For a time, we ruled Egypt. The Pharaoh Akhenaton and his wife Nefertiti were from our world. We attempted to reestablish essential lost technology, which is the technology that enables the movement of souls across space. A journey that takes eons in the physical can be accomplished in a few moments by a being in a state of energy. The Great Pyramid is a device that enables this. The Egyptian religion of the journey of the soul to the Milky Way is not imagination, but mythology based on lost science."

"And did it . . . work?"

He nodded. "It still does. At present, I can use it to return home, but nobody else can come here." He gestured toward the blackened console. "That new device had a lot of capability. Among the things it could do was transmit the entire record of somebody's DNA at faster than light speed. A clone could then be grown using stem cells and DNA matching. Using pyramids on both planets, the soul could cross from one body to the other. But that's all impossible now, because of what Michael Wilkes did."

"*Mike*? But why?"

"Before we can answer that question," Simpson said, "you need to understand a little more about why the grays are here."

"They're exploiting us somehow, I've always assumed. Feeding, perhaps, in some way that doesn't seem to hurt people but that they regard as absolutely essential to themselves."

"They're here because they're in terrible trouble," Crew said.

Simpson joined in. "They have one hell of a problem. Genetic. Only in the past few years were we even able to understand it. But when you do a really good genetic study on them, you find all kinds of breaks, inserted genes, genes that must be from other species, artificial genes—they're a genetic garbage can, is what the grays are. They're not actually alive anymore. The grays have replaced so much of themselves that they've become, in effect, biological machines. If you can believe this, the few original genes we have detected are at least a billion years old."

"A *billion*?"

"Or more. Maybe much more. What we're looking at with the grays is a species so ancient that it has used up its gene pool. As a species, in their entirety, the grays are dying of old age."

Crew continued, "Every gray we have ever recovered from crashes, a total of fifty-eight bodies over the last sixty years, has been suffering from this degenerative genetic disease, where the membranous nucleus of their cells hardens, until the genetic material that's stored there can no longer be used by the cell. Then the grays replace the affected organ with an artificial substitute. Over time, the individual becomes a sort of machine. They have even created a prosthesis for their brain."

"So, why are they dying? If they've become artificial versions of themselves, they're immortal."

"The more artificial they are, the less alive they are.

Knowledge and intellect transfer to the artificial brain, but not feelings. They've gained a sort of immortality, but at the price of losing their heart. And every gray is like this, and they all remember their lost hearts, and all they care about is getting them back. What they have now is not life, but the memory of life."

Rob had seen the Bob autopsy. He had been a living entity, but with things like a manufactured skin and metal bones, and a mind that was housed not in a brain as such, but in silicon filaments that filled his head in intricate patterns that looked something like Mandelbrot Sets. You could see, though, in the structures of the skull, that it had once contained a natural brain.

"So how does coming here help them?"

"The grays are trying to save mankind."

"What's that supposed to mean?"

"Oh, it's not altruism. They're getting access to our rich young gene pool. In return, they're going to save us from the environmental catastrophe that's going to ruin us. Together, both species survive. Apart, both die."

"Then why—I've always had the impression from Wilkes that they're evil."

"He and his friends are at the center of the linkage of corporations, governments, and individuals who currently control the world. He sees any threat to that structure as an act of war, and what the grays are doing is such a threat, big time."

"But what actually . . . are they doing?"

"That's the incredible part. The miracle. They know what needs to be done for their survival. They need access to our genes. And they know what needs to be done for our survival. We need to understand how to fix our planet and how to start colonizing other worlds. But what they *don't* know is how to communicate the information we need to do these things."

Rob looked from Crew's mild face to Simpson's careful, acute eyes. "Who does?"

"They have found a way to give a super-intelligent human being access to their collective mind. This, we believe, is why they were on the ground tonight. They've begun this process."

Rob felt his face flush, felt sweat breaking out under his arms. "And this person is . . ."

"It's a child. Bred over dozens of generations for extreme brilliance. The smartest person humanity can produce. When they bridge him to their collective, he'll be even smarter than they are. He will trump their genius and, they hope, figure out how to save us all."

"A messiah?"

"You could say that, I suppose."

"But this is all predicated on the collapse of our environment being a real thing. If it isn't, then they need us but we don't need them."

"It's real."

"It's not global warming, is it, because—"

"Global warming is one aspect of a very complex phenomenon. A sixty-two-million-year extinction cycle. The last time it struck, it killed off the dinosaurs."

"Which was sixty-five million years ago. So what is it, late for the bus?"

"It started right on time, three million years ago, when what is now Central America rose up out of the ocean. This destabilized ocean currents and led to what we have now, a devastatingly lethal oscillation between ice ages and warm periods. The number of species has been declining since before there was a single human being on Earth, and the climax has now been reached. We're finished, basically— at least, as far as nature is concerned."

"But why? And why sixty-two million years? I don't get it, who's behind it?"

"Ah, the silent presence. Nobody knows. The grays don't know. But they hope that their brilliant child will understand. They hope he will understand the universe, the work of God, as it were, because, unless he does, we are all going to suffer extinction, both species, for different reasons. Twelve billion vital, living minds, all hungry for life, for love, for children and all right about one thing: every single one of us, whether human or not, is exactly as important as he feels.

"The grays are going to arrive on Earth in force in 2012, around the time the planet comes apart at the seams. They've been racing against time for thousands of years, and now it's down to a clock that's ticking fast, and either they get that kid to figure this all out and fix the world, or both species crash and burn."

"This is beginning to sound—well, to be blunt, horrible. Truly horrible."

"You can understand the reason for the secrecy. For the grays' terrible threats."

"Keeping us from panicking and shooting ourselves in the foot."

"And them."

"So what has Mike got against all of this? And how can he stop them?"

"He and his buddies see this as an invasion, pure and simple. The grays are gonna show up in force and cream us and take our planet."

"Why do they believe that?"

"They don't know. Can't know. They fear it." Crew looked at Rob. "Do you fear it?"

"I'm not sure."

"Good answer. Truthful. Neither are we. But Eamon Glass—you know, he was the first empath—he felt that the grays did indeed need us, and if they need us, they aren't coming here to take the planet."

"But how can Mike and friends possibly stop them?"

"First, they kill this child. That throws the grays off their timetable, because there won't be time to breed another one before mankind goes extinct. They lose the tool they've been breeding across a hundred generations, that's endgame for them."

"But the other consequence—the environment falls apart and we go extinct. Where's the win?"

"Mike and his group—they call themselves the Trust—intend to save about a million. Who they regard as the best people."

"One million? Out of six billion?"

"There'll be a few survivals on the outside, but the million people the Trust save are going to be the core of a new humanity, as defined by the Trust, of course. Their million survivors represent every race they consider valuable, every DNA group, all chosen to ensure an adequate long-term gene pool. It's scientifically sound, certain to continue the species, and a nightmare of racism."

"But why would doing this stop the grays?"

"For the same reason that they're not coming to my world," Crew responded. "Too little genetic material to help them. They need to create a new genetic foundation for billions of their own people. That'll take a huge number of human donors. A million would be useless to them, so they'd go away and, presumably, die somewhere off in space."

"The Trust isn't stupid," Rob said, "and Mike's had unlimited access to Bob and Adam for years. He knows the grays as well as anybody."

"And he would rather see the human species essentially brought to an end than live with the grays on what we believe will be at least equal terms. After all, this person who's brighter than them, and thus able to control them, is going to be a human. They're doing that for a reason, to give us a basis for confidence."

"But if Mike's concluded that life with the grays wouldn't be worth living, I think we have to respect that."

"Evil is a funny thing. It comes out of fear. Mike and his people think of themselves as the saviors of mankind. But they're genocidal monsters."

Rob found the scale of the thing so large he could hardly think about it intellectually, let alone morally. He shook his head.

"Here's your question," Crew said gently. "The one we need to ask you. In your mind, which is worse? Die, as a species, or take our chances with the grays?"

"Think carefully before you answer," Simpson added.

The only possible answer was immediately obvious to him. "I don't have a right to make a decision like that. None of us do."

"You pass," Simpson said. "Any other answer, and you would have failed the test, as a result of which, you would now know too much."

"I came close, then," he said.

"I don't think so," Simpson said. "I've always respected you. You have a good, strong conscience. You realize that this decision has to be made by every individual human being. This child, when he grows up, is going to give us the chance to do that."

Rob thought of a question so crucial that he almost didn't want to ask it. He did ask, though, he had to. "Are you saying that they might give us a choice? I mean, if we don't like the idea of sharing our genes with them?"

"We won't," Simpson said. "We'll say yes."

"How can you be sure?"

"The grays will be here, billions of them, asking for life. We will say yes, it's human nature, because we are fundamentally good. And this child, grown up by then, will help us do it right."

"You know, I have another question. Why are we like we are? Why are we so much less intelligent?"

"We have less knowledge. We lost it during that ancient war, the basic knowledge of how the world really works, knowledge the grays have preserved intact. This is why we can no longer account for those engineering marvels you mentioned—Baalbek and such. We've literally forgotten how we did that."

Crew gave Rob a long look. "We're trying to sell you on something I sense you're still dubious about. That's how you see this whole conversation."

"You're not reading me right," Rob responded. "I don't see any alternative. We have six billion lives to save. It's a completely unimaginable responsibility, and this poor damn kid, boy, there is one hell of a lot on his shoulders. You know how I feel? I feel like I would give my life, without hesitation, to protect him."

"That might happen," Simpson said. "Because Mike will go after him if he finds out about him, and Mike is good."

"Then we've got to put him under arrest. Roll up these friends of his."

"We cannot even consider that," Simpson said. "They're more powerful than we are. Anyway, it would show our hand and we don't want that. We've been lucky in one respect, that Mike doesn't understand this child thing at all. He has no idea that the grays are even trying to save mankind. He's sitting back, confidently waiting for the extinction to ruin their plans. And they've played that like the experts that they are, warning him constantly about the environmental crisis, in order to make him think they're helpless to prevent it."

"What happens to this kid? Does he suffer?"

"Does he suffer? Being that intelligent? That alone? I don't think it's an answerable question."

"So we protect him. Can do. But why did they do this glowboy thing? Point him out like that?"

"It looks like some triad being bad. Not all that unusual. It's actually a signal to us, and it's full of information. It tells us that the child is right in the area of Wilton, Kentucky, and that they're going to begin the process now. It's up to us to do our part, find the child in our own way, and put down the kind of protection the grays can't."

"Which is?"

"Up close and on the ground, supported by good threat intelligence. Their ability to determine things like what's going on in a human social group is very limited. They'll be there to react if somebody jumps out of the damn bushes, but we're the only ones who are going to be able to see a threat developing."

Pete Simpson leaned forward. "Which gets us to your new mission. We need you to move your operations to Alfred AFB, Rob. Right now. Your orders are to identify and protect that child. We know that he's somewhere in Wilton. Possibly even on Oak Road, where the glowboy touched down. But don't be too sure of that. The grays are very, very careful, remember. Assume he could be anywhere in the region."

The three men fell silent then, each sinking into his own thoughts, all feeling the same sense of being swept up by a current that was easily powerful enough to drown them.

Through the last darkness at the end of the night, a black triangular object had been coming, flying just feet above the treetops, taking its time, moving in absolute silence. Fifteen minutes ago, it had arrived over the house. It hovered overhead now, enormous, darker than the night itself, a triangle three hundred feet long, two hundred feet across at its base . . . and six inches above the roof.

Inside the triangle, in a low-ceilinged cockpit, a woman in a USAF flight suit sat adjusting a sensitive device. Every word being said below was being recorded and transmitted with digital clarity.

Literally as they spoke, Mike Wilkes listened. He sat in the facility in Indianapolis feeding Lauren questions based on what he was hearing.

His mind raced. This child—dear heaven, it was the single most toxic thing on Earth, the most dangerous creature ever to live. He would lay Wilton, Kentucky, to waste.

Or no. He had to be certain that he'd gotten the right child. Absolutely certain. He needed to be careful, here.

He watched Lauren sitting in the easy chair she'd insisted on bringing into Adam's hellhole, watched and considered how to form his next question, which would be the most important one that, in his whole career of dealing with the grays, he had ever asked.

NINE

OVER THE THREE YEARS SHE'D been working here, Lauren had done what she could to make Adam's cell more endurable. Rather than the steel table and hard chairs that seemed to have been enough for her dad, she'd made a very unwilling Wilkes get her a Barcalounger and had a daybed installed. On the walls, she had a copy of one of Renoir's Aline and Pierre paintings, of Aline holding little Pierre in a way that she hoped one day to hold her own babies . . . off in the future when her life was no longer at risk and she was no longer tangled in an ever-growing web of secrets, and she could finally settle down to a husband and a family. There were also views of forests and mountains, intimate little waterfalls and another one that she especially liked, van Gogh's *Starry Night,* that seemed to contain, in some way, the same fiery and mysterious energy she found in Adam.

As Mike watched her, he reflected on just how careful he had to be right now. The grays must not find out that he knew about this little monstrosity of theirs. "I want you to transmit an image of the satellite photo again, Lauren," he said smoothly.

She closed her eyes.

"Lauren, pick it up and look at it. Do it right."

"I've already done it ten times! Come on."

"You barely glanced at it."

"Shut up and let me work!"

Her dad had been a guy you could settle down with after work and knock back a few drinks. In fact, Mike had wanted to bring him into the Trust. It was too dangerous, though. For some years, it had been obvious that the grays couldn't read minds well—not normal minds. But Eamon's mind was a different story, like hers. They had to be kept strictly unaware of any secret the grays shouldn't know.

Although the daybed appeared empty, Lauren knew that Adam was lying on it. She had learned to see him in her imagination, even though his tiny movements, synchronized to her flickering eyes, prevented her from observing him in detail.

Mike wanted her to be careful, so she'd be careful. She formed a thought series this time. First, a picture of a map of the state of Kentucky. Then a vision of the satellite image of the event in the field behind the Oak Road houses.

Nothing came back.

She formed another thought: *React, Adam.* She called up a sense of urgency, stared, tensed her muscles.

There exploded into her mind an image that at first seemed to make no sense. She was looking up at a towering, immense wall of ice, ghostly white and iridescent, blue against a deep blue sky. And then she heard a sound, a gigantic snapping noise that combined with a strange sort of sigh, as if a thousand people had simultaneously gasped.

She was on the upper deck of a cruise ship. They were glacier-watching. The deck was jammed with people . . . and the ice was curving slowly over them, bringing with it a shadow that turned the bright afternoon an eerie, glowing blue.

The ship's huge horn began to sound, thundering again and again. The whole body of the vessel shuddered as it strove to get underway, the propellers churning, smoke gushing from the stacks.

With a boom to wake the dead, a gigantic boulder of ice—an ice mountain—slammed down on the foredeck. The whole ship lurched violently upward and forward. Water, clear and frigid, surged over the bounding deck, and the passengers were hurled screaming into the waves.

Lauren looked up again and saw, dropping toward them, an even greater mountain of ice, an eternity of ice.

She was back in the cage. She asked Adam a question with her mind, felt the question in her heart: what does it mean?

Then she saw—

A supermarket, bright lights . . . voices bellowed, a little girl toddled past with a tin of sardines, a man swooped down, grabbed it, knocking the child aside. Screams came, merging with the bouncy shopping music. People clawed for bread, raced down long, empty aisles, hollow people, their eyes wild, ripping open boxes of uncooked pasta, gobbling it, throwing back raw oatmeal, eating from the mashed garbage on the floor.

Gunshots. Soldiers in dirty uniforms, tired young faces, terrified eyes, shot into the crowd—and people just sat there, staring like a dumb animal stares who has no idea what's about to happen. As they got shot, they crashed back with astonishing force into a shattered freezer, and then the soldiers passed down another aisle.

"What's going on in there?"

"I don't know! He's showing me some sort of tragedy."

"Wha-a-at?"

"Ships sinking, people starving in a supermarket—"

"Christ, will you get me what I need!"

"Damn you, Mike, what I am gonna get you is what I always get you. I am gonna get you what he has to give!"

Because Adam was showing Lauren images of the coming extinction, he might be aware of the conversation Mike had been listening to, which made continuing this way too dangerous. "Okay, that's it. Come out. We're done."

"I love my baby," she whispered, getting up from the Barcalounger. She reached out, touched the cool, soft skin of a hand that only became visible when she held it, the narrow fingers and lethal black claws fading when she withdrew.

Adam shot back an image of a mother nursing an infant, his standard good-bye. As she got up, he made one of his audible sounds, a cry like a shocked and despairing woman. Did he feel anything? She didn't know. But she did know that he was trying for sympathetic attention.

"Adam, I know you have a message for me connected with all these disasters, and I know I'm not getting it. However, we're asking you about a *specific incident,* and—"

She got no response from him. She knew why: he'd heard the words, but unless you formed your thoughts in your mind, he didn't understand you.

"Lauren, break it off!"

"Mike—sir—"

"Lauren, there's no time!"

No time? What the hell was he talking about? She had all the time in the world. And God knew, Adam had time. "I'm going to get this thing rolling."

"There is no time!"

But Adam had different ideas. Adam's mind was all around her, she could feel it. She closed her eyes, took a deep breath, and let herself go blank.

He came into her, as always, like a dog sniffing for a buried bone. Letting him get inside her felt kind of good, but also oddly sad . . . a sadness that he brought with him. He would go into her memories and kind of troll there, bringing up all sorts of things from her past, things she'd just as soon have forgotten, stuff done when drunk, that sort of stuff. He liked the intense things. Sort of ate them, she thought.

She let him go deep into a familiar little corner, the cardboard box experience when she was about ten, one of the first things she'd ever done that was related to sex. She smelled the slightly damp cardboard box again, saw Willy Severs's plump, white body, felt his hand go under her blouse—and then shut *that* door with a great crash.

She shot her question at Adam: the satellite image again, the town of Wilton, the houses on Oak Road.

For the split of an instant, she thought she glimpsed a boy's face, but it was not Willy Severs. Curly hair, slightly chunky, looked about fourteen or fifteen.

"I have something," she said. "A face."

"What sort of a face?"

"A kid. I asked him about Oak Road and I got the face of a kid."

"Bring it out."

Mike was all over her the moment the door closed. "Got what? What did you get?"

"They're interested in a child."

"Say more."

"He's a boy of fourteen or fifteen, curly hair, and another thing, I glimpsed a dog. He has a dog."

Mike became furtive. "Okay," he said, "that makes no sense."

"Yes it does. They're interested in this kid."

"Probably some kind of breeding issue. We'll never figure it out. You're dismissed. Operation complete."

He was lying and he was scared—and she was suspicious. "What's the deal with this child?"

"Look, I have to go to Washington and I'm already late. You're done, Lauren. Thank you."

She watched him leave. The one pleasant thing about her relationship with him was knowing that he wanted her, and denying him. She did it because—well, she didn't like him. Just did not like the man. She was not nice to him, couldn't be. Why, she thought, had something to do with Adam. Adam seemed suspicious of him, somehow. Wary.

"What's going on, Andy?" she asked as she came into the control room still drying her hair.

"The boss is sure as hell in a lather."

She went topside, and when the elevator doors opened found Mike just leaving. He was in full uniform, which was pretty unusual around here. He had his briefcase in his hand.

"You're moving fast," she said.

"Yep."

"Are you going to do something to that child, Mike?"

"Look, this is not your issue. Your issue is to communicate with Adam, and to take that job one hell of a lot more seriously than you do."

"How dare you."

"How dare me? You're the one with pictures on the walls down in that hellhole. That thing is a predator. It's a monster. It's not a damn pet, for God's sake, woman."

She made a decision. He was going to Washington. Fine, she was coming back here and going at it again with Adam.

She would get to the bottom of this without Mike around. Because, if this child was in some kind of danger due to her report, then she had a very clear moral duty: no matter the legal blockade her clearance created, she had to protect the kid. She would not be a party to murder, and she would not follow orders that she considered to be illegal.

She watched Mike hurry out to the parking lot, and take off in his latest car, a brand-new VW Phaeton. She knew the value of that car, she'd looked it up. He'd just driven off in half a year's pay. Where his real money came from she didn't know, but it sure as hell was not the United States Air Force.

TEN

THE SUN PEEKING OVER THE Warners' roof woke Katelyn. As usual, she rolled over, at first feeling entirely normal. She considered turning on the news.

And then it hit her: she was upstairs in bed, not in Conner's room where she had gone to sleep.

Dan chose that moment to slide an arm over her. Katelyn leaped away from him as if his body was on fire.

"Hey!"

"Conner!" She ran downstairs, ran across the kitchen, took his stairs three at a time, and burst in.

When she saw that the door to the outside was open, she stifled a cry. But the lump in the bed seemed entirely normal. She knelt beside him and peeked into the covers. Conner was deeply asleep.

She kissed his freckled cheek, inhaling the milky-sour smell of his skin.

Dan came in, went over and closed the door that led out under the deck and into the backyard. "Look," he said.

There was a puddle of water on the floor in front of it, standing on the linoleum.

"And outside."

In the sparse grass that clung to life under the deck, were numerous small holes. They looked for all the world as if somebody had walked there on stilts.

She went to Dan, looked down at the water, out at the peculiar holes. This was not right. None of this should be here. She rushed back to Conner, drew down his covers. Again she kissed him. She pulled him into her arms.

Conner moaned, then suddenly stiffened. "Mom?" he said.

Kneeling beside the bed, she held his face in her hands and looked into his eyes.

He asked, "What's the matter?"

She hugged him to her, feeling the heft of him against her. Her boy was on the verge of becoming a young man, and he was so beautiful, and you had to be so very careful not to let him know how beautiful you thought he was.

"Could you guys let me get dressed, here?"

The little boy who had cheerfully laid naked in her lap just a few short years ago now did not want to get out from under the covers in her presence, not even wearing pajamas.

She kissed his cheek. "Six months to your first shave," she said. "Mom predicts."

"The sooner the better." He looked at her. She looked back at him. He moved his eyes toward the door.

"Breakfast in ten minutes."

She and Dan went upstairs.

"What was that about?" Dan asked as she closed the door.

She whispered, "It's about his growing maturity. Problems controlling what's up down below."

"You think? Puberty?"

"Bright kids reach it early, so it says in the book." As they mounted the stairs, she saw the CONNER ZONE sign in his recycling bag and took it out. "The Conner Zone was so cute," she said.

"Cute is the problem," Dan said. "Part of it. The other part is being too smart in a world that glorifies the lowest common denominator. Conner's intelligence is not fashionable, and it's too big for him to conceal."

"Oh, I never want him to do that. How's your ear, by the way?"

"Not actually okay. I could stand to get an X-ray."

"You're kidding. On your ear?"

"Well, there's something there."

"Something *there*?" She reached up and touched the outer edge of the ear. "It's a little sort of a knot."

"I know what it is."

"Relax, Dan, I'm not the enemy."

For the past half hour, the smell of coffee had been getting stronger, and she went into the kitchen and poured them both mugs. Dan took his over to the table. She went into the pantry and got Conner's latest cereal, some kind of amaranth flakes thing. Conner had his own dietary ideas, most of them pretty smart—and pretty awful. He was a modified vegetarian except when Dan grilled steaks. Then he was a sullen but voracious carnivore.

There was no cancer of the ear, was there?

Conner appeared, poured himself coffee. She waited to see if he put the required amount of half and half in it. Did—but just a drop.

"Eggs?" she asked as she turned on the skillet.

"I'm going to be eating really pure for a while," Conner said. "No dairy, no alcohol."

"You don't drink alcohol," Dan said. "Better not."

"I mean, no wine with dinner."

"Wine belongs to the soul, son. No man can be fully himself without wine."

"The other kids can't drink it."

"Which is why they'll all be bingeing like the college students in a few years. Did you know that binge drinking among the young is unheard of in Europe, but common here and in the UK? What does that tell you—children have to learn wine early, get used to it. Which is why you'll continue with a glass of wine at dinner, thank you."

"I love the irony. Most kids would do anything to drink even so much as a sip. But I don't want to, so it's forced on me."

"Well, you get a glass. One glass. Which is mandatory."

"Do you want to have the fight now or schedule it for later? Because I will not be drinking wine."

Dan sighed. "I've got to go to the health center to get my ear amputated. Let's do it when I get back." He picked up Conner's cereal box. "I saw this lying open in the pantry last night. Are roach eggs okay for vegans?"

Conner took the box, poured himself some cereal. "Amaranth is one of a handful of dicots which photosynthesize directly to a four-carbon compound."

"Ah. So the reason you're now eating nothing but horrible-looking little crumbs is explained. You want that four-carbon compound."

"Actually, I want the protein and the lysine without meat, plus I get a designer-quality lipid fraction. I have the cholesterol readings of a twelve-year-old, you know."

"You're eleven."

"It's a joke, Dad."

"Ah. Of course."

Katelyn put down her and Dan's eggs and sat at the head of the table. "May I know the why of the vegan thing?"

"The aliens."

A silence fell, extended. "Are you about to piss me off?" Dan asked.

"I am eating pure because this neighborhood is in a close-encounter situation and it's the eating of animals that triggers the kind of fear response I experienced last night. I don't want to fear the aliens. I want to face them."

"Oh, boy," Katelyn said. "Dan—"

"No. No, I understand that I'm being baited. It's not a big deal, Katelyn." He watched Conner digging into the amaranth, and as he watched, he got angrier and angrier. He *was* being baited, damn right. Conner was masterful at it. And here he'd been the confidante, the father confessor, just yesterday. Now he was the enemy and his ear hurt like hell, to tell the truth, and he really did not need this just now.

"We had a visit from the grays, and they had an abductee aboard the craft, *and* the Keltons probably have video. A first in history. The world is changing, lady and gentleman, and I am preparing myself."

"What grays?" Dan asked carefully.

"Try Googling 'gray aliens' sometime. You'll find more than four thousand references. Plus, this business of a UFO descending with a screaming woman inside happened in Kentucky before. Moorehead, 2003, same situation, with one difference—no video. Lots of nine-one-one calls, but no video and therefore no story."

The sanctimonious singsong, the eyebrows raised to make the face appear absurdly credulous—it was all calculated to infuriate. Conner knew perfectly well how ridiculous Dan considered the whole UFO/alien folklore to be, and how damaging to the culture.

"Goddamnit, it was nothing but some kind of dope-inspired prank!"

"Dad, please. You're embarrassing yourself."

Dan's hand had slammed down on the table before he could stop it.

Conner seized the opportunity. "Right, go physical yet again, Dad. It'll make a juicy story for my psychiatrist-to-be. Another one."

Dan had spanked Conner exactly one time, when, at the age of three, he had rewired the toaster and caused a dangerous fire in the wall of the kitchen. It had been a single, sharp blow to the left buttock . . . which had been thrown back at him perhaps ten thousand times since.

"Conner, listen to me. I'm up for tenure, which the entire college knows. It's terribly important to us. If I don't get it, I have to resign, which means that we have to move to some other college where Mom and I can both get work, and she has to give up her own tenure here—it'll be a mess, son. And something like this—a UFO in the backyard—can ruin my chances. Marcie Cotton already wants to write me off. So please, for me, do not say anything about us seeing it for at least another few weeks."

Conner gazed off into the middle distance. "Prediction: the Keltons' tape, if it is halfway decent, will make this place famous. Prediction: Dr. Jeffers will make a total idiot of himself about it and he'll end up with walking papers. Prediction: you will not be damaged by this, but Dr. Cotton will still screw you to the wall."

Every time Conner used the word "prediction," a chill went right through Dan. Their son was never wrong. Actually, he found that he was so on edge and Conner sounded so right that he almost burst into tears—and was instantly appalled at himself. How could he possibly react like that? That wasn't him.

But then he thought—the pressure of the tenure conference coming up, the bizarre events in the night, the sleeplessness, Katelyn's waking up in near hysterics, this damned lump in his ear—of course he was on edge. Stressed. Big time.

"Look," he said, "thanks for a perfectly delicious break-fast. Tomorrow's my turn and it's waffles unless there are objections." He looked down at the still-gobbling Conner. "I'll make yours without egg."

"Fine."

"They'll be fascinating. I'm going to the health center, I'll call you with a verdict."

"Prediction," Conner said. "They will find a small object enclosed in a membrane made of cutaneous tissue. And, if you search your body, you will find an indentation where that tissue was taken from. It's called a witch's mark." He smiled up at Dan. "The grays have been with us for some time."

"Conner, this happened last night in a kitchen full of people. I hardly think the grays could have operated on me without anybody noticing."

"There was a moment—probably just a few seconds—when you were all turned off. The grays did what they did and turned you back on as they left. It's called missing time. It's the way they handle us. We're their property, you know. You know what the great anomalist Charles Fort called the world? A barnyard. The grays are the farmers, and right now they're doing a little farm work right here on Oak Road."

"Okay, I'll bite. What are they doing?"

"For one thing, they've got some kind of a plan for you, which is why they gave you that implant. You're in-volved, Dad."

"Let's look," Katelyn said. "I want to see this thing for myself."

But Dan did not want them to look at it. He retreated up-stairs and took his shower. Safe in the stall, shaving and soaping himself up, he felt his body for the sort of indenta-tion Conner had described.

Nah, there wasn't one. They'd X-ray him at the health center and tell him what he already knew: he had a cyst that was mildly infected. The doctor would prescribe a couple of weeks of an antibiotic, and if it got worse, he'd go in and open the damn thing up.

He had to wash his hair, anyway, so he sat down on

Katelyn's shower chair that she used for shaving her comely legs and—well, what the hell, he felt along both ears and across the back of his neck.

There was nothing there. Thank you, Conner, it's so delightful the two or three times a year that you're wrong. As he stood back up, though, he felt a very slight soreness in his right buttock. He felt back there, just above the cheek. As his fingers ran along the smooth, wet skin, he knew. He felt again to be sure.

Then he was having an aura, one of those odd sequences of perceptions—in his case, a vision of stars all around him from his childhood planetarium, followed by a feeling of floating—that were the prelude to one of the seizures like he'd had in childhood.

He leaned up against the side of the shower. "Katelyn," he managed to say. Not yell it, couldn't do that. "Katelyn."

The feeling of floating got stronger. It was uncanny, he even looked down to be sure his feet were still touching the floor of the stall. Then his eyes fixed on the drain, the silver circle of it with the water swirling down.

The drain became larger and darker, and now what he saw was a round black hole in a field of gleaming silver. Objectively, deep within himself, he knew that he was seizing. He felt nothing, you never did. All he could see was this opening that had been below him but was now above him, black and foreboding, getting bigger. It was like being drawn into the underside of a gigantic silver balloon, that was how the seizure affected his temporal lobe.

Then it was gone, *bam*. The shower was back, drumming on him. He coughed, gagged, recovered himself. Quickly, he rinsed his body, got out of the shower, and dropped down, still soaking wet, onto the toilet. Jesus God, he'd seized. After all these years, he had damn well *seized*.

In his late childhood, when the seizures had first been diagnosed, he'd been put on Dilantin. He had tolerated it well, and maybe he'd better go back on it. He hadn't had actual spasms while in the shower or he would have gone down, so he was still dealing with a petit mal epilepsy. That was on the good side. On the bad side, for this to return after so many years suggested that there could be some other syndrome present. For example, maybe there had been epileptiform tissue in his brain that had developed a tumor. Maybe the thing in his ear was indeed a tumor. It would not be a primary, that did not happen to earlobes. It would be metastase of a hidden primary, asymptomatic until it began, last night, to press a nerve.

If this was a distal metastase of a brain tumor, he might well be a dying man.

He toweled himself and dressed fast. He went downstairs and through the kitchen again, where Katelyn and Conner were still breakfasting, Conner now absorbed in NPR on the radio, *Meet the Press* on TV, and the *New York Times* "Week in Review," while Katelyn read the funnies in the *Herald Leader.*

" 'Zits' is great," she said as he headed out to the garage. "The father gets this—"

"Later. I'll call."

"Be sure they're open."

If they weren't, he was heading to the Wilton City Hospital emergency room. There was no way he could make it through another night without knowing what this thing was.

In the event, the health center was open and staffed by a nurse and a squeaky little doctor who appeared to be just a hair older than Conner. He was tempted to head on to Wilton anyway, but his paranoia was running full blast, and he feared a note to Marcie from some tenure inquisitor: "Subject refused treatment at College H.C., preferred Wilton."

Listen to that thinking, though. Paranoid. He was having seizures for the first time in over twenty years, and now entertaining lunatic paranoid fantasies . . . but how could he ask this freckled little boy with a sunburned skier's nose for what he really needed, which was a damned Xanax drip to take home with him?

"Doctor, I have a little cyst in my left ear that's giving me trouble. Mild trouble, but it's waking me up at night when I lie on my side."

He sat on the edge of the examining table while the doctor, if that's actually what he was, gently examined the ear.

"I'm assuming a subcutaneous infection," Dan said, aware

of his own nervousness. He wanted to also say that he'd seized, but he dared not do that. Paranoid delusions aside, if that got back to Marcie, it might indeed have implications.

"There's a mass," the young doctor said.

Dan felt the blood drain out of his face, felt his heart turn over. He was forty. He was dying.

"Let's do an X-ray," the doctor said.

He followed him back into the green-tiled, Lysol-scented depths of the health center. Dan managed to get enough spit up to talk. "What do you expect to find?" he asked mechanically.

"Have you been doing any sort of carpentry?"

"Carpentry?"

"There's a mass in there with something hard in it. I'm thinking a nail head. Something along those lines."

"Can you see a point of entry?"

"Not anymore. When did it start hurting?"

"Last night."

"That part of the ear's not very sensitive. It could've been there for a while, just recently become irritated."

They reached the X-ray room and the doctor turned on the lights, which flickered to life, revealing the same X-ray machine that had been there for all the years Dan had been involved with Bell College. Probably war surplus, and not from a recent war.

The doctor took four views of his ear and then he was sent off to the waiting area, an extraordinarily bleak little room with an anorexic gray couch against one wall, three plastic chairs, and two chair-desks for students who might wish to study while waiting for their bad news.

Dan would have taken out his iPod and listened to the *New York Times,* but his iPod was on his bedside. His choices were a coverless copy of *Bicycling* and the front half of a not-very-recent *Newsweek.*

Half an hour later, he began to fear that the young doctor, upon seeing the X-rays, had leaped into his car and rushed off to Wilton with them.

He went back into the depths of the place, where he found him sitting in a tiny office studying a thick textbook. "Oh, hi," he said. "Let's see if that e-mail's come in yet."

"E-mail?"

"Yeah, your X-ray's being read by our radiologist. He got it online."

Now, that was somewhat reassuring—a high-powered radiologist at another institution was reading his film.

"Here it is." He opened an e-mail. "Boy, these guys need their English translated into English."

"You can't read medical terminology?"

"I can't read a Sri Lankan's idea of medical terminology. Your radiologist is in Trincomalee. Actually sounds rather romantic, Trincomalee."

Dear heaven.

He reached across his desk and pulled out an X-ray folder. "This is interesting," he said. He put two of the X-rays up on a wall light. "You have a foreign object in your ear," he said, "as I suspected."

Dan stared at the X-ray. The object was a tiny pinpoint of light. He could hear Conner's precise young voice, "They will find a small object . . ." He asked, "Is it enclosed in a membrane?"

"A membrane? Not likely. Maybe a little calcification if it's been there for a while. I think it's a metal filing. It could have migrated from anywhere."

"I have a sore place on my buttock."

"Let's take a look."

He lowered his trousers.

"Nothing visible. Perhaps a slight indentation is all."

Once again, Conner had been exactly right.

"So, what should I be doing about this?"

"If it bothers you, I can take it out."

"You?"

He laughed a little. "Quite easily. It's not deep, it'll take five minutes."

He lay on the examining table and let the nurse swab his ear with iodine. They injected him a couple of times, and went in.

"Feel anything?"

"No."

"Okay, here it is. It's a white disk. A—whoa."

"What?"

"It just went—what the hell?"

"What?"

"I'm withdrawing."

"Did you get it?"

He was silent as he took a stitch in the wound.

"I did not get it," he said at last. "I got a little sliver of it before it migrated. It's down in your earlobe now."

He felt the lobe. "How can that be?"

"I'm not sure. It's not a normal object."

He had to say the word, hard as it was. "Cancer?"

The doctor laughed. "Cancers don't generally run like hell when you touch them with a scalpel."

"Was it, uh, a living thing, then?"

"Dr. Callaghan, I have no idea what it was. But I am going to do two things to put that question to rest. First, I'm going to put this sliver under a microscope, then I'm going to send it to the lab."

"Does this happen to people often?"

"First one I've seen. Foreign objects are a whole subdiscipline of trauma medicine. It's nothing to worry about, though. I wouldn't think twice about it."

They went into another room, this one containing a lab bench with a fairly decent microscope on it. The doctor prepared a specimen slide and put it into the viewing area. He lowered his face to the binocular.

Dan watched him, waiting.

He lifted his head. "Okay, off it goes to pathology."

"But—what did you see?"

"White material. Probably some sort of a protein."

"Why did it move? Is it a parasite?"

"Lord, no! Here—take a look for yourself."

Gratefully, Dan looked into the microscope. What he saw was shaped like a sickle of moon, and along the curved outer edge there was what looked like movement. "What am I seeing? It's still moving, am I right?"

"That has to be a light effect."

Dan adjusted the scope. Clearly, the thing had cilia on it, and the cilia were propelling it. He lifted his face. "Cilia," he said, "look."

The doctor barely glanced at it. "Well, call day after tomorrow, we'll give you the pathology report."

"But it has cilia on it that are moving. So it's a living thing, it must be. And it can migrate. What if it goes somewhere else? Into my brain or my heart?"

"There are no ear parasites like this."

And that ended that. Another two patients had come in, and the doctor was off to attend to their hangovers.

On the way home, Dan called and told Katelyn that he was fine. She asked him what they'd found, and he came, quite unexpectedly, to a powerful personal moment. He found himself shaking so intensely that he pulled over to the side of the road.

"Dan?"

"Sorry. It was a little something in there. They took it out."

"What sort of a little something, honey?"

"Not a tumor." He found that he very much did not want to tell her that Conner had been right. He did not want Conner to be right, and he never, ever wanted to ask Conner how he had known. "It was a little cyst. Took ten minutes to get rid of it. The main delay involved waiting for the radiologist to evaluate it . . . in Trincomalee. It seems we outsource our diagnostics to experts in the Third World. Or is it the fourth world? Is there a fourth world?"

"You sound a bit out of it."

"It's been a long twenty-four hours, dear. I'm coming home and I'm going to turn on the TV and watch Sunday golf and spend the afternoon in a coma."

All the way home, without knowing why and without being able to stop, he cried. There was no sound. In fact, his expression never changed, except for wetness flowing down his cheeks. He felt like an idiot, he never cried. But he couldn't stop himself now, because a tremendous sorrow was coming up from his depths, a hidden river exposed.

He remembered this so well, this anguish that he could not control. It had been a feature of his childhood, had come after his seizures.

He thought he knew why the syndrome had returned. This was probably the most tense period he had ever known in his life. He was not a particularly successful teacher. In fact, he was pretty much a failure. Bell wasn't just a holding tank for second-rate students, it was a refuge for dead-end teachers, too.

He had his good points. You could not find a more loving husband. You could not find a better man to father a kid as sensitive and exasperating as Conner. But he tended to the pedantic when he lectured. He was too careful, too humorless, too predictable.

Still, he had built a life for them at Bell. Conner's life was here. Katelyn was having a successful career in the sociology department. *She* was tenured, popular with students, had crowded classes. She was pulling down seventy grand to his forty-eight-five, also. It would not be fair for his failure to uproot her.

Tomorrow at ten sharp, he would have his final tenure review with Marcie. Of course, it wasn't the official word, that came from the tenure committee next week. But by the end of the meeting tomorrow, he'd know.

He drove past Marcie's house, noted that all the blinds were down. A signal? An omen? He drove on, circling blocks—but not Marcie's of course, God forbid—and forcing back these ridiculous, if thankfully silent, tears.

When he arrived home, he hoped to avoid Conner.

"I was right," his son said as he got out of the car. "I was exactly right."

"Conner, you were wrong. It was a cyst."

"Where is it?"

"Oh, brother. Son, it's in the garbage at the health center."

"Dad, do you realize what that is? It's an alien artifact! It's important, there's even a Web site about them. A lot of Web sites."

Dan tried to get past his son and into the house.

"Dad, it's important! You're involved in a close-encounter situation and—"

"SHUT UP!" He ran across the garage. "Will you just SHUT UP!"

Katelyn appeared. "What's the matter with you? What's going on out here?"

"Katelyn—oh, God. Katelyn, I'm sorry. I'm sorry, Conner. Please forgive me, both of you." He tried to smile.

Failed. Shook his head. "Look, Conner, you're always asking for space. I need some space right now. I need some, okay?"

"Dad, are you crying?"

"It's a mild allergy to the anesthesia."

"Dad's just had an operation, Conner. We need to back off."

"But Mom, he's letting them throw away an implant!"

"Goddamnit, there's no such thing! Conner, for a supposed genius, you can be an amazing idiot. A Web site on *alien implants* is your source of information? You urgently need to learn some discrimination, son. You can do calculus backward and recite Wittgenstein, and yet you come up with this garbage."

"Be careful, Dad. It was Wittgenstein who said, 'Our greatest stupidities may be very wise.'"

Dan knew not to pursue it. No matter how correct he might be, in a sentence or two more, Conner would win the argument. To avoid that, Dan went inside, took a relatively good Barolo out of the wine rack, opened it and grabbed a glass, and headed for the family room. Golf, decent wine, and deep, deep sleep were what he needed.

He'd gone over the top, of course. The boy was terribly sensitive, of course. Well, he'd apologize later. Conner got under your skin. He really did have a skill at that.

He poured some wine, drank it . . . and felt his ear. The damned thing had moved again. It had returned to its original site, under the stitch.

He considered screaming. But no, that would be rude. Instead, he poured himself another full glass and drank it down.

PART FOUR
THE HANGED MAN

Ah, love, let us be true
To one another! For the world, which seems
To lie before us like a land of dreams,
So various, so beautiful, so new,
Hath really neither joy, nor love, nor light,
Nor certitude, nor peace, nor help for pain;
And we are here as on a darkling plain
Swept with confused alarms of struggle and flight,
Where ignorant armies clash by night.

—MATTHEW ARNOLD
"Dover Beach"

ELEVEN

MIKE WILKES WATCHED AS, ONE by one, the members of the Trust filed slowly through a large white device that was set into the doorway to the conference room on the second floor of his Georgetown home.

As each trustee stood waiting in what was essentially a magnetic-resonance-imaging system reconfigured and re-tuned to detect very small metallic objects, Mike watched a whole-body image come into focus on a flat-panel display located beside the entrance.

"Come in, Charles," he said to their chairman, Charles Gunn.

"I'm wiped every morning at home," Charles said. "I had one pulled out of my damn neck last week."

"Uh-oh, hold it, Richard." The display showed a bright spot deep in the brain of Richard Forbes, the Trust's secu-rity chief. "They got one in your damn temporal lobe, buddy."

"Is it deep?"

"Oh, yeah. You're gonna need a neurosurgeon, big time."

"Well, guys, I'm out of this for the duration, then. I'll see you after my lobotomy."

There was nervous laughter. Brain implants were rare. They required an abduction, while an object that went in under the skin could be placed while the host was wide awake. All it would do would be to cause some pain, but there would be no wound, certainly no scar. The grays were, among other things, masters of atomic structure. They could walk through walls if they wished, and they could certainly deposit an implant under the skin without surgery. The terrifying thing about a brain implant was that it could be used for subtle mind control, detectable only by someone with profound understanding.

"They anticipated this meeting," Charles said.

"Yeah, they know damn well we'd want our security guy in a meeting called because of a security issue," Henry Vorona added as he came through.

Then Ted Cassius had one under his scalp. These were nasties, too, because that close to the brain, they could be used not only for monitoring, but for a degree of mind control as well.

"How long have you had this, Ted?"

"I got a splitting headache two days ago. Jesus, I should have known."

"We need to assume that you're both under mind control and we have to get your asses out of here fast." He opened his cell phone. "I'm calling for a Secret Service escort for both of you guys to Walter Reed. If you go under your own steam, you just might change your minds, as you know."

"Thank you."

Nobody else, thankfully, was implanted, and Mike finally was able to take his customary place at the conference table, second from the head on the left. Charles Gunn was head of table. Normally, he would not be at a meeting of the security-operations committee, but Mike had specifically requested his attendance.

Henry Vorona shuffled some papers as the Three Blind Mice took their places, three sour and mutually indistinguishable liaison officers from the main corporate groups that accepted delivery of the technologies and processes that evolved out of the liaison with Adam. They were Todd Able, Alex Starnes, and Timothy Greenfield, all in their forties, all looking like undertakers. It was their corporate dollars that funded the survival program. Creating the database of people who would be sheltered was costly, and monitoring their movements even more so. But those things were nothing compared to the cost of the underground shelters themselves, a hundred at half a billion dollars each, hidden around the world.

"Let's get going," Charles said. "I've brought a little patents-and-processes business to deal with first. Where are we with the plasmonics device?"

Mike was confused by that question. The invisibility fabric was deep in the pipeline. "Uh, do we need more from Adam? Because I wasn't aware—"

Tim Greenfield said, "We have a report, Mike. It's on its way to you."

"Then there's a problem, Timmy?"

Tim Greenfield's pate flushed. "It doesn't work."

"Well, that is a problem." The concept was a material that would reduce light scatterback to zero, thus rendering an object effectively impossible to see. They knew that the grays used invisibility cloaking in their abductions, in addition to their peculiar physical ability to lock movement with the slightest flickering of the eye, so their victim could not see them.

Adam and Bob had been queried on the cloaking, in the tiny bits and pieces necessary to extract information from them, for fifteen years. They had a ten-billion-dollar check riding on the success of the process.

"There's a compositional issue. Chemical. We need a real formula. What they've given us is not real."

So the grays had lied again. All of those years of work, those hundreds and hundreds of tiny, seemingly innocuous questions had led down another blind alley.

Not that they didn't have successes. "How are we doing with the electrostatic anti-friction shield?" Mike asked Todd Able, who was team leader on that project. He knew the answer better than Todd did, but he wanted to remind everybody that his work with Bob and Adam had resulted in its share of successes.

"It's deploying and we're looking at a ninety-seven percent decrease in friction across angular surfaces. If we could mine gravitite, we could fabricate non-aerodynamic spherical vehicles and we'd be looking at the same zero-friction profile we see in the grays' craft. All we'd be missing is their engine."

"The coherent mercury plasma can't be made more efficient," Henry Vorona said. "We're getting everything we can out of it."

Mike knew that well. Using a combination of research into ancient Vedic texts about the technology of Earth's previous civilization and questions to Adam, they had evolved a device that rotated a mercury plasma inside a powerful magnetic field, that reduced the weight of the craft that carried it by 40 percent. Simply knowing that the Vedic references to aircraft and weapons referred to actual devices had enabled scientists to proceed much more quickly.

"So what about gravitite? Progress?" Charles asked in his peculiarly cheerful voice, so improbable in a man who looked like the director of his own funeral.

"We know what it is and where it is, but extracting it is another matter," Mike said. He looked toward Henry Vorona, who was a substantial shareholder in a dozen companies that were feeding off the grays' technology. One of those companies, Photonic Research, had been mining for years in the same seams of iron in the southern Catskills that the grays used, pulling iron out of shafts directly adjacent to theirs, but failing to extract more than a few molecules of gravitite.

Henry said, "We're not going to be saving the human race with gravitite. We can pull up the iron and cut it up atom by atom, but we find one atom of gravitite for every three hundred billion atoms of iron. The grays must have a more efficient process, otherwise they would have used up every bit of iron on the planet to get a handful of gravity-negative product."

Charles now rested his eyes on Mike. "Colonel, if you'd like to go on to this security matter now."

Mike told himself that he wasn't frightened, but he was, he felt like a schoolboy about to get a thrashing. "We have a potential crisis that needs to be addressed immediately."

"Adam's not sick?"

Bob had been invaded by common household molds. This was why they kept Adam in an ultra-dry, ultra-clean environment. They were all terrified of losing their only captive gray. "Not that, thank the Lord, but something might be unfolding that could be bad for us."

Henry Vorona sighed. He was not a patient man and Mike could see an explosion building. He hurried on. "Basically, we've obtained information about a very unusual operation on the part of the grays. Spectacularly threatening, I am sorry to say. What happened initially was that the triad that works Pennsylvania and up into Canada came out of their boundaries and did an abduction in a college town in Kentucky."

"Okay," Todd said, "I'll bite."

"The grays have devised a way to communicate with mankind. To teach us how to save ourselves. They've been working on it for probably a couple of thousand years. And now, gentlemen, they are going to spring it on us. Of course, we save ourselves not for us, but for them. Mankind survives, but as a genetic milk carton for them. Slaves."

That brought total silence. These men had counted on the coming catastrophe to free their carefully selected fragment of humankind from the grays. None of them liked the idea of the disaster that they knew was coming. But they feared this slavery more. If six billion were alive in 2012, they would all be enslaved. If only a million were left alive by then, they would be left alone. So, at least, went the theory.

"So, get on with it," Henry Vorona snapped.

"Okay," Mike continued, "we've known for some time, based on the abduction pattern we've observed over five decades, that the grays are especially interested in children."

"Because they're small, easy to control, and emotionally rich," Henry said. "Easy to feed on," he added in a tone electric with contempt. Every man here shared one truth: he despised the grays.

"That does not explain the 'why,' which has always been our problem. The grays can outthink us. They're always ten moves ahead."

Henry slammed his briefcase, which had been open on the table. "That's it then. Let's all go home. Follow Forrestal out the damn window."

"I'm too old to jump out a window," Charles said. "Mike, you finish this. What's your problem and what do you need from us?"

"Well, wait," Tim said, "what about the scalar weapons program? We're going to have eighty of those birds up by 2012. We'll be able to induce the destruction of most of the species ourselves." He sighed. "God help us, I hope it doesn't come to that."

"You think they'll sit back and let us kill their cattle?"

"They haven't touched the scalar prototype."

"Because it's only one small weapon," Charles said. "It doesn't have the potential to affect their plans."

Mike continued. "The grays are doing something very inventive. What they've apparently done is to breed a child so intelligent that he can process and use the contents of their knowledge."

Vorona shook his head.

"You have a problem, Henry?"

"They've been preparing this from the beginning, then?"

"I found out about it early this morning."

"Mike, we've known about them for fifty damn years, and you found out *today*?"

"Look, let's not argue about me."

"I want to argue about you! This is not good enough!"

"Hold off!"

"You hold off! And you listen. Because this is urgent. Our whole damn program is in jeopardy. The freedom of the human species!"

"Because somebody didn't do their job," Alex murmured.

"Hold off, all of you," Charles said softly. "Go on, Mike."

"My expectation is that they're going to install something in him that links him to their collective."

"An implant does not a demon make."

"In this case, it does. This child's intelligence will enable him to use vastly more information than an average human being can."

Silence fell. He watched each face as each man explored the implications of this.

"Gentlemen," Mike said, "if this child survives, mankind survives. When the grays show up in 2012, dinner is served."

"Now," Tim Greenfield asked in his soft Georgia drawl, "we are absolutely sure that their coming is bad for us?"

"You cannot seriously entertain a question where we can't know the answer until it's too late. Good or bad, we can't take the risk!"

"Why not approach the child, get him on our side?" Todd asked.

"When we approach him, we approach the grays," Mike said acidly.

"So, do the child, Mike," Charles said. "Shouldn't be hard, not for a pro like you."

"I might remind all of you that every life I took because of this damned thing, I took under orders."

"I repeat, do the child."

"Which is why I'm here."

Charles slammed his hand down on the table. "You don't need our permission! For God's sake, Mike, this meeting is a waste of time. Do the damned child!"

"Charles, Goddamnit, will you please give me a chance to talk!"

Charles glared at him.

Mike continued. "My problem is that the grays are not alone in protecting this child. They have the help of some people within our own organization who appear to have come under mind control." He took his iPod out of his briefcase, plugged in its tiny speaker, and played for them the conversation that had taken place on Lost Angel Road.

"It's pitiful," Henry said. "Those are good men, all of them."

"The hard part is," Mike said, "I can see where their choice is coming from. There's a lot of life going to be lost doing it our way. A lot of life."

"You've made no headway finding this child, I presume."

"No, Henry, I have a description, obtained from Adam this morning. And I will undoubtedly find a child who fits it on Oak Road. And kill the wrong child."

Todd said, "Unless they've given you a description of

the right child in hope that you'll assume that it must be the wrong one."

"Kill all the children," Henry said. "And what in the world are we going to do with Lewis and Rob and Dr. Simpson?"

"Tell you what," Tim Greenfield said, "let's suck them up in the terrorist thing and ship them to Saudi Arabia. That'll do it."

"It will also bring in the CIA, AFOSI, and the FBI, not to mention the Saudis. We need a plane crash, an auto accident, a fatal robbery attempt, a nice heart attack, stuff like that," Charles said. "Take a year doing them. There's no hurry." He looked toward Mike. "The sort of thing you're expert at."

"The child is our urgent problem, and please let me repeat: the grays are protecting him—"

"—and so are our friends from Lost Angel Road, don't forget that, Mike."

Tim said, "Gentlemen—excuse me, Charles, but I think you're panicking, here. We have years to deal with this child, and—"

"We do not have years," Mike said. "Please get rid of that misconception."

"I'm sorry, Mike, but we have until 2012."

"WE DO NOT! GODDAMNIT! Let me tell you how this will work. The second they possess that kid or parasitize him or however you'd like to describe it, he is going to become invulnerable."

"Oh, come on!"

"I have spent the last fifteen years of my career sparring with Bob and Adam, and I am warning you, if we let that kid go *even a day,* we're done. They win. We will not be able to do a single thing to him. He will always outwit us. Good Christ, he's going to be *smarter than they are.*"

Alex said, "Let's put a nuke on the damn town. Pick up the phone and call the president."

"I can't imagine him agreeing to that," Charles said. "In any case, we need to keep this in-house if at all possible."

"Which gets me to my next question," Henry Vorona said. "Mike, you have a big rep. Given that you've been sitting at the bottom of a hole for fifteen years, may I know why we should believe you're qualified to go operational again?"

Charles said, "Henry, you surprise me. Mike is my choice and that ought to be enough. But if it's not, let me lay things out. Mike didn't always spend his days licking the heinies of those damn gray bastards down in that hole. He did a lot of hard, sad, wet work in the early days."

"Okay, I get it."

"No! You're questioning my authority, Henry. You've done it before and you'll do it again. That's fine. You want to run the show. Very ambitious. Maybe, if they vote me out and vote you in, you'll do okay." He looked around the table. "Do we want a vote of confidence? Gentlemen?"

No hand was raised.

He went on. "Suffice to say that Mike here had the unfortunate need, back some years ago, to become a master of untraceable murder. He's got quite a number of notches in his little cap pistol, am I right, Mike?"

"I've done a few," he muttered.

"Using everything from a chemical that induces cancer to a mind-control technique that makes people kill themselves. And he's never even come close to being caught."

Vorona smiled at Mike. "Then I'm relieved," the CIA representative said. "We can count on you."

Todd spoke up. "Obviously, the nuclear option isn't available to us, but I think Alex's concept is a good one. We could do a training accident, say, compliments of Alfred AFB, which is out there in Kentucky, if I'm not mistaken. Blow away the neighborhood with a stray incendiary, say."

" 'Then Herod, when he saw that he was mocked of the wise men, was exceeding wroth, and sent forth, and slew all the children that were in Bethlehem, and in all the coasts thereof, from two years old and under, according to the time which he had diligently inquired of the wise men.' " Wilkes paused. "But, of course," he added, "Herod missed. If we just do that one little cluster of houses, we might miss, too."

"However we do it, we have to do it now," Vorona said.

"Gentlemen," Charles said, "I think we've heard

enough. Mike, we need to find this child. Would it help if you had a TR?"

"A triangle is essential. It enables me to enter the community with minimal risk. The grays will inevitably discover me, but at least it can get me to the scene undetected. Once I'm there, I figure I have a couple of days." He stood up, signaling that the meeting was ended. Vorona was right about one thing: there must be no delay now.

"Wait just a minute," Vorona said. "You're not walking out of here without telling us how you're going to proceed."

"I think we have mind-control capabilities of our own that can be brought to bear on the situation. We can do this without revealing to the grays that we're responsible. *How* is my business."

"There's one system that works," Greenfield said, "the violence wire."

"Duty calls, gentlemen," Mike said as they started to filter into his living room for drinks. "There's no time, not tonight. There is no time at all."

He left, then, heading down to the garage in his basement. He needed to get to Wilton—which, of course, would turn out to be a trap. The larger question was how, exactly, did the trap work, and how could it be defeated?

If it could.

TWELVE

AS DAN ENTERED MARCIE'S OFFICE, he was enveloped in what he immediately perceived as an ominous silence. Behind her, the westering sun made a halo of her glowing russet hair. Her hands, holding what Dan presumed were his student evaluations, gleamed softly in the late light. Her skin was smooth and her features exotic, with large, frank eyes and lips that generally contained a hint of laughter—not the pleasantly sensual laughter that the face suggested, though. Marcie was first and foremost an administrator. She fired, gave bad news, and disciplined wayward professors for their crimes—drunkenness, sloth, and, of course, lechery.

He imagined her fingers touching him, and it was oddly thrilling. He blinked and shook the thought away.

She smiled, and he saw something unexpected: a sort of warmth.

"Given what I have here, it would have been useful to you," she said, "if you could have gotten a little more support from faculty."

"The student evaluations, ah—"

"I can't give you details, Dan."

"No, of course not." Student evaluations at Bell were held secret from professors, so that they could be used as a tool and weapon of the administration. "But they're bad, I assume."

She laid the paper back in the file from which she'd

taken it, aligned it with a long, deep red fingernail, and closed the manila folder.

From outside there came the distant strains of the Bell Ringers Band hammering away, improbably enough, at "Moon River," the sound carried off on the stiff north wind that had come up around noon. Voices echoed along the hall, the comfortable laughter of some succulent coed making light, no doubt, of a flapping faculty admirer.

"Marcie," he said. He stopped himself, astonished by a shocking and completely inappropriate sense of desire for her. She was doing nothing to seduce him. He looked at her right hand, lying there on the desk. If he reached across that two-foot space and laid his own hand on it, what would happen?

"Yes?" Her voice seemed almost to tremble. But why? Did she have to tell him no, and was she afraid to do that? But why should she be? He was no friend of hers and bad news was job one in this office. Poor student evaluations and no faculty support, open and shut case, toodle-oo.

"Marcie, look, we both know what's going on here."

She laughed a little, the nervous tinkle of a girl. "I think the problem is that your courses aren't sexy."

He had arrived at the edge of the cliff: poor evals, no support, now a negative on his courses. The next step would be, sorry, I cannot vote for tenure. "It's physiological psychology," he yammered. "Give me a couple of sections of abnorm, I'll bring my comments way up."

"That's unlikely until you're tenured."

"But I can't get tenured without good evals, and I can't get those without good courses."

"You're Yossarianed, then. As we all are. Bell Yossarians us all."

For a moment, he was at a loss. Then he remembered *Catch-22.* Yossarian was the character in the novel who was caught in a bureaucratic endless loop. Dan searched for something, anything, that might help him. He could drop a name. Pitiful, but it was what he had. "I knew a fellow when I was at Columbia—what was his name, Speed Vogel—who knew Heller."

She made a note.

"What are you writing?"

"Knew friend of Heller."

"Does it matter?"

"Not at all."

He found himself watching her lips, the way she pressed them together, the slight and fascinating moisture at the corners of her mouth.

But why? Was he going mad? How could he feel this way for this woman who was about to wreck his life?

Did he want this so badly that he was willing to whore for it? Probably, but why would she want him? She had her pick of faculty masochists, eager to roll in the hay with their punisher. And yet, the only thing that was stopping him from leaping across that desk was the fear that any such action would backfire.

"Marcie," he heard himself say, and he heard the roughness, the unmistakable sexuality in his tone. He almost slapped his hand over his mouth, but she looked up suddenly, blinking fast. Her eyebrows rose to the center of the forehead, her eyes filmed with tears that made them bright and awful.

"What's the matter?" she asked in a horrible, low tone that made him think she feared him.

He remembered, suddenly, his seizure dream, going up into the dark womb of the sky, the cave in the silver moon. He shook it away, frightened for a moment that he was going into aura again. But no, it was only a memory.

She cleared her throat, lifted her hand, and brushed her lips with the back of it, smearing her lipstick a little. "Yes," she whispered.

He said, "Is this the conference? My conference with my tenure advisor? We sit here staring helplessly at each other?"

"There's nothing to discuss, Dan," she said. She straightened herself, clasped her hands, and lifted her chin. She was beautiful, then, tragically beautiful. He could see her in the darkness, and she looked very afraid. But no, it wasn't dark and she wasn't scared. She looked across at him, her eyes steady. "It's just—obviously, you know the student evaluations—well, you know, they're often rather indifferent to the welfare of somebody they know has need."

"They know I'm up for tenure?"

She nodded, her little mouth grave, her eyes flashing. "Oh, yes," she said, and he knew, in that moment, that he must have her. He must do this, he could not help himself. He also knew that she was aware of the potential that existed between them. He went to his feet.

She looked down his body, then cleared her throat. Her cheeks had gone bright red. He stood before her like a little soldier at stiff attention. He said in his heart, *Katelyn, I am so ashamed,* but Marcie's rising flush told him that there would be no escape for him.

She lifted her hand off the desk and reached toward him, her fingers extending.

They froze, then, remaining like that, him pressing his thighs against the edge of the desk, her reaching to the air six inches in front of his midriff.

Tears poured down her cheeks. She whispered, her voice an unsure murmur, "What happened last night?"

Something in him, some sort of inner door, fell open. He remembered the blaring confusions of his boyhood, the stars passing his face, the field of silver and the black opening, gaping.

"You heard about that?" He backed away from her desk. Then he saw:

—A narrow steel cot, Marcie lying on it in heat, her face flushed and sweaty, her bush brown and touched as if by dew.

And he felt:

—His own nakedness delicious in the night air.

She gasped as if struck. "Dan," she said, "Dan." Her eyes widened, glistened, their green suddenly horrible to see, too glassy, too . . . hurt.

"Marcie, listen, uh—"

She stood up and came around the desk, entered his arms. She drew against him, drew close, and in the fur of his sweater he heard long and bitter sobs.

"I'm sorry," he said, "I'm so damn sorry."

She pressed herself against him harder. Then their lips

were touching, asking one another if there should be more. If she—of all creatures, she—could be admitted to his sanctum?

He laid his hand on her back and pressed her closer to him, and delivered himself to her kiss.

THIRTEEN

LAUREN DID NOT HAVE SEXUAL feelings about Adam, of course, and the idea of him having such feelings for her was repellent. But there was something else there. He liked to explore her intensities—sexuality, anger, passion, loss, triumph, her slight kinks . . . those little fantasies that she sometimes relaxed with, of helplessness and ardor. And her childhood. Adam moved through her childhood memories like a tiger prowling the tall grass.

Normally, he was curiously empty of emotion himself. You'd almost be willing to believe he was a machine, he was so—not cold, that's an emotion. Adam's heart was empty. But earlier this morning, when he had been showing her the images of the dying cruise ship and the supermarket full of the starving, she had felt such a powerful sense of disquiet that she'd gotten the idea that they represented a great fear of his, and therefore of his whole species. They were a collective, connected in some esoteric way across the whole universe. She thought it had to do with quantum interconnectedness. A gray could communicate instantly with a gray in another galaxy, but hardly at all with a human being.

She had come to feel that Adam's ceaseless quest to share her heart was central to his meaning, and probably the meaning of them all.

They weren't predators, like Mike thought, but people who had somehow become machines. They were smart enough to know that they were the most profound possible outsiders: they were functional, very much so, but had no access to the emotional universe that seemed to her to be the essence of being alive.

She lay staring at the living room ceiling, vaguely listening to Ted's golf tournament on the TV. What was it? The Masters? She enjoyed golf, the precision of it, the struggle, the inner calm that was essential, as well as beating her dear Ted at a game . . . which she managed occasionally.

He was her shelter in the storm of desperation that defined Adam. She wondered if the grays had lost their souls. Was that their problem—they'd once been more fully alive than they were now, and they were searching the universe for some way to regain themselves?

Adam rejected every effort she made to find out about his people, his world, any of it. If she tried to penetrate his mind the way he did hers, by latching onto the pictures stored there, all she'd ever get was white light. Static. He blocked her.

It was a little sinister feeling, truth to tell. What did he have to hide?

She became aware of a siren outside, which was certainly unusual for University Park. This was not a siren-oriented neighborhood, no way. The deep, booming horn that accompanied it announced that it was a fire truck.

Well, that was more believable. There were dorm fires over on the two campuses every so often, usually involving mattresses or common-room couches. Once in a blue moon one of the beautiful old U. Park houses burned. Still, it would be extremely serious if the facility was threatened in any way, so she got up from the couch, went to the front hall, and put on her jacket.

"Hello," Ted said as she passed through the living room.

"I'm going out. Back in a few."

He knew not to ask, of course.

When she reached the street, she smelled a faint tang of smoke. Okay, that was to be expected if there was a fire in the area. She got in her car and drove to the facility. She was appalled, as she turned the corner, to see three big fire trucks in the street.

Her mouth went dry, she began mentally reviewing the steps that had to be taken to protect the secure areas. Nobody, no fireman, no fire inspector, must go down that elevator.

As she pulled into the driveway, she saw that the house itself was not burning, but there were firemen in the drive. She fumbled frantically through her purse looking for her credentials. Mike was in Washington and Andy was off. They often left Adam alone. He was safe down there, and when he wasn't being interacted with, he lay as inert as an abandoned toy. If he began to move around, sensors would alert her and Andy, and they could watch him from their laptops. It had never happened, though.

She stepped out of the car and walked over to the firemen. Just the other side of their garden wall there was smoke.

"What's going on?" she asked.

"Grass fire, probably started by kids."

"It's not going to come over this far, is it?"

"No, ma'am. That's why we're here."

"Okay, thank you. Listen, I'm going to be in the house. If there's any change, please let me know."

She entered by the front door. Before going down, she went first into her office and turned on her computer. After it had voice identified her, she pulled up the feed from Adam's chamber.

Unlike the human eye, the camera simply saw what was in front of it. On camera, you could sometimes glimpse Adam. He could feel you watching, though, and would usually disappear in under a second.

She was shocked to find him pacing, the slim gray form speeding in a blur from wall to wall. At least he wasn't flying around like some kind of gigantic berserk blowfly.

Immediately, she went to the elevator, pressed her thumb against the print reader, and stepped inside. She dropped down into the pit. Quickly, she prepped, just covering her face and hands with emollient and leaving it at that. Her skin was as stiff as leather anyway. She didn't bother with an antihistamine shot, but she did stuff an epinephrine injector into the pocket of her slacks. Then she stepped into the lock, waited for the outer door to close, and entered the cage.

"Hi," she said aloud. She went to her chair, sat down, closed her eyes, and directed her attention to the physical sensation of her body. By thus removing her attention from her thoughts, she signaled to Adam that he could enter her.

He rushed in with all the eagerness of a dog leaping to its master's breast after a long absence . . . or a lion pouncing. It felt like both things when Adam came into her. This time, he didn't go to her sexual memories, but rather to earliest childhood.

She found herself back home in Philly, in Mom's study, and all the furniture was incredibly tall. She was gliding from chair to chair, and her heart was soaring. It was a place he'd gone to frequently, the moment she had taken her first steps.

She loved these memories Adam would bring up out of childhood's amnesia. Because of him, she had remembered her birth and even before, a sort of secret communion with her mother in the womb.

Then he went to a moment in the living room when she was about two, when she had stood watching the sunlight slanting in through the window, and listened to the voice of the sun singing a song whose words were deeper in her than even Adam could reach.

The message of these excursions into her earliest life was clear: see what I am about to show you with the open eyes of a child. She emptied her mind even more and waited.

Drifting in like a dream, she saw the Earth from above. North America was wheeling slowly toward the sunset. But the coastlines were changed. Florida was just a narrow spike, half its usual size. The Caribbean was mostly featureless blue. The whole East Coast was submerged beneath a brown scar of filthy water. Then she saw numbers, and she realized that these were a series of dates, ranging from 2012 to 2077.

She sucked in breath. She now understood the cruise ship, the starving supermarket: Adam was warning her about a great catastrophe.

"Oh, Adam," she said, "I'll tell the colonel. I'll be sure to tell him."

He began shooting around like a rocket, slamming into the walls with hideous, crunching thuds.

"Adam!" She leaped up out of the chair, but he was whizzing now, racing so fast she could hear the bzzt of his passing but not see so much as a glimpse of gray skin or the gleam of one of his huge black eyes.

At that moment, without the slightest warning, thick smoke came pouring through every air-conditioning vent in the room.

For an instant, she was frozen, her mind unable to take in what she was seeing.

The smoke roiled along the ceiling, and she saw that it was filled with glowing red streaks. The lights began flickering, grew dim.

"Adam," she screamed, "we've got to get out!" In two strides she was across the room. She fumbled open the cover on the bail-out switch and hit it with the heel of her hand.

Sirens erupted, the facility went to emergency lighting, and the door to the lock slid open. "Adam," she screamed, "Adam!"

The smoke came down like a curtain, turning everything inky dark. An instant later, the fire struck her head and neck with ferocious, terrifying heat. Covering her head, she dropped to the floor. "Adam! Come toward me, Adam, stay low!"

Nothing happened. There was bare visibility here, and it was hot and getting hotter. She could smell in the stink of the smoke the additional stench of her own singed hair. The next breath she took caused a reflex of a kind she didn't know existed. The choking was a fearsome weight slammed down on her back, the gagging like some sort of spring unraveling in her throat.

She backed out through the airlock and into the control room. Here, meteors of plastic were dripping down from the ceiling.

She was sick with dread, she knew that she had lost Adam, but she also knew that she had to get out of this place fast or she would be burned to death. The elevator doors were open, but she would not dare to enter it. Feeling her way along, she came to the door of the emergency stair. She reached up into the heat and opened it. As she went through, smoke gushed in behind her, and she only just managed to get the door closed.

Crying and screaming, she opened it a crack, but there was nothing but smoke and now also flames licking into the shaft. "Adam! Adam! Adam!"

The door began to crackle, and heat hit her in the face even though she was low, and she had no choice but to slam it again.

Crying and coughing, she began the long trek upward on the narrow circular escape stair. As she trudged along, pacing herself to avoid exhaustion, she wracked her brain to understand how a grass fire next door had spread to the facility. Sparks must have somehow entered the ground-level air intake and started a conflagration in the air-conditioning system.

Three-quarters of the way to the top, she dragged her cell phone out of her pocket, but it was still out of range. She continued on, reaching the surface so winded that she had to stop and catch her breath before she could even manage to open the door that led into the foyer.

She felt it, noted that it wasn't hot. She cracked it, looked out into the foyer. There were two firemen standing there. Above her head, thuds indicated that another man was on the stairs to the offices.

There was a rumbling from below and smoke came bursting up the stairwell. In an instant, it was fiercely hot, her eyes were burning, and she was choking again, even worse than before.

She had no choice but to act. She could not stay here. Again she opened the door. The intensity of the smoke increased at once. Behind her, the heat rose. Opening the door turned the stairwell into a flue.

The next instant, the door flew out of her hand and the firemen dragged her out, slamming it shut as soon as she was safe.

"Are you conscious?"

"Yes!"

"Okay, dizzy?"

"No, sir. My chest is burning."

"Is there anybody else down there?"

She wanted to say yes, she wanted them to try to rescue Adam. That could not be allowed, though. These men had no clearances. These men could not enter the facility.

She fumbled in her jeans, drew out her credentials. "That facility is classified," she gasped. "There's nobody else in it and it cannot be entered without authorization."

"This is a fire situation, lady. We're gonna go in there."

"No! It's illegal!" She struggled to her feet, went for her cell phone again. "I'm calling my supervisor." She punched in the colonel's speed dial . . . and got his message. "Colonel, there's a fire here, we're dealing with a lot of unauthorized personnel and I need somebody here to control this situation!" She hung up.

At that moment, Andy appeared. He came hurrying in and threw his arms around her. Then he held her at arm's length. "My God, you're burned, you have no eyebrows."

The foyer door burst open and fire gushed out with the ferocity of water from a burst main. They got out of there, and the firemen began deploying hose.

"It's totally out of control," she said to Andy.

"Where is he?"

"I couldn't manage to save him."

"Dear God."

"They mustn't find remains. We can't let them find remains."

"I know it."

Her cell rang. "It's him," she said. "Colonel, there's a fire in progress here."

Silence. Then, very calmly, "What happened?"

"There was a grass fire next door. When I heard sirens, I came over here from my place. The fire didn't appear to be serious, but I felt that I should be with Adam, so I went down. A few minutes later, the whole facility filled with smoke and fire. I've never seen anything like it."

"What's Adam's status?"

"He's still down there!"

"Is he dead, then?"

"I would assume so."

More silence. Then a sound that Lauren thought might be a cry, but it was so loud and so close to the phone that it broke up into a series of shattering electronic noises. Then she could hear him taking breaths. He said, finally, "Okay. You cannot let those people down there. Anything could be going on, this is outside the envelope."

"Sir, I can't stop them, they're ignoring my credentials."

"I'm gonna blow somebody's brains out if this doesn't get handled," he said, but so mildly that it didn't seem like the threat she knew that it was.

"Sir, where are you? Can you get here soon?"

"I'm an hour out in my plane, damnit! YOU handle it, *Colonel*." He sneered the word. Then he disconnected.

"He is one pissed-off guy," she muttered.

"Oh, yeah, he would be. You know what we lost here? We lost the most important thing this country possesses, that's what we lost. And that man is the person who has to take the heat for it. So he is gonna be pissed."

Mike couldn't pace in the plane, the cabin was too confined, so he sat rubbing the arms of his seat. He had to report this, he had to do it immediately. He said into the intercom, "I need the code box." This small, highly sophisticated device transmitted and received in quantum-encoded bursts that could not be decrypted by intruders.

The first officer brought it back from the equipment bay behind his station, then returned to the flight deck. Mike turned off the intercom, then glanced at the flight-deck door to make certain that it was closed.

He pulled out the red handset and punched in Charles Gunn's secure number. It rang once, part of a second time.

"Gunn."

"Charles, I'm in condition two-one-zero-one. Do you understand?"

"GODDAMN YOU!"

"I'm in the plane, for God's sake. It was Glass. Glass let a situation get away from her."

"Glass. Glass doesn't matter anymore. Glass is a liability and so are any other support personnel."

"I realize that, Charles."

"Well, act accordingly."

Mike replaced the phone. He stared, thinking. The grays were not sitting still, they understood that there was a threat, and the direction it was coming from.

Okay, first things first. Do the support personnel. Andy was a good man and that would be hard, but Lauren— pretty as she was, he was going to enjoy putting her down.

The Goddamn bitch had lost ADAM!

FOURTEEN

DAN HAD COME HOME REEKING of booze, of all the incredible things, and gone in the living room and begun playing the "Ode to Joy" from Beethoven's Ninth over and over again at blasting volume. He lay there now in front of the stereo in the dark, splayed out on the floor like a great, gangling rag doll. She'd wanted to put her arms around him and mother him a little. His mother had been mostly indifferent to her little boy, and she felt that he needed the reassuring support of his woman right now.

She knew, of course, what had happened: Marcie Cotton had ditched his tenure. She was scared, too, she had to admit, because they could not remain here on just her salary. So what was going to happen to them was that they were going to fall off the academic cliff into the stew of little, tiny colleges and junior colleges and spend the rest of their lives scrimping and scraping.

She looked at the clock. Eight-twenty. She went into the living room, turned on a lamp.

"Please."

"Dan, you've been in here for hours."

"Please leave me be!"

"Dan, no."

He did not respond.

She went on. "It's about time for Conner to get home and I want you to come down out of the tree and face this together." She had to bellow over the music. "Let's turn that off, now." She went to the stereo, flipped the switch. "Enough is enough."

He rose off the floor, then went to the bar. "What's in here? God." He came up with an ancient bottle of crème de menthe, left over from some distant summer party when they'd poured it over ice cream. Earlier, she'd removed the rest of the booze to the garage.

"You already stink of bourbon. I hope you didn't do this at the Peep?" The Peep Inn was the campus dive, where a professor most certainly did not need to get drunk.

"I did indeed. I consumed alcohol there, in the absurd hope that I could drink myself unconscious before the fall of night."

"Dan, we'll get by. Something good will happen."

Staring at her as if she was insane, he slowly shook his head. Then he bared his teeth and rocked back in silent, agonized laughter.

"I got promised tenure by Marcie Cotton."

She thrust her hands at him, connected with his chest. "Go *on*! You did not!"

He nodded.

"And you won't be getting drunk again, so it's forgiven. Now, Marcie told you? She actually told you this?"

He nodded.

"You're going to get a yes on *tenure*! Oh. My. God."

He stared at her, his eyes hollow, his lips hanging slightly open—an expression that said that this wasn't the whole story.

"If I needed punishment, how would you go about it?"

What an extremely strange question. "Excuse me?"

"If I'd . . . done something wrong?"

"What have you done? You've gotten tenure, that's hardly a matter for punishment. Is she sure?"

"Oh, yes." He closed his eyes, shook his head.

She realized, then, that he was trying to say that he had done something with Marcie Cotton. Or no, it couldn't be possible. You didn't go to *bed* for tenure, not even in this sinkhole.

"Dan, are you telling me—what? I'm not getting it."

"You're getting it."

"Damn you!"

The front door opened and Conner called, "I'm home, people," and Dan said, "I'm so damn sorry, baby. I'm so damn sorry!"

Conner breezed in. "Hi, Mom, hi, Dad. I have just been at an amazing editing session. The Keltons have an awesome video and they're bringing it over, and Paulie and his parents are coming, and there's a chance that—" He stopped, looked from one of them to the other. "Hello?"

Katelyn drew breath, drew it hard, trying mightily to contain the rage, the hurt that shuddered through her.

"Mom?"

She went to him. "I want you to go downstairs for just a little while."

"They got video of the UFO. Everybody's coming over to watch it on the big-screen TV."

She did not exactly want a convention just now, but obviously she couldn't prevent it. "You go down, and we'll make popcorn when they come."

"You sound strange."

She took him to the stairs and closed the door behind him. Then she went back to Dan, who was now slumped on the couch with his face in his hands. "You asshole," she said quietly.

"Hit me."

"Dan, I'm not physical. But what I would very much like is for you to go upstairs and gather your belongings and take them with you, and get the hell out of my house." She curtsied. "If you would be so kind."

"I don't know what happened! I don't know how to explain it."

"You screwed her for your tenure."

"I did no such thing!"

"And I find that grotesque. And equally grotesque that you confessed it. What happened to you, you're not this drunk blubbering jerk I see here! I sure as hell didn't marry *him*."

"Look, I want to ask forgiveness."

"It's that easy, you get drunk and you cry and what happens, I kick you around and yell a little and this violation of your sacred trust is forgotten? And if you go to go creeping off to sleep with her in the forenoon from now on, then what do I do? Just bear everyone in this miserable fishbowl knowing my—what's the word—shame, I suppose. My shame."

"It left me . . . vulnerable. Somehow, it affected me."

"What did?"

"That incident!"

"Something weird happens and therefore you go make love to Marcie Cotton?"

He shook his head, waved his hand at her. "I—it made me . . . want her. I don't know why, but it did. I relate the two things."

"What in hell are you saying?"

"I don't know!"

"Dan, I'm an orphan to the violence in my family, and you to the neglect in yours and, Dan, nobody but another orphan can heal either of us, this is why we're together. But you—you've taken something from us, and it is profound, Dan, because trust has a different meaning for people who suffered from betrayed childhoods."

"It wasn't over the tenure. It was—" He shook his head. "Oh, my love, it was like some demon flew in and sweated us with his fire. I think, being so tired, so surprised and relieved—I just suddenly found myself in her arms."

"Don't tell me about it! For God's sake, Danny, have some mercy!"

He slumped yet deeper into the couch. He looked so tired, so sunken, nothing at all like the rippling, robust husband she adored. Had adored. He looked like somebody who'd fallen victim to a vampire, shadowy about the eyes, gray of skin.

Her stomach had grown tight and sour with fear, her own skin was so cold she shuddered. This had been her rock, this marriage, in its honesty and the richly sensual capsule of its love. But how could she let him touch her now? How could she bear it?

"Momma, what, exactly, is wrong?"

"Conner!"

"Because something is and I need to know."

"Conner, please."

He came into the room. "You two are fighting and I want to know why."

Figures appeared on the deck, looming up out of the dark, flashlights bobbing.

Conner went to the door. "This is a chance for me. Don't wreck this."

Dan got up, started to kiss Katelyn on the cheek, wisely thought better of it, and greeted the Keltons.

"You need to see this, folks," affable John said. "It really is genuinely odd."

"It's not what it seems," Dan said. "It's explainable, trust me."

"Dad, it's not," Conner said. "That's the whole point!"

Dan went into the kitchen and picked up the phone. Chris answered on the third ring. "Have I woken you up at nine-fifteen, old man?"

"We were out with the 'scope. It's a good night for the Crab Nebula."

"Speaking of nebulas, the Kelton clan has arrived with what's probably a pretty nebulous video of that prank."

"Prank?"

"The affair of the fiery balloon."

"That could be historic footage."

"How so?"

"You saw somebody in the field, buddy. And then you didn't. I think that somebody was an alien."

He had indeed seen somebody. It was also further support for the prank theory, but they could get to that later. "When you come, you might think about bringing some spirits. *Mon femme* has stripped our bar." He hung up the phone, then returned to the living room where the crowd had surrounded the gigantic TV. "We gather round the campfire," he said, "and see shapes in the sparks. And thus the mythologizing begins." He sat down. "The Jefferes will be here directly."

Paulie Warner burst in from the kitchen, followed by his parents and then Chris and Nancy. The energy in the room exploded as the two boys excitedly traded speculations. "It's the grays," Conner yelled, "they're doing an operation right here at Bell!"

"Okay, Conner, sure," Paulie said.

Terry said, "What we actually have is some unexplained video."

"Edited," Dan added. "Most carefully, I'm sure."

"Not really," John Kelton said, his voice sharp with annoyance. "It's actually just pulled out of the camera. Not edited at all. There's no reason to edit it."

"We copied it onto a DVD," Terry said as he dropped the gleaming disk into the player's open tray. "Beyond that, you're seeing what the camera saw."

The player absorbed the disk. This was followed by blackness, then a couple of flashes.

"Fascinating," Dan said.

"Just wait," John snapped.

There was a sound of gasping, then crunching. "That's us running," Conner said.

"You were really there?"

"Conner was there," Dan told Paulie.

Another flash, then a blur. Dan was beginning to think that this might be pretty minimal when suddenly the screen filled with light. And with screaming—as terrible, as powerful, as it had been the moment it happened. Silence fell. Paulie sat close to Conner, Dan was pleased to notice. He heard his own voice shouting, then saw himself and Conner in the light of the thing.

"Conner, you were *right there*!" Paulie whispered.

It was the eeriest thing that Dan had ever seen. Two faint seams were present, one running the length of the object, the other around its center. Behind the thing, something seemed to be moving in the light, almost as if it was climbing out of an opening that was concealed by the object's bulk.

"There's your culprit," Dan said. "Nancy, be prepared to ID a student who needs disciplining."

The object rose a bit and seemed to shimmer.

The woman's voice, which had been screaming and then silent, now cried out more clearly and a cold horror shot through Dan as powerfully and unexpectedly as a lightning bolt from a silent sky. "My God," he said—whispered.

"What? What, Dan?" Conner was pulling at him.

"Don't miss this," Jimbo said.

In the flash of a single frame, the object disappeared leaving behind it the fleeting shot of a figure, barely visible in the dark. The figure seemed to turn, but it all happened so quickly that you could see little. There was silence, blackness. Dan heard his own voice say that he didn't think they were alone.

"It *is* the grays," Conner shouted, jumping to his feet. "I told you, Paulie, it's the grays!"

"Yeah, you're right," Paulie said. "I gotta go to the john." He headed out of the room.

Dan hardly heard them. His mind was reeling. Because Marcie had been involved, he had recognized her voice in that last scream. But what could it mean? Had she pulled the prank? Maybe she'd gone insane. It would fit with the bizarre seduction, maybe even vindicate him in Katelyn's eyes . . . eventually. That was going to be one hell of a siege.

But then he thought, what if it *wasn't* a prank? What if Chris and Conner were right, and some sort of genuine anomaly was unfolding? Perhaps he and Marcie had both been traumatized by it. Psychological trauma was well known to drive people to sexual activity. It even had a popular name: battlefield syndrome. He was confused and, frankly, afraid. He wished he hadn't drunk all that booze at the Peep. He felt lousy, his head was pounding, and now he had this bizarre, impossible thing to consider.

"Boys, can you slo-mo the last little part?" Chris asked. "The figure?"

Terry stabbed a couple of times at the remote, and the figure appeared again, frozen, its back to the camera.

"Let me juice the contrast," Terry muttered.

The scene became lighter, the figure more clear.

"Is that a balloon?" Katelyn asked.

"It's the head, Mom."

As Terry shuttled the image forward frame by frame, the figure turned in short jerks, until its face was visible in a blurred three-quarters view.

Total silence fell as every person there reacted to the image. It was not clear, far from it, but anybody could tell that this was no disguise and no inflated toy. The one fully visible eye was black and slanted, gleaming. It gave the creature a breathtaking look of menace. The lower part of the face was complex with wrinkles, like a very, very old human face might be, the face of a man deeply etched by the trials of his time. There was the tiniest suggestion of a mouth, little more than a line.

With another flick of the shuttle control, another frame appeared. Now the mouth had opened slightly, and the sense of surprise it communicated was so vivid that it was eerie.

Another flick of the shuttle and the figure was gone.

Dan found himself feeling his ear and remembering what Conner had said. Dear heaven, what if this was real?

His mind rebelled. It just could not be true, because if it was, then he was involved and so was Marcie. But why? In the name of God, *why*?

"Look at that," Paulie said as he returned. He went to the glass doors and stepped out on the deck.

Conner followed him. "It's them," he said softly, his voice trembling.

"Jesus, it might be," Jimbo said.

A glow rose behind the stand of pines that separated the house from the field beyond.

Dan went onto the deck. The glow was smaller, but it was still very damn bright, and was indeed out in the field.

Were they in contact? Aliens had chosen to land in a little college town?

It just did not seem possible. No matter what was happening, that was not the whole story.

Then he saw stars slowly wheeling around him—an aura, another one, the third in two days. Maybe if he could get to the couch, they wouldn't notice the staring emptiness of petit mal. Hardly able to navigate through the sea of stars that now surrounded him, he somehow found the couch, nearly sitting on Maggie's lap.

"Slow down, buster," Katelyn snapped.

"Sorry! Sorry!"

He slumped back. Before him was not the gleaming sliver he usually saw, but a room. There was a person there—a child. She was exquisitely beautiful . . . and recognizable.

He cried out and the seizure was over.

"Dan!"

"Sorry!"

"Dan, aren't you hearing me? Stop the boys!"

Then he realized that Paulie and Conner were outside and running like two mad things toward the field, flashlights bobbing.

The world seemed to stop. Harley and Maggie looked up at him, their expressions identical, eyebrows raised, slight smiles playing on their faces.

Chris said, "This could be it."

Katelyn burst out the door and went running down the stairs. Dan followed.

"Come on, Conner," Paulie yelled.

"Calm down," Conner yelled back. "Stay together!"

Dan was aware that the Warners had come out onto the deck, and were quietly standing and watching. Then he saw Chris beside them. "You better come down here," he shouted.

It all seemed to be happening in slow motion, as Chris came across the deck and down the stairs.

Dan ran after Conner and Katelyn, moving more slowly through the woods because he had only the light of the object to guide him.

When he broke out into the field, he saw an extremely bright light, but it appeared to be more of a pinpoint. He could see the silhouettes of the two boys close to it, and Katelyn coming up behind them.

"We mean you no harm," Conner yelled. Then, "*Nous vous voulons dire aucun mal.*"

"Conner get back," Katelyn shouted.

"Come to meet us," Paulie cried. His voice almost bubbled.

Dan ran harder. The children should be very damn afraid.

"Wait! I'm getting a mental communication," Conner said. "They want us to come closer."

"Hold hands, buddy!"

The two boys went forward—and suddenly the light went out. "Run, boys," Dan shouted.

Then he heard laughter, a lot of young laughter. There was more laughter behind him, and he turned to see the Warners breaking out of the woods. They were laughing, too.

"Aw, shit," Chris said from the dark. "I never win."

There were flashlights up ahead, and as Dan arrived, he realized that he was surrounded by kids, and they were laughing and jeering and shining flashlights on Conner, who was trapped in the center of a circle of derision.

It had been a prank, and it looked as if most of Conner's classmates were here.

Conner put his hands over his head as if he was being stoned by the voices. Katelyn ran around the outside of the circle, trying to part it, to get to her boy.

Harley and Maggie Warner came up chuckling amiably. "That's our gasoline lantern," Harley said. "It came back from Neptune just in time."

Dan closed his fist, pulled back—and just barely managed to stop himself from decking Harley.

"He-ey," Harley said. "It's a joke. An innocent practical joke. They've been planning it all day. We need something to cut the tension, man!"

"At my son's expense!" He was not as careful as Katelyn, who was still trying to gently push kids aside. He grabbed a fistful of somebody's jacket and hurled what turned out to be a girl to the ground. As she screamed and cursed at him, he waded in and reached his son.

"Get out of here," Conner shrilled, "please just get out of here!"

"Conner, come home," Katelyn said, joining them. She looked around them. "You're pitiful, all of you!"

"Asshole!" came a muffled yell from the dark. "Bitch!"

Their arms around their boy, Katelyn and Dan headed for home. As they passed the Warners, Dan said, "You stay away from our place and keep that fat troll of yours away from our son."

"Dan?" Harley called after him. "Hey, man, stay loose."

When they returned to the house, Chris was already back. He and Nancy were replaying the video.

"It's real, you know," Chris said.

Conner started to run downstairs.

"Hey, wait." Chris caught up to him. "Hold on. We have historic footage here. Come on back, take another look."

"Dr. Jeffers, I really can't right now."

"Forget those kids, Conner. The Warners are idiots, and the Keltons haven't got the faintest idea what this actually is. This video is one of the most precious records ever created by the human hand."

Conner was silent. Dan saw why. Tears were pouring from his eyes. But he raised his head. He said, "Could I possibly be homeschooled?"

Dan's heart almost broke, but he said, "You have to learn to face it, Conner. To gain control."

"Don't be ridiculous," Katelyn said. "He does not! And the fact that Harley and Maggie keep letting these things happen is a big part of what's wrong with child-rearing these days. They're passive, they believe in the mythical wisdom of the child, but children are savages and they need boundaries or they turn mean." She threw her arms around Conner. "You're the exception, love. You *are* a miracle, and if they can't handle that, then they're scum. That's all."

Conner sighed. "Mom, they happen to be people I have to spend every day of my life with." He moved away from her. "So, Dr. Jeffers, what have we got?"

"Come on. We'll go frame by frame, from the top, making a note whenever a new point of proof is present in a frame. Hey, you could count the rivets in this thing if it had rivets. There's a lot here. This is wonderful, convincing footage."

Dan hardly listened. He was in a state of complete turmoil. He had to understand about Marcie, and he did not. He just did not get it.

Then he did. "I remember," he said.

"What?" Katelyn snapped.

Dan got out of there. His stomach felt as if it had just filled with a foamy storm of acid. He dashed upstairs and into the bathroom.

"Dan," Katelyn called, following him.

She found him on his hands and knees over the toilet, barfing like a sick dog. He rose to his feet and started yanking paper off the roll to clean up the considerable quantity of yellow froth that had missed. He worked furiously, perhaps not yet aware of her presence.

"Dan," she said as she went down to him. She took the paper from him and flushed it away. They knelt there awkwardly, face to face.

"It's impossible," he said. "It has to be impossible." How could he tell her what he thought he was remembering? He had not only been in some way connected with Marcie two nights ago, it was worse than that. His childhood seizures hadn't been seizures at all, they had been memories so extremely strange that it hadn't been possible to recognize them for what they were. "We're lab rats," he said, then got sick again.

As she nursed him through it—rather bravely, she thought—he gasped, "I'm sorry, I'm sorry," and it meant a whole lot of things, and she wasn't real sure what all of them were. He got up, shook his head.

"Are you okay?"

"We're in some sort of trouble."

"Oh, yes."

He took her in his arms and held her. "This goes deep," he whispered, "real deep."

She wasn't sure she should, but she remained in his embrace.

"No matter how bizarre and how impossible it may seem, it had something to do with them."

"Something to do with whom?"

"Them! It was Marcie screaming in that thing."

She leaned back, looked at him.

"I recognized her voice—it was all crazy with fear, but it was her yelling, it was certainly her."

Katelyn could not think of how to react. She wasn't even sure exactly what he was trying to say. And yet the screaming had sounded vaguely familiar to her, too. She knew that he was right. It had indeed been Marcie—in the thing, with the alien, and absolutely terrified.

"How did she . . . seem?

"'*How did she seem?*' My God, that's too small a question! 'What in the name of all that's holy is going on here' just begins to approach it. When I walked into her office, that sour, rigid woman was—oh, Lord, totally changed, love. All soft and steamy and really, really sold on me. That cold fish. As if her personality had been totally revised overnight." He paused. "Which is exactly what did happen, in my opinion."

"Aliens did something to Marcie because—why? What does this have to do with the price of beans, Dan? Because you are an Irishman to your core and you might be a dull lecturer, but you can sing a song to a lady, and I think I'm hearing a damn clever one now."

"I'm telling you the truth!"

She backed away from him, looked at him out of the corners of her eyes. "You're telling me aliens—which you have always until ten minutes ago thought were utter bullshit—made you do it. I don't think I'm going to buy it, Danny-O. Nice try though. On the fly like that, very impressive."

Inside herself, though, she was much less sure. It seemed to her that she'd had more than a glimpse of an alien down there on that video. She'd seen, ever so vaguely, into an aspect of life that she had never even dreamed existed. There was somebody behind the scenes, it appeared, stitching things together, and they were taking an interest in this neighborhood and most specifically, she thought, in this family.

"Katelyn, I have to tell you something. I believe that I

was brought into that thing. That I was with Marcie in there. Because I have memories of that."

"Oh, come on."

"I have *memories*!"

"Okay, don't have a cat. So, when did this happen? While I blinked my eyes, maybe? Remember, I was there most of the time. And you did not go into that thing. In fact, if you had, it'd be on the video."

"Do you remember that you went to sleep with Conner afterward?"

"I was scared and so was he. I didn't want him left alone down there."

"And when you woke up, you were up here. In bed up here . . . and we saw those marks, that strange water. What if they were tracks, Katelyn?"

"Holes in the ground?"

"After we came back and went to sleep, that thing returned. It brought her back after they'd knocked her out or whatever they did to her. And for whatever reason . . ."

"No, Dan, the aliens did not make you do it. That will not fly."

"OKAY!"

"Keep your voice down!"

He pushed on, because a lot rode on this, his whole life with her rode on this. "The thing is—"

"Dan—"

"Listen to me! You listen, because this is bizarre and impossible but it is real, and you need to wrap your mind around it."

"I need to wrap my mind around your infidelity and I will not be talked out of it! Come on, Dan, at least respect my dignity as a human being."

"Katelyn, that's your melodrama showing and I accept that. Self-dramatization is a characteristic of people scarred by traumatic childhoods."

"Analyze yourself why don't you, my self-obsessed little boy."

"I take that. And I accept that what I did was wrong no matter what the explanation."

"Okay, now we're getting somewhere."

"Now will you listen?"

"All right. The star people made you do it. I'm fascinated."

"I remember seeing her on a sort of black frame cot, and we were—something was happening." He shuddered, then went to the sink and slugged water.

"What would that have been? Alien foreplay?"

"It was horrible! Katelyn, *horrible*! They—I remember some kind of sparks, and we were——oh, God—some sort of arcane thing where I kept seeing these sparks and hearing, like, her inner voice, her memories, her—like some kind of inner scent . . . the smell of her soul."

"Was there a rectal probe involved, or is this even kinkier?"

"I deserve that. Sure I do, but—"

"What, Dan? Don't talk in riddles, please."

"When we were kids . . . I saw another girl under the same circumstances . . . with them. A girl that was you."

"We didn't even know each other." And yet, she did have certain disjointed memories that were really strange, that she had always thought involved child abuse by one of her mother's many boyfriends. She did not mention these memories to him, though, not just now.

"We knew each other, but not in normal life. We knew each other very well . . . because they made sure we did. They made this family, Katelyn. We're damn lab rats is what we are."

"Oh, come *on*! Look, we have guests, I'm going downstairs, plus the ever-alert Conner is going to figure out that we're fighting again and do you really want him involved?"

"He is involved! He's heavily involved. Katelyn, don't you get it—why he's so brilliant, so off the charts—he's *theirs,* Katelyn."

"Oh, I don't think so. I really don't think so at all, because I seem to remember something about an epidural and a hell of a birthing struggle and he is *mine*! MY DAMN SON!"

"Shh!"

"Don't you shush me! First the aliens made you fuck that slut for your tenure, professor prostitute, then you dare to tell me my son is some kind of pod person? You're fucking certifiable, is what you are."

"I didn't say that. Of course he's our son. Our flesh and blood. Who sweated through that labor with you, who spent seventeen hours, *breathe, breathe,* who kissed your sweat and prayed with you? Who was there, Katie Katelyn, and is still here and will always be here, if you let me—and if you don't, will live still, yes, but will also be dead?"

She looked at him. He looked at her. In that moment, something, perhaps, about the vow of marriage itself that is sacred reasserted itself, and the union decided to continue on . . . at least for the while. "Was that a question?" she asked.

He raised his eyebrows. She raised hers. He opened his arms. She went in.

"Something so complex has happened—it's like I've glimpsed a level of life that's normally hidden, where there are other motives and meanings, that never normally come to light. And somehow, Marcie and I—and you and I, Katelyn—are connected on that level . . . and it's all to do with our boy, somehow, I know that. I know it and I love him and I love us, Katelyn, oh my God, so much."

"We've got to be with him," she said.

They walked together from their dark bedroom. Out the east window, which overlooked the field where the thing had appeared, an enormous moon was rising. By its light, silver with frost, she could see the whole field, wrapped now in the familiar mystery of an ordinary night. She looked up toward higher space, the glowing dark of the deep sky. There were stars, a few, battling the flooding moonlight.

Perhaps he was right. Maybe his struggle was, in some way, true. Maybe a shadow was there, one that you couldn't see, but that was nevertheless very real, the shadow of an unknown mind from a far place.

He came beside her, put his arm around her. "They're watching," he whispered.

She leaned against him, wondering what the future would bring. He might be going mad. It happened to people in middle age, and for a psychology professor to become psychologically abnormal had a certain irresistible irony to it, did it not?

Then again, maybe aliens were the answer. Certainly, the video was odd and disturbing. It had provided him an inventive excuse, she had to give him that.

"Come on," she said. She pushed away from him, and went back downstairs to rejoin the tormented odyssey of her son.

PART FIVE
THE MINISTERS OF DEATH

No man is an island, entire of itself. Every man is a piece of the continent, a part of the main. If a clod be washed away by the sea, Europe is the less, as well as if a promontory were, as well as if a manor of thy friends or of thine own were. Any man's death diminishes me, because I am involved in mankind, and therefore never send to know for whom the bell tolls, it tolls for thee.

—JOHN DONNE
"Meditation XVII"

FIFTEEN

LAUREN WATCHED THE COLONEL AS he moved back and forth, back and forth. She'd never seen him like this, all of his rigorous professionalism gone, his eyes flickering from place to place like an animal looking for escape from a cage.

"Where's Andy? Andy is supposed to meet us here."

"Andy is gone."

"And you don't know where, of course."

"No, sir, I had no idea he would leave."

"You know your problem, Lauren? You're naïve. Relentlessly damned *naïve*!"

"I—sir, I did everything I could. I only backed out of there because I had no choice."

"You didn't think to detain Andy?"

"Of course not! Why in the world would I do that?"

"You don't have the whole picture, I grant you that. With all his years in the hole, working with you empaths, Andy knew a little more than you do."

"Has he, uh, what has he done?"

"Run, you damned fool!"

"Don't you take that tone with me."

He gave her a look that made her step away from him. He'd never been a pleasant man to work with, but he seemed violent now, and she did not like this, she did not like it at all.

They were standing in his smoke-stained office. The fire

department had saved the house, but the facility below was a total loss.

"I want to know the truth of this thing, Lauren, and I'm sorry to say that I don't think I'm getting it from you."

That made heat rise in her cheeks. She did not like her own professionalism challenged. "My report is correct in every detail."

"Don't you understand what happened, even yet?"

"Of course I do. There was a grass fire, it spread to the air intake, and flammables in the air dryers ignited. That's the official verdict and it's also the truth."

"Then where's Adam?"

"Excuse me?"

"You do understand that there were no remains."

"Well it was incinerated, then. He was, I mean. All they pulled out of there was ash, anyway. Black, sodden ash, I saw it."

"It's been gone through and there are no remains!"

"He burned! *Burned*!" And she was crying. Thinking of him. "He had a beautiful mind, you know. Incredibly beautiful."

"The skeleton is made of a metal that's quite indestructible. But we did not find that skeleton down there, and the rubble was sifted through screens. It was very carefully gone through, Lauren, so I think you must be lying to me."

"You're beneath contempt, you know that?"

He backhanded her. The blow came unexpectedly, a flash in her right eye. For a moment, she was too stunned to understand what had hit her. Then she did understand and a torrent of pure rage filled her. "That's a violation," she said, trying to force the anger out of her voice, "and I'm going to put you up on charges for it."

She realized that he was laughing in her face, then that he was withdrawing a pistol from underneath his tunic. She was very quick of mind, which is one of the reasons that she was effective with Adam, and that quickness enabled her now to recall the rumors that people could get into lethal trouble in these deep black programs. Within perhaps three seconds of the weapon appearing—in fact, before he even had it fully out, she had turned and left the room.

Leaping down the stairs, she brought all of her considerable athleticism to bear. She hit the floor, staggered—and heard a gigantic roar. She knew what it was: a shot. He was trying to kill her. She dashed across the hall as a second shot crashed into the wall beside the door. It was close, she could feel the heat of it on her cheek. He was a damned good shot, getting that close from that far away with a .45.

She got the door open and another shot rang out. She ran down the sidewalk and out into the middle of the street. She had to get this out in public, that was her only hope, and keep enough distance between them to make a hit a matter of luck. Fifty feet, at least. Closer and he would not miss.

She ran down the middle of the street, zigzagging and not making the mistake of looking back. Damn this neighborhood, it was too damn *quiet*! Just one car, please, just one damn car—but there were none.

Maybe not all of Dad's nightmares had been about the grays, maybe he had also feared this sort of thing happening to him one day.

Then, as she rounded the corner, a lovely Mustang with two coeds in it appeared. "Help!" She stood in front of them waving her arms. "Help! I need the police! Help me!"

As they swerved around her, she yelled into the car, *"Help me!"*

They did not help her and she ran on. Almost immediately, she heard the growling of a powerful engine and the whine of tires. He was turning the corner.

She raced down the driveway of one of the large homes and threw herself down behind the garbage cans beside its garage. Hiding there, barely breathing, she heard a car stop. It was him, it had to be.

She dared not look, dared not move, found herself hardly able to breathe. She had never been this scared, never remotely. She could almost literally feel the sensation of the gun pointing at her.

She heard footsteps on the driveway, soft, quick . . . and then a loud click and some muttered words. A woman was there. Her remote control hadn't worked.

She brought her car into the garage and the door began closing.

Lauren sobbed, stood up, started toward the house—and in that moment Wilkes's Phaeton came snarling up the driveway.

She turned and ran, crashing past the garbage cans and down the side of the house, across the expansive backyard where an elderly man struggled with a broken gate. "Call the police," she shouted as she darted into the alley.

Behind her, she heard Wilkes snap, "Official business," to the old man. Curse him, the bastard was in uniform, too. She would get no help.

She moved to the end of the alley, darted across the street and into the next alley. She pressed herself back into a tangle of bare bushes, hoping that he would miss her.

A moment later, she saw him come out of the other alley. The gun was now concealed. He was breathing hard, his chest heaving. He looked up and down the street, then toward this alley. He stared a long time at the big shrub. He was looking right at her, but apparently couldn't see her.

Then he took out the gun. He went down on one knee and braced it toward the shrub. She got ready to run. He snapped the barrel—and she froze. She bared her teeth, fighting the urge to break cover like a terrified pheasant. You did not need to do what he'd just done to cock a .45 automatic. Therefore, he'd done it for effect, to frighten her into moving. He was guessing.

Finally, he stuffed the gun under his jacket and began hurrying away.

A moment later, she heard his car start. She moved deeper into the alley and crouched down behind the edge of a shed. She could not be seen from the street at all. She called Ted on her cell.

"Hey, bad girl."

"Teddy, love, listen to me and listen close. Never go back to my apartment. Never, at all, for anything."

"What the hell are you saying?"

"Okay, Ted, I know how this sounds. But you'll be in terrible danger if you go back there. Don't even come in the neighborhood."

"Lauren?"

"I'm not ditching you, I'm warning you. There's terrible

danger, Ted. It has to do with my work, and I am extremely serious. If you go back there, you will be tortured and you will be killed. You just forget it, you forget me, you go on with your life."

She broke down, then, so badly that she held the cell phone away from her ear and gritted her teeth to keep from sobbing.

"Lauren, what's going on?"

She forced back the tears. "Where are you now? No—don't tell me! I shouldn't have asked, not on this phone. Look, you can help us both. Go to the Air Police. Tell them that Colonel Wilkes threatened us with a gun. Both of us!"

"He didn't."

"He did, he threatened me, he shot at me."

"Jesus!"

But the Air Police weren't going to be able to help. They couldn't reach into a black program like hers. He would end up confronting all kinds of questions he couldn't answer, and probably confronting Wilkes into the bargain. "No, I'm not thinking straight. Don't go near the Air Police. Move back on base and just go about your business. You'll be left alone."

"Lauren, I love you."

"Oh, Ted, no you don't. You were going to, but it hasn't happened yet because I ditch guys before it does happen, and stuff like this is the damn reason. You obey me on this. You trust me and you obey me."

Silence.

"Ted, promise!"

"You can't tell me a thing, can you?"

"Not one thing." She closed her cell phone, leaned against the wall of the shed for a moment, then continued on.

She went down the alley to the next street and crossed it quickly. She continued this process, going down one alley and then the next, until she arrived on North Meridian at the edge of University Park. She went into a Starbucks and moved about looking at the coffee machines and CDs, staying well away from the front of the store.

She thought that Colonel Wilkes might well have license to kill her as a security risk. In fact, he would never have pulled his gun if he hadn't known for certain that he would get away with it.

She remembered, suddenly, a story Andy had told her. At the time, it had seemed like so much scuttlebutt, the kind of thing that went down over beers. Now she knew that the tale of the code experts who were lobotomized on retirement, as lurid as it was, had been a veiled warning.

Andy was gone because he'd understood the situation they were in the instant he found out what had happened. He was running, probably even had an escape plan all worked out for himself.

She had no such plan, and zero confidence that she could survive very long at all in this situation. She had no operational training at all. Beyond the basic attack-and-defense maneuvers and gun skills she'd learned at Lackland, she was not capable.

If she had Adam, though, things would be different. If she brought Adam back, instead of being a liability, she'd become an asset again.

If Adam wasn't dead, and Wilkes had been certain that he wasn't, then where was he? Given how fast he could move and his ability to make himself so hard to see, he must have escaped without her seeing him go. Left her behind to die.

No, not Adam. He was always ten moves ahead. He'd have known that she would escape on her own. Or maybe he hadn't wanted her to, or hadn't cared.

Nobody had ever told her much of anything about the way the grays functioned, whether they had bases or satellites or even exactly what they were, for that matter. So how would she go about finding somebody that weird, who had all these special powers and abilities?

She could try remote viewing for him, but that only worked if you were completely calm, and anyway, she wasn't much good at it. All she was good at was making pictures for Adam and seeing the ones he sent her.

She couldn't reach him that way, either, because that only worked from a few feet away. Oh, she could sense things about Adam from a distance—sort of intuit them, but there was no mind connection over distance that she'd ever experienced.

So where did that leave her? She couldn't very well go looking behind houses and in trash cans. There was no point at all trying to find Adam. Adam was lost to her.

She was at a loss, getting so frantic that tears were forming in her eyes. This feeling of being trapped was just hideous and it was panicking her and making it hard for her to think clearly.

She decided that there was only one real option open to her. She had to go in. She had to go straight to Wright-Pat and actually file a complaint against Wilkes. She was within her rights, the man had shot at her. If she was a liability, fine. The more public she became, the safer she'd be from the shot in the night.

When she saw a bus pull past and stop at the corner, she hurried out of the store and got on it. It would go downtown, she was fairly sure. "I need to get to the Greyhound station," she told the driver.

"First stop on Illinois, walk two blocks, you'll see the sign."

"Thank you." She took one of the seats in the very last row, because there were no windows beside it. She sat wondering what she might do, where she might go. She thought carefully.

She knew that there were other aspects to the operation. Somebody watched for violations of the agreement with the grays about who they could involve themselves with. But who? She had no idea and no way of finding out.

Again, though, she might find out more at Wright-Pat. Officially, she was stationed there, on detail to the facility. Given that the facility was now inoperable, she couldn't be said to be violating any orders if she returned to base. In fact, that was likely her legal requirement.

She saw that they were passing her condo. She looked up toward her windows, thinking that all her stuff was there and maybe she would never see it again, or her cute little car that was still parked at the facility or any of her old life, not Ted or any of her friends.

As she looked away, she felt a sudden shudder go through her body. And she was *in* the apartment. Vivid. Real. Her bed still unmade, yesterday's skirt on the floor of the bedroom, a flat beer open on the kitchen counter. All of it, just as it was.

Then she was back in the bus.

She knew it immediately: Adam was there, Adam was in her apartment! She jumped up. "Let me off! Let me off the bus!" She hurried forward. "Driver, you have to stop!"

"Express to downtown," he said.

Idiot! She thought fast. They were a quarter of a mile away, the place was likely to be watched, she should not risk this. But it was her best shot, she was sure of it. "If you don't stop this bus, I'll throw up on your head!" She leaned over him and started gagging.

The bus was stopped and the door was open and she was running back up the street toward the condo. She was insane to be risking this, of course, but Adam was there, he must be, he had to be. That was Adam's mind broadcasting to hers, it was totally and completely unmistakable.

As she ran, she looked for Mike's Phaeton but didn't spot it. Maybe she'd outrun him.

No, don't be a fool, assume only the worst. You didn't need operational training to understand that.

She went into the cleaners next door. "Hi, Mr. Simmons," she said.

"Hey, Lauren—"

She ducked behind the counter and headed to the back of the establishment.

"Lauren?"

"Hey, Mrs. Fink," she said to the seamstress as she passed her sewing station and went out the back door.

She ran up the alley and then took the stairs down to the trash room, and opened the steel outer door with her passkey, which fit all the building's outside locks. Going through into the basement, she hurried past Jake Silver, their handyman.

"Miss Glass!"

"Hey there, Jake, taking the back way today." She went to the elevators and pressed the button.

"You ain't supposed to come through there. That's not a door, Miss Glass."

The elevator opened and she got in without responding to him. She started to punch seven, thought better of it, and took the car to the top floor, nine. The corridor was silent, the air smelling faintly of cooking. She went down to the fire stairs and took them two flights.

Her own corridor was just as quiet. She formed a thought—Adam's face, with a feeling of question attached to it.

Instantly, there came back another thought—an image of her own face. It wasn't Adam's usual signature, but it was certainly an image from him, she could tell by how it felt when it appeared, bursting out into her mind like a television picture.

She opened the door and went into her flat. She stood in the doorway with the door still open behind her. From many, many questions she had put to Adam, she knew that whoever she really worked for was attempting to understand and use the process of communication by mind. They had even had her test the range, which was about a quarter of a mile, and could pass through anything except a certain type of electrical field, which was used at times to isolate Adam in the cage.

She looked toward her bedroom. Everything was as she had seen it in the bus, every detail. In the back of her mind, she had been worrying that this was some kind of trick on Mike's part to draw her here, so now she closed the door and double-locked it—as if that would keep him out for more than a few seconds—and moved deeper into the apartment.

She'd never been with Adam outside of the cage and on one level she was fascinated to find out what this would be like. Hunching her shoulders to express an atmosphere of question, she moved into the center of the living room. With a faint click that made her gasp, the heat turned on. "Hello," she said. "Adam?" Simultaneously, she projected an image of his face—well, not really his face, because she'd hardly ever actually seen it except in glimpses, but a sort of generic face, long and thin, with big, black eyes.

There was a sound behind her. She turned, but there was nothing there. "Please don't hide," she said. "I need you, now."

Another noise came, behind her again. She turned, and for a moment could not understand what she was seeing. There were two small creatures, each about four feet tall, standing near the broad picture window that crossed the front wall of the big living room. She was appalled at how insectlike they looked, shocked by the gleaming eyes, the expressionless faces, the gracile forms. Insectoid children.

As she stepped forward they turned into two great vultures, black, their red and terrible eyes glaring, their huge beaks open, their wings spread in warning.

A scream pealed out of her, totally involuntary, and she jumped away—only to feel something leap on her back. It held her arms down with an iron grip, its legs pressed against her hips. She could hear it breathing, an absolutely regular sound, like some sort of machine.

Frantically, she projected an image of herself on her knees, then went down as best she could. She made an image of herself as a little girl.

The two vultures postured, screaming, their wings spread wide.

She projected an image of a beautiful garden, then of her and Adam sitting together, then of Adam with his head in her lap—imaginary, of course, she'd never seen him so close.

One of the grays before her became itself again. The other turned into an enormous hooded cobra, coiled against the wall, its head raised a good four feet off the floor, the hood extended, its tongue licking the air.

Then the one that had grabbed her disappeared.

As she had at first with Adam, she sat down, closed her eyes, and cleared her mind. She brought a long-ago trip to the seaside to mind, the blue waves, the smell of suntan oil, the seagulls crying. "It's okay," she said, "I know you're scared. I'm scared, too. But Adam is my friend. I love Adam." She opened her hands on her knees. "I want to help you."

The cobra swayed. The other gray stared at her. The one behind her slid its long hands around her neck.

She made an image of Adam again, then of the ruined facility, then of Wilkes shooting at her, then of her running through along an alley. She fired these off fast, one after another.

The cobra struck at her—and was suddenly a gray again, hanging in midair before her. She fought to quell her terror. The gray disappeared, but not completely. The three of them were racing around her, moving so fast through the air that they were blurs.

She got an image of Adam running, then rising into the sky in a shaft of shimmering light.

In return, she made an image of Adam in the light, then of herself in a coffin. She imagined Mike Wilkes closing the coffin with a bang.

Then she said, "Take me with you," and imagined herself in a shaft of light, going up.

The blurring movement stopped. The condo suddenly seemed empty. Then she saw, in her mind's eye, Mike's Phaeton pulling up down front. He was here.

He was coming—but they were helping her! She blanked her mind as completely as she could.

Immediately, she saw a satellite photo of a small community, a big light in a field behind it. Then an image of a little boy, not the one Adam had shown her, but another child, and Adam was standing behind him. Then Adam stepped forward and went *into* the child. For a moment, they were superimposed on one another, then the child threw his head back and got this look on his face of ecstasy . . . or was he screaming? When he was quiet again, his eyes were like two headlights, with fire glowing out of them.

The vision was replaced by another one of Mike, this time in the lobby waiting for the elevator.

She made an image of him blowing her brains out, which caused something to happen, a feeling of movement, in fact, of rushing.

When she opened her eyes, the world was a blur. Then she saw the city wheeling below her, then the sky, its hard

winter-blue glowing, then she heard a great, crashing noise
and a building rushed up toward her.

She stopped, there were water noises—and a man was
sitting in front of her. He stared up at her, his eyes bulging.
"WHAT IN HELL?"

She wasn't in her apartment, she was in a men's room, in
a closed stall, face to face with a guy sitting on a toilet. She
stared down at him. He covered his midriff with his hands.

"Get out of here," he rasped. *"Get out!"*

"Sorry, uh, sorry, I took a wrong turn."

She opened the stall and left the men's room as fast as
she could. Behind him, she heard him yell, *"What the
fuck? The fuck! Hey!"*

She was in the Greyhound station. *Thank you,* she said
in her mind, *thank you from the bottom of my heart.*

She hurried to the ticket window, bought a ticket for
$25.50 cash and immediately got on the waiting bus, which
was due to leave in four minutes. The windows were tinted,
which was good. There were already a number of other passengers, so she felt at least somewhat safe—as long as the
guy in the men's room wasn't going to Dayton, that is.

They had rescued her, those weird, fierce little beings,
the only grays she'd ever even glimpsed except Adam. They
had been waiting for her there in order to save her.

It was just awesome. Beings from another world were
involved with her and they wanted her safe, and now she
really began to feel better, because they were not about to
be thwarted by Mike Wilkes.

They had taken her in one of their vehicles, they must
have. It had seemed—well, like flying, and it had been so
damn wonderful because it had saved her life, and she began to laugh and cry at the same time.

When she opened her eyes an old man was right in her
face. "How'd you do that?" he asked.

"Excuse me?"

"You got in my damn toilet."

She thought quickly. There were other passengers
around. "Sir, please."

"No, she come in my toilet. Outta nowhere! She come in
my toilet."

"I don't know what's going on," she said.

The driver came back. "Sir, you'll need to take a seat or get off the bus."

"I was sittin' there mindin' my own business and all of a sudden, *wham*! How'd you do that?"

The grays obviously did not know the difference between ladies' and men's rooms. They'd dropped her in a place from which she could emerge without suspicion. Except, it had been the wrong one.

The driver got the old guy seated toward the front, and warned him against returning to the back of the bus. He'd just have to live with what he'd seen.

As the bus started off, Lauren leaned back and closed her eyes, her whole body filling with a delicious relief. "You helped me," she whispered, "thank you for helping me."

An old lady smiled at her. "He helps me, too," she said. "Jesus helps us all, isn't it wonderful?"

"Wonderful," she said, "really, really wonderful."

She had a couple hundred dollars in her wallet, so she would not leave a paper trail. As far as her apartment and possessions were concerned, until this situation was brought under control, she was not going near them again.

If Mike had the backing of the Air Force, then she couldn't escape anyway, could she, no matter what she did? So this was the best course of action. She would surface at Wright-Pat and hope his powers were limited.

The bus was running a bit early, so she found herself presenting her regular Air Force ID at one of the guard stations of the gigantic base before eight in the evening. She was directed to the Wright-Patterson Inn, where she obtained a room. Rather than waste time and take risk, she at once called the Law Enforcement Unit and reported Colonel Michael Wilkes's assault with intent to kill on her person. She stated her location and that she was slightly injured due to a blow to the face.

She then went to the unit and filled out a complaint against Wilkes, getting more and more furious at him as she did so. The man had shot at a fellow officer. If she could manage it, she would see him in that secret Air Force detention facility he was always talking so much about, where they kept all the crooks with high-level clearances. Sonofabitch.

One thing at least: she would no longer be working for him, because his operation was over. No more Adam, no more detail. Great, as far as she was concerned. She'd had it with the whole mess. Let her get back into procurement, anything but this.

But they'd told her, three years ago, that there was no exit.

An Air Police captain came over to her. He was carrying her complaint form. "You're Colonel Lauren Glass?"

"Yes."

"Lady, Colonel Glass is a KIA."

"A KIA?"

"She died yesterday in a facility fire in another city, and I want to know what this is supposed to be about."

Her heart missed a beat. KIA? If he got that to stick, she was outside the context of the whole military infrastructure. No chance of getting him up on charges, no ability to use Air Force facilities or appeal for protection.

"Ma'am, I'm gonna need to ID you."

Did she have her credentials? Yes! She fumbled her wallet out of her purse, handed the card to him. "Excuse me," he said, taking it.

She made images of herself with a gun to her head, of herself lying in a coffin, but the grays did not respond. It was the range issue, again. Did they even know where she was?

She heard a car stop outside the guard station. She went to the front and looked out the window. An awful coldness crept into her gut as Colonel Robert Langford's tall form got out and headed her way.

Him! She had to run. She whirled. The desk officer was watching her, his eyes narrow. Behind him was another door. She strode across the room, passing the sergeant's counter.

"That's off-limits, Colonel," he said.

She broke into a run and got out the door. Where to go now? Ted's apartment was on base, but it was a good mile away. She took off down a sidewalk, heading toward a big hangar. At least there would be people around. At least when they got her, there would be someone to remember.

Then she saw a general's jet sitting on the tarmac, its engines turning over. The stairs were down, and two officers were talking at their base. The plane was either landing or taking off.

She took a chance and went over to it. "This isn't General Martin's plane, is it?" she asked.

"General Cerner."

"Finally!" As she went aboard, they barely glanced at her, then returned to their conversation.

There were three officers in the plane, a full-bird colonel, a major, and the general. "Sir," she said saluting, "Colonel Glass. I need an urgent hitch to D.C. It's classified, sir, national security."

He looked up from his seat. "I'm reading a lotta levels of bullshit in what you just said, lady."

"Sir, it's extremely urgent."

"Who's your commanding officer?"

"Sir, I'm not at liberty to tell you that, but I can commandeer this aircraft."

"Don't give me that kind of guff. I've been in this Air Force a while, girlie. But what the hell, fellas, who wouldn't want to take boobs like these to thirty-thousand feet?"

She swallowed her outrage, managed to construct a seductive smile.

Then she noticed something. He wasn't looking at her. In fact, his eyes were practically glazed over with fear.

She turned—and there stood Colonel Langford with a pistol in his hand. "We'll take care of this," he said.

"Be my guest," the general replied.

"What in hell is going on?" the major asked.

"A prisoner is being taken into custody," Langford snarled. "Come on, Miss Jacobs." He glanced past her. "She's not even Air Force. She's pulled this hitch trick for the last time."

"My name is Lauren Glass," she said as he marched her out of the cabin. "I am a colonel and I've been listed as a KIA. I am alive, General, remember that when you read her obit, Colonel Lauren Glass is alive!"

"Don't even think about running," Langford said when

they reached the tarmac. "I'll have the Air Police on your tail in a matter of seconds."

She walked ahead of him.

"You're a problem," he said, "a very serious problem."

She felt the gun in her back. So the stories were true. Black ops had their own special way of solving problems, and Lauren Glass, as the colonel had just said, was a problem. She thought, with a curious sort of detachment, that she had reached her last hours of life. It was a sickening, trapped moment, and yet oddly peaceful.

She had avoided marriage, and now she regretted that. She'd never felt a child in her belly, nor the pain of giving birth. She regretted that, too. It was so very odd, this feeling. Not awful at all. The end of all responsibility, the end of the need to run.

Too bad the grays couldn't help her now. She tried sending images of her with Langford's gun in her face, but nothing came back. Too far away.

She wondered if he would kill her here at Wright-Pat, or take her somewhere else. Maybe it was even an official killing. Probably it was. So there'd be some stark room somewhere, and a steel coffin waiting. "I'm ready," she said. If he was planning to move her, maybe there would be a chance to escape. She might feel oddly peaceful, but if she could get away, she sure as hell would.

"It's going to be easy, then?"

"What choice do I have? You've got me."

"Yes," he said, "I do."

SIXTEEN

THE MOMENT HE HAD REALIZED that he'd lost not only Adam, but also the two handlers, Mike had raced back to Washington. There was only one way to fire somebody in an organization this secret. Nobody was retired. You were either actively involved in the Trust or you were dead . . . and Mike understood and agreed completely. You could not risk even a rumor getting out that mankind was on a death watch, or that there was an organization that planned to save only a precious few, or that any part of the U.S. government was involved with aliens, not when there were such dire threats associated with revealing the secret of their presence.

Mike explained to Charles Gunn how Andy and Lauren had gotten away.

"That was damn stupid."

"I don't think—"

"Andy moved fast, you couldn't help that. But we'll pull him in. The empath is another matter, Mike. You were stupid to shoot, but an asshole to miss."

"Charles—"

"Shut up, I'm thinking."

"Charles, the gray is at large."

His eyes fixed on Mike's face. His lips opened, then he closed them. He suddenly grabbed a pen and a pad of paper and started writing.

"Charles?"

The writing became scratching, then trenching, then he rose up like a tower and ripped the pad to bits. He rushed around the desk and loomed over Mike. "Goddamn you."

"Charles—"

"Goddamn you!" He paced, then. "I have to think."

"Do me, Charlie. Get it over with."

"Boy, that would be a pleasant way to spend an hour or so, you stupid piece of shit. I've defended you, but you are fucking incompetent. You and that fancy house of yours, your theft that I've ignored all these years. Not to mention those special passes to the shelters that you've given your crook friends."

That would wreck him, to withdraw those bribes that were also such superb blackmail. His every defense industry contact would turn against him. He'd be a ruined man. "Charles, those people—some of them are essential—"

"The hell they are. They're gone. History. And so are you, Mike. There's no way you're getting anywhere near one of the shelters. When this planet's environment collapses, you're gonna be in the wind. You live with that, now. You live with that."

By which Charles actually meant that he had just allowed Mike to live. He had expected to die in this room, right now.

Charles asked, "Do you think Glass could be hiding Adam?"

"I went to her apartment first thing. No sign of anyone there. I think Adam's been recalled. The moment they realized that we were aware of the child, they pulled the plug."

"Because you asked the wrong question." Charles dropped down behind his desk. "They've got us in check, here."

"They always have us in check."

"We have to locate this child."

"It's in Wilton."

"You know that?"

"Crew said they were signaling him. So he could play his role."

"We've got to scorch the earth, then. Langford, Glass,

Simpson, Crew—they've all got to be done. But first, find and kill that child."

"We have this Oak Road group with a grand total of six residents under the age of eighteen, so that's our target. But we can't approach them directly or we get the grays on us like a bunch of infuriated hornets. The key is to identify the right child without getting so close to him that the grays become aware of us."

"We have the children's test scores? IQ tests?"

"Unfortunately, the school they all attend doesn't do IQ tests. Too elitist or too P.C. or some damn thing. They're all bright kids. Professors' children."

"What about the public schools in the area?"

"Their gifted and talented programs have a hundred and sixty kids in them. Highest IQ is 160. We don't know how smart the grays want their poster boy, so they're a possibility that needs checking."

"Let me ask you this, then. Do you have a plan?"

"I think the child will reveal himself to us."

"How?"

"He's got to be spectacularly bright. A freak, like."

"What if he's ordinary? We have only that tape to tell us he's going to be some kind of a genius. Maybe Crew and Simpson knew you were listening. Maybe the tape is a lie."

"Then we're already defeated, Charles."

"Do you think that?"

"I think they're going to be mighty careful and mighty ferocious. Look what's riding on him—their whole species. And ours."

Charles shrugged. "Don't tell me you're disloyal, too."

"I've been to India, I've been to Vietnam, I've see the brainless, gobbling hordes of human filth out there. No, I believe in what we're doing with every cell in my body, Charles. This little band we call the Trust, is the most noble, the most courageous, and the most important organization in human history."

Charles gave him a twinkle of a smile. "You know what Stalin did when his little commissars were too eloquent in their praise? He had them shot."

"Then do it, Charles! Get it over with!"

"I can't, Goddamn your soul. You know that I've been defending you from Henry Vorona for years. Ever since CIA saddled me with him, in fact. If I tell the others just how royally you've fucked things up, I'm gonna end up sitting on a vote of no confidence, and guess who's gonna join you in hell? No, Mike, I'd like to see you good and dead, I have to admit that, but I damn well can't, because the bullet that goes through your head goes through mine, too."

"Charles, I'm going to fix this."

"You'd better, because you are talking about the entire human species being enslaved, Mike. Because that is what this is about. Somewhere out there, they're coming. And they will do this. They will do this, Mike. Just remember one thing, we have to get that child before they change him, because if we don't, God only knows what kind of abilities and powers he's going to have."

"I need people. I need backup."

"You can't have a damn soul!"

"Charles—"

"I can give you equipment and I can give you money, but *not people*. The second I do that, Vorona finds out and both of our throats get cut."

Mike had assumed that he'd have a trained team of experts. But he could see Charles's point all too clearly. Unless he fixed this, and did it quietly, they were both dead men.

"What's your plan, Mike? I want to know your exact plan."

"Forget Adam, forget Glass, Langford, all of them. Go for the kid now, fast, next twenty-four hours. Then worry about everything else. Use the TR to get me into Wilton with absolutely no chance of detection."

"The grays will know you're there."

"Not right away. Remember, I've seen this mind-reading business up close for years. Distance is a big issue. They're not going to find me until I'm physically near the kid. But that's the one place I'll never be."

"You're a sniper or what?"

"There will be no direct approach to him whatsoever.

But he will be killed, Charles. Coming from me, I know it's not worth much to you, but I do guarantee it."

To his credit, Charles made no comment, but the expression on his face eloquently communicated his contempt for what he undoubtedly regarded as outrageous braggadocio on the part of a proven incompetent. "You know how to access the TR?"

"Yes, sir. You'll recall that I set up the security."

Charles turned around in his chair. The Capitol glowed in the distance, the Washington Monument beyond. "What do you think this'll be like in a thousand years, Mike?"

"In a thousand years? If we succeed, it'll be the holy city, the center of heaven."

Charles said nothing more, and Mike took that as a signal to leave, for which he was very damned grateful.

He had a good plan, and if he acted quickly enough, he thought there was a reasonable chance that it would work. The important thing was to push all consequences out of his mind. His life being at stake was bad enough, but looking at the larger picture was enough to freeze a man's soul.

As he drove to National Airport, he called his personal travel agency and booked the next civilian flight he could, which was Delta to Atlanta. He parked in long-term parking, then went to the ticket counter and got his ticket. He bought a newspaper and went to the gate to wait until the agent arrived. He did nothing out of the ordinary.

When the agent appeared, he checked in and selected his seat.

Having set up this false trail, he then left the airport and hailed a cab, which he took to a small office building a short distance from his house. He descended into the garage, took out some keys, and started another car. This one was a Buick from the mid-eighties, nondescript compared to the Mercedes he kept here in Washington.

He drove to the Beltway, then took 95 up to Baltimore, exiting onto 695 toward Owings Mills. An hour and a half after he left the garage, he was exiting onto Painters' Mills Road. As he drove up Caves Road, he entered a more isolated area. He turned off onto an unmarked road and soon came to what appeared to be a construction zone. From here, the road appeared to be impassable. He took a right, and it turned out that what looked like brush was something quite different. The car moved through the brush and trees as if they weren't there—which, indeed, they weren't. This was a state-of-the-art holographic projection, one of the most advanced camouflage devices in the Pentagon's arsenal. The design had come from Adam. It was deployed sparingly, out of fear that the press would get wind of it. If the origin of any of these technologies was discovered, the whole deception would become unglued.

The result of this was that certain select areas of military technology were stunningly ahead of public understanding. To accomplish his purpose, he would use an array of that technology.

Central to his plan was a device that lay in a large underground hangar in these woods. Its development had taken forty years. It had cost perhaps a quarter of a trillion dollars, paid for by misuse of the gigantic criminal enterprise known officially as the "black budget" which was really a cover for making select people rich at the expense of the American taxpayer, by using national security to conceal the theft.

The TR, or Triangular Aircraft, officially designated TR-A1, had also cost the lives of scientists who had come to a fatal eureka moment. When they realized that they were working on alien technology, they became too dangerous to be allowed to live. Test pilots had died, too, perfecting its capabilities, as had engineers who had suffered mercury poisoning in the fabrication of its extraordinarily toxic power plant.

The reason for the extreme secrecy was twofold. Not only did they have to protect this device from the public, they had to protect it from the grays. They had gotten every kind of lie from Adam and Bob, most of them infinitely subtle, and as a result had gone down a thousand blind alleys and consumed literally vast wealth, indeed, so much wealth that every American citizen, for the past fifty years, had worked a fourth of his life in support of the development of technologies he wasn't even allowed to know existed, let alone gain any benefit from.

He came to a certain spot in the narrow roadway where the radio, which he had tuned to an unused frequency, suddenly began to make a faint, high-pitched sound. He stopped the car, got out, pulled back a stone that lay at the roadside, and pressed his hand against a silver disk that had been concealed beneath it. A moment later, the small hill before him opened. He drove the car in.

Inside, it was absolutely dark and silent. The only light came from a single red bulb, glowing softly. As Mike strode toward it, the outlines of an enormous object became visible immediately above his head. It was a triangle, totally black, measuring hundreds of feet on a side.

Its power plant involved the rotation of a ring of a coherent mercury plasma at extremely high speed, reducing the overall weight of the craft by 40 percent. The rest of the weight reduction was accomplished with a very old technology. The triangle had to be as large as it was because, for the rest of its lift, it relied on helium. It contained the most sophisticated surveillance and camouflage technology known, but it was not much faster than an old-fashioned dirigible.

Years ago, it had become obvious from Eamon Glass's talks with Adam and the stories told by Mr. Crew, that mankind had lost a very sophisticated civilization to a ferocious war that was fought some time around fifteen thousand years ago. The combination of the use of devastating weaponry and the rise in sea levels that had taken place when the last ice age ended twelve thousand years ago, had first pulverized and then drowned this civilization.

It lived on only in myth, most notably in the Vedas of ancient India. But there was almost enough information there, in the descriptions of Vimina aircraft, to reproduce the power plants of the distant past. Careful questioning of Adam and Bob had filled in the missing pieces of information.

Large though they were, the TRs, of which there were ten on the books and two off, were no more difficult to fly than a small general aviation aircraft.

As Mike continued toward the faint red light, his head was just a few inches from the lower surface of the craft. The light marked the entrance, a simple hatch that was slid open by hand.

He withdrew the ladder, which gave a bit under his weight as he climbed aboard. He took the long tunnel to the flight deck, pulling himself along on a stretcher as the crew had in the old B-36 bomber.

This flight deck, though, was very different from what a bomber pilot from the fifties might have seen. It wasn't even meant to be flown by a pilot, but rather flown *in* by a reconnaissance expert. The plane all but piloted itself.

Mike used a penlight to find the code panel, and input the thirty-three-digit code that activated the craft. A moment later, its amber control panel came to life. The basic aircraft instruments were there, of course, airspeed, bank and turn, altitude. There were others though, that were not so familiar. Most of these involved the craft's extraordinary surveillance capabilities.

Mike keyed Wilton, Kentucky, into the autopilot. He pressed the three buttons that activated the plasma. Behind him, there was a distinct "pop," the loudest sound the device would ever make. The altimeter began to wind up—but not far. It was a very unusual sort of altimeter, because it could measure anything from thousands of feet to inches. The plane's operational altitude was, essentially, ground level. Unlike a cruise missile, it did not rely on comparing a picture of the terrain it was crossing to its memory. Instead, it had the intelligence and the instruments it needed to examine the terrain it was crossing, and adjust its altitude accordingly.

He watched the altimeter rise to 60 meters, then felt a slight shudder as the ship's propulsion system, which used the Earth's magnetic field, slowly began to impel it forward. It took ten minutes for him to reach top speed.

The craft sought out forests and mountains, only rarely slipping across a town, and never a city. From ten feet away, it made no sound at all.

The flight from Owings Mills to Wilton covered 433 kilometers and took just over two hours. As Mike flew, he prepared instrument after instrument, most of them gained from his own hard work managing the empaths, extracting bits and pieces of information from his grays.

Sound, in the craft, was as carefully managed as all other emissions. Even switches had been carefully damped so that pressing a button made nary a click. The fans that controlled the craft's altitude were entirely silent, designed so that the air they emitted was always exactly the same temperature as the air they took in. Just as it had no sound signature, and at night essentially no visual signature, it also had no heat signature and no radar signature. Even the pilot's body heat was dissipated by being used in production of electricity.

The TR could fail; if the mercury plasma malfunctioned, the craft would be incinerated inside of a second. During development it had happened many times. There was never anything left, only ash drifting in the sky. In 1980 in Texas, some civilians had been close-up witnesses to one of these failures. One of them got cancer and filed a suit against the U.S. government, but the judge was prevailed upon and the case went nowhere. The civilian died soon thereafter, thankfully.

He flew on. When he was within thirty miles of Wilton, he flipped another switch, and something happened that would have awed anyone who had not expected it.

This was a technology that they had developed by analyzing the stories of a close-encounter witness called Travis Walton, whom they had also discredited in every possible way, making a national joke out of him so that the public would never be convinced by his tale.

Why the grays had taken him on a ride was not clear. But they had, and on that ride, they had made their ship disappear around him, so that he appeared to be floating in the stars. Such a capability would be extremely useful for a reconnaissance craft, and Eamon had gradually obtained from Bob knowledge of how to design materials that would change their opacity by the simple application of heat. He pressed a button and was rewarded with the apparent complete disappearance of everything around him except the control panel itself. He floated now over the broad hills of eastern Kentucky, a man alone in the night sky.

The ship was on a course that would take it directly over Oak Road. He had only to watch the world slipping by fifty feet beneath his feet. He saw horses running in the moonlight, he passed over an elegant farmhouse and barns, so close that he felt as if he could have reached down and touched a weathervane. He smelled nothing of the night air and felt nothing of the cold, because the temperature within the ship was carefully controlled. There was a heat signature, of course, but it was no greater than that of the breath of a swooping owl.

The ship's voice said in his earphone, "Two minutes."

He turned on the camouflage. This drained electrical power, but also provided an additional level of protection from notice from above and below. It consisted of thousands of tiny light-emitting diodes served by cameras on the upper and lower surfaces of the ship. From below, an observer would see the night sky under which the ship was passing. From above, the image that was projected was of the ground.

"One minute."

He saw light ahead, winking in among the trees. Soon a small neighborhood of tract houses appeared. He stopped the ship. Now he activated the infrared sensors, trained them on the first house in the tiny development. Two adults, one registering 98.6, the other 97.9. An infant, registering 99.1.

The ship was so low that it was buffeted by gas fumes coming out of the furnace chimney. He "opened" the house by activating the whole array of surveillance instruments.

An ultrasensitive receiver read the electroencephalograms of the occupants, and provided a readout of their state, whether awake or asleep, and a level-of-awareness index. One adult was fully awake. One adult was registering mostly Alpha. Dozing, according to the computer's interpretation. The infant was profoundly asleep.

It seemed to him that he was not likely to be dealing with an infant, because this child would surely need to be at least fairly mature by 2012.

He went to the next house. In it, he saw two adults. Deeper in the structure was another person, perhaps a small adult, perhaps an older child. The two adults were physically motionless but their minds were alert. He deployed the microphone system. He heard a familiar voice, and for a moment was shocked. How could he know somebody in that house? Who would it be?

Then he realized that it was Grissom. They were watching *CSI*.

In the basement, there was another sound, a continuous noise identified as a small electric motor. Could it be a shaver? No, it was moving over too broad an area. He visualized the movement and immediately had his answer. The person in the basement was using a model train set. Therefore, it was not a small adult, but a child.

He moved to the other two houses, then, gathering the structural plans into the computer, identifying approximate ages and sexes of the occupants.

When he was finished, he had all the humans and all the animals. He then found the open space behind the houses that the grays had used on their revealing foray. He dropped down into it. He wanted to step on the actual ground, but he must not leave the ship unless necessary. It had been designed to allow the occupant to reconnoiter on the ground, and was intelligent enough to protect itself, even for extended periods, but still, no chances were to be taken unless they were essential.

He increased altitude to a thousand feet, then went online again. Using Expedia, he found motels in Wilton. He input the address of the local Days Inn and was carried there.

He then observed the local terrain for heights. It turned out that the top of a grain elevator was the highest point in the area. He flew until he found it, an enormous structure in the center of the small community.

He went close. There, on one of the silos, was where he would place his antenna. Nearby, he saw a field. He dropped down.

Putting the ship's remote into his pocket, he slid back along the access tunnel and climbed out. The ship would find a hiding place on its own. It would not go to altitude, but rather would hide just above the surface somewhere, probably back in the hills that surrounded the town. When he looked up, even though he knew that it was there, and not but a few feet overhead, he could not see it.

As it departed, he felt the brief wash of one of its altitude control fans.

He crossed the field, then walked into the lobby of the Days Inn.

"Hey," he said to the sleepy clerk, "got a room?"

"Yes, sir," the young man said, coming out of the tiny office where he had been watching TV. Mike had a dozen false identities to choose from. He checked in under the name of Harold A. Hill, salesman. It was one of his favorites, because nobody ever wants to talk to a salesman.

He went through the lobby and crossed a bleak courtyard to his room. He entered it, turned on the light, and used the bathroom. Naked now, he slipped into the bed.

Tomorrow morning, he would scout the town for a Radio Shack. To complete his mission, he needed a few commonly available items. He lay down and closed his eyes. He was deeply tired. Deeply, deeply tired. Curse Lauren and Andy, who were both out there in the wind doing God knew what. The grays were on the warpath and extremely dangerous.

He wished he *was* a damn fool salesman.

PART SIX

CHILD OF HALLOWS

Our birth is but a sleep and a forgetting:
The Soul that rises with us, our life's Star,
Hath had elsewhere its setting,
And cometh from afar:
Not in entire forgetfulness,
And not in utter nakedness,
But trailing clouds of glory do we come . . .

— WILLIAM WORDSWORTH
   "Ode on Intimations of Immortality
   Recollected from Early Childhood"

SEVENTEEN

CONNER HAD WAITED ON THE steps for Paulie to leave school. Usually, they would be carpooled home by Mom or Maggie, but that had obviously ended.

The thing was that Paulie, leader of the Connerbusters though he was, also remained the only real friend he'd ever had. He had to reach him somehow, and he thought that the way to do it was still through the idea of the aliens, despite what had happened. If they were real, then maybe he could contact them somehow and get them to come back, with Paulie as a witness.

It was an audacious, insane idea, but there were more than a few Web sites out there put up by folks who were doing just that, and posting video of the UFOs that had turned up. He'd communicated with one or two of them and gotten detailed instructions about how to do it using, as one of them had put it, "a flashlight, patience, and a serious interest in meeting them."

All day at school, he had kept to himself. There was nothing else he could do, not without triggering some sort of additional humiliation. As it was, everybody had gotten up from the table and moved when he sat down for lunch. He had eaten alone, ostentatiously and purposely reading a book none of them could begin to understand, *Physics from Fisher Information*, a rather basic text, actually.

He had considered going the total eccentric route, perhaps refusing to speak anything except Latin and dying his hair purple or something. But that would just justify his isolation, and he did not really want to be isolated. Faint though it might be, there remained the possibility that some girl might some day do just slightly more than run screaming when he drew near. Amy, for example. After all, they had an embarrassing past in the woods, did they not? It had, when he was ten and she was eleven, involved the revelation of body parts, back where the little stream flowed and the bluebells nodded along its banks.

He had been thinking fairly carefully this past couple of days about what actually *had* happened the other night. What did the Keltons' video really show? The answer to that question, he thought, might be far less obvious than it seemed.

It was possible that the legendary grays of Internet fame actually were involved, but only very remotely.

Although the Search for Extraterrestrial Intelligence people claimed that the chances of finding a signal from another world was vanishingly small, that was incorrect. They were actually pretty good—about 0.4 percent a year.

He thought that, if somebody actually had appeared here from another planet, they must be desperate. It would take vast resources to cross interstellar space, and huge amounts of time. Wormholes and such were science fiction. The reason was simple: it was theoretically possible to bend space until two distant points touched, but the amount of energy necessary was unimaginable. To bend the United States until, say, Phoenix and Buffalo touched, would be child's play by comparison. Faster-than-light transmission of signals was indirectly possible using quantum-entangled particles, but the movement of structured physical objects at hyper speeds was out of the question.

So, if they were here, they had come at less than light speed, probably far less, and thus even a journey from Centauri A, the closest sun-like star, would have taken many years. Internet scuttlebutt had the grays coming from Zeta Reticuli, a double star. Such a situation would make for planets with lots of seasons and some really eccentric orbits, but it wasn't completely impossible.

All of these thoughts danced in his mind even while, at

another level, he considered his father's straightforward advice to confront the kids who were tormenting him. Dad was no genius, but his advice could be relied on, and Conner intended to take it.

"Paulie," he said as he came down the steps, "hey."

"Hey, Conner."

"Would you like to come over?"

Paulie stopped. He stared at him like he was some kind of bizarre animal. He was flanked by two of his most unpleasant new friends, Kevin Sears and Will Heckle. "'Course not," he said.

"The video's real, Paulie. We all ought to respect what it means. The event happened."

"I wasn't there, Conner, I didn't see it."

Conner was pleased to hear the anger and disappointment in his voice. This was precisely what he had expected. He had taken Paulie exactly where he wanted him to go, and now he would win him back. "You know I can fix things," he said. "Maybe I can fix that."

"How? Build a time machine?"

"What if I could get them to come back?"

Will Heckle burst out laughing. A smiling Kevin shook his head.

"No, wait," Paulie said. "I want to hear this."

"I can call them," Conner said, "with you as a witness."

The boys were not laughing now.

"If I do it, then will you agree to cancel the Connerbusters?"

"Oh, sure. Sure, Conner."

"Come over after supper and spend the night. You'll meet the grays."

"What about us? Can we meet the grays, too, little boy?"

"Not yet, Kev."

Kevin grabbed his jacket, loomed over him. "Kevin to you."

Conner stared right back. "Okay, Kev, I'll make a note of that." Finally, Kevin released him. Conner turned and went down the steps, looking for Mom's car in the line out front.

On the way home, he wondered what the odds were of Paulie showing up. Actually, he thought, they were excellent. In fact, he would show. But the larger question was, how in the world would he get the grays to come to the party?

He also knew that he would get resistance from Mom, so he said nothing in the car. In fact, he waited until after dinner, until just before Paulie would appear.

"Incidentally, Paulie's gonna sleep over tonight."

She stopped clearing the kitchen table of dishes. "No, he isn't."

"Yes, he is, Mom. He's been invited and he is."

"No way, Jose."

This did not surprise him, but he pretended that it did. "Mom, come *on!*"

"Conner, no! You're groveling."

"Mom, I have arranged a sleepover. Simple as that."

"I don't want any Warners in this house, not Paulie, not Amy, not the parents. Especially not Maggie and Harley. You find other friends."

"Then let's move into town! I'm twelve miles from the nearest other kids my age."

"You're so handsome when you're mad," she said.

"God, the condescension. All right, let's come to a compromise. I invited Paulie. He didn't say yes or no. If he comes, he comes."

"Why did you invite him?"

"Because, Mother, if you diagram the social configuration of my class, you quickly discover that Paulie Warner is at the center of every major structural orbit, and, in fact, I am not going to make any headway with anybody until I have solved my relationship with him."

She almost burst into tears, to hear him applying his genius to a problem as trivial as being accepted by some little bully with a room-temperature IQ. She went to him and hugged him. He came to her with raglike looseness, neither willing nor unwilling.

"You know something that's going to happen in a couple of years, Conner? In a couple of years, Paulie, who looks like a little dump truck, is going to be running after girls and getting nowhere. They're going to be all over you. You're sweet, you're smart, and you look like a movie star."

"That's then and this is now. What about my compromise? Fair?"

He'd won, of course. She couldn't very well call the Warners and tell Paulie not to come, only to find that he hadn't been planning to anyway.

Since last night, Conner had been using the same technique of meditation the Internet contact mavins used, and intended to make the same flashlight signals toward the sky that they did, and at the same time, 3:33 in the morning. One of them had craft showing up about 70 percent of the time. The other had never had a failure in two years, and had hundreds of hours of video, including a photo of the palm of a long, thin-fingered hand with claws pressed against a window. Conner had gotten the guy to upload a high-res file of this photo to his personal FTP site where he usually collected dissertations and things, and had analyzed it carefully.

Using a very conservative extrapolation algorithm, he had been able to bring out the fingerprints. They were absolutely remarkable in one respect: they had completely symmetrical whorls. He'd thought at once, *if a machine had fingers, they'd look like this*. The design wasn't a digital trick, it was actually on the hand, and it was self-consistent, too. He'd measured it micrometer by micrometer. It was a real print, all right. Maybe the Keltons had gotten the first somewhat clear shot of a gray; this guy had definitely gotten the first fingerprint.

Mom and Dad were having all kinds of hush-hush conversations about the grays and about their friend Marcie Cotton, who, Conner had understood from their transparently cryptic comments to one another, had been the person screaming in the craft the other night. No matter how well they hid it, even from themselves, Conner could see that the incident had terrified his parents. Therefore, he certainly had no intention of telling them that he planned to attempt to vector the grays in.

"Just one thing," his mom said—and he instantly anticipated one of her little zingers. "I want you guys to sleep upstairs. We don't want you sleeping alone in the basement anymore."

"I don't care for those beds," Conner said smoothly, hoping to deflect this zinger. "Also, we're going to be doing gaming until late."

"Not downstairs you aren't."

There was a crash and Paulie came banging through the back door. "It's snowing," he yelled. "We're gonna be sledding in the morning plus Gestapo Torture Fest came from Games Unlimited!" He brushed past Katelyn and went pounding downstairs, Conner hurrying along behind him.

She went into the living room, where Dan had been watching the Kelton boys' video again and again. As she walked in, he froze the blurry image of the hydrocephalic with fly eyes on the screen.

"I don't want the boys sleeping in the basement," she said.

"God, no."

"And turn that damned thing off, it's hideous." When she sat down, he got up from the far end of the couch and moved closer to her.

Before she realized it, she'd reestablished distance between them.

He did not try again. Instead, he gestured toward the TV. "I've had them with me all my life. I've never had a seizure. It's been memory, traumatic memory of this. Which I need you to understand, Katelyn."

She wished he hadn't brought it up. She wished it didn't hurt so very much. "Understand what?"

"About Marcie! Which is connected to this."

"That again. Dan, you screwed the woman."

"We were made to do what we did." *As,* he thought, *were you and I, my precious heart and fellow breed animal.*

"Okay, I'll bite. If the devil made you do it, why? Why does he give a damn about you and Marcie—and me, for that matter? He's a busy devil, he's surely got more important things on his mind."

"I cannot even begin to answer that question. I don't understand any more than you do. All I can say is, if they wanted me to get tenure, then whatever they did more than worked."

"I should say. It got you tenure and a mistress." She heard Conner's voice rise downstairs as they reached some sort of crisis in the shrieking video game that Paulie had brought.

Angrily, she shook away a tear. She didn't want to feel like this, all tragic over her marriage. She wanted to feel angry and full of righteous self-justification. She wanted to be strong enough to march off to a lawyer, if that turned out to be what her heart wanted her to do.

Dan reached out across the distance. "Hey," he said.

She turned away.

He sighed, got up, and went into the kitchen. As she came in behind him, he drank down a glass of wine in a couple of huge gulps.

He turned, looked at her. Dear heaven, she was as beautiful as an angel. What had happened, here? He was getting really scared, he was beginning to think that he'd ruined his life by being honest with her.

He touched the thing in his ear . . . and touched, also, his memory of seeing her as a child. He looked into her eyes, saw the sorrow there.

"Oh, God, Katelyn, you've got to accept something. The aliens—"

"No! Shut up!"

"You shut up! You listen!" He touched his ear again. "You know what this is? This is an implant. I got it right here in this kitchen. Right here, right in front of everybody and God only knows how they did that."

"Dan, I can't handle this. I warn you."

He went to her. She turned away from him. "Katelyn, they brought us together when we were children, for God's sake!" He touched her shoulder. She pulled away. "I remember you, Katelyn, in a white nightgown. I remember— oh, my God, they've been with us all our lives."

She shook her head, waved her hand in front of her face.

At that moment, Conner burst in. "Can we take the DVD down?"

"Be my guest," Dan said.

"Be careful with that, the Keltons'll kill you if you mess it up."

"We will," Conner said as he raced off. Then he returned. "Plus, we need a flashlight."

"A flashlight?"

"Check the snow, see if it's stickin'!"

Dan got a flashlight out of his toolkit and gave it to him.

"Okay, listen," Conner said to Paulie when he returned to his basement lair. "I'm reasonably sure that they've been in here. In this room."

Paulie's eyes opened wide. "They have?"

"What's interesting is I have a screen memory—"

"Which is? Remind me."

"Paulie, you've gotta quit. Right now."

"Quit what?"

"I can hear the laughter in your voice. You've seen the video, you know this is real. So trying to laugh me out of court is wrong. And that Connerbusters thing, Paulie, it's incredibly corny. It's the sort of thing that happens in third grade, not middle school."

"It's just a joke, Conner. If you didn't take it so seriously, nobody else would, either. You gotta be more mature about these things. Kids are assholes. You get a few more years on you, you'll learn to roll with it."

Conner said, "You want me to crack that game?"

"Jesus, yes. Can you?"

"You know I can. But you have to promise me, Paulie. We've been friends a long time. All of our lives. You stop dumping on me."

"Is that why I'm here? To get begged? Because I'm not the one you need to beg. You need to beg every guy in the class, Conner, because they all think you're a complete schmedlock. The schmedlock of the century."

"Paulie, if you quit, they will quit, which you know very well."

"You got guts, I'll say that. You crack the game for me and the Connerbusters are on hold for a week. You vector in the grays, and I'm your puppy dog." He pulled a Nikon digital camera out of his backpack. "Six megapixels. Detailed pictures should be worth a fortune. So, when do they show up?" He looked at his watch.

"The exact time will be three-thirty-three," Conner said. He realized that he was setting himself up for something. The odds against him felt huge.

"Okay, then, let's synchronize watches."

"My watch—"

"Conner, everybody on planet Bell Attached knows that your Christmas watch automatically sets itself to the Naval Observatory time signal once every twelve hours. So let me rephrase that, let me synchronize my ordinary watch to your awesome one."

"Paulie, you want this watch?" He started to take it off.

"Conner, you just do not get it. I don't want your watch. If you're gonna get people off your back, you need to stop bragging and showing off. Everybody knows you're a genius. Half the school are geniuses. Maybe you're our major genius, I don't know, but kids don't like having their faces rubbed in the kind of shit you dish out."

"I'm not understanding you."

"Like night before last. You actually tried to communicate with the aliens you thought were out there in English *and* French. That was so lame, Conner."

"I hadn't realized that."

"Well, try K-Paxian next time. I'm sure you're fluent in that, too. Now, little boy, if you're gonna crack Gestapo, crack it and I'll suck your toes."

"Conner!" Katelyn called.

"Okay! Okay! In a while."

"It's after ten."

"So, little boy, we gonna get tucked in by mommy?"

"No, we're not at your house, little boy. Come on." Conner went across the room and out under the deck. He was outside before he asked himself why he'd done this. He'd just suddenly felt like coming out.

Paulie joined him. "Wow, is it ever *snowing*! Look at this!" He danced around, then went down on his back and made an angel. He leaped up. "It's butt cold, we need our coats."

As he ran back inside, Conner pointed the flashlight upward and flicked it on and off. As he'd learned, he varied the signal, three long, three short, two long, two short. The beam revealed a whirling maelstrom of snowflakes, dancing, racing before the wind. The air was sharp with smoke and the tang of ice. Off to the west, thunder rumbled. Con-

ner went on signaling, even though it was nowhere near
3:33, even though it felt hopeless, even though Paulie was
probably right and he'd dreamed up the whole thing.

"Lame-o, Connner! I mean, you really are trying. You
believe this."

"Shut up."

Paulie brushed Conner's head with his hand. "Ah, little
boy's getting all covered with snow, isn't he?"

Conner stopped signaling. A light glowed around them
just then. It didn't last long, but it came from above. "Oh,
Jesus," Conner said. He started signaling again.

"It was lightning."

"They're here." He looked up, letting the snow pummel
his face. "You guys," he whispered, "come on down."

Suddenly and without a word, Paulie took off toward the
house. Then, in the distance, Conner heard the Keltons'
dog Manrico set up a howl. He looked in the direction of
the Keltons' place . . . and saw, standing at the edge of the
yard as if they'd just come up out of the woods, three kids.
They had really big heads and their eyes were terrible in
the reflected light from the house. "Paulie!" Conner whispered. But Paulie was standing under the deck, as still as
death "Paulie . . ."

Then he saw that they had a lantern. He looked at it,
glowing in the snow, the interior flickering orange.

"Mom," he called, but it came out as a whisper. He
fought to form the word. "M-o-o-mm." It stayed in his
throat.

They came across the snowy lawn, sort of floating just
above the ground, floating and flickering.

Conner was terrified beyond anything he'd ever thought
possible. It was freezing-cold fear, a fear so deep he had
not known that it could exist.

Had he been insane? Why had he done this?

The thought crossed his mind that this was yet another
joke, but then he heard them, a buzzing sound like huge
flies, a sound that was really, really strange, that was not of
this world. They remained out in the gushing, swirling snow.

The lantern wasn't a lantern at all, it was a very black
metal thing with glowing holes in it that sort of looked like

eyes, and it seemed to Conner as if it was sort of alive, too. The three aliens came closer, moving swiftly and accurately now, no longer floating and flickering. They were like wolves in the snow, now, and they were clearly interested in him.

And then there was something on his shoulder, as light as if a bird had landed there. Almost too scared to move, he looked down. A hand was there, with fingers like long, thin snakes, and black claws.

EIGHTEEN

CONNER HAD TO RUN, HE had to get out of here, but then the world distorted, seeming almost to bend, and the glowing thing was right in front of his face and he was staring into the orange light inside where there were millions of glowing threads. They were just threads of light, but he couldn't look away from them, he had to keep staring.

One of the creatures pulled his shirt front up, and he felt something pushing against his chest and getting hotter and hotter and he couldn't stop it and he had to because it was burning him.

The snow swirled and lightning flashed and there was a loud snap like a wire had come down and was spitting in the yard.

Suddenly Conner realized that he was alone. He was standing in the snow and he had to get back inside because somebody was out here who should not be, and he was in danger.

He'd seen black eyes and orange light, terrible light, but the rest of it was all confused. Had he met the aliens? He wasn't sure. Or no, he was sure. He hadn't. He'd pointed the light at the sky and everything, but they hadn't shown up.

He opened the door. He walked past Paulie who, without a word, went into the bathroom and drank glass after glass of water. When he came out, he was transformed from a posturing preteen into the little boy he had been as recently as last summer. "I want to go home," he said quietly. Then he ran upstairs.

Conner ran after him.

Paulie burst into the living room. "I want to go home," he yelled.

"Paulie?" Katelyn asked.

Paulie looked toward Conner, his face soaked with tears. Conner went closer to him. "Hey, man?"

"Don't let him near me!"

Katelyn got to her feet "What in the world did you do to him, Conner?"

Conner shook his head.

"Here, come here to me, Paulie, honey. I've dealt with a lot of scared guys in my time, honey." Katelyn took him by the hand. "Now, we are going into the kitchen, fellas, and guess what we're gonna do? We are going to make a big, old-fashioned pot of hot chocolate flavored with brandy. Would you like that?"

"We have brandy?" Dan asked.

"I'm not allowed to drink."

"This is a very tiny bit, Paulie," Katelyn said as she drew him toward the kitchen.

"Hey, guy," Dan said to Conner.

"Yes, Dad?"

Dan patted the couch cushion. Conner sat down beside him. "Conner, did you—no. Better way to do this. What did that to him?"

"Dunno. He was okay, then he wasn't."

"Did you, perhaps, have a fight? It was awfully noisy down there at one point."

"No. No fight."

"No, that wouldn't make him cry. What made him cry, Conner?"

"Homesick, maybe?"

"No."

Conner's chest hurt. He tried to sort of move his shirt away from it to not have anything touch it.

Dan saw, and lifted it. "What's going on here?"

"Nothing."

"Yeah, there is. Katelyn, could you come back, please?"

Conner heard a voice, *Hello, Conner.*

"Hi."

Dan said, "Hi what?"

Be quiet!

He started to talk, but it was like somebody had grabbed his throat from the inside.

This is real, Conner.

A coldness raced in Conner's veins. This was somebody that was *inside* him, somebody else alive, *in him!*

"Katelyn, something's not right here."

Don't tell them, Conner.

She came in.

"Look at his chest."

"Conner, what have you boys been doing?"

Paulie had followed her. She turned to him. "Paulie, you tell me. Have you boys been playing too rough?"

"No, Mrs. Callaghan."

"Mom?"

"Son, you're all skinned up! You look like you've been sandpapered, so I want to know what you were doing."

Conner had no way to respond. He wasn't sure why he was hearing this voice, only that it was not being heard by anybody else.

That's right, Conner.

Mom and Paulie returned to the kitchen, followed by Dan. Conner hesitated a moment, then hurried after them. He was trying not to be scared, because this was the real thing, this was contact. But he was not just somewhat scared, he was so scared that he was actually dizzy.

He knew what had been done to him: they had put a communications device in his chest.

Right again.

The kitchen was filling with the smell of cocoa and it seemed so wonderfully comfortable it almost made him burst into tears. He ran over and threw his arms around his mother's waist and tried not to let Paulie hear him crying.

"What is the matter with these boys?" Katelyn asked.

"I think it's called nervous energy. Running on fumes. When's your bedtime, Paulie?"

"Whenever."

"I repeat the question, Paul Warner. When is your bedtime?"

"Nine-thirty."

"It's already ten forty-five," Dan said. "You must be tuckered out."

"Conner's an eleven o'clock guy," Katelyn said. "But you're tired, too, right?"

"I'm tired."

Paulie nodded into the mug of hot chocolate that Katelyn had just poured him.

They drank their cocoa in silence, and the voice did not recur. Conner began to hope that it had been an auditory hallucination, because if contact was going to mean you had a voice inside you, that was going to take a whole lot of getting used to.

He'd read most of his father's abnormal-psych texts, so he hoped it wasn't an early symptom of schizophrenia, the curse of the excessively intelligent. Even though that might actually be better than having an alien communications device buried in his damn chest.

He and Paulie did not argue about going to bed upstairs. There was no way that either of them were going anywhere near that basement again tonight. In fact, Conner considered proposing to Dan that they brick the thing up tomorrow and just forget about it.

After they were both in pajamas and had their teeth brushed, Paulie said, "I'm sorry about not believing you."

"About what?"

He put his arms on Conner's shoulders and pushed his lips close to his ear. "The aliens! I saw them. I saw the whole thing!"

"Forget it, Paulie."

"*Forget it?* Are you nuts! I saw aliens in your yard, man, three of them!"

"We don't know what we saw."

"Hello? You were the big believer. You were the guy who was vectoring them in."

"Maybe I made a mistake."

"Maybe you didn't."

They left it there, and soon Paulie was asleep. Conner watched the night, listened to the snow whispering on the windowpanes, and wondered how the world really worked.

There came that voice again, very quick, trembling with something like fear and something that, oddly enough, sounded to Conner like a sort of awe: *Soon you will know.*

NINETEEN

CHARLES GUNN PULLED UP TO the presidential safe house on Embassy Row. The mansion had been acquired during World War II when the Roosevelt Administration was concerned that Hitler might develop a long-range bomber and attack the White House. Successive administrations had continued to use it, and during the cold war, tunnel access had been added across the mile that separates it from the White House. Now it functioned as a very private presidential enclave, at present ostensibly owned by Washington insider Larry Prince, but actually under the control of the Secret Service.

He walked quickly to the door, which was opened as he approached. A young man in a dark suit, with an earbud in his ear and the bulge of a small machine gun under his jacket, stepped aside and let him through the metal detector. Another young man fell in ahead of them, and the three of them proceeded silently down the hall, then turned right into the president's ornate office.

The president didn't know it yet, but he was going to provide a diversion that would, hopefully, deceive the grays into looking in the wrong direction for the source of danger to their evil little child. It might well mean that the president would himself be killed, but to Charles this was of little consequence.

He was watching the news and paging through a speech. "Hey there, Chester," he said without looking up, "just give me a second, here." Then, a moment later, "Pull up a chair."

"It's Charles, sir," Charles said as he sat down.

On the wall of this office there were paintings chosen by FDR, the most spectacular being a Nicolas Poussin, *Landscape with St. John on Patmos*. As Charles knew, and as FDR had certainly known, the geometry of the painting resolved into a date: 2012. That this was the year of tribulation had been known by the secret societies that had created western civilization literally from the very beginning. The date had been handed down through the Masonic community from the ancient Egyptian priesthood who had divined it by looking through the last, clear glass of man's old, lost science: a window into the future. This had been at Abydos in Egypt, and some of the other things they had seen had been commemorated on beams that held up the temple's roof to this day.

"So," the president finally said, "how are you gonna make me miserable today, Charles?"

"Mr. President—"

"You never come here with good news. All your good news is secret. So, hit me."

"The grays are acting against us in a major and very bizarre way."

"The grays are acting bizarre? You're kidding. I sit here astonished."

Charles had constructed his lie carefully. "Sir, they're going to do something that will reveal to the public the fact that the government's been concealing their presence for sixty years. They're going to destroy our credibility."

The president pointed a finger at his own temple.

"Exactly. They're trying to undermine the government. First, the public becomes aware that they're real. Second, people tell about their abductions. Third, it's discovered that we're helpless. Chaos follows."

The president was silent for a moment. "And, for some reason, you can't get control of this situation, which is why you're here. First, tell me why it's out of control. Second, tell me what you need."

"It's not out of control."

"Then why are you here?"

"Sir, I need a TR-A. I need to surveil in the area where this disclosure event took place."

"You have TR-A1."

"Mike Wilkes is using it. He's on detail out there now, but he needs backup."

"Okay, you've got another TR. I'll cut orders for you to have access to one. What else?"

"I need some people killed, *tout de suite*."

"Just do what you gotta do."

"You need to be aware that one of them is Mr. Crew."

"Oh, fuck."

"Exactly. Our friend from the beyond is not our friend."

"He's—what's he done?"

"He's giving the grays support."

"Next."

"I need one other thing."

"Hit me."

Charles smiled. "I don't want to hit you. I want you to hit Wilton, Kentucky, with an earthquake. Enough to disrupt the place and reduce the college that's there to rubble."

The president stared at him for some little time. "Why?" he asked at last.

"We need a diversion so that we can clean up all the principals. We need it to look accidental. All the folks who were present during the disclosure event."

"I see." He looked down at the top of his desk. This time, his silence extended even longer. When he spoke, his voice was soft with what Charles knew must be pain. "You know, it feels like the best day in your life when you walk for the first time into the White House as president. President of the United States—wow, and wow again. Then you find out the secrets, and you spend the rest of your life in mourning."

"Mr. President, this will be a very localized hit. It's not going to activate any fault lines, nothing like that. We'll see significant disruption and a few deaths, obviously. It will be a cover for us to sterilize the area. We'll confiscate all original video, and deal with the people who were firsthand witnesses. We have assets already at work who will get a local physics professor who saw the thing to debunk it. Our media people will see to it that his message gets spread far and wide. But the damage and the deaths will be the minimum necessary, let me assure you of that. I feel the same way you do about the American people, of course."

"You're assuring me that this will not do any more than the minimum damage necessary?"

"Absolutely. It will be very precisely contained. We'll have a TR directing the pulses from the immediate vicinity of the target."

"And the grays are not going to react adversely? That is one limb I sure as hell don't want to go out on."

"Sir, again, there is no way. They are not going to be able to connect the dots, as it were."

"I'll redeploy the scalar weapon."

"Thank you, sir. I'll call you when I need it fired."

God only knew what the grays would do to the president after he unleashed a scalar pulse that devastated the whole center of the United States and threw all of their plans awry. One thing was certain, Charles planned to stay far, far away from this particular moron after he pulled that particular trigger.

"I have a state dinner in an hour. I gotta go over to the rathole and put on my monkey suit, and spend the evening with the prime minister of Thailand—whose name I will never, ever learn to pronounce—who is here to whine at me about some damn thing or other."

He stood up. The interview was at an end.

MIKE WILKES LAY IN HIS motel room trying to do anything except worry about the next few days. He had a difficult, complex task, and if the grays detected him, he was going to be something worse than dead meat. Over the years, they'd found bodies of people who had been attacked by the grays, mostly airmen who'd gone too close in the early days, when Truman was still trying to shoot them out of the sky.

They would have their lips cut off, their eyes and tongues gouged out, and their genitals removed. There would generally be seawater in their lungs, no matter where the bodies were found. The grays would cut them up, drown them, then leave them as warnings. The grays could very definitely be crossed, and this particular action was certain to qualify.

He really did not feel so comfortable right now, sitting in this dismal little hole of a room and, frankly, waiting to start getting cut to pieces by somebody he couldn't even see. He'd long held that the grays couldn't read minds beyond a few feet, and that they had trouble even understanding what was going on in the human mind. But lying here on this bug-ridden bed watching Jay Leno wish he could suck any part of his guest, Drew Barrymore, he feared that the opposite might be true.

His only chance was speed. If he could get this done by tomorrow night, he could be back in D.C. by noon on Wednesday, and maybe he would be okay. *Maybe.*

AT ALFRED AFB, THE FLIGHT line was being used for foul-weather training runs, and the sound of engines being fired up and jets screaming off into the night could be heard clearly in the disused office block where Lauren Glass and Rob Langford had been together for hours. Since he had caught up with her last night, he had not let her out of his sight.

And now that she'd understood that there were two opposing groups within the Air Force, she was glad that she had ended up with Rob. She had never liked Colonel Wilkes, and had not been surprised to discover the danger he posed to her.

She sat across from Rob in the office, watching the snow sift past the windows. She was exhausted, and she was hoping that he would soon let her rest.

He remained formal and distant, though, and showed no sign of either becoming more at ease or of offering her a place to sleep.

She wished it was not so. He was a lovely man, handsome in a way that made her want him, simply and frankly. His eyes were gray and intense, but also had a sort of wide-open look to them, as if he was as friendly as he was dedicated. They were the eyes of somebody who worked hard, but, she thought, also liked to have fun.

He did not trust her. There was a secret he wanted to tell her, but he was wary. If he decided that she was the enemy, what then?

She knew what then. She just didn't want to think about it.

"Tell me again about your relationship with Adam," he asked. In all these hours, she had not refused to answer a question, no matter how often he had repeated it. She knew this interrogation technique. She would let him use it. She would cooperate fully.

"I've been with somebody who shared the life of my soul," she said. "I don't think he was a predator like Mike said. Losing him has left a hole in my life, almost as bad as when my dad died."

"That's not what you said the last time."

"I'm being creative."

What you said was, "They aren't predators, but I think they're missing something they know we have, and they're trying to get it."

Rob could not take his eyes off Lauren Glass. It wasn't just her beauty, it was the trembling, delicate play of emotions in her eyes as she spoke about Adam. He could see that the love was genuine, entirely so. But there was also something furtive about Lauren, as if, on some level, she might be lying to herself, and might at least sense that.

This long, repetitive interrogation was leading to a judgement. When he was finished with it, he would draw his conclusions and her life would either continue or it would not. He wondered if she knew, decided to assume that she did. "So tell me, are the grays a danger to us? How do you feel about that?"

"I guess I miss Adam more because I know he's somewhere. If he'd died in the fire, that would have been cloture, you know." She fell silent.

"That didn't answer my question."

"It did, indirectly. If you want a precise answer, I have never been able to figure out exactly what the grays are here for, so it's pretty hard for me to tell if they're a danger.

I mean, they look like aliens. God knows, they act like it. But I've seen the Bob autopsies. They're partly biological and partly manufactured, and they have no brain as we know it. Just all those threads of glass in the head. But far, far fewer neurons than we have. So why do they think so well? We don't know. And since we can't say what they are, we also can't assign motive. Those are my thoughts, anyway."

He watched her. He didn't know exactly what he was waiting for—perhaps for some mistake, the nature of which would only reveal itself when she made it. Potentially at least, this woman could play an important role. He had no doubt that the grays had maneuvered her very neatly out of Wilkes's hands and into his, and he had understood that it was so that she could perform a function with the child. *Teaching*, he thought.

She asked him, "Listen, do you know anything about them? Like, where they're from? I've always asked Adam about that but, you know, he doesn't tell you much."

She wasn't afraid of him, and that was good. "We don't know anything about where they're from. We do know that there are a lot of them out there, and they're on their way here."

"So the DNA thing is true?"

"You know about that?"

She nodded. "Mike told me that they've used up their DNA and they want ours."

"That's part of it."

"So this is the reconnaissance element of an invasion force and we should fear them."

"I didn't say that. I think they may also be our only chance of avoiding extinction."

Her lovely mouth opened. The tip of her tongue, a soft, pink pearl, ran along her lips and withdrew. "Are you— uh . . . no." She shook her head. "Wow. That's big."

"The calculations are correct. There's going to be a tremendous environmental breakdown. In fact, it's been building for eons. We're at the climax."

She sat there, staring at him.

"Lauren?"

"What about babies?"

He shook his head. "Nobody makes it . . . except your friend Mike and his outfit. Have you ever heard of the Trust?"

"No."

"The way they've got it set up, about a million people will survive, chosen by the Trust—Mike and his group."

"But then the grays will get them. They'll have gained nothing."

"That's not how it works. We have reason to believe—to know—that the grays will give up on us unless there are billions of us alive. Smaller numbers will be of no use to them. The reason that Adam left when he did is that something has come to crisis, and Adam is apparently involved. Man and the grays are both in danger of extinction, and they're trying to save us all. Your boss and his friends are trying to prevent that so the grays will go away and leave the Earth to their million elite."

He watched her thinking, saw the pain in her eyes, the shock . . . saw a young woman's face reflect fear for children who had not yet been born. "What happens . . . if the grays get their way?"

"Lauren, a very long time ago, there was a war on this Earth. A great civilization fell. When it did, we lost our knowledge of how physics really works. We set off down a road of ignorance that's led to where we are now: all six billion of us trapped on an overburdened and dying planet. Meantime, the grays are so ancient that they've used up their DNA. Without each other, both species go extinct. They're looking for a sort of marriage: they get access to our youthful DNA, we get access to their brilliant minds. Everybody survives."

"But how? What happens?"

"Lauren, it's my growing belief that you are one of the most critical human beings now alive on this planet, because you are a big part of the answer to that question."

Suddenly, she looked every inch the soldier. Her eyes flashed. Rob thought, as always, that the grays had chosen well. She would be able to do this. He made his decision about her, after all these hours, in that split second. The

grays had given her to him so she could be the child's empath, it was the only explanation that made any sense.
"You'll be a sort of teacher, Lauren. An interpreter, if you
will."

"Of who? Of what?"

"I don't want to be mysterious, but it's best that we let
this unfold in its own time."

"That's hard."

"So be it, duty is duty. I have one further question. Do you
know how to hide? I mean, on a trained, professional level?"

"Why in the world should I hide? Colonel Wilkes had no
right to do what he did, you said that yourself. He's up on
charges."

"He's also very powerful. More powerful by far than we
are. He's dangerous, Lauren. I hope you understand that."

"He's trying to kill me, of course I understand it! But I
have no idea how to hide."

"You got this far. That's saying something. A hell of a
lot, in fact."

"If I'm a KIA, then I have no Air Force standing. If I'm
already dead, he can kill me without fear of penalty."

"We're going to hide you, Lauren."

"I wish the grays were here."

"Keep trying to contact them."

When they went outside, the snow of earlier had stopped.
The base was very quiet, the flight line now shut down.

She noticed that he moved very quickly, striding across
the base to the carpool. He had a car of his own, but he req-
uisitioned a staff vehicle instead. "This is part of staying
hidden," he said. "I'll exchange this for another staff vehicle after I drop you off."

He took her to a Days Inn, which appeared to be about
the only motel in this small town.

Thus it was that Lauren ended up in the room next door
to Mike Wilkes, an event that had not been orchestrated by
the grays, but was not entirely chance, either. Rather it
emerged out of the fates of both species, human and gray,
as they rode the dark rails of their destinies.

Mike heard voices next door, a man and a woman. He
took no notice.

Rob wanted to stay with Lauren—he told himself, to protect her. But he had work to do, because if he didn't find Wilkes, not only was Lauren going to be in trouble, the rest of this thing was going to come apart. He could not imagine the consequences if the grays were thwarted, dared not even think about what might happen.

As he drove back to his office, Mike Wilkes and Lauren Glass both lay on their beds unable to even think of sleeping, their heads separated by just six inches of drywall. Lauren's mind whirled with the astonishing secrets she had learned, and, as she sank into exhaustion, also with the image of Colonel Rob Langford, who appeared to her as a sort of angel, powerful and good and strong enough to take her the way she loved to be taken, and give her the babies her whole heart and soul told her that the future needed.

Mike would doze for a moment, then see Adam looming up, his insect eyes glaring. Then he would start awake and toss and turn, and nuzzle his gun close to his side.

Far overhead, in a sky that had cleared magnificently, strange stars hung over the town. The Three Thieves had been joined by Adam, and the first phase had been accomplished. They were counting the hours, now, the minutes, the seconds, the nanoseconds until they acted again, and Adam entered Conner, and became part of him, and either it worked or it did not.

It was an amazing time, truly, with six billion human lives and six billion gray lives hanging in the balance, in the quiet of a little town, in a dark corner of a small state, in a strange and faraway place called Earth.

PART SEVEN
LOST LAND

There was a child went forth every day,
And the first object he look'd upon, that object he
  became,
And that object became part of him for the day, or a
  certain part of the day,
Or for many years, or stretching cycles of years.

—WALT WHITMAN
"There Was a Child Went Forth"

TWENTY

CONNER AND PAULIE WOKE UP late and had to rush to get to school. When Paulie saw Conner's mixture of amaranth flakes, wheat germ, and unsweetened live-culture yogurt, he did not ask for an explanation, but gratefully ate the bacon and eggs that Dan, wearing only green boxer shorts and huge, fluffy slippers, provided to him. He was fascinated to watch Conner eat what looked like upchuck.

Conner had called in aliens, which was damn amazing. But now here he was gobbling down this fantastically geekish food. Nobody could eat like this and get away with it. Paulie had an obligation to uphold the reputation of Bell Attached as a cool school.

"So, what's your lunch?" he asked Conner. They'd stop by his house to pick up his, which would be Cheetos, a ham sandwich, and a power bar.

"My lunch?" He went over to a little plastic greenhouse that was sitting on the kitchen counter. "Ah, excellent. *Sprouting* alfalfa, I'm happy to say. Some organic hummus, which is really pretty delicious if you'd like to share, buddy."

Aliens or not, Paulie saw that the Connerbusters had to continue.

"Sounds great, but I've got my dumb old ham sandwich waiting for me at home."

Dan listened to the boys with only half an ear. Conner had somehow managed to bring this off, it appeared. He was more socially resourceful, then, than he seemed. All to the good.

During his own wakeful and uneasy night, Dan had made a decision. Once he was tenured, he was going to do the unthinkable. He was going to circulate his resume, and he was going to concentrate exclusively on schools in large cities far from here. An untenured professor was an academic beggar. But a man operating from tenure was more significant, even if he came from the lower ranks of colleges.

The reason he was going to do this was that he wanted to get his family as far from open spaces and dark, abandoned nights as he could. Preferably, he would raise his remarkable boy in a Manhattan tower, some place like that. Conner was vulnerable, and Dan's instinct was that moving to a more populated area would protect him.

As for Katelyn, she was in the process of putting Marcie behind her. She dressed for her morning round of classes while listening to the males crashing around downstairs. She would not have believed Conner's skill in recapturing Paulie. She'd been furious with him last night, but now she was proud of her son.

She hurried downstairs to be in time to give her men good-bye kisses—accepted with dear brusqueness by her son, with hopeful eyes by her husband.

She let him hug her. This family was her responsibility and her achievement. She was not going to let it go awry simply because he'd done something foolish and she felt humiliated. "Men are fools," her mom had said, "expect the worst." As, indeed, her dad had been, disappearing on them the way he had, effectively orphaning her and widowing Mom.

So far, her mother's advice had never been wrong.

AT THE DAYS INN, LAUREN Glass was awakened by a tapping on her door. She was shocked, then frightened. Then she remembered the code that Rob had given her, and recognized the pattern of taps. As if a motel room door would keep out Mike Wilkes or whatever goons he might send.

She still had no clothes but what she'd been wearing when Mike had attacked her, so she went into the bathroom and wrapped herself in a towel before cracking the door.

"What time is it?"

"Six-fifty. We've got to get started."

"What are we doing?"

"Trying to figure out where the kid is, if he's really here, or if this is some kind of a feint designed to throw Wilkes off, in which case we can concentrate on the issue of you. But we need to solve the child question first."

His life before hers, that was clear enough. "The grays aren't protecting this child?"

"We're not in communication with the grays anymore. As you know."

"I do indeed. And I have to tell you, I just don't see them as really understanding how jeopardy functions in our society. They know how the brain works, but I don't think they understand reality the same way we do. We need to assume that they're going to be blindsided if this child is attacked."

MIKE WILKES WAS RETURNING TO the motel from the early run he took every day when he saw, from a distance of about a quarter of a mile, two people get into a USAF motor pool car in the parking lot and drive away. A man and a woman, but too far away to see their faces. He noted that they'd been parked directly in front of his room.

He decided that some sort of Air Force investigative unit must have been activated, no doubt because of what had happened last night, when Lauren Glass had appeared at Wright-Pat after he'd listed her as KIA.

He put in a cell phone call to Charles. "Hey there, sorry I'm so early. Yeah, it went fine—at least, the trip was fine. Look, there are a couple of officers in mufti sniffing around. I haven't gotten a close look at them, but I have the feeling that they're an arrest team. I need that handled, Charles."

He hung up quickly and did what he now had to do with his cell phone, which was to take out the battery and throw the whole instrument in a ditch. You might as well paint yourself purple as carry one of these things. If you had a cell phone, turned on or turned off, they could track you from twenty-five thousand miles overhead with the Watch-Star satellite.

He had probably a dozen cover identities. He didn't even remember them all. Some of them were essentially perfect, provided to him by the Defense Intelligence Agency. They would stand up to the most rigorous scrutiny. Others, thrown together as needed over the years, were less reliable. But all except two of them were on file somewhere within the U.S. government.

So, at the moment, he had only the two to choose from. He decided to stay with the salesman he'd used last night. He found a gas station, went in, and asked the attendant for directions to the nearest rental car agency. He had about twelve hours to perform a whole complex sequence of actions, then the night to do the really challenging work.

The Three Thieves watched Conner leave home and be driven to school. So far, there had been no threat against him. They wanted to be closer to Conner even than the collective demanded. He was their creation, too, and his mind was like a garden of jewels. They wanted to partake of his rich feelings, but they dared not, he was too precious to disturb in any way.

Because, as a species, they were so close to death, the grays were particularly terrified of it. Their main body was alone in the immensity of space, no longer protected by a home planet and a parent star, their own having long since perished as victims to time. They traveled now in an engineered world on what many considered a hopeless quest, and their collective mind dreamed of oblivion, and worried about it, and clung.

The Thieves had spent much of the night hanging over the town, listening to the people they could hear through implants, trying to ascertain if any of them might seek to harm their treasure.

Last night, they had carried out the instructions of the collective and prepared Conner to receive the extraordinary implant that was going to be given to him.

The fragment of the collective the humans called Adam had been assigned to man some years ago, with the hope that Adam, through exposure to them, would evolve structures in his mind that would enable him to do something that no gray had ever done before—indeed, that was only an idea, a theory, perhaps a hope and maybe a forlorn one. They wanted him to meld into the boy, in effect, to implant his entire being into Conner and become part of him.

Now Adam lay waiting in an empty barn, on the floor of a disused horse stall. Later, when darkness fell, he would complete his mission. Death was in this for him, but a very strange sort of death. It would not be the oblivion that was at the center of the long, complicated drama that obsessed the collective, but rather the surrender of self in a sort of living death. Once his thoughts and knowledge became part of Conner, he believed that he would disappear entirely.

He listened to the dripping of the old barn and the rustle of beetles in the hay, and dreamed formless, uneasy dreams.

The Three Thieves were fascinated and horrified by what Adam was being called upon to do. Like every gray, in the privacy of the self, they regarded it with horror. Superficially, though, they were grateful both that he was trying and that they didn't have to.

The grays in the scout group had various human genes, this and that, whatever they'd been able to use, and were much healthier than the ones in the main body. The Three Thieves, for example, had human blood, vivid with life, not the dank artificial goo that sustained most of those in the main body. They had taken this blood and adapted their bodies to it, and used it now as their own. It made them quicker, smarter, and also, they thought, more able to understand man.

The Three Thieves watched Conner from above as he moved about in his school. They wanted to get closer, but could not go into a crowd and remain invisible. They could lock their movements to no more than two or three pairs of eyes. So they could not enter his school, they could only watch. This was why grays worked at night, when people were alone.

CONNER HAD SLEPT A RESTLESS, frightened night, and now sat in history class bored senseless because he had realized that his teacher did not understand the events in the Napoleonic Wars that he was teaching. The French loss of the Battle of Borodino in 1812 had led inevitably to the political structure of modern Europe, and discussing the way that had happened would have been interesting. Instead, he had to listen to stupefying trivia about General Kutuzov's bad feet and Napoleon's good lunch.

His chest hurt. He remembered some kind of fire, but he had not been burned. He knew he had seen the grays, but it all now seemed curiously unreal, like it had happened to somebody else, or not happened at all.

This disturbed him. He knew that he had seen them. He remembered them, though, in the unstable way that you remember a dream. He understood that this was because the experience had been so strange, but it still troubled him. He wanted these memories. He knew that the grays were here for a reason and they were obviously interested in him. But what was the reason, and why him?

At the ten-fifteen break, he caught up with Paulie before he had reached the protection of Kevin and Will. "Do you still remember?" he asked.

Paulie stopped opening the combination on his locker. He stared down at his feet. "Yeah," he said in a low voice.

"Paulie, I'm scared."

"I wasn't when we got up, but I am now."

"Yeah, the same thing's happening to me. I don't want to go home. I don't want to be there at night."

Paulie looked at him, his eyes hollow. "I was gonna restart the busters," he said, "but I'm not. You're having too rough a time. But I don't want us to be together again, Conner. I don't want ever to see those things again, not ever."

"I can't handle it, either!"

"Yeah, you can. You're as smart as any alien. That's why they're after you, I think. Because you *can* handle it."

Conner's throat closed and tears welled in his eyes. "No, I can't," he said.

FAR ABOVE, THE THREE THIEVES felt his fear, and drew closer together in their own disquiet. What was the matter with him? Was he in danger? Helplessly, they watched the purple fear flowing up out of the shimmering haze of feelings that hung over the school like a many-colored smoke. They could tell it belonged to Conner by listening to it. They could also talk to him, but dared not. Last night, they had done something with him that the grays had never before managed with human beings, which was to form words in his mind that he could hear and respond to—words, not images.

They dared not do that now, because it might panic him and that must not happen.

Conner went to his physics section at the college, hurrying along the snowy walk that linked Bell Attached to the campus, and wishing that he was safe inside some building and not exposed to the watchful, dangerous sky.

TWENTY-ONE

THE SUN WAS HIGH IN a thin haze by the time Mike reached the Enterprise rental car agency that was tucked between the Wal-Mart and something called Goober's Used Trucks. He considered buying a truck instead of renting a car, but he didn't have but about six hundred dollars in his wallet. Too bad, a purchased vehicle would be a hell of a lot more secure than a rental, which any expert could trace, no matter what sort of identity he used.

"I'd like a car, please," he said. He pulled out the Harry Hill driver's license and credit card.

"Missouri," the agent said, looking at the license.

"Yes, sir. Here trying to sell the college on some new band instruments."

"Well, good luck. Pardon my French, but they're tighter than a witch's tit over there. You want a Grand Am?"

"A Grand Am is good."

"Looks like we're gonna get some serious weather tonight. If you want, I've got a Volvo. It's three-sixty a week. Front-wheel drive might be useful, though."

This was certainly true. "Yeah," he said looking at the sky. "It sure might." He took the Volvo.

In his top pocket was the remote control that would summon the triangle, which was laying by in some concealed draw somewhere in the hills. The trouble was, it connected through the MilStar communications satellite, and the second he used it, whoever was looking for him would know both where he was and where the triangle was.

Once he had the car, he went through a drive-though and got some food. It was too dangerous to stop and eat, lest some sort of horrible serendipity expose him to those two investigators. Professionalism in a situation like this was defined by attention to detail. He also knew from long experience that going without food was a mistake when you were dealing with complex and stressful issues.

AIR FORCE CHIEF OF STAFF Samuel Gold was ushered into the presidential executive office next to the Oval, which was open. No matter how often he passed near that room, he was always inspired by its history. No matter which president happened to be sitting at that desk, the power of the office was so intense that it was like a kind of scent around them all. Gold saw the presidency of the United States as the greatest governmental institution ever devised to expand human freedom and happiness. So he was especially concerned about this order he had come to discuss.

"Sir," he began, "I won't take up but five minutes of your time. I am requesting confirmation of an order received at oh-nine-hundred today, directing—"

"I know the order," the president said. "You're to prepare to fire the scalar weapon."

"Yes, sir! I just—sir, what you may not know is that this weapon is not stable. It's still in development."

"The tests have worked pretty well."

"Yes, sir. But you're going to fire it into the New Madrid fault line."

"Oh?"

"Mr. President, this thing is going to devastate the entire central United States. You might see half a million deaths and trillions of dollars in damage. Sir, if I may ask, why do you need this?"

"General Gold, you can't ask. But I do want you to put a hold on that order until further notice."

"Yes, sir, thank you, sir."

"Thank you for coming in."

Gold's thick neck flushed. He went to his feet, saluted, turned, and stiffly left the room. The president watched until the door was closed, then called for his next meeting to be delayed. He went out into the Rose Garden, bleak in winter, and stood a long time alone and in silence. To slow his pounding heart and damp his rage, he sucked long, deep breaths. And it passed, and he returned to his work.

MIKE WILKES'S NEXT STOP WAS Bell Attached School. They were all college families on Oak Road, so he could be reasonably sure that the children attended Bell, which went from kindergarten through high school. He wasn't concerned about the Jeffers infant. The grays needed their instrument to be ready by 2012, not in twenty years. That left the two Kelton boys, Paul Warner and his sister Amy, and Conner Callaghan. There was a fair chance that he'd find his candidate among these children. If not, then he'd expand his search. He would not fail, that was unthinkable.

The school was housed in two elegant old redbrick structures on the edge of the Bell College campus. The place was certainly beautiful, with its tall white columns and broad sports field behind the main complex. As he walked up the long sidewalk to the main entrance, he reached in his side pocket and turned on his Palm Pilot. Tucked in beside it was the remote that would call the triangle.

Now the Palm would record the emissions of any computer in any room he entered. He would be able to access that computer again from the parking lot. If they used paper files, he'd find a way to physically invade them.

He had held the belief for many years that a person with sufficient training and resources quite simply could not be thwarted. Today, he would put that theory to the test.

As school was in session, the doors were locked. He identified himself over the intercom as "Dr. Wenders," interested in enrolling his children in the school.

He was admitted by a student volunteer and led to the principal's office. Mary Childs was a quick-voiced woman, big and ready to smile.

"Dr. Wenders," she said, thrusting out her hand. "I thought I knew everybody on the faculty."

"I'm not on the faculty just yet. I'm considering an offer, so I'm trying to get the lay of the land."

"Oh, okay. How can I help you?"

"My son is a rather special case."

"All right."

"He's extremely bright."

"So is everybody here. The whole school is a gifted-and-talented program, essentially."

"At nine, Jamie devised a muon detector that won a Westinghouse commendation. His IQ is over two hundred. As you know, even in a very accelerated program, students like this can pose some special challenges."

"We have such students."

"I'm surprised to hear that. They're relatively rare."

"Oh, we have one or two."

"That's very reassuring. How do you approach their needs, if I may ask?"

"Certainly." She turned aside and began typing into her computer. "Here," she said, "we devise special enrichment programs to address the needs and strengths of each child."

"Could I see such a program, something you've developed for a two-hundred-plus student?"

"We don't actually do IQ tests, but there is a student who we've identified as hyperintelligent, and we've devised a special program for him."

"Could I see that, please?"

"Well, I can show you the program itself, I think—just a minute, let's see if I can print out his curriculum without his identity. Yeah—no, it's not gonna let me do that. Here, I'll read it."

As she read off a list of the special tutoring, the accelerated reading program, the various high school and college language, physics, and math classes the child was attending, and his grade-point levels, Mike knew that he had almost certainly identified his kid. If he was also among the Oak Road families, then it was final.

"That's certainly very impressive."

"It's an advantage that we've got the college right here, of course. His college-level courses are just a short walk away."

That little slip told him that it wasn't a girl. Mary Childs was easy to handle. "That's a very impressive program. I don't think my son's in as good a situation now."

"Where are you, if I may ask?"

Here was a chance to work his list a little more. He chose the professor with the most candidate children. His response rolled out smoothly. "I'm at Mabry in California. I'm in history."

"Then you know John Kelton, our department head."

"I certainly do. He sent me over here, in fact. But he didn't say anything about his boys being like my son."

"No. But we do have one actively matriculated. That program is in current use, I can assure you."

Another two off the list. Nice. That left Paul and Amy Warner and Conner Callaghan among the Oak Road possibilities. But the information had come at a cost: at any time, this woman might mention "Dr. Wenders" to John Kelton. Probably, it would amount to nothing more than a moment of confusion between them, but if it went further, it could be dangerous. "I haven't actually resigned from Mabry yet, so if you don't mind . . ."

"Of course, I understand perfectly. Not a word."

"May I take a tour? Just look in on a few classes? We'll be in middle school."

She conducted him through their science lab first. Among the things it contained was a truly elaborate tangle of lab glass, with three retorts bubbling happily away. "Oh, boy," she said, striding over to the rig. "This should not be left on unattended." She looked quickly around the lab. "Conner?"

Silence.

"That boy, he's always doing this sort of thing. This is supposed to measure the body burden for some-odd-thousand pollutants found in common foodstuffs. But he can't just leave Bunsen burners on like this."

"This is your super-gifted one?"

She laughed. "Please keep *my* confidence, too!"

"Of course."

"The Callaghans have their hands full with this one. He's absolutely awesome. But this experiment's going to have to be moved to Science Hall, we can't have this in our lab anymore. Look at some of that glass!"

"I've never seen anything quite like it."

"Oh, I'm sure it separates each molecule into a different container or something. Probably has five original inventions floating around in there. *And* he speaks French, German, and Spanish and, God love him, Cantonese."

"He must annoy the other students."

"Let's put it this way. If yours comes in, he will be eternally grateful to you for a companion who runs at the same speed."

"My son isn't in this kind of overdrive, but he's close enough to where I can guess that it'll be a relief for both of them." He glanced at his watch. "I'm off to see the libraries," he said. "I want to thank you for your help. You've moved Bell to the top of my list."

"Which is where it darned well should be. We're the best little overlooked and ignored college in the United States."

In other words, a perfect backwater for the grays to hide their bright little baby, Conner Callaghan. On the way back to her office, he said, "I'm seeing a rather high class density."

"I don't think so."

"That class back there—I saw about thirty kids."

"Where?"

"Back opposite the lab."

She shook her head. "Let's check that out." She went into her office and did just what he needed: called up a class list. "Nope. Twenty-two in sixth-grade English B. And that's high for us. We try to stay around eighteen."

Back in his car, he opened the Palm and tapped the screen a few times. He was out of Wi-Fi range, so he attached the antenna to the Palm and was soon looking at her computer's desktop. The class list was still there. He down-loaded it to his Palm's memory.

He had his weapon, now, as well, in the form of that list. Armed with it, he would not need to go near Oak Road to carry out his plan, nor would he need to be anywhere near Conner Callaghan when he died, nor would it appear to be an assassination.

But he would go to Oak Road. Two could play the grays' lying game, and he planned to trick them into be-lieving that he had bought into their deception. He knew that Conner Callaghan and Paul Warner were in middle school, and that the description given to Lauren was of a high school student. That meant that it was one of the Kel-ton boys. So Mike would enter the Kelton house and only the Kelton house. The grays would think that he had swal-lowed their bait.

What he was going to do there and elsewhere in the community did not involve directly killing anybody. Nor was the process in any way extracted from the grays. It had been invented during World War II, in fact, by a Dr. Anto-nio Krause, who had brought it from Auschwitz to Dr. Hu-bertus Strughold's operation in Texas as part of Operation Paperclip in 1947.

By now, it was part of CIA routine. Field-tested, reliable as rain. The only difference between what he had to do and how a field agent might function was that he didn't have a neat little surgical kit and would have to devise his own.

He drove down to the county seat. He needed a good map of the community, as well as the large property that surrounded the Oak Road development, in addition to a look at the plans of the houses.

By the time he reached Somersburg, the thin light had gone. The sky was dull now, the sun pallid. The air had that empty coldness that portends a blizzard. He was glad of the car he'd chosen. A lot of this work had to be done to-night, and he absolutely could not get stuck, not at any point.

He went into the small county records office, and up to a clerk who sat behind a counter playing Texas Hold 'Em on a computer. He froze his screen and looked up.

"Any luck?" Mike asked with a smile.

The clerk raised his eyebrows as if to say that yes, he was having some luck, which meant only one thing: he was having no luck. "What can I do you for?"

"I've seen a large farm out Oak Road east of the town, and—"

"One, that's the Niederdorfer farm. Two, they aren't sellers."

"I'd still like to take a look at the plat, if I may."

The clerk got up and came back with a large black record book. Mike took it to one of the three tables in the room and opened it. He familiarized himself with the layout of the farm, and noted down the longitude and latitude. In the car, he would use his Palm Pilot to go online and get a topo map. Unlike a cell phone, a Palm Pilot could not be specifically identified just by using it in a wireless context, as long as it was effectively firewall protected, which his was.

He then went to the pages that contained the little Oak Road development. He copied the plat numbers of each property, then went back to the clerk and asked for the blueprints of the houses.

"You looking to buy?"

"Not sure. I want to see what kind of construction I'm looking at in the area." This office was too small and this man was too inquisitive. He would remember every detail of Mike's visit, which was really damned unfortunate.

He finished drawing a diagram of the Kelton place, then returned the book. "I'm looking at the wrong area. Is there an Oak *Street* in Wilton, maybe?"

The clerk consulted a map of the community on the wall. "No, not up there."

"Well, thank you then." He cursed himself as he left. This had been sloppy. His problem was that he was too used to power.

He sat in his car, letting the Palm look for a network. Sure enough, it found one—the town clerk's. It was WEP encrypted. Good, WEP was easy. The software was online in ten seconds, the encryption solved.

He got a topo of the entire eastern half of the state, then

went offline and zoomed to the Wilton area. The map was from 1988, but Oak Road was there, and the houses. He saw the way the land worked, coming down in a series of ridges. Across Oak Road was an old rail line, and beyond it a very large forest. Half a mile behind the houses was Wilton Road, with the field where the glowboy had come down visible between them.

He found one hill with an elevation of a hundred and eight feet, but it wasn't enough to cause him a problem. His choice of the grain elevator for his antenna and transmitter was the correct one. As the trap that would lead to the death of the kid was sprung, the evidence of its existence would be destroyed.

His next step was to buy the various items that would have been in an operative's surgical kit. Everything was important, but the most important was a small reel of narrow-gauge copper wire that would provide both his transmitter's antenna and his receiver's. He also needed a radio transmitter, an X-Acto knife, electrical tape, and, from a drugstore, a topical anesthetic and that old reliable, ether.

He got everything except the drugstore items at a Radio Shack he found in an almost derelict strip mall. There was a chain drugstore down the street, where he picked up a fairly decent tube of anesthetic. The local druggist was able to sell him a bottle of solvent-grade ether.

He drove until he found a rural area, where he opened the transmitter carton. He read the schematic and specifications, opened the back of the transmitter with the tool pack he had bought, and modified the circuit board by bypassing a couple of resistors. The unit would now transmit at a far greater power output than allowed by amateur equipment. Carefully, he stabilized the connections with electrical tape.

He returned to Wilton, driving the quiet country road in an unhurried manner, listening to the radio and making certain that he violated no traffic laws. He passed the motel, observing nothing unusual. His room opened onto the parking strip, which was now empty. He drove to the end of the block and turned. To his right was the field he had come down in the night before, now covered with a new dusting of snow. Snowflakes drifted slowly out of a hard, gray sky. The field was empty, and there was no sign of any tracks, human or vehicular, in the new snow. Beyond the field stood the immense grain elevator.

He drove past the elevator and then turned into its concrete loading area. It was abandoned at this time of year, and the large bay doors were carefully padlocked. He went to the personnel entrance and opened it by sliding a credit card between the door and the jamb. Nobody expected an empty grain elevator to be robbed in a small town, so the security was extremely light.

Inside, he went to the control room. It was simple enough to understand. The conveyor that moved the grain from trucks into the silo was what he was interested in. He descended to the cellar and threw the switch that turned on the power. Then he went back to the control room and started the conveyor. It screeched and clanged, then began to rattle along doing exactly what he wanted it to. Its tubs threw off dust every they time bounced. Overnight, the constant motion of the conveyor would fill the whole enormous space with a volatile haze. Explosive dust like this was the reason that elevators were not run when the weather was too dry.

Later tonight, he would return and set up the transmitter.

He left the grain elevator and drove out into a neighborhood. He found a corner lot with a house set back on it. The place was silent and dark, the family obviously off at work. He turned into the driveway, parked, and went up to the back door. He tapped on the glass.

A dog barked, came rushing to the door, his claws clattering on the kitchen floor. As he barked furiously, his face kept appearing at the lower edge of the door's window. He was a big dog, he thought some sort of hound, maybe a coonhound. Whatever, a big, mean dog was just what he was looking for.

He had learned how to handle dogs years ago, when he was a young officer and had been in training for the Air Police. But he would not risk tackling the Keltons' mutt without a practice run. The dog was one of the few weapons man had against the grays. They could not control a dog's mind. They hated and feared the dog.

He got the door unlocked after a small struggle with the mechanism. After soaking a handkerchief with ether, he pulled it open.

The dog rushed him, of course, and he clapped his hand over the snout and grabbed the animal by his scruff. While he was still struggling, Mike pushed his way into the kitchen. By the time he had closed the door with his heel, the dog was limp.

He spent a moment examining the skull, then cut into it about two inches above the right eye, making an incision so tiny that it hardly bled. He inserted a half-inch length of wire into the incision. Now he covered the wound with a little anesthetic. The dog would feel no pain when he woke up. Later, the wound would look like an insect bite, if it was noticed at all in the animal's fur.

He was about to leave when he noticed a faint sound coming from the back of the house. A television, a soap opera. Moving swiftly and quietly, he was quite surprised to find a man, big, in his fifties, asleep in a chair in the family room.

A nice chance to practice. Working gently and swiftly, he dropped the man into a deeper sleep with the ether, then wired him, too. He did not hypnotize this man. He had no way of knowing what the name "Conner Callaghan" might mean to him, if anything. To direct an assassin at a target, the assassin had to have a means of identifying the target. This was why most of Mike's subjects would be kids from Bell Attached School. Conner would be killed by somebody who knew him. It would look like a particularly vicious and crazy version of a school shooting.

He looked at his watch. One-forty. So, around breakfast time tomorrow, these two would be the first to enter a state of rage.

———

THE GRAYS WERE DEPLOYED ACROSS Earth in strict and carefully guarded territories. In the United States, they even adhered to the agreement they had made with the humans, and minimized their activities so that the Air Force would not come buzzing around and annoy them. In the rest of the world, they observed no such strictures.

It was difficult to reach into the human mind, but it was not hard to communicate with each other. The collective was growing excited, almost holding its breath, as the time for the attempt drew nearer. They did not know what their creation would be like, could hardly imagine a mind greater than their own. They felt a sense of worship and hope, and the Three Thieves an even more intimate wonder, because, as his guardians and his link to the collective, they were closest to him. Indeed, the feelings toward Conner were the strongest any gray had known in eons. And the hope, now that they had come this far and were so close to success, was very intense.

The other scouts, a million of them who had been scattered throughout the galaxy searching, had started racing toward Earth at 99 percent of the speed of light as soon as it had been understood what a perfect fit man was, a species that needed the grays as much as they needed man.

Inside the gigantic artificial world that was the main body, creeping along at half light speed, the sorrowing ranks stirred with hope so intense that they thought that a plague of suicide would overtake them if they failed.

When one of the lucky thousand scouts here on Earth tasted of a human dream, or licked the suffering off the soul of a prisoner or swam in the delicious sea of discovery that defined a child, all the billions quivered with joy, and all longed, themselves, to once again have such feelings of their own.

So, when it became clear that a particularly dangerous satellite was moving from one orbit to another, and that its new orbit would park it twenty-five-thousand miles above Conner's head, the whole mass of the grays fluttered with unease. They knew exactly how this satellite worked, they had seen it built. Had they wished, they could have built a similar instrument based on much more elegant principles, and with it shattered the planet.

They would never do that, of course, not to precious Earth, to precious man. They knew that there must be a way to revive their souls, to make their lives worth living again. Locked somewhere in the human genome was the secret of man's vitality. Conner would find this spark, and understand how to enable the grays to share it.

At least, that was the dream. But if this atrocious weapon was fired at him, maybe the dream would end.

The collective directed a triad to attend to the thoughts of the president. Ever since Harry Truman had, in 1947, ordered his airplanes to shoot at the grays, all presidents were routinely implanted. This made their minds easy to hear, with the result that their most private fantasies, desires, and actions were part of the vast public entertainment the grays had constructed for themselves by implanting humans.

This was one of the main reasons they abducted human beings, to implant them so that they could enjoy them from a distance. Thus some of the most peculiar and most intense people, the ones with the most colorful fantasies— usually deeply hidden—were actually among the most famous creatures in the universe.

This president was a marvelous *seraglio* of sexual invention and hungry, innovative desire. His thought processes were more conventional. Sexy he might be, but he was also an efficient man.

Listening to the flowing whisper of words and watching in their own minds the flickering mass of colors, fantasized human body parts—long feminine legs and white, full breasts, mostly—and the low growls of desire that were the mental "voice" of his subconscious, they saw that he was uneasy about Charles Gunn's murderous request. But would he deny it? Of this they could not be sure. Mind control was not a reliable tool. Also, they did not like to interfere in the action of human will. They had wrecked their own independent spirits by creating their collective. They would not also wreck man's independence with excessive use of the tools of collective thought.

But this was one time that it was necessary. They began to work on the president's mind, to touch it with images of the suffering the scalar weapon could cause.

As the collective mind of the grays concentrated on the president's decision, they failed to address the building crisis in Wilton, or to see just how serious it was, and Conner's death began to come closer and closer yet, as the fatal hours passed.

TWENTY-TWO

ROB LANGFORD PUT DOWN THE phone. "We've got orders," he said to Lauren. "First, we are to assume that Colonel Wilkes is in the area, second that he is definitely here to kill this child. We are to protect the child at all costs, and deal with Wilkes in whatever way is required."

"What does that mean?"

"Find him, kill him."

"Wait a minute on that. Are these orders in writing?"

"No, they are not."

"I don't think murder is such a hot idea. I mean, if you don't have a written order that is definitely legal, that is way out of line."

"Let me deal with Wilkes. You concentrate on the kid. That's the way it ought to be, anyway. What we are going to do is uniform up—or rather, I am—and pay an official visit. We will seek cooperation from the parents."

"How far along is Mike? Do we know?"

"We do not."

"What if these folks don't like the Air Force?"

"Our objective is simple. It is to determine if there is an extremely smart child living on Oak Road. If not, then we extend our search to the local schools. Assuming we identify the child, we provide information to the parents and put them under surveillance protection. We must not do anything that might cause these people to resist the approach of the grays to the child."

They went to the traveling officers' quarters where Rob had a suite. She remained in his small living room while he changed.

Rob was an attractive guy, and she wanted, she was finding, to do more than sample him the way she had been doing with men since she'd started this job. In fact, she could get serious with this guy. In fact, she thought he was the best man she had ever met.

He was also the most dedicated to his mission and the most businesslike.

They drove off the base and through fourteen miles of slowly worsening weather, passing through the town and going onto the Bell campus. On the way, they phoned all four Oak Road houses. They got three answering machines and a non-answer. So everybody was where they were supposed to be, which was working at their various occupations on campus or attending school.

"We'll try the physics guy first. His discipline fits best, I think."

"The baby's not our target."

"No. It could be one of the two teenagers, the Keltons, unless Adam was lying to you. The other three children seem too young."

"He was lying."

"Maybe Oak Road doesn't even figure in it, then. Maybe the whole thing was a feint in anticipation of some discovery they knew Wilkes was about to make. They directed his—and our—attention to Oak Road because it doesn't matter."

She felt a shiver of unease the moment the words were out of his mouth. "My sense of it is that Oak Road is very damned important."

"They don't make mistakes."

"Adam made one. He killed my father."

"That's true enough."

"So they do."

"What do you think they'll do if they lose the child?"

She thought about it. "I get a feeling of tremendous rage."

"Are you in touch with them now?"

"I'm not sure. I think I might be." She shuddered. "Sometimes I feel sort of as if I am. As if I'm part of a great sorrow. I think that's the heart of the grays, the way I perceive their collective being."

"That's chilling."

He turned the car into a parking lot, beyond which was a neat white sign with black lettering, SCIENCE HALL.

It was a towered old brick pile, Bell's science center. The enormous windows were designed to gather light, from back in the days before electricity had come to rural Kentucky.

According to a schedule affixed to his door, Dr. Jeffers had been teaching until five minutes ago, so they waited in his office. He had no secretary and the door wasn't locked. Inside, it was surprisingly uncluttered for an academic's lair.

"Uh oh," Rob said, picking up a book from the professor's desk.

"We have to expect them to be in a tizzy about UFOs. Look what just happened."

"Well, we have to stay far from that topic."

Ten minutes passed. Rob remained composed but Lauren did not wait well, and she got progressively more and more nervous. How could he be so collected? He was like too many military people, in a certain deep way resigned to fate, a fault that, in her opinion, came from living by orders.

"Maybe we should try the school," she said, somehow keeping herself from screaming it at him.

At that moment a short, quick man came through the door. His eyes fixed on Rob's blues. "Hello?"

Rob went to his feet. Smiled. Extended his hand. "Good afternoon, Dr. Jeffers, I'm Colonel Langford."

"The UFO!"

"Excuse me?"

"You're here about the UFO, yes?"

Rob shook his head. "I'm not aware . . ."

"We saw a UFO. There's videotape. Our whole neighborhood saw it. There was an Air Force jet chasing it."

"Uh, I don't think we do that."

Rob was really very impressive at this.

"We're here to talk about gifted students."

"Gifted students?"

"There's a new program, and we're informing science departments all over the country. Seeing as you're head of the physics department here at Bell, and we've got Bell on our list, we decided to come on over."

"On your list?"

"We're from Alfred," Lauren said. "I'm in procurement. He's—"

"Traffic-control supervisor. I make sure our trainees don't run into each other. We've volunteered for this mission, actually."

"What mission is it? I'm not understanding."

"The Air Force is looking for a few very gifted, very extraordinary students. Unusual. Freaks, even. That smart."

"This is Bell College, nobody here is smart. I'm not even particularly smart. In fact, I'm not smart at all, and certainly my students aren't. They're a bunch of idiots, actually."

"Ah. We always thought—"

"A beautiful campus does not mean smart. It only means lots of red brick and white columns."

"What about that other school?" Rob asked. "The professors' kids?"

He leaned back in his desk chair, stared at the ceiling. "Actually, my neighbors have a sort of monster. Aggressive, peculiar, frenetically loquacious for age eleven. Builds remarkably detailed model trains."

This didn't sound promising to Lauren, but Rob said, "Should we interview him? It could mean an appointment to the Air Force Academy."

"Somehow I don't see Conner in a uniform. He's . . . anarchic. I really find him quite disturbing, but now that you mention it, he is pretty much of a genius."

Now it sounded promising. "Can we meet him?" Lauren asked.

"His father's over in the psych building. Daniel Callaghan.

Or he could be off fucking some administrator. Apparently he does a bit of that."

What a bitter man this was. Bitter, mean little man. "So he's a monster and his father's a womanizer. Has he got a mother, or has she killed herself?"

Rob shot her a frown, but she couldn't help it. This was a very nasty little man, and she wanted him to know it.

"Surprisingly not. Actually, I'm being mean, which I suppose is what's got your back up. I am rather frustrated, I'm afraid." He held up the UFO book. "I believe in this, which has demoted me from CalTech through the middle Ivies to Bell. I thought you were here about our astonishing, wonderful UFO. I thought everything was about to change. Instead, you're here for some totally conventional and annoying reason. The Callaghans would never let that precious child of theirs anywhere near the military. At least, I hope not. I suppose I was trying to scare you off, to preserve them from a temptation I don't actually trust them to resist. Truth be told, he's the most marvelous human being I have ever encountered, and I bless the day we happened by sheerest chance to move next door."

She knew for certain, then, that they had found the child of the grays. She thought of all the generations of effort that must have gone into his creation, of the struggles in the night, the long and careful thought of those strange, exquisite minds, and all the people who had suffered their bruising attentions, all for this person with the euphonious name of Conner Callaghan.

She knew, also, that she had more than a little of Adam still within her, whether due to some arcane connection devised by the grays or from her own beating heart, but she felt at that moment that, without question, she would give her life to save him.

Rob had flushed and grown silent. In his silence, he had taken the book from Professor Jeffers. *UFOs and the National Security State,* he said. "What does this mean?"

"Essentially that another academic has been marginalized for promoting folklore as fact. However, it's actually an expertly written and devastating indictment. By careful and scholarly inches, it proves without question that the government is engaged in a cover-up of the UFO phenomenon. So what would you do with him, Air Force people, shoot him, get him fired, trump up some charges against him?"

How extraordinary to sit here and see this man suffering like this for a truth he believed in—and to know that he was right, to know it better than he did, and to still lie to him, and curse his innocent soul and condemn it with your lie.

"Dr. Jeffers," Rob said, "we'd like to thank you for your time and help. We'll contact this family in due time. Who knows, perhaps Conner Callaghan will solve the mystery for us." He handed back the book. "I've always thought that the Air Force hid a lot of things that it shouldn't. Maybe about this. But it's not my lookout, unfortunately."

He gave the wild-haired professor a grin that made his face explode into gleaming, twinkling boyishness.

On the walk to the parking lot, the snow was more persistent.

"That was pitiful," Rob said.

"Why don't we just tell them?"

"You don't know? Even yet?"

"Sure I know. You tell people that something is going to invade not only their space but their actual, personal bodies, they are going to panic. I'm panicked, just thinking about it. If there was any viable alternative, I'd take it."

"I think that's how we all feel. But our next step is to meet this family. Because if we found this kid, we can be sure that Mike has found him, too."

"Maybe the grays will attack him."

"If he showed up with a gun they'd probably abduct him and barbecue his damned brain. But what if he's more indirect? They have their limits, Lauren, as you must know."

"Look, I don't know how to protect him, either, okay! And it's winter, it's snowing, and it's starting to get dark, so one of us had better come up with an idea. How about it, boss?"

"I'm not the boss. You're the one closest to the grays. You're the boss."

"Fine. I say we go out to Oak Road. Take it from there."

First they returned to Alfred. Rob threaded his way around to the parking lot closest to his billet and went up to change again. After Jeffers's reaction, he no longer felt that the uniform was such a good idea.

She sat in the car and listened to the radio, which told the story of the onrushing storm.

TWENTY-THREE

"HI, CHRIS," KATELYN SAID. SHE was quite surprised to see him. The Jefferses usually called before they came over. As he entered the foyer, snow swirled behind him and he brushed off his coat. He looked extremely solemn, she noticed. "Are you okay?"

"Where's Conner?"

"Downstairs designing a train wreck. He had an unpleasant day, apparently. Why do you ask?"

"We need to talk. Where's Dan?"

"Dan," Katelyn called, "Chris is here."

"Yo. Hey there," he said coming in from the kitchen. "Whassup?" Then he saw Chris's face. "What's wrong?"

They went into the family room together. The TV was blasting. Katelyn turned it off.

"I got the classic visit from the Air Force today."

What was he talking about? "What visit?"

"You're not conversant in the UFO literature, of course. You've never read a word of anything I've given you."

"That would be correct," Dan said.

"I got a visit from the Air Force." He looked from one of them to the other.

Katelyn had no idea what to say. She was at a complete loss.

"All right, let me background you. There is this legend that when somebody has a serious sighting or gets video or something like that, the Air Force secretly investigates. Do you follow that?"

"Yeah," Dan said. "Of course."

Katelyn felt kind of queasy. She wasn't sure she wanted to hear this.

"Okay, so I went back to my office after class and who's there but this Air Force colonel and this woman—my God, this *woman*!"

Not another one down, Katelyn thought. "Is Nancy at home? Is she aware of this woman?"

"Yes, she'll be over in a minute. The baby's going to sleep. But I didn't want to wait, and you'll see why in a second. Just listen. Okay, so I come in and the colonel is looking at *UFOs and the National Security State,* which I believe I foisted off on you last summer."

"Okay," Dan said. "Ended up on the shelf with *Trailer Park Ghosts,* and *Bigfoot: First American,* I'm afraid."

Chris's voice had a curious, measured quality to it, so different from his normal tone that Katelyn felt a twinge of concern that he might be sort of crazy just at the moment.

She did not want him to be crazy here. She and Dan were trying to work their way past the Marcie incident and having trouble. She wanted to let him make love to her, but so far had been unable. Unable just a couple of hours ago.

"Anyway, I have a prediction. These two folks are going to show up right here at this house sometime very soon, and they are going to ask to meet Conner."

That focused Katelyn at once. "That'll be the day," she said.

"The man is this very big, tough-looking type. But fatherly, sort of. You know this guy is in on the secrets the second you lay eyes on him. Very imposing figure, indeed. The woman—well, you have to see her. She radiates something and it is weird. If I ever saw anyone who might be an alien in human form, it's this woman. She has these big, staring eyes and she is very, very still. She just sits there staring at you, and you get these bizarre feelings, like she's penetrating your mind, somehow."

This was all beginning to sound more than a little crazy, even for Chris. "You're scared," she said. "Tell us why."

"I didn't realize at first what was going on, and I slipped. I told them something I don't think I should have. About Conner being a genius."

"But they were there asking about the UFO," Dan said, "so what does it matter?"

"Oh, no, they never mentioned the UFO. Of course not. That isn't the way these things are done. They were asking if we had any physics geniuses at Bell for some kind of Air Force program."

Katelyn laughed, she couldn't help it. He glared at her, though, and she stopped.

"I've had enough laughter," he said in a low voice. "The point is—"

"They didn't actually mention UFOs, though?"

"No, Katelyn, they did not."

The phone rang. Katelyn got up and took it in the kitchen. "Hi, Nancy."

"It's snowing too hard, I'm staying put. Has he told you?" Nancy asked.

"He thinks the Air Force is interested in Conner because of the UFO. He's not making a lot of sense, Nancy." She did not tell her that he sounded like he was on his way around the bend, not with a little baby for her to worry about. Anyway, he'd probably be fine in the morning. He had these flights of weirdness every time a big UFO report appeared on one of the crazy-person Web sites he haunted.

"The reality part is that the Air Force is looking for geniuses for some sort of program of theirs," Nancy said. "The Chris part is that they're secretly investigating UFOs."

"Well, then, I'm glad he told them about Conner. Conner could use more stimulation."

"Be careful, Katelyn. This is some kind of military thing. I'd make certain that you can supervise Conner at all times."

Katelyn had no real problem with the military. But then again, she would protect Conner and Conner's mind from any kind of intrusion at all. "For sure," she said.

"Is Chris drinking, by the way?"

"No, he didn't ask and I didn't offer. Dan got tanked at the Peep the other day and I loaded the liquor into the garage attic."

"Over the Marcie thing, yeah, I heard."

God, this was such a little place! "You mean, the fact that he got tenure?"

There was the briefest of silences, then Nancy said, "Congratulations, by the way."

"We're holding off on the official celebration until after the official announcement. You want me to send yours home?"

"Yeah, please. Before the UFOs come out."

She went back into the living room, where Dan and Chris were staring at each other like two people at a funeral. "Momma called, Chris. Time to go home."

"Katelyn," Dan said, "I'm what they call an abductee, and so are you."

She sat down. "That again. Okay, Dan, it has to do with folklore, not with reality. There's nobody being abducted by aliens because there are no aliens, at least not here at the moment. I'll grant that the video is strange, but we are in no way involved."

The doorbell rang—and sent a shock through her. Silence fell. Dan jumped to his feet, strode off to answer it.

Katelyn brushed past him. "I'll get it."

She swung the door open.

A QUARTER OF A MILE away, Mike Wilkes crouched watching the Kelton house. He was freezing cold, despite the fact that he'd bought boots, gloves, and a black Eddie Bauer jacket. He knew the house's layout, and by nine he also knew that the boys both slept in the same room, that the dog was a Doberman, and that nobody in the house was in good enough condition to match him, despite the boys' age advantages.

Lights flickering drew his gaze to the road. A car came, moving slowly in the snow. He slid back a little, lest the lights reflect on the lenses of his tiny, light-amplifying binoculars. He did not recognize the vehicle, but he could see two dim figures inside.

The lights went out abruptly, and he was sure that it had stopped around the bend. That would mean that it was either at the Jefferses' or the Callaghans' house. That was of interest, and he had to find out. He left his position but remained behind the tree line as he worked his way to a location that would enable him to see the last two houses on the road.

OVERHEAD, THE THREE THIEVES SAW the radiant energies of all the bodies on Oak Road. Given the alteration of the deadly satellite's orbit, they were on full alert now. Below them, they observed the shimmering darkness that was Colonel Wilkes moving among the trees. The Thieves were uneasy about Wilkes being out here. But he showed no interest in the Callaghan house. The collective had instructed them to let him proceed, as long as he didn't threaten Conner directly. In fact, it was eager for him to proceed. Maybe he had bought their little trick.

MIKE RETURNED TO HIS ORIGINAL position. He had wanted to see if it was a motor pool car. It was not. Not only that, it was in front of the Jeffers house. His conclusion: continue with his plan.

KATELYN WAS THUNDERSTRUCK TO SEE the very people that Chris was talking about standing on her stoop. They were snowblown and miserable looking, and she immediately let them in.

In the family room, Chris, smiling tightly, introduced them. He was at least partly right about the appearance of the Glass woman. She had huge eyes, but they worked well in her face. She was a beautiful woman, and Katelyn knew instantly that her friend Colonel Langford was head over heels in love with her. Was she weird? Not at all.

They began a spiel about a special Air Force program for the very brilliant.

"Now," Katelyn said, "let me get this straight. You put Conner in this tutorial program. But he does or doesn't have to commit to the Air Force Academy?"

"Oh, no," Miss Glass said, "no commitment at all. What

will happen is that I'll visit Conner daily and work with
him in these accelerated concepts we've been referring to."

"And back we go," Dan said, "around the circle again.
Let me be blunt. We want, in writing, an exact description
of what you intend to do with Conner. And we want to be
physically present at all times when you are with him."

"And why don't you just tell the truth about this?"
Chris said.

Lauren Glass turned to him, and for an instant Katelyn
saw a flicker in her eyes that was most definitely not normal. Katelyn thought she knew why. This girl was also
super-bright. There is an aura around such people. They
are not the same as the rest of us.

"The truth is that we're in trouble with some important
classified problems, and the country needs its very best
minds to work on them."

"Is it weapons?" Dan asked.

"Sir," Colonel Langford said, "I can only repeat that we
cannot go into detail."

"Not with us," Katelyn said, "but with our eleven-year-
old son. I don't think so."

"Yes!" Chris said. "Way to go!"

Katelyn watched Lauren Glass grow very still, then saw
her lips go into a line and her face become pale. The big
eyes glittered with suppressed rage.

"Folks, I'm sorry, but I think we're ready for you to
leave," Dan said. "Because I think that you're here because
of that UFO and aliens and abduction and all that sort of
thing, and the fact that you're trying to involve our son just
plain scares me."

"Me, too," Katelyn said. She stood up. "So let's just call
it a night, shall we? And don't come near our son, because
if we find out you're trying to approach him, we're going to
report you to the police."

They gave each other frantic glances. "Ma'am, sir—we
can talk to him. We can approach him. We have the right."

"Okay, that's it," Dan said. He went out across the hall and
upstairs, and Katelyn suddenly knew what he was doing.

"Dan!"

"Ma'am, your son is the most intelligent human being

presently alive," Lauren Glass babbled. "Please listen to us, because I am uniquely capable of teaching him what he needs to learn."

Dan came rushing back with his hand thrust in his pocket.

"My gun is bigger than your gun," Colonel Langford said with frightening nonchalance. "I want to see that thing on this table right now." He pointed at the coffee table. "Right now, Dan. Do it!"

Dan took the pistol out and put it on the table.

"You're right," Langford continued. "This does have to do with certain extraordinary secrets."

"At *last*," Chris said.

"I remember me and Katelyn being brought together when we were kids. Being brought together in this dark, womb-like place. And I think you might know something about what this was."

"I have some odd memories, too," Katelyn said. "But nothing . . ." She trailed off. She didn't know what more to say.

"We believe that you were abducted together, so that, by a process we don't understand, you would inevitably later marry and have Conner."

Katelyn's mouth was so dry that she could hardly speak. She didn't remember anything about any aliens when she was a kid, and she hadn't even known Dan back in Madison, but she had gone from being furious at these people and scared because they were obviously a couple of stinking liars, to a sort of nauseated dread. From the dark, in other words, to the very dark.

"And Conner is the smartest person in the world," she said.

"There could be others, of course. But he must be among no more than a very, very few. Certainly, in this country, yes."

"That part doesn't surprise me. But as far as me and Dan—I met Dan years after we lived in Madison. So that's all conjecture."

Again, Lauren Glass smiled. She was a person with a thousand different faces, it seemed to Katelyn. This one combined what appeared to be contempt with anger, thinly masked beneath the grin. And the more you looked at her eyes, the odder they got.

"Conner's a staggeringly good physics student," Chris said. "He's doing advanced graduate-level physics at the college and his work is . . . well, beautiful. The grasp of math is a lovely thing to witness."

Langford spoke, his voice dense with authority. "Dr. and Mrs. Callaghan, what has happened here is that your child is intended to be the point of contact between mankind and a very old, very brilliant, and very advanced galactic civilization."

Katelyn felt suddenly horribly dizzy. Then a sort of bomb seemed to go off within her. Did this mean that Chris's nonsense . . . wasn't?

Something came rising up from deep within her that seemed like a kind of release, as if some part of her had been in a trap and was now free.

To her own amazement she reached up so quickly that she didn't have a chance to check herself, and slapped the colonel across the face.

Nobody said a word. Then Dan began to shake. For an instant, it seemed as if he was having a full-bore seizure, but it emerged into silent laughter. His eyes were closed tight, tears filling them.

Lauren Glass had cried out softly when the slap had taken place. Now she sat still and silent, rigid in her chair.

Rubbing his cheek, the colonel said, "It's an understandable reaction."

"I'm sorry! I just—Dan, will you stop that!"

He took a deep breath. Another. "What do we do?"

"What do you do?"

"With our little boy? Who is he? Who are we?"

"Let me give you a piece of advice," Langford said, "you just take things as they come. Don't worry about anything happening to your boy. He's well protected."

"He needs to be protected?" Katelyn asked. But then it seemed a rather obvious question. Of course he needed to be protected, and so did his secret. "I don't want anybody told this."

"Oh, no. Not at all. We tried to avoid telling even you."

"This should be public knowledge. It's immoral to hide it." Chris's face was alight with zeal and excitement.

Katelyn had a sudden, chilling thought that he might go on TV with that stupid video the Keltons had made. "Conner's life probably depends on hiding it," she told him. "Think about it. Think how many different fanatic groups would want him dead. How many governments would fear his power."

"I hadn't considered that."

"Announcing the most amazing railway accident in the history of this or any other century!" There stood Conner, his shirt smeared with model paint and his tattered engineer's cap on the back of his head. He glared at them. "Doom on the railways. Come and seeeee . . ." Then he saw the two strangers. "Oh. I'm so sorry." He came into the room.

"This is our son, Conner," Dan said. "This is, uh, Mr. Langford and Miss Glass. They're from the, from, ah—"

"We're from St. Francis Parish, Conner," Colonel Langford said. "Soliciting for a fund drive."

"I don't guess this is the right moment for a train wreck, then. It's quite amazing, though."

"Conner has a train set," Dan explained to the two wondering faces. "He often builds staged railroad accidents."

"I guess Catholics wouldn't approve, somehow," he said. "We don't actually go to church—or, oops, perhaps—"

"We know that, Conner."

Conner took a step back. He had noticed a sense of winter that clung to them both. They were not pleasant people to be around. But all suspicions immediately dropped away when the colonel said, "We'd love to see the train wreck."

"Great! I've been working very hard."

"Conner, did you do my homework?" Chris asked as the adults followed him down into his basement room.

"*Absolutment,*" he said. "I've got a new way of integrating the calculus, boy-o."

"What are you talking about?"

"I have *no* idea! Look at it and see if it flies." He crossed his room, picked up a badly tattered notebook, and thrust it into Chris's hands. "And now, may I present, the Wreck of Old Ninety-seven." He looked up at Lauren. "It's a metaphor," he said, "of my day."

"Conner, this is beautiful," she said, looking over the train board. "Oh my God, Rob, look at this. Look at the detail!"

"Glad you like it," Conner said. There was something in his voice that Katelyn knew well. These two were going to get a surprise.

OUTSIDE, MIKE WILKES HAD BEEN forced to return to his car, which was hidden about a quarter of a mile away. The snow was getting more persistent, and he couldn't risk it becoming immobilized. He had processed a few of the kids in the town, but he needed the night to finish his work. He wished the damn Keltons would go to sleep. He pulled the car out into the road and drove it for a distance in the giving snow, getting it onto the crown of the road. There would be no plow through here tonight. He decided that he had about an hour. After that, he was going to be forced to abandon this part of the plan.

Not good, possibly even fatal.

WHILE THE COLLECTIVE WORRIED ABOUT the president, the Three Thieves worried about the fact that Wilkes was still close to Conner.

Adam was with them as well, preparing himself for what would happen tonight.

He detected a familiar voice. Lauren was nearby. He shifted his interest away from Wilkes. The collective wanted to let him make his mistake, and that seemed a good idea. But Adam needed Lauren away from here, too, and soon. What was to be done required absolute privacy.

He sailed across the snowy fields and into the yard behind the Callaghans' house. There he built a vivid picture of Lauren's car being covered with snow. He sent this like a drift of smoke into her mind.

AS THE TRAIN MOVED AROUND the tracks, Conner made sound effects, screeching and huffing. Then he touched an edge of track, which sprung open.

"It broke," Lauren shouted.

The next instant, the wonderful black-and-brass steam engine, spewing smoke, struck the sprung track and bounded off into the superbly modeled little town. It churned down the main street crashing into stores, snapping light poles, and sending figures flying.

"Wow," Rob said into the silence that followed this remarkably realistic effect.

"Why did you do this?" Lauren asked the boy.

"So I can build it all up again a new way. Hey. I just got this flash. Are you people gonna want to get back to town tonight?"

"Well, yes, we live in town."

"Then I see in my mind's eye your car getting slowly buried. Or, actually, quickly."

THOUGHTS HAD TO BE PUSHED into Lauren's mind, but the child just sucked them up. Adam regarded him, a smiling, strutting little thing, the aura around his body vastly more complex and colorful than those around the others.

Adam prepared to die.

TWENTY-FOUR

CONNER WOKE UP—AND REALIZED instantly that he was not in bed. He could hear wind and he seemed to be standing.

He opened his eyes. White flying dots. Cold. A leathery thing beside him. This was all impossible, so he closed them again. He opened them for just a second, saw darkness and millions of white dots, and closed them again, tight.

He surveyed his situation. The strange church people had left, he'd gone to bed in his upstairs room. Mom had come in and stared at him and gone all eerie. She'd cried for no apparent reason and Dan had come and they'd hugged each other, then gone across the hall to their room. Sometime after that, he'd fallen asleep.

Without opening his eyes again, he tried to decide what was happening to him now.

Then he knew: he was going down the street in the snow, but he wasn't walking, he was sort of . . . flying.

Which couldn't be real, therefore he was asleep.

Again, he opened his eyes. He could see the house, which was drifting back behind him. This looked like a dream and felt like a dream, but it sounded and smelled like the real world.

Perplexing, in other words—not a dream, yet not possible.

For a second he thought he heard the living room clock chiming, but it was the wind clattering pine branches in

Lost Land, which was what he had named the big woods across the street.

The woods were drifting closer, home farther away. There were three big leathery heads bobbing along around him.

He gasped, started to scream, then forced himself back under control. He had to stay calm, this was contact, it had to be handled with all the skill and intelligence he possessed. *You're up to this,* he told himself.

But he was being *taken.*

Okay, this was bad, he was being kidnapped by these guys, no question, no way to get around it. Is kidnapping ever good? If you're going to be straight, why not just ring the doorbell?

He realized that he was hearing something odd in his left ear, a sort of deep whine, if such a sound could exist. He reached up and touched an earbud. Then he saw that one of the big-headed creatures had an MP3 player. There was no music coming out, though, just this odd noise.

He ripped the earbud out and immediately fell down in a big puff of snow. For a second he lay trying to understand just how this worked. It was *sound,* sound that had caused him to defy gravity. Okay, there had to be some kind of harmonic—or, no, was he crazy, he'd figure the damn thing out later!

The creatures swirled around with their mouths open and their hands on their cheeks. They were not menacing looking. In fact, far from it. They looked scared, too. Then one of them thrust the earbud at him—not toward his ear but toward his hand.

He looked down at it. They hovered and wobbled their heads.

Please, came a sort of nice-sounding voice, the same one he'd heard in his head during the encounter with Paulie.

No, it wasn't on, not out in the woods with no explanation. He ran back toward the house as fast as he could go.

What can we do to help you stop screaming?

He's not screaming, you fool, he's running!

He ran faster, his legs pumping. "Dad! Mom! Help me! Help me!"

The creatures buzzed around him like giant flies. The one with the earbud buzzed along ahead of him, face to face, holding out the earbud.

The house was farther away than he thought. It was hard to make progress in the snow.

Then the creature made a sort of thrust at his head. *Sorry! Sorrrysorry!*

The earbud was in again and he was all of a sudden running in midair. He yanked it out and hit the ground and got up and ran again, his feet crunching in the snow.

He got to the front walk, vaulted the gate, landed in the snow, fell and got up, then slipped on the icy stones and fell harder, rolling off into the drift-choked front yard. He went slipping and sliding up the walk, his feet stinging from the cold. He reached the door, pulled on the handle.

Locked. He rattled it. "Mom! Dad!" He dragged at it. "Oh, please, please . . ." He saw the doorbell under its little light, and moved to press it.

We have to!

We can't!

Conner, come on!

Go in him, you idiot! NOW!

Conner then felt something that few human beings have ever felt. He experienced the sense of something moving inside his own body, slithering up from his gut as if alive.

OF COURSE, THE THREE THIEVES could have turned him off with a little whiff of gas, and taken him wherever they cared to take him, but that was not what this was about. The collective had known that Conner would need to be tamed.

HORRIFIED AT WHAT HE WAS feeling, Conner looked down at himself. His chest and belly were visible, his pajama top having blown open in the wind. Something glowed through his skin, and it was coming up from his chest toward his head. Bright light shone out of his body in the shape of the thing, a snake that twisted and turned inside.

He cried out, he clutched at his chest—and the thing shot into his head and the cry was stifled. His head glowed for an instant so brightly that the whole front yard was lit up. The icicles on the windows reflected blue light brighter than a flashbulb.

Then it was dark. *Real* dark. Because Conner was not anywhere anymore. He was not looking out of his eyes, it didn't feel like. What it felt like was so odd that he could hardly believe it, but the truth was that he seemed to have been swallowed by his body, as if he'd gone down into his own stomach.

This was all so totally new that he could not even think about it, let alone explain it. In truth, he was being affected by a simple electromagnetic field that was being applied with great care to about two million specific neurons in his brain. It wasn't magic. There is no magic. There is only the unknown—in this case, a very old and experienced science possessed of a great knowledge of how bodies and brains work.

Objectively, he recognized that it must be some sort of illusion. Even so, the fear was a claw clutching his heart.

He felt his body turn and begin to move away from the house. No amount of effort would get him back into his head or enable him to regain control of his movements.

He tried to call to Dad, then, in his rising panic, to the police. Nothing worked. He could not make his voice turn on. Despairing now, he thought of how very, very sad his parents were going to be, never knowing what happened to him like this.

Somebody help me. Please, somebody!

We are helping you.

He felt himself turn, felt his feet dip into the snow, felt it blow against his chest.

Now I will remove myself from you, the voice said. *Do not run again.*

In a moment, he began to go up through his body. In another moment, he was seeing through his eyes again.

The wind blew, the pines moaned, snow flew. He had been taken deep into Lost Land, so deep that there was nothing around them but pines. No lights, no houses, just the pale glow of the snow.

We're the Three Thieves but we didn't steal you.

Yes we did.

Shut up!

"Okay . . . I hear you."

Nobody moved.

He was well aware of the mystery he was facing. Remarkable, indeed. Then he saw movement in the woods, and a fourth gray appeared. He was not squat and kludgy like these three. He strode on long legs and his head was more in proportion. Coming through the snow, he was as graceful as a dancer.

He stopped behind the three and raised a long, thin arm, sort of like an Indian chief or something. Conner noted: no muscles. Therefore the skin itself must contain millions of micromuscles.

He took a step toward him. Conner took a step back. He came closer.

Conner yelled as loud as he could: "Get away! Get away from me!" Then he clapped his hands over his mouth, actually surprised at himself. But there was more than one Conner in here, and the other one, the little child alone in the woods, was still really, really scared and did not care about the fact that this was contact, it was historical and damn awesome that it was *him* doing it or any of that.

The other Conner took over and ran, he just ran, he didn't care where, deeper into Lost Land, past the great, frowning trees, into the tangled places where nobody ever went.

The more he ran, the more the panicked Conner replaced the curious Conner, and the wilder and more frantic his flight became.

Soon he began to feel his feet burning. He was getting cold. When he wasn't around the grays, he needed more than just pajamas out in this blizzard. Something they did had been keeping him warm. Curious Conner thought, *Heat without radiance or forced air or anything. I wonder how they do that?*

And he slowed down a little. Now his breath was coming out in huge puffs and his feet were really burning and it was meat-locker cold.

Sobbing like an infant, he stumbled to a halt. He forced the tears down, and finally stood trembling from the cold, rubbing his shoulders.

The wind roared in the trees, and a big gust stung him head to toe with snow. Cold this cold felt just like being burned and he screamed into its howl, but his loudest cry was so small against it that he could hardly hear it himself.

This was idiotic. He was here to think, not cry like some idiot. So okay, he turned around and around, trying to get his bearings.

No bearings.

He hopped from foot to foot to keep the agony down. But it didn't work, he was barefoot in the snow in the middle of a blizzard and wearing cotton pajamas. He was quite familiar with the dangers of hypothermia. If he'd known the temperature, he could probably have calculated to the second just how long before he lost so much reason that he could no longer hope to survive.

He had never thought much about dying before, but he thought about it now because it appeared that it was going to happen to him. He was already getting numb and that was a really bad sign, it was a sign of death coming, he knew that. The next step was the final sleep.

"Dad! Mom! Hey, I'm lost out here! Hey, HEY!"

Ridiculous, meaningless effort.

"Grays! Hey, I'm here! I'm willing to negotiate! HEY!"

Nothing.

How could such a smart kid turn into such a moron? He'd just blown contact, and probably frozen himself to death in the process.

When he tried to walk, his legs wouldn't move. Muscle spasm due to advancing hypothermia.

He did not want to die before he'd kissed a girl or had a paper published, or even driven a damn car.

His pajamas snapped in the wind, his face got more and more caked in frost, and he prayed his usual prayer, "Any

God who happens to be real, this is Conner Callaghan and I could use some help. Thank you! Uh, *really* use it!"

The world around him seemed to grow quiet. He looked down at his right hand. He could see the snow hitting it and bouncing off, but he could no longer feel anything. But he did feel something really funny, a sort of jittering in his heels. It spread through his feet, and he noticed it in his hands, too. Then it went up his arms and legs, bringing with it wonderful warmth like a really good blanket would if he was cold and Mom came in and tucked him in.

Then a face popped out from behind a tree, huge eyes, tiny mouth communicating surprise, fear, concern all at once. *Boy,* Conner thought, *do they ever look like bugs.*

Oh, no.

"I won't run, relax. As long as you keep me warm, consider us friends."

What's he saying?

I have no idea.

Striding out of the snow on his long, thin legs, came the tall gray. As he came closer, Conner could see that his body shimmered with light, as if he was swathed in flickering, ever-changing rainbows. His eyes gleamed with bright reflections of the trees around them even though it was night, almost as if they somehow enhanced light. Then he saw this beautiful figure in the creature's eyes, a person blazing with light of a thousand different colors.

He looked around him, trying to see this person. Then he moved his hand, and saw that it was him. He looked down at his own arm, and the glow wasn't there. Only in the eyes of the gray. He knew about auras, that they were a faint electrical field emitted by the nervous system. The gray's eyes were somehow amplifying its visibility.

As the tall gray came closer, the three short, squat ones buzzed nervously around him.

Okay," Conner said, "my name is Conner Callaghan and I'm going to do this. I hope."

Talk to us in your head. Form the words in your mind, but don't speak them aloud. We will be more easily able to hear you, then.

He sounded actually sort of okay. An ultra-precise voice

that appeared right in the center of your head, as if you were wearing earphones. He felt for that earbud, but it was gone. "How are you doing that?"

I can't hear you!

"WHAT—no. Uh . . ." *How do you do this?*

I don't know. You're the only person we've ever managed it with. With the others, we have to use pictures. They can't hear us talking.

He was quite close now, so close that Conner could see that he had faint, white hair on his head and a wrinkled face.

I am old. We are all old.

Where are you from?

Endless time. We are so old we've lost our history.

What is your mission?

You are my mission.

What does that mean?

There was no response . . . except there was. He hung his head.

Are you . . . crying?

I think so.

Why?

He shook his head, then held out his hands. They were long and the fingers were like snakes tipped with claws. Slowly, his own hands shaking, Conner reached out to him. They stayed like that, their fingers an inch apart, both of them trembling.

The three others came closer. They hovered around the taller one, bouncing slightly in the air when a gust of wind came.

The tall one touched Conner's cheek with the softest finger he thought you could ever feel. It did not just touch you, it made vibrating electric contact with your skin.

Little colt, not ten minutes ago, my touch would have made you run again. But you do not run.

Am I going to get to go home?

Home . . .

You're crying now.

The gray lay down in the snow. The three others hovered over him. Something then happened that was completely beyond comprehension to Conner. They had a black object that turned out to be a jar, which they opened, screwing the top off in a flash. Out of it they drew three gleaming butcher knives.

As Conner watched in stunned astonishment, they cut open the tall gray like Dad gutting a fish. The knives made a ripping sound.

He struggled. They were killing him.

"Stop it," Conner shouted. *"Stop it!"*

One of them turned toward him, brandishing his knife, and Conner backed away, holding out his hands, trying to convey that he would not interfere.

They opened the gray from his featureless groin to the top of his head, splitting his whole body in half. Inside was a swirling mass of lights in a million, million colors, and Conner recognized them. They looked like an immense star field imaged by the Hubble Space Telescope. They looked like the whole universe, somehow contained inside the body of this gray.

They lifted it out, and it wobbled in the air between them, the universe in the shape of a gray, snow swirling around it, flakes blowing into it and away into the vastness of the stars.

There was humming, voices that sounded both innocent and wise, and the notes were so beautiful that Conner gasped aloud, and wanted to cry because this was the richest, the most lovely sound he had ever heard. It was a sound with a scent, almost, as if the flowers of heaven had bloomed.

THE LITTLE GROUP OF GRAYS with Conner were by no means the only ones who were witness to what was happening. On the contrary, there was vast witness in the huge device that carried the main body toward Earth. The gigantic sphere was now two light years away and had been decelerating almost since 1947, when it had turned in the direction of Earth. Large though it was, with its thousand-mile diameter, it was still far too small to be detected by earthly telescopes. In fact, it probably wouldn't be noticed until it was actually in orbit around the planet, because its surface was black, designed to absorb any and all light energy that might reach it.

Inside, a tiny sun glared in a strangely constricted sky. In fact, this was a miniature star just six hundred feet across, built by the grays and capable of shining steadily for a million years, at which time it would explode and instantly vaporize the whole sphere. If they hadn't made it long before then, it wouldn't matter anyway. There would be nothing left in the sphere but dust.

Its inner surface was landscaped to an exact replica of the grays' desert home, with cities made of white houses, domed and looking like adobe. A shield moved around the central sun, bringing fifty hours of darkness every fifty hours to each part of the sphere, the same amount of day and night that the grays had known at home.

As they needed nothing and ate nothing, the grays had no economic life. They had freed themselves from sexual reproduction an epoch ago, then discovered that pleasure is founded in desire, and without reproductive needs, desire fades.

They would have gone collectively mad in this trapped chamber, had they not been able to venture with the earthly triads into the mind of man.

They watched now, sitting in their houses, their heads bowed in concentration, as Adam gave his whole being, all of his experience, all of his knowledge, all that he was, to Conner.

An outline of the child's body stretched across their strange sky, a body filled with stars, and with it came the wind and the night and the snow.

Slowly, as they listened and felt, one of them and then another, then more and more, raised his head and came to his feet. The tall, gracile ones, the short, squat ones, all of them in their unimaginable billions, raised their heads.

Then they ascended from their white cities, rose into the air, and began to fly like so many soaring eagles, and it became clearer what was happening. These creatures, who could neither laugh nor smile, were doing the only thing they could to express an emotion they had not known in many a long age: they were dancing with happiness.

THE STRANGE FIGURE WENT ROUND and round Conner, its head getting smaller, its legs and arms thicker, its body like a fluid of stars, taking on a different shape, the shape of a human being, and getting brighter, too.

Each snowflake that touched the thing now went up in a tiny puff of steam, and it was beautiful, the smoking snow and the brightness, and the humming of the thing as if the wind itself had learned to sing.

Conner began to quake down inside his stomach and up his spine and everywhere, even in his toes and in his eyes, and he realized that the thing was vibrating, too.

"Momma . . ."

The thing came closer to him.

"MOMMA!"

Then the humming was all around him, it was in him and his chest was vibrating with it, and he felt as if he had risen off the ground or gotten very large, and for an instant the snowflakes that had looked like stars around the thing were around him, and were, instead, a whole tremendous universe of stars.

Then it was dark again and Conner had fallen down in the snow. He could not rise. He was completely weak, and when he closed his eyes, he saw the universe in his head, and he saw it, too, when he looked at his palms, in his hands, stars swirling inside his skin.

The three grays pushed at the tall one until his body closed up again. Then he rose in the air between them, and the four of them ascended, wobbling and buzzing, into the storm.

"Hey! Hey, you! I am *still willing to negotiate*!"

It got cold again. Conner could no longer see stars inside himself. The wind howled around him and he screamed in agony and clutched his pajamas around him.

Whump whump whump whump.

Up in the snowy sky, a shadow, black and huge. Then light shining down, a glaring blue-white searchlight beam.

The light shone so bright on Conner that he could hardly look into it. He knew that it was a helicopter, and that it must be here to rescue him, and he got up and wallowed in the snow, into a clearing among the pines, waving and waving and waving and yelling with all his might, "I'm here, I'm here!"

Wind from the rotors hit him and with it came ferocious, lung-shattering cold. He screamed, covered his head, and turned away from the blast.

"Conner! Conner Callaghan!" a voice shouted, barely audible over the churning of the helicopter blades and the screaming of the wind.

It was a man in a helmet, not a gray, coming down a rope ladder from the chopper. He had on a faceplate so you couldn't see his face, but he sounded strong and, above all, normal.

The helicopter roared off into the storm and was gone. The guy knelt before Conner on one knee, and quickly wrapped a space blanket around him. "I'm going to take you home, boy."

Conner threw his arms around the man, who held out his big gloved hands. "Come on, buddy." Conner was not a small kid, but the guy was really tall, and picked him up easily. "We need to warm up those feet real quick."

It felt so good to be carried that Conner just leaned his head against the guy's shoulder, and let himself be cozy in the space blanket. As the guy strode along, he watched the woods slip away behind them.

"Conner, lots of new things are going to happen to you, I suppose you've realized that."

"I'm sort of getting that feeling."

"You're going to have a teacher. You met her earlier tonight. Lauren Glass. I want you to know that you can count on her absolutely."

"Who are you?"

"Somebody else who's concerned with your well-being."

He could feel that it was true, that there was goodness radiating from this man like heat. "Man, I'm glad you found me." He closed his eyes.

"Sleep, child," the man said, and held his head against his shoulder.

Then somebody was shaking him. He stirred, pulled at the blanket—and shot straight up in bed. "Dad!"

"You're having a nightmare, son."

"I was . . . outside. I was outside and—" It felt so good to see Dad there that he just threw his arms around him. "Listen, it was no dream. *No* dream! I was out in the woods, with—"

Conner no!

"What?"

"Conner? Out in the woods? Go on."

"I mean, uh, in the dream. Obviously. Look, let's go back to sleep."

Conner lay back in the bed. Dad lingered. Good, let him stay.

Why not tell him? Conner asked.

In time, Conner, in all good time.

The voice was different, Conner noticed, bigger, somehow, echoing.

Who are you?

The collective.

Okay. What is the collective?

Conner, we are nearly seven billion, and we need your help.

"You're kidding!"

Shh!

"What? Kidding about what?"

"Let's go to sleep, Dad, okay?"

"Sure, Conner . . . of course."

He could hear singing, then, the same tune that he had heard in the woods. He sensed, but in an indistinct, unformed way, an immense shadowy sea, that seemed to be made up of numbers and words and this deep, fleeting song. It was knowledge, he decided, so high and fine that it was a music, totally simple, utterly pure.

"Something's happening to me, Dad."

Dad had tears in his eyes. "Conner, you look like stars."

"I do?"

DAN COULD NOT UNDERSTAND. HE saw his son, but his son now appeared to be a child made of the stuff of the night sky, a child whose body was somehow shining out of the planetarium of his own boyhood, and he heard a song from his boyhood, a beautiful voice humming *"Suo Gan,"* the song by which his own mother had seen him off to sleep when he was scared, just come back from a journey into the dark.

He sat on the bedside, and met the music with the words in the old Welsh tongue of his mother's people: *Huna blentyn yn fy mynwes, Clyd a chynnes ydyw hon . . . sleep, my child, at my breast, 'tis love's arms around you.*

Slowly, as Conner fell into sleep, the stars in his body faded as if with the coming of morning, and Dan was left with his boy gently breathing, lost in the deep sleep that blesses and heals childhood.

Katelyn came, and he stood up. "A miracle," he said. "Katelyn, a miracle." He embraced her.

"What do you mean?"

He could not explain it, not as it had been. "I just think you gave me such a grand kid."

She leaned her head against his shoulder. Arm in arm, they returned to their own bed.

Outside, the storm howled wild, and the footprints of the man in the mask, who had carried Conner home all unseen, and entered the house by stealth and returned him to his bed, slowly filled with snow.

TWENTY-FIVE

AS THE WEE HOURS WORE on, Mike drove the car yet again out of the snow, and went to check the Keltons. He was very annoyed with this family, who were so damnably late to bed. But this time, there was only a single dim light showing out of the upstairs bathroom window.

He trotted out into the broadness of the road. In the distance, he saw a flash and thought perhaps he heard a shout carried away by the wind. A long minute's careful watching and listening brought only the hissing of snow and the moaning of the wind.

He glanced up at the sky. According to the radio, the storm would not abate until morning. That was important to him, because his tracks had to be covered.

He proceeded up the rougher edge of the property, where there would be flower beds in a few months. Any remaining suggestion of tracks would be harder to spot here. He moved to the back of the house, then examined the doors and windows. He found an unlocked window. Carefully, he examined it for any sign of an alarm system. Finding none, he slid it open and pulled himself into the house.

He closed the window behind him. Standing absolutely still, he got used to the sounds of the place. He prepared some ether. His first challenge would be the dog. He was awake now, but would soon fall asleep again, as long as his odor didn't reach the dog's nostrils. The reek of the ether would cover it, however.

He closed his eyes and listened. He had to locate that animal or he had to back out of here. He moved farther in, through the dining room, to the foot of the stairs in the front hall. The dog was sleeping on the landing. The instinct of the watchdog is to block the path.

He took a step, another. Could he get around the dog? He took another step. Now he was on the step just below the landing, looking down at the animal.

The step across him was too long. So Mike had to use the ether. He came down on his haunches and laid the soaked cloth ever so gently over the animal's muzzle.

He waited. The dog's breathing deepened. Now it began to rattle in his chest. Mike could kill the dog. He'd enjoy that, he detested dogs and their reeking shit and their brainless fawning over people who weren't worth a damned glance. Like this family of fatsos. But the dog was too useful. First, the grays couldn't control the minds of dogs. Second, he could—and to great effect.

More confident now, he went to the top of the stairs. The parents would be the lightest sleepers, so he implanted and hypnotized them first. This hypnosis was a simple process, taking only a few moments. The secret of it was that the words were chanted in a rhythm that caused them to be perceived by the subject as his own thought. These people would wake up in the morning thinking violently about Conner. When they came into range of his transmitter in town, the irritation to their temporal lobes would cause the anger to become an uncontrollable obsession.

He went next into the boys' room and did them with equal efficiency.

Just like that, and very neatly after the agonizingly slow start, his mission on Oak Road was accomplished.

THE THREE THIEVES ALL HEARD it at the same time: breath sliding through nostrils, getting louder. Then they saw Wilkes leave the Keltons' house. *Very well*, the collective said, *let him go*. There was a flicker of suspicion, however, when no soul drifted out of the structure. If Wilkes believed that the Kelton child was his target, why had he not killed him?

Of course, he would want to attempt to deceive the grays. He would not want them to know he had done the murder. He would have created some sabotage within the structure that would make the death seem an accident.

The collective had one of the Three Thieves physically observe Wilkes depart in his car. The Two listened to the brown moaning of his mind as he drove away. And then the world was once again silent, and he rejoined his brothers in carrying Adam into Conner's sleeping form.

Adam was not yet fully depleted. There remained in him structures of thought that would organize Conner's mind. These structures were the core of him, held in immensely complex fields of electrons that rested in permanent superposition. As such, they were both in Adam and were Adam, and were also everywhere in the universe, and potentially capable of tapping all knowledge. This core could not be implanted in Conner until the rest of Adam's being had settled in him, or the core would burn the boy's nervous system like an out-of-control nuclear reaction.

The transfer of this last material would result in the permanent annihilation of Adam—in fact, this was the essence of Adam, the part of him that felt real and alive. Here and now, is when Adam would feel actual death.

He was scared. In fact, so were the Thieves. This was the unspeakable thing that, as emotionless as they were, every gray still feared, the final end, wherein even the memory of self disappears and all the long years lived without emotion, and thus without meaning, slide away into useless nothingness.

The whole collective watched, breathless and sorrowful, each one hoping that Conner would find a way to save them, that after this death there would be no other.

The Thieves crossed the yard and slipped into the house via the basement door, and rose quickly through the darkness to Conner. They spread Adam's body, now thin and as pale as a wraith, and guided it over Conner.

Adam had wondered how this would be, to die into another. He'd feared it, and out there in the woods, he'd cried. *Do it.*

He felt himself dwindling into the boy, sifting downward as lightly but as inexorably as dew. All that had enabled him to relate to and understand man, what he had learned from Eamon Glass and Lauren Glass, slipped away into the sleeping child.

He had given Conner all he knew, and his ancestors knew, of the universe. Now he gave him himself. As each tiny bit of his being detached and flowed into the hungry new nervous system that was spreading like a fire through the boy, he felt not regret but an abiding joy, an emotion that he had not known he *could* feel.

Thus, as he died, this ancient creature regained all that time and age had taken from him, the once-rich spirit of the grays with its love of truth and appreciation for the glory of the universe.

It had been eons since a gray had *felt*. Now, though, Adam's experience hummed across the gulfs of space, and the whole collective felt with him the anguish and joy of his death.

They sang in their chains, the grays, as they felt, each of them, a taste of hope that they had not experienced since the day they left their planet and began this long dark journey through the nowheres of the sky.

Simply because they were there, water in the vast desert of his heart, the first tears Adam had ever shed—and his last—were tears of joy.

IMAGES FLASHED ON THE WALLS of Conner's mind, of the long and improbable histories of man and the grays, dancers in a secret dance whose steps were measured in eons. He saw that we, as a species, had lived before, that we'd had another civilization and another science that had worked by different laws, in a time when the light of the human mind had been brighter. He saw the tragic, lingering evening that we have named history, and heard along it the forlorn chanting of the Egyptians as they built boats that would never reach the sky, and the grim, rising roar of human voices that signaled the onset of the modern world, and the ignorant hordes that now marched the Earth, suck-

ing every green blade and morsel. As this vision swept
through him, he listened to the booming drums of time.

And so it was done; Adam, ancient in his days, fulfilled
a destiny that was also a tragedy: he died. The last light of
the wraith flickered in the air above Conner's bed.

Then it was dark.

FOR BETTER OR FOR WORSE, this phase of the grays' mission
was complete. They searched for memories in Conner's
mind that would shield him from the huge thoughts that
now lay hidden within him. Time would be needed before
he could bring them forth and put them to work.

Looking through the house, they saw where he had put
most of his effort, into his splendid trains. They planted his
consciousness in one of his own superbly painted plastic
figures. This would give him an unforgettably vivid dream.

CONNER FOUND HIMSELF IN HIS own toy railroad town, under his own streetlights, and everybody else was horrible
and plastic, staring at him with painted stares. The sidewalk under his feet was plastic, the trees made of foam. A
shrieking rose, and his own train screamed past, impossibly immense, electric fire roaring under its wheels.

He was right in the middle of the street and he couldn't
move. The plastic faces of the people around him stared,
expressionless. Then he saw a huge, glaring giant looming
back in the shadows of the sky, saw his own hand, now gigantic, come down. He heard a length of track screech as it
came loose.

He was trapped in his own train wreck, somehow part of
one of the plastic people, as stiff and still as they were. He
wanted to run, he was desperate to get off this street because he knew what would happen. But he could not run.
He watched in fixed horror as the train's headlight flickered
among the trees to the left, as it came roaring around the
bend, and with a curious grace leaped off the track and
sped toward him, its wheels churning, the headlight a cy-
clops eye.

Then a warm hand was on his forehead.

Mom was there.

"Hey, mister," she said, "you're gonna wake everybody on Oak Road if you don't stop running that train."

"I—oh, wow, I dreamed I was in the train set during the wreck!"

"*In* the train set?"

"I'd become one of my figures. I couldn't move and the train came right at me!"

She hugged him. "Oh my love," she said, "Mom and Dad are always here for nightmares."

He felt the depth of her love, then, with a power that he never had before. He adored his mom, she was the most beautiful, the smartest, the nicest—she was like Dad, very much the best.

Unseen now, the Three Thieves guided his mind back to a memory of a certain spring day long ago, when the lilacs were bobbing on the lawn and the leaves all were new, and he had come from glory, a tiny, secret spark, and gone gliding down into the house and saw her sleeping, her belly big, and gone closer, and entered into her, and lay, then, in the cradle of her womb.

"I love you, too," he said. It felt so good to hug her, it felt like floating halfway to heaven.

DAN ALSO REMAINED AWAKE ON this restless, uneasy night. He was determined to prevent the aliens from abducting his son. As he listened to Katelyn speaking softly to Conner, he felt an isolation that made him sad. She had been trying to forgive him, he knew, but there was a coolness in her now that even his most tender efforts—kissing her, speaking to her of love—could not seem to cure. He loved them, both of them. And yet, he did not feel free to join them across the hall, when they were in such intimate communion.

To avoid dealing with his couple crisis in the middle of the night, he turned his mind to what the Air Force people had said. Strange, strange stuff. Lies, of course, on some level.

He would protect Conner from them until they told him the truth. There were dark corners in this world, and Conner was not going to fall into one, not as long as his dad had anything to say about it.

Too bad Katelyn couldn't handle the idea of being an abductee. What of it, it happened to all kinds of people, just read the books. The notion that people only remembered their encounters after being hypnotized by UFO researchers was, he had discovered, a lie, and a sinister one at that.

And yet, she had a point. No matter that he now believed it, because these two officials had confirmed it, how could anything like this be real?

He closed his eyes, but sleep did not come. Sleep was far away.

His mind returned to Katelyn. She had said that she was past it, that she understood. They had made love again, and it had been sweet, but not as sweet as ever. There was a thin sheen of emotional ice that just would not melt, and he thought now, at this vulnerable hour, that maybe it was the beginning of saying good-bye.

Too bad he hadn't been able to keep these thoughts away. He opened his eyes again. She was singing in there now, in her high, haunting voice, a lullaby. It was better than the one *he* had sung, and he was sure that it was helping Conner more.

Did she secretly want separation, perhaps even divorce? No—and yet, maybe yes. Maybe she hadn't articulated it to herself, not thus far. But she would. He feared that she would. She was the best person he had ever known. How had he *ever* busted this up? You were not going to find another Katelyn, mister, not in this lifetime. And Conner— how could he live without Conner? Conner claimed a huge part of him, would of any father. He couldn't give that up. Fatherhood and husbandhood had become his meaning.

He heard her stirring out of Conner's room. Rather than confront her now, he feigned sleep. He heard her come close, felt her sit on her side of the bed, and heard her sigh. Then she slid in beside him. She turned her back. He lay in silence for a time, then reached over and touched her shoulder.

She didn't offer any sign that she was even aware of his touch. The night drifted on. In a little while, though, he was aware of movement in the room. When he opened his eyes, he was surprised to see Conner.

Silently, his son came to the bedside. He looked down at them. Dan had seen him before as a child made of stars, but he was ordinary enough now.

"Conner?"

The boy smiled a little, said nothing.

Katelyn stirred. "What's going on?"

Conner reached over and took her hand, and then took Dan's hand, and held their hands together. They remained like that, silent in the deep night, a family sailing the ocean of the unknown.

PART EIGHT
SECRET SOLDIERS

Or ever the silver cord be loosed, or the golden bowl be broken, or the pitcher be broken at the fountain, or the wheel broken at the cistern.

Then shall the dust return to the earth as it was: and the spirit shall return unto God who gave it.

—ECCLESIASTES 12:6–7

TWENTY-SIX

CONNER HUNG AT THE EDGE of the playground, as far from the other kids as he could get. He'd left message after message at home and on Mom and Dad's cells, but they hadn't responded yet and the bell was about to ring and he'd have to go back near the other kids, and he could not bear that.

If he got close to the kids, like, three feet away, he could hear extra voices that were extremely disturbing, because he knew the voices were the kids thinking. What was worse, they hated him, a lot of them, and that hurt his soul.

He remembered last night perfectly well. He'd had something done to him by the grays, using a science so high that he couldn't even begin to touch its meaning. They had changed him, though, and he was marked, and would forever be marked, by the greatness of that hour.

Will had said as Conner came out onto the playground: "Hey, Conner, how's it hangin'," smooth and easy, but his inner voice had screamed, *I'd like to get a knife and cut your heart out, you stupid asshole!*

Look at them playing around now, laughing, horsing around . . . and glancing at him from time to time, sly glances from Will and Kevin and David Roland, from Lannie Freer—even sweet Lannie Freer—who had imagined, that she was going to come up behind him and tap him on the shoulder and spit in his face when he turned around.

She'd done it, too, she'd tapped him on the shoulder and

he had run, it had been like a nightmare knowing what she was planning.

Not all the kids had those thoughts. Paulie didn't, thank God for little blessings. He was only thinking how scared he was of Conner. He was thinking how to convince his parents to move, and feeling sick inside every time he so much as glanced Conner's way. Then he'd smiled and said, "Hey, pal, I ditched the busters, okay? They're gone." He'd snapped his fingers and said, "Poof!" and his mind had said, *Get away from me, you're a monster, get away!*

Then a familiar car appeared at the end of the street. It turned, came this way. Conner tore through the gate and down the middle of the street. The moment Mom stopped, he jumped in.

"Honey, what's the matter? Do you have fever?" *He doesn't look sick, he looks terrified. If they've been hassling him, that damn Paulie, my poor little guy, he's too damn small for eleven, the baby . . .*

He looked at her. Most of the time, her mouth hadn't moved. He pushed up against the door, but it wasn't good enough, he could still hear that sorrowing voice and he didn't want it to be that way, he wanted his mother to see him as strong and confident.

"Conner?" *What's the matter now? Oh I'm so tired, the damn kid . . .* "Honey, what's wrong? Why are you looking at me like that?"

Her face smiled but that was no smile, he knew the truth of it, he knew that his mom wasn't close to being as happy and contented and full of energy like she wanted him to think. She was terribly upset and so tired that last night she'd dreamed about her own funeral.

"You won't have a funeral!" he shouted.

"What? What funeral? Conner, what's the matter with you? Why do you want to go home in the middle of the day?"

"Mom," he whispered, "I love you so."

"Oh, honey, I love you so, too! What happened, honey, why do you want to leave school?" *Why can't he get along, oh but I do love you, I do love you my gray eyes.*

How could he tell her that the kids wanted to kill him? The thoughts came back to him, the ones imagining that they would shoot him, the ones imagining that they would kick him to death, knife him, choke him, but smiling, always *smiling*. How could he tell her about that?

Mom pulled the car over and stopped and turned toward him. "Honey," she said, reaching out her hand, "honey, now, what's the trouble? Why do you need to go home, what happened? What happened at school, Conner? Did Paulie and his friends give you a hard time? Because if that damned kid—"

The angry thoughts that accompanied these words were like brands burning into his skull as she talked. She wanted to slap Paulie, to shake Maggie Warner until she broke her neck, to wade into the class slashing with a sword.

"Mom! No, Mom! It's not that, it's not Paulie. Paulie was okay to me today. It was better than it has been, actually."

"Then why aren't you on your way into English Lit? Why did you tell me it was an emergency, Conner? You terrified me! I adjourned my seminar and came over here as fast as I could. But you're not sick and you're not hurt and you're not in trouble with the kids. So why am I here, Conner? Please tell me."

He tried not to listen to her thoughts, but he did listen, and she was thinking *what is wrong with my child?* and that thought was making her scared.

"Mom, I need to be home."

"Then it's not an emergency? You're just—"

"I need to be home!"

She sighed, then put the car in gear. Then she turned around, heading back toward the school.

"It's an emergency!"

"All right, tell me what the emergency is."

He could not tell her he could hear thoughts, hers included. How could he? He said, "I'm afraid I'll go insane on you, unless I can go home and get some private space."

She took a sharp breath. Then she stopped the car again and sat there for a moment in silence. *Look at his face! He looks insane! Oh, God, he looks like his great-gran. Could it be that he's schizophrenic, too, will we be cursed now with that? Help him, help him God.*

He smiled a glaring, hollow smile.

"Come on," she said, "whatever, you can take the rest of the day off. Let's go home and game together. Would you like to game with me?"

They played a lot of Myst: Uru together but he didn't want to. "You never told me we had schizophrenia in the family."

She was silent for some time. When she talked, her voice lilted like it did when she was trying to hide something. "What makes you ask that?"

He had to watch her lips to see if they were moving, or he was going to keep giving himself away. If Mom knew he could hear her thoughts, she was going to withdraw from him. Not right away, but over time. Anybody would, because of the invasion of privacy. He hunched close to the door, stared out.

"What makes you ask that particular question right now?"

"Uh, it was in science."

"They were talking about schizophrenia in science? Why was that?"

"Abnormal-psych module."

"Dan would be fascinated." *Oh, my Dan, I need you now.* Conner clapped his hands to his ears and forced the scream that urged to get out to become a hiss through his teeth, *sssssss!*

Mom's neck flushed, she gripped the steering wheel, she glared straight ahead. Then she sort of shook it off. She started the car and they continued home.

"Mom, it's not Dad's fault."

"What isn't Dad's fault?"

"Mom . . . you know. It's not his fault."

She almost ran the car off the road. Then she looked at him with her eyes bugging out and her face bright red. *What is this?* Her hand came out and she grabbed his shoulder and she turned him to her. "What did you say?"

"Nothing. I'm sorry."

She stared at the road, tears rolling down her cheeks. "Conner, I think I know why you're feeling so bad. You're feeling so bad because you know about Marcie."

He did not exactly know, not the name. But now he did, because the instant she uttered the word Marcie, a huge complex of thoughts and feelings had poured out of her. They were frightening adult thoughts about sex and things he knew little about, and they made him feel like he was prying into his mother's deepest privacy, and he didn't want to but could not help it.

"Conner, has she been at the house? Has she been there when I was gone?"

He shook his head. She'd turned onto Starnes, which meant that they would be home soon and he could get away into his room and get out of this hell of *thoughts*.

"She has, hasn't she, Conner? You answer me!" *He better not lie because if he lies, he's not my son, not anymore!*

"Oh, Mom, no! NO! I'm not lying and I am your son, I love you so much, Mom, you have no idea!"

She looked toward him. Her eyes were full of tears, now. "You're reading my mind."

He could not lie to her, he would not do that to his mother. But he wanted to, he wanted desperately to. He remained silent.

"You know what I'm thinking!"

He still did not answer.

In her face there were suddenly other faces, flowing one and another to the front with the lazy assurance of carp drifting up from the shadows of a pond. She was a shimmering mass of changing eyes and lips and shapes and hair. She whispered in a voice quite different from her ordinary voice, that he recognized as her soul's voice, her *real* voice, "I know what you're doing and we don't do it, Conner, we hide this. This is a secret of the soul."

Just then they turned onto Oak and then into the driveway, and Conner was very, very glad to open the car door and get out of there, and run downstairs and get some space and not have to listen to thoughts.

"Conner?"

"Gotta go to the bathroom, Mom!"

He raced into the kitchen from the garage, then headed across the family room toward the door to the basement. He took the stairs three at a time and dashed across to the bathroom and shut the door.

His mother followed him. "Conner, are you okay?" *If this is locked . . .*

"Fine, Mom!"

He is not. "I'm coming in."

"Mom, I'm on the pot!"

"Oh, for goodness sake, I'm your mother."

The handle turned, and in the gleaming of the brass he saw people moving in bright rooms. His vision focused and then he was *in* one of the rooms. The Keltons were there and they were in a state of rage, fighting and screaming and pushing each other around like battling animals. Pictures were falling off the walls and their dog was all contorted trying to bite himself—and then Mom came in and she came down to the floor where he had fallen, and he saw a boy walking away down a lane lined with flowering trees and dappled by golden sunlight. He knew, then, what had thrown him to the floor, what agony. That was the lane that led to the land of the dead.

"Mom," he whispered, "I'm in danger."

She held him close to her, and he knew that he had seen something that was going to come soon. When the sun was low in the sky and the bare trees shuddered in the wind, everybody on Oak Road, him and Mom and Dan, Paulie and the Keltons and everybody, even the animals— everybody who lived here—was going to face death.

TWENTY-SEVEN

"THEY'RE FINISHED," CREW SAID. "I observed it to completion, then took the boy home myself."

"When did it happen?" Rob Langford asked.

"Last night, just at two. They instilled Adam's content into the child. It looks like it went well."

"So Adam is gone?"

Crew heard Lauren's grief. "You and Adam have a long future together. You'll find him in Conner. He'll seem like a sort of shadow, I'd imagine, a little like seeing the ghost of the parent in the child."

"But he's . . . in there?"

"Adam is no more. What's in Conner is his knowledge, and the structures of his mind."

"Then my friend is dead."

"I don't think you really have a word that describes his state. He's not alive. He hasn't possessed Conner, he's given himself to him. But there is so much of him in there, of his personality, his being, his—well, essence, I suppose is the closest word—that you're going to feel, when you're with Conner, that you're also with your friend."

"Is that reassuring?"

"It's meant to be."

"Then that's how I'll take it, but what does it mean to Conner? What's he experiencing? He seems like such a very intense child."

"He's confused and afraid, I would think. He'll have

powers he doesn't understand, and that's going to really throw him. Knowledge that seems to have come out of nowhere. It's probably going to be about as stressful as human experience can get. The whole family will be stressed. Extreme stress. Psychotic breaks are possible."

"Have the grays factored that in, do you think?" Rob asked.

"That's a hard one. What do you think, Lauren? What sort of insight do they really have into the human mind?"

She thought over her time with Adam, remembered how profound the communications difficulties had been. "Anything might happen," she said. "My guess is that he'll go into meltdown."

"Then you'll have to help him keep his sanity. He'll be able to communicate smoothly with you, while he's going to find fear in every other mind he touches." Crew glanced at his watch. "I had a little conversation with Dr. Jeffers this morning. Unless this alien sensation is quieted down, Conner's going to have a really rough time." He turned on the TV. "That boy has to have the chance to grow up in peace."

The local station came on, and there sat Dr. Chris Jeffers, blinking into the lights like a disinterred mole. They ran what had become known in the media as the Oak Road Video. It had been on CNN, Fox, even ABC and the BBC. It was all over the Internet, of course.

DAN SAT BEFORE HIS TELEVISION watching *Local Edition*. After Chris had called him, he'd come straight home to see it. Chris had said that his appearance would be a big surprise, but he scarcely believed what he was seeing, his good friend blithely lying like that on TV. The spot might be on a local afternoon newsmagazine buried at 3 P.M., but it would be picked up worldwide. The media had committed itself a long time ago to the notion that the grays were nonsense. They had not liked being shown to be wrong when the Keltons' video was broadcast. The backlash would be ferocious.

Their own dear Chris had become a voice of authority,

and he was lying. It also made Dan jealous as hell, but that he suppressed. Firmly—or, in any case, fairly firmly. "Hey, Katelyn, you think this'll get him a better job?"

"Nancy says that CalTech is reconsidering him."

"Now, that is impressive."

"You don't sound impressed."

"He's lying for dollars, here."

"Well, I—"

"Don't you think that people have some sort of right to know this? My God, he's dirtying his soul, and look at him smile. It's revolting, Katelyn."

"If he tells the truth, what happens to him? The press went to him, remember. They demanded a statement from the head of the physics department. He has no net and a baby to feed."

"He's the believer, and now listen to him."

She went into the kitchen, kicking the door closed behind her. He listened to it swing, and it surely felt like rejection.

IN WILTON, MIKE WILKES BRACED close to the wall of the convenience store. Stinging snow blasted him as he fumbled to make his call. He didn't want to do this again, but he had to. "Hello, Charles."

"Mike! Is this line secure?"

"I'm on a pay phone. I tossed my cell. Any word about this investigation, Charles?"

"I don't see a thing from this end. I'd say that there isn't one."

That was wrong. "I saw them, Charles."

"Well, they weren't from any investigative body I can tap, and I think I cover pretty much all of them, Mike."

So the danger was still out there, and it was beyond the ability of Charles Gunn himself to detect.

In that instant, Mike decided that he had to cut off all contact with Charles. Without another word, he replaced the receiver. He would not communicate with him again until the operation was complete.

He glanced at his watch, then stepped away from the phone. Time was wasting. There was work to do.

He drove through the streets of the town. Too bad this car didn't have tinted windows. A little thing like that could have been so helpful.

He approached the grain elevator carefully. The snow had not been plowed in its drive, only on the road in front. He got out of his car and surveyed the situation. There would be tracks, no matter how he approached the entrance. If a gust of wind blew snow over them, that would simply be a matter of luck. Time was flying, though, and soon these people weren't going to be concerned about a few tracks in the snow.

IN THE OFFICE AT ALFRED, Lauren considered again what Crew had been saying. It looked as if the grays had won . . . whatever that might mean. "So, if Conner—if he's now this extraordinary person, does that mean that Mike's finished? That Conner will always be able to stay ahead of him?"

"Conner is like a newborn baby, confused and frightened and in need of support. Right now, he's more helpless than he was before it happened." He glanced at Rob, who said, "I've had my team in the Mountain burning satellite time looking for Mike. So far, no joy."

Crew took a cell phone call, listened for a moment, then disconnected. The two of them waited, but he said nothing.

AT THE CALLAGHANS', KATELYN RETREATED into the kitchen, largely to get away from watching Chris. He'd warmed to his subject, lying so well that it became agonizing.

Dan came in. "You know, the wonder of the whole thing is that they really are here. I mean, what a thing to know."

"I wish we knew what they wanted with us and I wish especially that those strange military people weren't involved. They make me think it's all terribly dangerous, and Conner is vulnerable in some way that I can't quite understand and that scares me. It's affecting him, too, Dan, and it worries me. I almost thought he was reading my mind this afternoon."

"In what sense?"

"He kept answering my thoughts. It was terrifying."

"Was it—do you think . . ."

"I don't know!"

At that moment, Conner appeared. His hair was a mess, his eyes were swollen, he shuffled along in a bag of a T-shirt. Katelyn tried to hug him but he stared at her fixedly for a moment, then shook her off.

He looked from one of them to the other, frowning.

"What?" Katelyn asked.

"Don't be afraid," he said.

"Are we?" Dan asked.

Conner was watching this sort of darkness that kept flickering between them. He could hear Dad moaning inside himself. Mom's inner voice was crying and crying, like a little lost girl. The darkness flickered, grew more intense, seemed to come out of them, then toward him like a shadow full of claws.

He clapped his hands to his head and shut his eyes and screamed with all his might.

"Conner!"

"You have to stay married, you have to! Mom, Dad, don't you end this family, don't you dare!"

Katelyn stared at him, too amazed even to try to comfort him. His face was bright red, his eyes were swimming with tears, but his voice—his *voice*!

Dan stood slowly, staring at Conner as if he could not understand what he was seeing. "Hey, there, Conner. Take it easy, son."

"You're not leaving me, either one of you. I need you, do you understand? I NEED YOU!"

"Conner, hey! You're outta line!"

Conner pointed at him. "No. You are out of line. Both." He turned and ran from the room. A moment later, music came roaring up from his basement.

"Two-thousand-one time," Dan said. Katelyn came to him. They stood, staring toward Conner's door, silent. He wanted to kiss her, but he was afraid he would feel that coldness again.

From downstairs, Conner's voice came again, a boy's voice but full of something else, something that neither of

them could really identify—a strident roar, fierce and
brooking no opposition. "Do it," he cried. "DO IT, DAD!"

"How does he know?" Dan whispered.

She shook her head.

Dan kissed her hard and clumsily, like a scared teenager.

She did not close her eyes. When he stopped, he saw
tears welling and rolling down her cheeks, and reached up
and touched them away.

They embraced, but not like lovers, like people in a
small boat in great waves.

IT WAS FREEZING ON THE roof of the grain elevator and Mike
was concerned about frostbite, as well as slipping due to
numb fingers.

He had waited until the light was leaving the sky to
come out here. This time of year, the sun hung low in the
west by four, and he hoped nobody would chance to look
up and see the figure on the roofline installing an antenna.

When the transmitter was up and running, he got off the
roof, sliding badly at one point, so far he thought he'd go
over the edge. But he caught himself in time.

Even back inside the structure itself, it was frigid. Also
dusty. He coughed a little, and held a handkerchief to his
face. Leaving the conveyor running overnight had been
more effective than he'd thought possible. He was in a haze
of dust, and since the temperature wasn't much above ten
at the moment, the humidity would be effectively zero. He
should have picked up a face mask at some hardware store.
Well, he hadn't, so he'd just have to live with it.

He hoped that nobody would make the Volvo. As far as
satellite surveillance was concerned, they had probably located his cell phone by now, so they'd be certain he was here.

He wished he believed that this was all going as well as
it seemed, but he had been dealing with the grays for too
long to be anything but extremely uneasy about doing
something they did not want done. If they'd been more
open in their opposition, he would perhaps have felt better.
This way, he could not know where he stood.

ACROSS TOWN, HIS FIRST LITTLE experiment came to fruition. Gene Ralph Petersen had run Petersen Texaco for thirty-one years, and his dad had run it before him. Before it was a garage, it had been Petersen-Michaelson, a stage stop, livery stable, and smithie. Just now, Gene was in the kitchen of his house behind the station. He was rustling up some coffee and fried ham. Ben, his dog, paced nervously. "You want out again, guy, in all that snow? It's ten degrees out there."

Ben stared at him, stared so hard that he stopped what he was doing and stared back. "Ben? Boy?" Was the dog having some kind of a fit? "Hey, Ben!"

When Gene took a step toward his dog, his lips lifted, he let out a window-rattling growl and he leaped at his master like a wolf leaping at a fawn.

Gene was not in any kind of shape at all, and he fell back against the stove, his arms windmilling. He hit the frying pan and the ham flew up in a mess of scalding grease, and he felt fire searing his back as the dog came at his throat.

Like a volcano that had been building pressure, Gene erupted. He grabbed the hot frying pan and slammed Ben with it, but Ben was filled with unstoppable rage, and got a piece of his neck and shoulder before he beat him off.

Screaming, his own teeth bared, he lunged at the dog, and the two of them went down fighting.

They fought and blood flew, and fingers were torn off, and the dog's muzzle was shattered with the skillet, but finally the dog won. Gene lay on the floor, his eyes glazed, his face gray. Ben, his companion of fifteen happy years, bent down and pressed his bloody muzzle into the face of the master he had adored, and ripped it to pieces.

PART NINE

A CHILD IS DYING

Because I could not stop for Death—
He kindly stopped for me—
The Carriage held but just Ourselves—
And Immortality.

—EMILY DICKINSON
   "Because I Could Not Stop for Death"

TWENTY-EIGHT

TWENTY-FIVE-THOUSAND MILES OVERHEAD, an event that would have riveted the attention of every man, woman, and child on Earth—had they known— was taking place. A large and complex satellite, totally black but visible in the brutal light of the sun, was approached by a small, egg-shaped object. This object shone silver, but it was not what it appeared to be at all, a small spacecraft. It shimmered as it approached the satellite, changing into another, much more complex shape. This swung around the satellite and fitted itself neatly over the end that pointed toward Earth.

Inside the satellite, relays sparked, and on its surface tiny rocket nozzles spat bursts of flame. The orientation of the satellite turned away from the snowy center of the United States and toward the line where the land ended, and the coastal waters of the Atlantic began. Then they turned it farther, out over the Atlantic, far from where it could do any harm.

The object released from the satellite became an oval once again, and darted away.

LEWIS CREW BREATHED HARDER THAN he would like, a lot harder. Earth's air had just a half percentage point less oxygen than home, but that difference had a definite effect. Also, his lungs were not accustomed to the pollution here, and they had been deteriorating for years. Now they boiled

and bubbled when he ran. He knew that Wilkes had come
in here within the past half hour, the kids in the Mountain
had called him and confirmed that. Wilkes's car had been
identified as a rented Volvo early this morning, and located
via satellite ten minutes later. Since that moment, his every
move had been tracked.

But why in the world was the man in a grain elevator?
Crew had tried to understand but he did not understand,
and that frightened him badly. He stood gasping, watching
Wilkes climbing down a catwalk from far above.

Still trying to catch his breath, Crew squatted, tightening
the muscles in his legs and back, concentrating his energy
into his solar plexus—then let go, springing up, the wind
rushing past his face, leaping at Wilkes.

He grabbed the catwalk, felt it shake, heard it clatter.
Wilkes stared from the far end, wary, ready . . .

And then he shook the catwalk violently. A wave came
down it, causing it to collapse under Crew's feet. He tumbled through the air and hit on his back. The catwalk
wouldn't have collapsed like that unless Wilkes had done
something to it. It had been a booby-trap and Crew had
fallen for it. Wilkes jumped lightly down.

They had been sixty feet apart, one as ready as the
other. Now they were thirty feet apart and Crew was on his
back, struggling to catch the wind that had been knocked
out of him.

Wilkes straddled him. Crew thrust himself to one side
and rolled out from under his feet. Wilkes stumbled and
shook his head—and moved off, disappearing into the
murk of dust that filled the huge chamber.

Crew peered after him. This was a catastrophe. He prepared to be shot. He had lost. He took the warrior's pos-
ture, legs apart, ready. He peered into the dust, tried to
listen over the maddening clatter of the conveyor.

Strangely, Wilkes didn't shoot. But why not? He was
alone here. Had Mike not realized that?

"Okay, men," Crew said just loudly enough so that he
would be sure that Wilkes heard him. "If I go down, fire
into the flash."

To his left were the four huge storage vats, each fifty feet high with a diameter of thirty feet. To his right and soaring overhead was the elevator itself, an enormous contraption of pulleys and chains driving the bucket conveyor, which rose to a height of about seventy feet, and could be directed into each of the storage vats. Farther off in that direction was a locked office that contained the elevator's controls. The conveyor was running. Why was not clear.

Slowly, Crew began turning around. If Wilkes didn't act, he would head for the door he had come in. The dust would conceal him, too. He was fast, he might make it.

He went deeper into the way of the warrior, gathering his energy along his spine. He had a small pistol in his side pocket, but the grain elevator had been a clever choice, given that he couldn't see four feet in front of him.

Mike must realize that the longer he delayed, the greater Crew's chance of escaping.

Then he saw him, and not two yards away. Wilkes's eyes were baleful, sparkling, rock steady.

Crew leaped at him, extending a powerful punch as he did so. Mike took it in the face and lurched back. But he righted himself, and before Crew realized what was happening, Wilkes's hands slid around his neck. His fingers felt like steel cables, crushing into his neck, making his head pound, pinching off his breath. He sucked as much air as he could manage, and then his windpipe was closed. Wilkes must have seen him gasping. He had targeted this weakness.

Crew got an arm free from beneath Wilkes's weight, reached up, and tore at his ear. For a moment, nothing happened. With all the strength he possessed, he pulled harder. Wilkes growled through his bared teeth. His head twisted to one side, slowly, slowly. Then, suddenly, Crew could not breathe. He saw blackness coming around the edges of his eyes, deep, warm blackness.

Eight thousand miles away in Cairo, the pyramids lay beneath a night sky choked with smog. Around them, the city roared, an onrushing cataract of light and noise. A furtive jackal that haunted the edge of a nearby slum raised its head, cocked its ears, and whined. Dogs in the flat houses that hugged the pyramid compound began to pace.

An old man who had been tending a smoky kerosene heater paused, looked up, then got a ladder and climbed up to his roof.

Crew drew up both his legs, and kicked Wilkes so hard that he flew into the air. He hit hard but rolled, moving with distressing agility. Crew fought for breath, managed to pull himself to his feet. His throat was partly crushed. He cut off the pain as best he could, concentrating his attention in his crashing heart, willing it to beat strong and steady. He waited, watching for movement in the dust, insisting to himself that he would not die here.

After a time, he began to hope that the silence he was listening to was the silence of death. Had he won? He watched a last shaft of sunlight creeping across the part of the floor he could see, sunlight that rendered the wheat dust golden. The smell of this place, the dry, faintly sweet odor of grain, reminded him of home.

He closed his eyes and concentrated on getting strong enough to get out of here. Only after some moments did he become aware that there was breathing that had not been there a moment before, and that it was very close.

Wilkes hammered him in the face so hard that Crew saw an explosion of lights, immediately followed by a curious sort of darkness. He tried to raise his right arm but it would not come up.

Fingers explored around his neck again, this time with tremendous speed and power. With a shuddering crackle, his windpipe was collapsed.

In Cairo now, feral dogs howled, jackals yapped and paced, and the old man in his white soutane and fez crossed his arms over his chest in a gesture that would have been familiar to the pharaohs, and bowed his head toward the Great Pyramid.

Closer to the structure, a guard looked up from his charcoal brazier and frowned. He called to his companion. Both turned toward the pyramid. They saw, along its vast side, a spatter of pure white sparks. Coming as if from the throat of the Earth itself, a vibrating hum shivered the two men from within.

They ran.

Crew was dead. He was still moving, but nothing would enable him to breathe again. Mike watched him, smiling with an artist's gentle amazement at his completed work.

Crew's air hunger increased. His thoughts were distant and unreal. The anguish of suffocation made him frantic, made his sphincters release, and he shat and pissed himself, and rolled in agony on the floor.

Mike positioned himself and kicked Crew so hard that his head, flying back, caused his neck to snap. He looked down at the sprawled body, then pushed at it with his foot to confirm the obvious.

He went to the door, opened it, and took two small bottles out of his trousers. One was cracked and oozing. Carefully, he collected the thick liquid in the palm of his hand. He poured the dark purple contents of the other bottle onto the floor, making a tiny hill of the crystals. Then he poured the glycerin from his palm over the potassium permanganate. He stepped out through the door and was gone.

As he sailed the ancient lays of the Earth, Crew felt absolutely nothing. Objectively, he knew that he was dead, but this had lost its importance.

In Cairo, the pyramid flickered with blue light. People came out onto the roofs of houses, stopped their cars in the streets, stared at the midnight spectacle. Dogs barked wildly, jackals sang, tourist camels boomed, and horses tossed their scruffy manes.

Crew knew he had reached the place of ascension, he felt it as a warmth caressing him. All pain fell away and all memory of pain.

A tourist who had bribed the guards to let him spend the night in the king's chamber leaped out of the sarcophagus as it filled with blistering incandescence.

The old man on his roof moved round and round in an ecstasy of graceful concentration, dancing a dance that had been handed down across the generations, not among the Arab invaders of Egypt, but in the secret Sufi ways that were drawn from the old religion, the hidden science that had last sent souls across the chasm of space when Akhenaton and Nefertiti had gone home.

A light so great that it dimmed the glare of Cairo itself

then filled the air. The very stones of the pyramid glowed as if on fire from the inside.

People screamed, dogs howled, the jackals writhed in agony.

Then, darkness.

All returned to normal. The old man bowed again toward the pyramid. Smiling a toothless smile, he went back down to tend his broken heater.

An image formed in Crew's memory, of the scents and lights and caresses of home. He turned his face heavenward, following the golden thread of love more and more swiftly. Soon he saw a gentle rain of stars, and knew that this was the passing void of heaven itself. For a few timeless moments, he traveled the perfect physics that was long ago devised for the journey of souls.

Then he saw the wheeling immensity of the galaxy, a crystal conflagration of stars in blue, white, red, yellow, green, large and small, spread across the silence.

Below him came the gigantic horizon of a planet, as he sailed out of darkness into the sunlit side. Now he saw broad lands, farms in silver morning.

He let the weight of his love draw him downward. Soon he could make out individual farmsteads, their thatched roofs clustered together beneath ancient trees. Then he could see, far away, the White City shimmering on the horizon, and carts in the roads going toward it laden and returning empty. Dropping closer, he could hear the great auris singing as they passed one another on the road, and their drovers humming the tunes that gentled their raucous dispositions.

He came to his own farm, saw it spread below him, its fields rich with bowing wheat. The love he felt was so great that it made him glow, and he heard voices rise below. They could see him coming, a shaft of light dropping down out of the sky. He heard his sons' shrill voices and his wife's cries of alarm and joy.

Then he was over the cool room, set partly in the earth, where his return would take place. He dropped down though the roof, which felt like a sort of smoke of straw. Below him now was a body on a stone table. It was his own body, indistinguishable from the one the humans called "Crew." It was naked, this body, lovingly groomed.

The next thing he knew, he was looking out of its blinking eyes. The room was lit by flickering candlelight. He inhaled. Perfect air, clear, faintly scented with the odor of his wife. He lay naked on the familiar stone table. His wife, looking tired in her sweated muslin work clothes, gazed down at him.

She bent to him, then, and kissed him long, and he was home.

TWENTY-NINE

A FLASH FILLED THE AIR, as if a gigantic flashbulb had gone off in the sky. Conner began to count, "One, two, three, four—"

"What the hell?"

"Shh! Six, seven—"

A long roar rolled in, full of thuds deeper than thunder.

Conner looked from Dan to his mother. "The grain elevator just exploded," he said. It had to be that, unless somebody had dropped a very large bomb on little Wilton, Kentucky. Nothing else in town was big enough.

The phone rang. Conner snatched it up. "Hey, Paulie! I know. Okay!" He pointed out the kitchen window. Katelyn saw a great mushroom of smoke rising in the direction of Wilton.

Within a couple of minutes, a horn started honking out front. "It's the Warners," Conner yelled. As he stopped at the hall closet to get his jacket, Dan grabbed the video camera.

Katelyn did not want to be trapped in a car with the Warners. She went out behind Dan and Conner. "We'll take our car," she called. But Conner jumped into the Warners' backseat with Paulie and they were off. She and Dan went into the garage and got in their car.

"Thank you," he said. "I consider that a rescue."

"What in hell happened in town, and how do we know it's the grain elevator? What if it's terrorists?"

"In Wilton, Kentucky? Anyway, Conner's always right."

He stepped on the accelerator, seeking to stay close to the Warners' speeding van.

MIKE WILKES WAS JUST STARTING his car when the blast took place. There was a gigantic roar and a flash like a sheet of silver-white filling the whole world. Frantically, he switched on the ignition. The car was already in motion when a large piece of the elevator's tin roof struck it, smashing the windshield and caving in the roof to the point that Mike was lucky even to get the door open. As he crawled out of the ruined car, a segment of conveyer buckets slammed into the snow a foot away. He slid under the car, then, and waited while debris rained down.

When it finally stopped and Mike came out, he saw that the car was a complete wreck. Worse, he could hear sirens. He had to get away from here.

The elevator was burning furiously now, the fire heating his back even from this distance. At least he had accomplished his objective. In a little town like Wilton, a spectacle on this scale would draw everybody who could move, and especially the kids. As he had intended.

He loped in the direction of a line of abandoned stores across the street from the elevator, and ducked down an alley. As he did so, a small fire engine came up and stopped, its horn blaring, its siren whining. It stopped beside the Volvo. As the siren ground down, firemen jumped out and examined the car. An instant later they all looked up—directly toward Mike.

His tracks, of course, his damned tracks in the snow.

He turned and ran, ducking down an alley and out into a disused rail yard. A glance backward told him that the antenna still stood, taped as it was to the tank farthest from the collapsed roof of the elevator. The transmitter would be doing its work, now, and would continue until the tank itself disintegrated.

He threaded his way across frozen tracks. He could not escape, of course, not slowed by the snow and chased by men who were not injured.

It had been Crew in there, *Crew*! They would find the

body. With arson and murder charges against him, the Trust would disappear from his life. Worse, nobody would know for certain if the kid had survived.

CHARLES GUNN'S PHONE RANG. HE picked it up, was told by a young voice that there had just been a major explosion in Wilton. He input his code into a satellite access node on his laptop and chose the correct satellite, then zoomed until he had a clear shot of the town from above.

There was smoke pouring out of a large building. He recognized three circular storage tanks. A grain elevator. He sat staring at it for some minutes. What might it mean? Was Mike in trouble or was he succeeding? He was not reachable by phone, so there was no way to tell.

At that moment, his six-year-old daughter came in. "Mommy says to ask if you want coffee."

He drew his little girl close to him. As he nuzzled her flaxen hair, he punched numbers into his phone. "Mr. President," he said, "the time is now."

"Is it?"

"Yes, sir, we needed it some time ago."

"And it's going to be a purely localized thing?"

"Oh, absolutely, sir. Minimal damage."

"Thank you, Charles." The president hung up.

Charles looked at the phone. What did this mean? He hadn't cancelled the order, surely. No, he would have said something to that effect . . . wouldn't he?

His daughter asked, "Was that the *president*?"

He kissed her.

"Mommy says you're very important. Are you very important?"

"What's important to me is being your daddy, punkin." He lifted her into his lap. She gazed into his eyes.

She frowned. "Are you upset, Daddy?"

He hugged his little girl.

MIKE WILKES NOTED THAT FIREMEN were not only chasing him now, they were making radio calls, and he could hear a higher-pitched siren, then another. They were getting the police.

He'd run out of options. He pulled the plane's remote out of his pocket and activated its GPS. He stopped long enough to input the code series that brought the plane to life. At each stage, he got a positive response. It was out there, thank God, and intact. Then the ETA came in: four minutes and twelve seconds before it could reach this location. *Way* too long, damnit!

LAUREN WAS FAIRLY SURE THAT she could sense Conner in her mind. What was amazing about this was that he was nowhere near this base, he couldn't be. She'd been able to perceive Adam's mind from no more than a few feet away. "I sense something," she said to Rob. "The boy is . . . agitated."

"He's seen the explosion. How do you feel him?"

"It's like remembering somebody in present tense, if that makes any sense."

"Is he in jeopardy?"

"I'm not sure. He seems agitated."

He called Crew's cell phone again and again got his terse recorded message. Then he phoned Pete Simpson.

"We identified Wilkes's car. We located him in the town. I told Lewis immediately. The Mountain says that Wilkes's car hasn't moved from behind the grain elevator."

Rob thanked Pete and hung up. He gazed out the window. On the horizon, there was smoke. "Look, I'm going to go into town."

"I'm going with you."

"Not with Mike at large. I need to get this situation into focus for me first."

She let him go.

BEYOND THE RAIL YARD MIKE could see the center of Wilton. Cars came this way, and twenty or thirty people hurried up the broad street that crossed the rail yard and went past the elevator. At least one or two of them were bound to be

among his human bombs, and they were walking right into
the range of the signal that would trigger them . . . as indeed, was the whole community.

His bait was working efficiently. There was now little
question in his mind but that the child would die.

Outside, the crowd came closer to the burning structure.
Nobody could see the antenna, let alone imagine that it was
there, or how extraordinarily dangerous it was.

The streams from the firemen's hoses made sleet, which
slicked the ground. Sliding, Mike ran toward the crowd,
picking out a woman who was hurrying along with her
daughter.

"Hi there," he said as he trotted up to them.

Her eyes widened as she looked at him. "He's hurt," the
little girl said.

"Oh my God—here, I've got my cell." She began to
rummage in her purse. A police car roared around the corner and came straight toward them across the rail yard.

He grabbed her shoulder, drew his gun, and thrust it into
her face. "Shut up," he yelled. "Don't move!" He glared
down at the little girl. "You move and your mommy gets
her head blown open."

The little girl began making a shrill, desolate noise.

Two minutes and eight seconds before the TR would arrive. Getting aboard would be a near thing. He'd have to
carry the kid.

"Take it easy," one of the two cops approaching him
called.

"Don't move an inch! One inch and she's fucking
dead!"

The woman gobbled in her throat.

The cops froze.

The little girl screamed at the cops, "Help my mommy!"

They stayed like that, and a standoff was just what he
needed.

Finally, a warning warble came from the plane's remote.
Mike was brushed with warm wash from its fans. There was
no frost visible, because the dehumidifiers would be working to remove every trace of moisture from that exhaust.

With a swift and controlled motion, he reached around the mother and wove his fingers through the girl's hair. She howled and kicked and turned red as he dragged her. The remote was chiming, two discordant notes. He thumbed the hatch control.

"Jesus Christ," one of the cops yelled as the stair came down, apparently out of clear sky. But then, of course, with the eye drawn to it, they could see the plane, a faint outline, its lines visible where the camouflage worked imperfectly. It wasn't designed to be invisible from this close, not if you were aware of its presence.

Dragging the little girl by the hair, with her mother walking along, her hands out, begging, her eyes wild, full of tears, he backed up to the ladder.

The child scrabbled at his hand in agony. An odor of urine rose from her twisting, struggling body.

All in one motion, he dropped the girl and climbed into the ship. He jammed at the remote, but not fast enough, he had a cop on the damn ladder. The man was looking up at him, trying to bring his gun to bear.

Mike fired directly into his face, which exploded like a smashed pumpkin when the jacketed Magnum bullet blasted it. The body dropped away and the ladder came up as Mike slid to the cockpit and dropped into the seat.

He hammered buttons, preparing one of the twelve diversions the plane carried. It would eject in ten seconds. Outside, he heard a shot. The plane was not armored in any way and that would do damage, for certain. Immediately, he got an alarm on one of the sixteen exhaust fans. As Mike took the ship up two hundred feet at a sharp angle, the damaged fan shut down.

The diversion ejected. This was an extremely bright plasma, which would draw the eye of everybody in the area. Gunfire erupted as the cops, deceived into believing that the glaring orb was the ship, shot into it.

Resistant to the Earth's natural electrical charge, the coherent plasma shot off into the sky faster than a bullet.

"Holy God," a voice yelled.

"That was a Goddamn UFO!"

Every eye was scanning the sky in the direction the diversion had gone. Mike turned the ship and moved off, quietly working his way out of town.

THIRTY

ON THE OTHER SIDE OF the building, where the main fire deployment was under way, the firemen continued unrolling and charging hose. A burning grain elevator wasn't going to be extinguished. It was a matter of standing by, making certain it didn't spread, and letting it burn itself out with as little damage to its surroundings as possible. So their main interest was the roof of Martin's Feed Store nearby, and the John Deere tractor dealership across the street, not the elevator, which was sending flames at this point well over a hundred feet in the air.

"Captain, we gotta go in there," one of the firemen said.

"Don't do it, Harry, that's an order. You're gonna see the walls go any minute." He grabbed his bullhorn. "Okay, folks, back it up! Get those cars outa there!"

CHARLES GUNN CALLED THE WHITE House. "Mr. President, I need that scalar pulse, sir. I don't understand why it hasn't gone in."

"I don't want to do it, Charles."

Charles's heart quietly skipped a beat. "Excuse me?"

"Charles, I'm not going to pull the trigger on Americans just on your say-so. It's not enough, Charles."

It was as if he was talking to a different man. "Mr. President, the whole future of mankind is riding on this."

"You didn't tell me the truth, Charles. I know the kind of damage this is going to cause, and I'm just not going to do it. How dare you lie to me like that."

"Sir, I didn't—"

"You lied and you were willing to destroy the lives of millions and wreck the country! You're gonna have to find another solution, Charles, this one's too expensive, and I have to tell you, I've got a problem—a major problem, Charles—with your even recommending such a course of action. You don't walk in here and do a thing like this, ask me to wreck my country and try to trick me into doing it."

Charles hung up the phone. He had to take a tremendous personal risk if he was going to cut false orders. There was plenty of precedent for it. Dean Bracewell had done it back during the cold war when he'd moved elements of the Sixth Fleet from the Mediterranean to the Black Sea in violation of *détente* in order to pull an asset out of Roumania. The problem was, there was no real way to accomplish it without getting caught. Reagan had been furious at Bracewell, yelling at him, "The next time you try to start World War Three, mention it to me, first!"

Given the magnitude of what Charles was going to do, there would be more than a White House tantrum. At the least, he'd go to jail for life. Maybe he'd even suffer the death penalty.

So he'd get Henry Vorona to do it. It would be easier for him, anyway, given that he was active CIA. He'd tell Vorona that the president approved, but wanted the orders to flow this way.

Problem solved.

DRIVING TOWARD TOWN, KATELYN AND Dan had fallen into another silence. Despite Conner's pleas, she was beginning to feel that Dan had just sort of slipped out of her soul. She should have found forgiveness for him, but she simply had not been able. Halfway to town, with the smoke now towering before them like a storm in the evening sky, Dan silently took her hand. She let him, but could not think why.

IN THE WARNERS' CAR, CONNER tried to keep the thoughts of
others out of his head, but it was hard. He kept feeling like
somebody else, also. One moment he was himself, the next
he seemed to have a huge, complicated memory of things
that had never happened to him, of flying in the stars, of
being hideously lonely, of something that was terribly, terribly wrong. Except one thing was not wrong: he remembered Amy who was sitting right beside him, as if he'd
known her for a thousand years. He remembered her in life
and between lives, in the green rambles of death, planning
this life together.

He shuddered. How could he be thinking about things
like this? He knew the secrets of the dead and the ages,
knew them certainly. In a flash, he could see back huge dis-
tances in time, to bright inexplicable fortresses and death-
serpents swarming ancient skies.

And he could see the people around him, really *see*
them, and it was wonderful and terrible, it was very terrible, because their secrets were as much a part of him as
were his own.

It was like spying on their souls, he decided, looking
across the walls they had built around their soft central
needs.

"That is so awesome," Paulie said, looking at the rising
smoke.

"Yeah," Conner agreed. It was an act, though. To appear
to be himself as he had been, he had to pretend.

His memories of last night were foggy but he knew that
something very incredible had happened.

"Dad, can you step on it please?" Paulie asked.

"We gotta watch the snow."

At least they weren't all full of hate. They were thinking
about the grain elevator. Mr. Warner was worried about not
getting there in time for Paulie to take pictures. Mrs.
Warner was making plans to keep the boys from going too
close. She was telling herself that she'd yell at them if she
had to. In Paulie's mind there was nothing but smoke, fire,
and eager excitement.

Conner put his hands over his face and totally relaxed, blowing out a long breath. His bones seemed to tickle, and the feeling of the air on his skin changed. He had to learn to tune this stuff out. He'd messed up with Mom and Dad, shouting at them about their marriage secrets.

He could hear their inner voices especially well, Dad's perfectly. He knew that this was because of Dad's implant, and he felt a question now: somebody—was it called the collective?—was asking him if he wanted others implanted. They would implant anybody he wished, and he would be able to hear their thoughts perfectly, no matter where they were.

He shook it off. It hadn't been a voice, but more thoughts entering his mind that were not his own, like smoke joining other smoke.

He tuned in to Dad by simply wanting to hear him. There came a tremendous burden of woe, a river of Mom's face and her skin, long streams of memories, such happy memories, of walking down Oak Road in the summertime, of moments in bed that he modestly turned away from, of a train trip they must have taken before he was born . . . and then this sad, sad thing that had happened with Marcie Cotton—

—and he saw why: the grays had needed the family to stay here in Wilton, and they had made certain that Marcie would give Dad tenure. He saw the two of them whirling round and round in a dark place together, saw sparks of golden soul mingling, and understood what had happened.

It made him angry at the grays, because they had hurt Marcie and Mom and Dad just to get what they wanted. *You better understand that I'm calling my own shots now,* he said in his mind.

Instantly, there flashed before his eyes a vast wall of gray faces, eyes gleaming, arrayed in rows as far up and as far down as you could see.

He cried out in surprise.

"What's the matter?" Paulie asked. "Scared?"

"Nah."

As Mr. Warner, stuck behind a truck, slammed his hands

against the steering wheel the color around him changed. The air flickered with red and then took on darkness, especially around his head. He hammered on the horn and flashed his lights.

"John!"

Purple light filled the car, gushing off both Paulie and Amy. Conner saw it coming out of himself, too, pulsing out of his chest with his heartbeat. He looked down at it and told it to go away, and as it did, so did the fear he had felt at Mr. Warner's outburst.

"Sorry, sorry, folks. That guy was intentionally hassling me, he—Jeez, it's Len Cavendish, too. He must have gone nuts. I hope he can still unstop sewers."

Conner watched the familiar Cavendish Plumbing truck weave off down the road. Tim Cavendish had been in the passenger seat, and he had locked eyes with Conner, and Conner had heard a thought, *kill,* directed at him.

He shook his head, trying to shake away the feeling of it, and the memory it had evoked of the awful time in the playground at recess.

Since it was impossible to hear thoughts and see emotions, both of which he was doing, he decided that when he got home he would go online and learn everything he could about schizophrenia. *If you're schizophrenic,* he thought to himself, *you have to diagnose yourself and figure out a treatment protocol. If you need medical attention, you have to tell Mom and Dad.*

He would start at the *New England Journal of Medicine* and read all the recent monographs on childhood schizophrenia. Then he would go into the neutraceuticals literature. If there was a cure or a useful treatment, he would find it.

As the sun dropped lower, the western sky turned dull orange behind the skeletons of trees.

A car coming toward them suddenly sped up and smashed into the rear of the car in front of it. As they went on down the road, Conner could see the two drivers get out and start fighting like maniacs. There was a lot of black haze around the cars, the evil smoke of their rage.

He had the strange, sickening feeling that it was some-how connected to him, as if the cars had been . . . after him. On their way to Oak Road.

That must be part of the schizophrenia, a paranoid aspect. There were drugs that controlled schizophrenia itself, but not paranoia. Paranoid-schizophrenia was still difficult to manage.

He had known for years that he might be susceptible to problems like this. He squirmed in his seat next to Paulie. He did not want to see his beautiful mind destroyed. He watched purple fear gushing out of his chest like a water-fall, and disappearing down through the floor of the car.

He decided that he was definitely going around the bend.

They got to the fire and Paulie practically threw him across the street getting out of the car. He was tremen-dously excited, racing toward a cluster of their friends, waving his new camera, and yelling.

Conner noticed more of the black haze, and saw that Will Heckle was as black as night. Was he coated with smoke or something?

Conner was afraid of Will. That was not right, that he would look like that. He stayed close to Paulie. "Awe-some," Paulie breathed, looking up at the massive structure with flames shooting out of it.

It was a marvelous fire, but Conner really did not like the way Will and now Steve Stacy and another of the older kids were looking at him. A lot of people sounded crazy, their thoughts roaring like a maddened troop of chim-panzees screaming at each other in the zoo. He began to look around for his parents, to cast for his dad's thoughts in the screaming turmoil around him. *Dad* he said in his mind. But, of course, Dad couldn't hear him, that was just the schizophrenia talking.

KATELYN HEARD A CRACKING SOUND a good deal louder than the fire. Then she saw, at the far end of the elevator, that somebody was down, and a cop, young Tory Wright, was standing over him. "That looks like Dr. Bendiner," she said.

"It is Dr. Bendiner. I wonder what in the world—"

Tory Wright skullwhipped the old man with his night-stick, and Dr. Bendiner's head flew from one side to the other with the blows.

"My God, he's going to kill that old man!" Katelyn yelled. She started to run toward them. The rest of the crowd totally ignored what was happening. Then two townies started fighting, and a fireman suddenly threw down his hose and stalked away, leaving it spraying like some mad snake, the brass head a lethal projectile.

"What is going on here, Dan?"

"We've gotta get Conner." He looked around, but it was hard to see through the icy haze being generated by the spraying hoses. "Conner!"

Katelyn saw Marcie about fifty feet away. She froze, not knowing if she should go to her or what she should do. Marcie looked at her. A slight smile trembled in her face, vulnerable, ashamed. She took a step forward.

Katelyn did the same.

"Katelyn, forgive me. I don't know what happened. I can't explain it and I'm deeply ashamed, Katelyn."

As the fire roared and the water thundered, the two women embraced.

"Something happened, Marcie," Katelyn said

Sleet swept over them. "I know it, I had—oh, Katelyn, what's going on? Something is *not right*!"

Without warning, the hose the fireman had abandoned seemed to rear up before them like a cobra. Katelyn leaped away, but it smashed into Marcie's face and slammed her to the ground.

"My God, it hit her! Help her," she screamed at the fire-men. *"Help her!"*

Dan saw she was badly hurt and ran to her, and found her jaw shattered and blood bubbling out of her mouth, and her eyes filmed and uncomprehending. "Marcie," he cried, going down to her. "Help me, this woman is dying! She's dying!"

Katelyn saw a fireman staring . . . but not at Marcie. He looked off into the crowd, into the blowing ice haze. She looked around again for Conner, still did not see him. She ran to Dan. "Dan, we've got to help her!" But Dan heard something, he heard it in his left ear, as clearly as if a radio had been turned on there. It was Conner's voice: *Dad, I need you!*

The implant—he realized that it was there for Conner, to help Conner. He went to his feet. "She's beyond help. Katelyn, Conner is calling us, I can hear him, it's the implant, Katelyn. We've *got* to find him!"

CONNER STOOD ABSOLUTELY STILL, STUNNED by what he was seeing. Kids, adults, a lot of people, were looking not at the fire but at him. They were stealthy but they were very definitely surrounding him. He could hear a sort of grumbling whisper, as if they had lost all humanity, and turned into snarling animals that had only one enemy on this earth . . .

This was not making sense. It had seemed sort of understandable at school, but not here. Nobody should care. They were here to see the fire of the century, not to go after some kid. Turning slowly round and round, he watched them. Any moment, one or another of them was going to jump him. *Kill,* he heard, once or twice, but most of the thought was more primitive than words, it was an incoherent snarling, and every time he moved, it rose, got more sinister . . . and they came closer.

AS CHARLES GUNN REACHED THE flight deck of TR-A4, the control surfaces flickered to life. Immediately, he turned on the plasma engine and watched the batteries charge. Because it was daylight, he'd need to use camouflage the whole way. He was going to Wilton himself. He wanted to be low and close, there just wasn't any other way. Also, there was a possibility that he might be able to reach Mike using the ship's super-secure sideband system that was capable of keeping TRs around the world in touch with each other, and was not accessible to outside tracking.

Henry was working on the scalar weapon orders. He'd probably be able to start pulsing in about an hour—unless, of course, the president, who was by no means stupid, had taken steps to close the many back doors into the Pentagon's operations system.

"Charge," the plane said in its soft female voice.

"Deploy shield."

"Done."

He hit the button on his throat intercom. "How do I look?"

"You're ready to proceed, sir."

"Open the doors."

As he watched the monitor, the huge hangar doors opened. He would move out, then go straight up to minimize the number of people who would observe a very strange phenomenon—a gigantic triangular shadow, apparently cast by nothing. A close look would reveal the ship, but protocol required daylight takeoff to use full plasma and all fans to ascend to fourteen hundred feet immediately. At this altitude, the shadow would be too diffuse to be seen except from the air, and the air above Andrews was, because of this operation, at present entirely clear of aircraft.

"Sir," came a voice in his earphone, "return to the hangar, please, sir."

It was base ATC. What in the world were they doing interfering? "Excuse me?"

"We have new orders, sir. TRs are grounded effective immediately."

The president had closed the operation down. Charles acted with characteristic speed and decision: he immediately took the TR up. Inside of thirty seconds, it was completely undetectable, not by radar, not visually, not in any way at all.

Incredibly, his cell phone rang. For a moment, he was furious. Voices inside the TR were damped, but if Andrews had deployed its sonic scanners, they might pick up that ring. He fought it out of his pocket and opened it.

"Charles, I'm being arrested," Vorona's voice said. "He's pulling us in, all of us."

Charles thought fast. Then he saw, instantly, just how to

contain this. "Henry, stay calm. Do you have the scalar's codes?"

"Yeah, but they're busting in my door right now!"

"Give me the codes."

"This isn't a safe line, this is—"

"Do it!"

"Code of the day is B Bravo C Charlie Z Zero G Gremlin N, then one niner one in six three three eight nanosecond timed sequence."

The line disconnected. Okay, his next act was to activate sideband. He had the TR moving away from Andrews at its top speed of 320 mph. "Mike?"

He waited. Nothing. He punched up the signal-seeking equipment. "This is TR-A4 for TR-A1. Mike?"

There was a carrier out there, but Mike wasn't answering. Maybe he wasn't aboard the TR.

Charles decided that he had to trust Mike to do his job. His first priority now was to save the Trust.

A TR was richly endowed with communications. In fact, an entire subset of controls for the scalar weapons would turn on as soon as it was fully deployed. This way, a TR could stand in close and watch the effect of scalar pulses that it was triggering, and make fine adjustments in their strength and angle while remaining entirely unaffected by the earthquakes they were causing on the ground just a few feet below.

Charles went into the plane's operational manual and read as he flew, pressing buttons on a console.

Far overhead, rocket servos on the scalar weapon began once more to fire as his commands redeployed it. He had no idea that the grays had sabotaged its previous deployment, but this didn't matter because it would seek to its new coordinates from wherever it happened to be. As he worked, its long, black snout swept back across the blue of the ocean, back to the land. It stopped, then, and with tiny bursts of the servos, began to move about as if it was hunting for something.

When a city appeared below it, the motion stopped.

On the TR, Charles watched a screen. He pressed buttons, and the image became clearer. He zoomed again, and the image was clearer still: he had pointed the scalar weapon directly at Washington, D.C.

He turned the plane on its axis and headed directly into the D.C. no-fly zone.

THIRTY-ONE

INSIDE THE GRAIN ELEVATOR, THREE figures, all dressed in silver protective gear with full hoods and gloves, moved carefully across the broad floor. Nobody on the outside was aware of the presence of Colonel Robert Langford and this specialized crew.

Dr. Simpson had phoned him while they were driving into town. "If he's dead, you will need to collect tissue, Colonel Langford. I want cell-rich tissue. Do it the way the grays do, take the eyes, the lips, the genitals. We are going to need to build a clone of him."

He'd wanted to ask why, but knew that he had no need to know, and therefore didn't waste his breath. So what he had said was what duty demanded: "Yes, sir."

"We're looking at imminent structural failure, sir," a voice crackled in Langford's ears.

"I know it." He lifted an electronic bullhorn to his lips. "LEWIS! LEWIS CREW!" His loss, in Rob's opinion, would be greater than the loss of the gray that had departed the Indianapolis facility. Adam was so deceptive and complicated, there was no telling what anything they got from him really meant. But Lewis was as straight as they came, and he knew many secrets. Maybe his story about coming from another world was even true.

A rumble from above drew his attention. Like a gigantic missile, a flaming beam arched down and hit the floor in a

shower of sparks. "Careful, guys," Rob said, "we can't af-
ford any attrition, here."

"I've got an organic mass." Captain Forbes raised his
viewer away from his face mask.

"Oxygen-level warning," Airman Winkler announced,
meaning that he had five minutes before compulsory
withdrawal.

Langford moved through a forest of fallen, burning
beams to reach Forbes. At his feet was a corpse. "Okay,
let's collect tissue and pull out."

It was so badly burned that it looked more like a black
log than a body.

"Holy moly, Colonel!"

"Take it easy! Gentlemen, let's bag this." It affected him
deeply to see Lewis this burned. The poor guy was almost
unrecognizable, but not completely. What a way to go,
what a rotten death for that good man.

High above, a roar started.

"Move it! Now!"

PAULIE AND CONNER STOOD SIDE by side. Conner stayed
close to the Warners, because they were not having these
weird thoughts, not like the others, and they didn't have
shadows around them. They were shimmering with what
he had come to see as normal colors of life.

The others came closer. He looked for his mom and
dad, didn't see them. The haze from the spray and the
smoke was like a fog bank full of looming shadows, the
roar of the fire and the rumble of hoses, and strange,
echoing cries.

He dared not move, dared not call out. In his heart,
though, he begged for his mom and dad, begged them to
get him out of here.

Paulie and his family had no idea that anything was
wrong. He innocently pointed his video camera at the
burning elevator. Amy took pictures with her cell phone.

The whole wall of the building was now smoking. It
shuddered and made a sighing sound.

"**HE'S CALLING US,**" **DAN SAID.** "I hear him clearly."

"You can hear him? How can you hear him?"

"Katelyn, I told you, it's the implant, and I'm sure that he's in terrible trouble."

"I can't hear him! Why can't I hear my child?"

"You don't have an implant."

"But that's—"

"We'll sort it out later." He moved off, trying to see ahead through the smoke and haze and gathering dark. "Conner! Conner!"

CONNER DECIDED THAT, NO MATTER how it looked, half the town could not be coming after him. They didn't even know him, most of them. So this was paranoia. He would not allow himself to react to a symptom as if it was real, he wasn't *that* paranoid . . . yet.

Nearby, two people leaped into their cars and began driving this way.

Harley ushered the kids away. "They're pulling out too fast in this ice," he said.

Then one of them skidded into the other, and they both went spinning around, slamming into each other and bouncing off amid a flying shower of glass.

"**DID YOU SEE THOSE CARS?**" Dan yelled to Katelyn. "Conner! *CONNER!*"

They moved through the nightmare murk, both calling his name again and again.

As she walked beside him, struggling with him in this bizarre nightmare situation, she thought, *If he has to, he will give his life for his family.*

As if the sudden, deep love this realization made her feel had opened a door, she remembered being in a dark space, remembered it quite clearly. At her feet there was a round opening. Far below, she could see water in the moonlight. A boy was beside her, his dark hair scattered across his forehead. His eyes were scared, but he was so attractive that a shiver went through her when she saw him. She remembered reaching out to him, and in that instant knew it was Dan when they were children. She felt then the most exquisite, most deeply poignant sense of memory that she had ever known. Without being able to put it into words, but just feeling it, she saw the role she and Dan had to play in what she perceived as a plan of some sort that she could not even begin to understand, but that involved Conner.

"Dan, we have to find him!"

"I know it." Then he pointed. "Katelyn, there!"

He was not thirty feet away, just visible through the swirling ice haze. And Kenneth Brearly, a Bell tenth grader, was standing in front of him pointing a pistol at him.

Conner disappeared behind a billowing mass of haze from one of the hoses. "Conner!" Katelyn bellowed, "Conner, run!"

DESPITE THE DANGER OF BEING seen by Wilkes or somebody under his orders, Lauren left the office and moved closer to the base perimeter. She had no car and dared not draw from the motor pool.

She had to get to Conner, she knew that, but how? It was miles to the town, there was no bus. She'd tried to call the cab company, but there hadn't been any answer. Everybody was at the fire, no doubt.

That fire was bait, she was certain, set by Wilkes to draw the whole town. Conner was an eleven-year-old boy, he would be there. Mike would kill him and make it look like an accident.

She pulled out her cell phone and called Rob again. It was a futile gesture. She tried to somehow reach out to Conner, attempting to communicate with him via her mind.

Maybe he heard her and maybe he didn't, but she certainly felt no response. She looked down the long road that led to the town, to the gigantic smoke cloud, magnificent in the fading sun.

FOR THE FIRST TIME IN so long their memory of it was nothing but a few dim sparks, the Three Thieves felt love. They felt it fiercely, hanging over the burning building, for the child down there in the mist, who glowed gold in the dull, swirling crowd of other souls.

They saw, also, the antenna and the signals flaring off it, impacting the red flaring implants in the heads of people in the crowd. That antenna was connected to a transmitter, it must be, but the live voltage would be too low to make the wire visible to them. They hung far above, their small oval ship out of sight above the smoke, watching Conner. And they saw, suddenly, somebody with a gun.

Help me, they heard Conner's mind saying.

They felt something strange within them, the beating of the heart. And they understood at last why Conner was calling for help, what all these strange signals meant: Wilkes had used a primitive form of mind control to turn dozens of people into assassins.

KENNETH WAS AN HONOR STUDENT, an Eagle Scout, and a very proud young citizen, and he was absolutely terrified at what he was doing. He remembered some kind of a nightmare with this strange, whispering man in his room and he had woken up crazy like this, and he knew it was crazy, but he could not stop himself, he'd been turned into a killing machine, and the worst of it was that he just needed to kill this geeky middle schooler and do it NOW!

He kept losing him in the haze, but just for a second or two, so he was getting closer fast; then he found a clear shot, he raised the pistol, he aimed—and, Jesus. What the hell was *that*? Or no, he hadn't disappeared, he was still there. He was four feet away. He could not miss. He pressed the trigger, which did not go back. He stopped, cursed himself, thumbed the safety off, and raised the pistol again.

Conner looked into his eyes, down the barrel of the gun—and felt his body begin making tiny movements, very quick, tiny movements that seemed somehow linked to the kid's vision.

Kenneth started to pull the trigger—and this time Con-

ner cleanly and clearly disappeared right before his eyes.
There was no obscuring haze. He was just gone.

Then he saw him again, flickering back into existence as
he shook his own head, as if that had been enough to make
him visible again. Now he would not miss.

Dan tackled him from behind and he went down without
a sound. The pistol flew off into the murk, and the next
thing Kenneth knew, the world was dark.

"Dan, don't kill him!"

"He's just knocked out. Where's that pistol?"

"Oh, God, Dan, *look!*"

Linda Fells did not know why she had brought her dad's
deer gutter. She loathed the ugly, hooked knife, hated it
when he brought home does to carve up. But now she had
to use it, and she knew on who and even though she was
screaming in revulsion and fear, she marched toward Conner Callaghan, raising it as she went.

She screamed and shook her head, trying to get rid of
these thoughts, but the thoughts only got stronger and
stronger.

Dan ran toward her with all his might, but he tripped on
a hose and went sliding on the ice, screaming for Conner to
watch out, that she was behind him. Katelyn howled,
"Conner, Conner," and struggled as if through mud, crossing the slick of ice, hoses, and fallen people that lay between them and their boy.

THE THREE THIEVES MOVED DOWN toward the roof of the
grain elevator. They had to reach that antenna and the
transmitter connected to it, but the collective was horrified
to see that they could not reach it unless they descended
into flames and certain death. But they couldn't die, they
mustn't. No other triad was prepared to replace them. This
had not been anticipated.

The One said, *We have to save him.* The Two said, *We
have to save ourselves.* The Three leaped out of the craft
and dropped down through the air. As he fell, a great mass
of fire enveloped him and the whole collective howled his
pain and his loss. He saw fire all around him, a red haze.

He felt his bones growing hot, felt essential processing systems in his body begin to boil.

He reached the lip of the great tank. The whole structure was unstable, he could feel it shaking, could see the flames licking at it. It would not last long, but even another moment was too much time. He ripped off the antenna, pulling it away from the concrete lip of the huge tank to which it had been affixed.

As he looked for the transmitter, a great tongue of fire enveloped him. His skin began to pop and shatter, his limbs to shake, then to gyrate wildly as millions of micromotors lost control of themselves. He broadcast, *Alarm, alarm* as he felt himself ceasing to function. He dropped the antenna, which went sailing off into the flames. His left eye exploded in a shower of sparks. He fell farther.

The One went after him, dropping also into the flames, attempting to save him, struggling against the fire. And he, too, caught fire. His head exploded in a flashing mass of sparks.

The antenna was gone, but not the transmitter. It remained taped to the lip of the tank, its red diode gleaming, still sending its signal—although weakened—to every one of Wilkes's killers.

The Two took the craft up fast, faster than a bullet, all the way to the edge of space.

CONNER FELT THEM LEAVING HIM. *Don't go*, his mind cried, *don't cut me off*. But he was cut off, there was now no sense of the presence of the collective within him. He felt it as a silence at the center of his being. "Come back to me," he screamed, but the Thieves could not hear him, not the dead, not the frightened, confused survivor far away.

DAN AND KATELYN REACHED CONNER at last.

"Mom, Dad, something's wrong, we have to go!"

"Oh, Conner, dear God, Conner, I couldn't find you!" Dan said. Katelyn threw her arms around him. "Let's go home now," she said. "Right now!"

"Hi, Mrs. Callaghan."

Katelyn backed away from the girl. She knew what was in her hand, she had seen it.

"Stay right there," she told her. "Don't you come near him!"

The girl stepped closer. She was a pretty girl with a sweet, open smile. "There's nothing wrong, Mrs. Callaghan."

"Then what do you want?"

"Nothing."

"Why are you carrying that knife?"

The girl raised it and leaped straight past Katelyn. Conner stepped to one side and she slashed down where he had been standing. Snarling, she raised it again, looking around as if she couldn't see him.

Katelyn grabbed her arm, then Dan leaped on her from behind and got the knife out of her hand. "Who are you? What the hell's the matter with you?"

The girl crumpled, bursting into tears. Here and there other people, freed by the weakening signal, began screaming, holding their heads, throwing down weapons.

ON THE ROOF OF THE grain elevator, the metal skeletons of the two grays smoked and sparked in the licking flames. They moved, though, flickering and twitching, as if they wanted to stand. High above, the Two concentrated, his head down, his hands over his face.

One skeleton actually rose a few inches, stretched an arm toward the transmitter, trembled, and fell back. The bones fell into the the maelstrom. Now the other moved a little—its hand scraping along the lip of the tank, then touching the edge of the transmitter, the black claws scrabbling at its power switch—then falling to a jumble of gleaming metal bones and black claws. The tiny red diode on the transmitter remained lit.

At that moment, the grain elevator collapsed, leaving only the three enormous tanks standing. The light on the transmitter flickered, went out—but then came on again, glowing steadily. Huge pieces of concrete began falling off the tank.

INSIDE, ROB AND HIS TEAM threw themselves into the cellar where the elevator's motors were housed. A massive tongue of fire roared at them from above, coming through the hatchway like a living, questing monster, grasping for their lives. The space was long, the far end collapsed and burning. The floor above them groaned, ready to buckle. He thought he had perhaps twenty seconds to get these men out of here.

THE CALLAGHANS BEGAN MOVING AWAY from the debris, Katelyn and Dan shielding their son as best they could.

As they headed for their car, Jimbo Kelton came over to them. He was smiling.

"Hey, Jimbo," Dan said, "watch our backs, we—"

Jimbo lifted his arms over his head and brought a rock down on Conner.

Conner ducked, but not fast enough to avoid getting hit in the shoulder. A stab of pain went through him and he cried out.

Jimbo raised the rock again. Then another rock hit Conner in the neck and bounced off. It had been thrown by Mrs. Kelton, and she and Jimbo were both gathering more projectiles, fragments of lumber, of tin—anything to throw at him. Their faces were gray, their eyes watery and crazy.

As a third rock hit Conner, he ran toward the car. Now Terry Kelton tackled him and tried to drag him down, but he pushed him off. Catching up with him, Katelyn grabbed his jacket and dragged him toward the car as Dan fought off the Keltons, screaming and kicking, backing toward the car.

"Dan, John has a rifle!" Katelyn shouted as she and Conner reached the car. "Run!"

Conner jumped into the back of the car and crouched down on the floor. His head and his back throbbed where he'd been hit. Katelyn and Dan got in and slammed the front doors. As they pulled out, a rock hit the back window, transforming it into a haze of cracks.

"What in damn hell is the matter?" Dan yelled.

"Look, please, I'm sorry, I know I did something, and I'm so sorry."

"You didn't do a damn thing, son."

As they drove away, Conner came up from the floor. He sat hunched against the door, staring out the window at the bizarre scene, which faded quickly into the gathering winter evening.

They went toward Oak Road, turning up Wilton, taking the lonely way.

"This is a mistake," Conner said.

"What do you mean?" Dan asked.

"The lonely way."

THIRTY-TWO

LAUREN WAS ALMOST INSANE WITH worry and fear when at last a two-car convoy appeared at the main gate. Rob's car was in front, a Cherokee behind full of specialists in fire control gear.

As he pulled up, he opened his window. "We're not out of the woods, and I need you right now."

She ran around and got in the car. The Cherokee headed off into the base.

"Why in hell didn't you call me? My God, I almost lost my mind."

"You had orders, Colonel."

"*Orders?* Dear God, the military mind is—oh, forget it. What's our situation?"

"Crew is dead and Wilkes is at large. He may have made an escape in a stolen TR."

"What's a TR?"

"Classified vehicle," he replied tightly.

"He killed Lewis Crew?"

"Details later, we've got a hell of a situation back there. I don't know exactly what else he's done, but we've got to get that kid to safety or we're gonna have another dead body on our hands right away."

At that moment, the base siren sounded and the guards began closing the gates. Rob turned the car around and headed back toward town.

"What in the world is going on?"

"It seems that Wilton is rioting."

"You're kidding."

"They're killing each other."

She closed her eyes, playing move after move, and came to a conclusion: "Wilkes couldn't identify exactly which child, so he did something that would turn the whole place violent, in hopes that all the children would be killed."

"One possibility. Another is that he did identify him but was scared to take direct action because of the grays, and is using this as a diversion."

"But the family—they're miles out of town."

"They came to the fire, I know that, I identified the car. They are not there at this time, however."

"Oh, boy."

"Yeah, we're in trouble."

"And you're certain about Mr. Crew?"

"He's in a bag on his way to Wright-Pat."

"Was he really from another world? Is that true?"

He glanced at her. "You might as well accept that there is no final truth in this thing. Not ever. This reality, more than any other, changes depending on the way you look at it. As far as I know, the man could be from Chicago or Denver or anywhere. But he was a good man and a useful man, which is the bottom line on Lewis damn Crew."

Rob stopped the car. They had come around the curve in the highway which opened onto Main Street. Smoke rose from at least four different fires. A man shot a rifle from the roof of a store. Groups of people ran through the streets, most of them armed with hunting rifles. Sirens howled, and, as they watched, a garbage truck backed at full speed into the front of the First Church of Christ. Its steeple, bells pealing, tumbled over the truck and into the street.

Rob flipped open his cell phone, speed-dialed a number. "The situation in the town is deteriorating fast. You'd better get the governor on the horn, General, because the place is gone. He needs the National Guard out here, the state cops won't be enough."

A Buick packed with kids snarled toward them, its tires leaving smoke in the street.

Rob turned the wheel full right and jammed the gas pedal to the floor. A second later, the Buick passed behind them and raged on, swerving to snap fireplugs. Screaming laughter could be heard, full of terror.

Rob pulled over to the side of the road. "We can't drive through that."

"No."

"We're going to have to cross the town by helicopter, locate the child on the other side. And I think we need to just move him. Get him out of here."

"What about Mike? What about the group? Won't they keep trying?"

Rob looked at her for a long moment. "I never said this would be easy."

DAN DROVE HARD, TRYING TO get back to Oak Road before the craziness spread there if it was going to. He would defend his family with his pistol until they could leave this place. For the Callaghans, Wilton and Bell College were history, and to hell with his precious tenure. Bell would probably fall apart now anyway. Who would send their children to a place like this?

"Conner," Katelyn said, "do you have any idea what's happened to these people?"

Dan thought it was a fair question to ask this child who had changed so much. You could see it in his face, a new steadiness in his eyes.

"It has to do with me."

At that moment there was a snap and the car shook.

"What was that?"

Conner knew that it was a bullet, he'd felt the hate of the person who'd fired the gun. He pressed himself down below the level of the windows.

"Conner?"

"It hit the left fender just above the tire."

"What did?" Mom asked.

"A bullet."

Dan increased their speed. "Conner," Katelyn screamed, *why?*"

That wasn't the right question, he knew. They needed a different energy to survive this. Fear would not save them.

He needed the Three Thieves. Now that they were gone, he saw how they'd been his link to the collective, and how important the collective would be to him in the future. He also saw how they helped him now, watching over him, doing the small, essential things that had saved him.

Giving their lives for him.

There was a bang in the front, and the car swerved over to the side of the road. Dan tried to keep it going, but it slurried all over the place.

"That's a shot-out tire," Conner said.

"I know it," Dan snapped.

Mom turned around, and he had never seen her look like that. Her eyes were like shattered glass.

Mom and Dad were panicked. He had to get away from them, he could not let the bad decisions they were going to make kill him.

"Stop the car, Dad."

"I can't do that, my God we're being fired on!"

Conner breathed hard, bit his lips to keep the sobs in, then opened the door and threw himself out into a snow-bank. He rolled like you're supposed to, and proceeded to hit Mr. Niederdorfer's fence so hard he saw stars. He heard the car growling, and as he got up he saw it skidding around in the snowy road, its right front tire now also in shreds.

A whisper flashed past his face, followed by an echoing crack. Far down the road, he could see a car with some-body standing on it. That person had a rifle, and he was lifting it to aim again.

He needed to get to the trees on the Niederdorfer land. He hopped the fence and trudged off in snow up to his waist.

Mom burst out of the car. "No, come back! Conner, no!" She leaped the fence, surged ahead like some kind of raging lioness. Then Dan came plunging through the snow behind her. He closed the distance even faster than she did.

"You've got to get back in the car! In the car, Conner, it's our only hope."

"Trust me," he said, reaching for her hand. He looked to his father. "Trust me, Dad."

Then he heard somebody else coming fast, their breath whistling.

A glance over his shoulder revealed Jimbo Kelton surging through the snow with superhuman power. In his right hand was a big axe.

Conner ran. He could only hope his parents would do the same. There were thousands of acres of forest out here that would significantly improve the odds. Staying with a disabled car was obviously not the best move.

Then the trees were around Conner and he could dart and twist and turn and get through them fast. But Jimbo was bigger and faster, and Conner knew that it would not be long before he caught up.

He got to a clear space and ran for all he was worth, then veered off, trying as much as possible to avoid dislodging snow from the branches of the pines all around him, and stepping in places where the snow on the ground was lightest.

LAUREN SAT BEHIND ROB AND the pilot as the chopper moved quickly over the mad town. There was a sharp snap, then a ping, then another.

"Incoming," the pilot said.

"Bastards," Rob muttered.

A vibration started. "Sir, I took rotor damage off that rifle fire," the pilot said into the intercom.

"Keep it in the air."

"Sir, I need to return to base immediately."

"Keep it in the air!"

"I'll go down, sir!"

"Even if you end up crashing this thing, you have to get me where I'm going."

"This is my bird sir, and I've got to return to base!"

"Captain, our lives are not as important as this mission. None of us."

"Sir—"

"This is the single most important thing this Air Force has *ever done*! We cannot, I repeat, *cannot* fail! We must put at least one effective on the ground in the right place and nothing else matters, do you understand!"

"Yes, sir! Losing altitude, sir!"

"Down there," Lauren shouted over the roar of the chopper.

He saw it, an elderly blue car smashed into a fence by the roadside, and the trenches of runners leading off toward the woods. Three trenches, the one in the middle smaller. From another direction there came a fourth trench.

"I don't like the look of that," Rob said.

"The family's being stalked."

"Exactly. One—no four. Four other tracks." He pointed, and Lauren saw them, too, four distinct lines in the snow, all coming from the direction of a station wagon parked about a quarter of a mile behind the Callaghans' vehicle.

"Sir, I am losing control of this bird!"

FIGHTING HIS OWN CONTROLS, MIKE Wilkes managed to move the TR over Wilton Road. At this point, it was the only route to Oak Road, because County Road Four forked off from here. If the Callaghans made it out of the maelstrom in town, he was going to have to take the boy out personally, and damn the consequences. The problem was the TR. It was leaking gas, losing lift. At some point, the computer would conclude that it was going to crash. It had a self-destruct mode that would vaporize it in seconds, and anybody inside as well. In the operational models, there was an elaborate escape mechanism that could fly the pilot hundreds of miles to safety, but it was not present in this stolen prototype.

Then he had seen two cars coming. The one in the rear was the Keltons' wagon. Ahead of it had been the Callaghans.

When the Keltons had fired on them, he had experienced a surge of relief. This might yet work, and work well . . . or so he had thought.

Now, he wasn't so sure. He slid slowly over the woods, looking down, unable to determine the exact situation.

There was a distant roar as the last of the elevator tanks

collapsed like great, drunken giants, leaving a pall of white
dust on the golden western horizon.

So the transmitter was done, now. How much longer
would his assassins last? Maybe as much as an hour, some
of them, but most would revert to normal almost immediately. The nice ones.

He unbuttoned his holster and dropped the ship to
ground level. He moved slowly past the Callaghans' car,
making certain that it was absolutely disabled. As he was
ascending again, he noticed that the Keltons' wagon was
occupied. Their dog was in the back, barking to be let out.
The animal would not revert. Unlike a human being, he
would remain savage for the rest of his life.

He climbed down onto the road and opened the wagon's
rear door. He didn't need to break the glass, nobody had
thought to lock this car.

The animal snarled at him, then began to come forward.
Quickly, he returned to the TR, and turned toward the forest. Alarms were tinkling in the cockpit.

He would stalk Conner and watch, and if the Keltons
failed, he'd go in for the kill.

CONNER, DARTING THROUGH THE WOODS, heard a helicopter.
Then a shot clipped a tree beside his head. He threw him-
self down as another three bullets hit all around him.
Jimbo, about a hundred yards away, roared, "Way to go
Dad, I've got him now!"

Very suddenly he was swooped down on and arms went
around him. "Mom!"

As Katelyn's arms closed around him from behind, she
cried out with joy.

"Mom, no! Mom, we have to keep on!"

"Honey, it's the Keltons, it's our friends, honey."

Then Dad was there and he was not confused at all. He
scooped Conner up and ran like hell.

But a shot crackled and Conner felt his dad's whole body
lurch. With a gasp, Dad went down. Conner disentangled
himself, but not before Jimbo arrived, his face purple, the
axe flashing. Light the color of pus flowed out of his eyes.

"Get back in the woods," Dad said.

Jimbo hurled the axe, which slammed into a tree, its handle ringing from the vibration of the blow. Then Conner heard the helicopter again, this time very loud. He looked up.

INSIDE THE CHOPPER, LAUREN REALIZED that it was counterrotating. She knew that this was the worst possible thing it could do short of losing its blades and falling like a rock. The forest whirled, then she was thrown against the window and almost out the open door. The world was racing now and she could hear Rob howling in rage as the pilot made the engine shriek, and the trees came closer and closer. She watched, mesmerized, until finally they were sweeping past twenty feet below, all immaculate with snow.

In herself she became quiet. She was not afraid. She thought, *It's a perfect world,* and peace overcame her.

"Go! Go! GO!"

"What?"

"Jump, woman! Jump or burn!"

There was fire all over the place. Where had that come from? Then she knew that the chopper had hit the trees and she'd been stunned. The pilot cried out and began to struggle, and was enveloped in flames.

She leaped out into a frigid cacophony of snapping pine boughs and sighing snow, snow that took her into itself like a freezing womb. In summer, the fall would have killed her, but she went down now in a curtain of snow, and struck the ground almost silently.

She got to her feet, looked around. "Rob?"

Then she saw him. He was bleeding from his back and both arms and his hair was burned off, but he went charging off anyway. She started to follow him—and then saw out of the corner of her eye a blue flicker as small as the flutter of a bird's wing. It was not spring, there were no birds.

It was a child's blue car coat, over there through the trees. "Rob, this way!"

Lauren ran out into a small clearing, and there before

her was a tableau, for the instant frozen as if by the cold: a
boy kneeling in the snow, his face flushed, pleading
silently toward a much larger boy, who stood with froth on
his mouth like a mad dog. In his hand was an axe.

A man lay in the snow, the red of blood around him. Dan.
Lauren ran toward them.

THE AXE CAME DOWN, CAME with blinding speed, like the
striking head of a snake.

Katelyn saw Dan grab the handle of the axe in both
hands, and in doing so give Conner time to get to his feet
and stagger toward the deeper woods. Jimbo roared with
frustration as he took off after him.

She ran to Dan, knelt over him. His eyes met hers. "Help
him," he said, "help our son."

She looked toward the woods, got up, and ran on.

Rob struggled frantically for his gun, and Lauren saw that
he was fighting an arm so broken it was almost snake-like.
His lips twisted, his face went ashen, but he used it anyway,
getting to the weapon, dragging it out of the holster.

"Your left hand," she screamed. "Rob, your *left* hand!"

He raised it past his body so she could see the useless
hunk of meat that dripped there. She saw his chest heaving,
saw a froth of bile appear between his lips, but saw him
still struggling, still trying to raise that pistol.

WHEN MIKE SAW ROB APPEAR at the edge of the clearing
where this thing was coming to climax, he pulled the TR
back quickly. Rob was familiar with the TR and he just
might spot it despite all the optical camouflage. As he maneuvered the craft, a soft female voice began a countdown.
"Alert. Destruct in thirty seconds. Alert. Destruct in
twenty-nine seconds . . ."

Mike hammered at the controls, increased the velocity
of the plasma, the speed of the fans, and brought the lift
level inching back up. "Countdown ends." For a moment,
he sat absolutely still, hardly breathing, but the countdown
did not resume.

He activated the secure communications system. It didn't matter much if the Air Force found him now. They were going to be too late, and he needed to let Charles know the situation. "This is TR-A1, I am going to burp coordinates."

"Negative that."

"Charles! Can you reach me?"

"Three hours."

"I've got progressive damage. This thing is going in sooner than that."

"Do you have the kid?"

"Just about."

"Mike, the president's arresting the Trust. Until further notice, consider yourself a fugitive."

What in hell had happened? The president couldn't arrest the Trust, could he? Mike wasn't sure, but he was sure that he had a battle to fight, so he forced the issue out of his mind and instead concentrated on working the TR closer to the boy. He took out his pistol.

CHARLES GUNN, STILL OVER WASHINGTON, did not like that "just about." To him, that meant that the child was not secure, and if that was true, he might never be secure. Charles must not end up in the situation that had destroyed *der Wolf* in the forties—a two-front war. For the Trust, one front would be this monster of a child, using his powers of mind to stay ahead of them and undermine their plans. The other front would be the president and his powers of arrest.

He had hesitated to do what he now knew he must. He'd hidden the TR by hanging in a wooded draw in Rock Creek Park. He rose up to the level of Glover Bridge and headed down Embassy Row. He cleared his vision. It was as if the plane around him had disappeared, except for the three control panels and his immediate seating area. He moved low over the buildings, stopping above the Prince Mansion. Just a few voices. Very well, the president was in the White House.

As he aimed the TR down Massachusetts Avenue, he opened a small cover under his right hand, revealing a black button. He adjusted his altitude, then activated listen-

ing devices. Much clearer voices filled the small area, a
press officer on the telephone, two Secret Service agents
chatting about their house cats, the First Lady discussing
colors with her dressmaker.

Finally, he heard the president's voice in the Oval Office
talking to somebody through an interpreter.

He pressed the button. He held it down.

THE WHITE HOUSE KITCHEN WAS organized pandemonium.
Last night had been the Thai prime minister. Tonight, it
was the sultan of Qatar, the second state dinner in a row.
The pastry chef was the first to notice something awry: a
meringue was shaking wildly. Then he realized that he was
shaking, too.

In the press room above, Press Secretary Roger Armes
said, "We appear to be—" as ceiling tiles began to come
down. Then the lights went out, immediately replaced by
emergency lighting. Voices rose, shouts and screams, and
some of them terrible screams.

In the Vermeil Room, the portraits of all seven first
ladies fell at once. A moment later, the ceiling followed. In
the Oval Office, the president, his chief of staff, and two,
then three, then four Secret Service agents were thrown
with ferocious energy to the floor along with the elabo-
rately robed sultan and his translator. The Resolute Desk,
made from the timbers of the *HMS Resolute* and used by
such presidents as FDR, Kennedy, and Reagan, now
crashed with a crackling thud into the floor. A moment
later, the walls came in, and the whole contents of the office thundered through into the Blue Room below.

From thirty feet away, Charles watched the carnage, directing pulse after pulse toward the building. The private
apartments on the roof shuddered and caved in, then the
whole West Wing sank away into a cloud of dust.

Charles traveled over the mess, heading for the Mall. He
moved just inches above the Reflecting Pool, aiming
toward the Washington Monument.

High above, the long snout of the scalar weapon now
glowed bright red. Every time Charles pressed the button

in the TR down below, the red fluttered brilliant white, and a ball of light shot toward the Earth.

Tourists screamed and ran across the Mall as the worst earthquake to strike the area since the Mississippi embayment in 1811 rumbled and rattled. The Washington Monument swayed, its sheer marble facing dancing with cracks. Inside, more tourists scrambled down the stairs.

The monument came down almost gracefully, sinking into its own base as it disintegrated. Marble is a soft stone, and does not stand up well under stress.

Charles circled the collapsing monument, then moved toward the Capitol. Far overhead, the scalar weapon's servos emitted flashes as it made fine adjustments.

Congress was in session when the balconies swayed like hammocks and crashed down into the house chamber. Fortunately for all except the observers, few representatives were actually in attendance.

The Senate was not so lucky. A ceremony honoring a retiring senator was under way, and three-quarters of the senators were present when the chandeliers began to fall, exploding into the chamber with horrendous loss of life.

The quake, finally finding a fault line, spread through the area. The tunnel to the Senate Office Building caved in. Then the Anacostia Bridge fell. Everywhere, people strove to keep their feet, tried desperately to avoid falling monuments and falling ceilings.

Charles continued his mad ballet, paying special attention now to the Pentagon. Inside, people held onto their desks or clung to doors and walls, but the tough old structure would not come down.

Finally, Charles took his finger off the button. At monitoring stations around the world, the pens of seismographs returned to normal. But the record was clear: an earthquake measuring 7.3 on the Richter scale had struck Washington, D.C. Strangely, the epicenter was located very close to the surface, rather than the three to ten miles beneath it that was normal. Stranger still, no fault line was known that could account for the highly localized event, which had been centered, for all practical purposes, on the White House. And yet it appeared to be entirely natural.

Henry Vorona, who had been in a car on the Anacostia Bridge when it collapsed, drowned with the two men who had arrested him. He died furious at Charles and at life, but also relieved, because he knew that the Trust would now certainly survive.

The president died, too, crushed beneath the desk he had so proudly accepted as his own, never dreaming that he would come to his end behind it—or rather, under it.

Charles grabbed altitude and headed off west-northwest as a flight of F-16s scrambled from Andrews screamed past him, their engine noise practically blowing out his ears.

"Mike, are you still up?"

"Just about on the deck."

"What's the status of the kid?"

"Unknown."

"Goddamn you."

TERRY AND JOHN KELTON CAME out of the woods, both with high-powered rifles. As they strode past Dan, Terry knelt and fired into the trees.

Lauren leaped through the snow—which here had drifted as high as her chest—leaped and struggled in a slow-motion nightmare, feeling the cold of it sear her in places where she had never been cold. She clawed on anyway, because she knew without fully understanding that this was one of those tiny, secret moments on which a whole future turns.

She saw John laugh and stride forward so powerfully that the snow seemed to part for him like the Red Sea, as if he was helped in some way by the purity of evil itself.

"Rob," Lauren screamed. "Rob, *shoot*!"

Rob struggled to raise his gun, his whole body shaking with the effort.

Three of the Keltons zeroed in on Conner. Lauren saw that they were converging with a fourth, a boy of about fifteen. She recognized him from that last session with Adam: he had the hair, the face, the build of the image of the boy that Adam had put in her mind and that she had described so carefully to Mike.

"Oh, Mike, you are good at what you do." He had turned the grays' own decoy into one of Conner's assassins.

She broke free of the drift and ran hard, but all the hunters except the fifteen-year-old were too far ahead of her. "Rob," she shouted in his direction, "Rob, stop them!"

Rob stood as still as if he had frozen, and Lauren feared for a moment that he had done just that, but that limp, flopping arm still came up, still carried the heavy pistol. He grimaced in agony, his face now lined with bars of frozen blood.

She watched the shattered arm rise impossibly higher and higher, the gun wavering in it. Then she launched herself in a final burst and took down Jimbo. He exhaled with a whoosh and fell, and she grabbed his shoulders and kept smashing his head into the ground as hard as she could, so hard that it soon packed the layer of snow beneath it and began to make thudding sounds, and his eyes began to roll.

Rob raised the gun higher. Higher. And kept raising it up right *past* the hunters. "ROB! ROB, WAKE UP!"

Rob's face worked, his eyes rolling. She looked up to where the gun pointed and cried out, astonished, a red-hot knife of terror stabbing her heart as she saw, just a few feet overhead, a gigantic shimmering triangle that looked so much like the sky above that she hadn't noticed it before.

The gun blasted and Rob hissed through bared teeth in his agony as the kick flashed torment down his arm. With his mangled left hand he shoveled snow against his face to force consciousness back, and fired into the thing overhead again and again.

"Alert. Auto destruct in ten seconds. Nine. Eight—"

As Mike twisted the controls, the TR wheeled away from the clearing, its huge wing skimming the treetops, leaving behind billows of snow.

"Five. Four."

He slid down to the hatch. The treetops were five feet below him.

He leaped. As he did, he felt a fierce blast of heat from the dying TR. He crashed down among the wide pine branches and landed hard in a billow of snow. He checked himself, got to his feet—and realized that his ankle was broken.

Rob Langford stood not ten feet away. Mike's pistol was gone, but he began to hobble toward Langford anyway.

"Rob, you've got to help me."

"I can't do that, Mike."

"Rob, you don't want the whole human race loaded with chains. You're too good a man to want a thing like that."

"They're not loading us with chains, Mike, they're giving us wings."

"How the hell would you know?"

As Rob stood staring at him out of filmed eyes, Mike dragged himself closer.

He watched as if in a balletic nightmare as Rob's pistol slowly rose from his side, clutched in a hand that looked like gnawed meat, and braced by a burned claw.

The pistol came to bear. He saw Langford's teeth grinding, his eyes squinting with effort. He was almost on him now, just a couple more feet.

But the hammer went back, and he knew he had lost.

THIRTY-THREE

THE GUN WENT CLICK. AGAIN, click. Langford dropped it into
the snow and Mike reached him, shoved him back, and
pounded him in the face with all his might. But Langford
was also a powerful, resourceful man, and he fought back,
finally hurtling Mike off him with his feet, sending him
sprawling in the snow.

Mike tried to get up. He pushed at the ground and struggled with all his strength to raise himself but he could not.
More than just an ankle was broken, he knew that from the
blood frothing his lips.

Then a fist came down, and the lights went out.

Somehow, Rob got to his feet. Somehow, he moved
toward the clearing. He hoped that Wilkes would be out, at
least for a couple of minutes. But he knew the colonel. The
colonel was one to be reckoned with.

Screaming in agony, he forced his mangled hand into his
pocket. As he got a fresh clip into his pistol, he gagged,
bent double, and retched from the agony of using the hand.

Step by agonized step, he moved toward the tableau in the
clearing. His uniform hung in tatters, blood gushed down
his right arm and left a frozen trail in the snow. Now the gun
came back up, this time pointing toward John Kelton.

John raised his rifle but he was not a military man and
Rob got off the first round, which sent him flying back
thirty feet into the trees. It hadn't been a fatal shot, Rob
saw, as John clutched a bleeding shoulder.

Snow cascaded down around Terry, who cried out when he saw his dad go down. Mrs. Kelton came rushing through the woods screaming.

Good, Rob thought, they were distracted. He prepared to shoot them both the moment he had clear lines of fire.

Dan lay in the sanctity of his wounds, looking into the peace of the darkening sky. He remembered Katelyn on the catwalk in the secret world of their childhood, when the grays had stitched their lives together. He remembered her thin summer nightgown, and that face, Katelyn in the summer of her girlhood, became what he would take with him if now was when he traveled on.

Lauren got off the inert form of the Kelton boy she had taken down. In that moment, Rob appeared. He looked through his one unswollen eye. Like a stone, the pistol dropped from his hand. His head lolled to his chest. "The others are coming," he slurred. "Got to stop them, Lauren."

As he toppled forward, Lauren shouted, "Somebody help him!" But there was nobody to do that. Rob was so caked with frozen blood he looked like he was wearing the uniform of a butcher.

She went down to him and embraced him, telling him that she would save him. She ripped off her own parka and put it under his head. He smiled a little. "You're gonna freeze your ass," he said. Then his eyes closed in the way people's eyes close when they are dying and she cried out again, "Help us, somebody help us!"

Suddenly, the eyes opened. They bored into hers. "You've got work to do, soldier."

Crying, begging God for his life, she picked up his pistol and ran to her duty in the woods.

It was dark and silent in among the trees. She peered ahead. Every time she moved, snow came in cascades off the pines. But the movement of others was easy to follow, because their passing had done the same thing.

She listened.

At that moment, a shocking and, she thought, totally inappropriate thing happened. She was plunged back into her babyhood, and was walking again for the first time.

That was Adam's signature!

But Adam was dead, so—

She saw movement in the woods—a shadow back among the branches that had a great, soft eye like a deer.

At that instant, Conner, who was running blindly, saw Lauren's face in his mind just as clearly as if she'd been on a TV screen five feet in front of him. Her eyes were full of a very special sort of light, pure blue as the sky, tinged at the edges with a million other colors, the richest, most beautiful light he had ever seen.

She saw him, also, in that moment, as if at the end of a tunnel of light that wound through the trees.

She struggled forward in a haze of cascading snow and whipping branches, and the light gleamed on the snow, elusive, disappearing at moments, then coming again.

Before she could reach Conner, though, a figure was there. The older of the two teens. He had a rifle and he was pointing it. Then Conner came into view. The kid turned toward him.

Lauren raised Rob's pistol and in one motion fired, and the shooter flew into the snow and lay still. Then she moved toward Conner.

He turned toward her, looked from her face to the pistol—and literally disappeared before her eyes.

She still saw him, but only in her mind's eye, standing there staring fixedly at her. Like Adam had done, *exactly like Adam*!

She went down on one knee, put the pistol in the snow, and said, "Conner, Conner, I won't hurt you." She projected an image of herself hugging him. Instantly, an image came back into her head from Conner, of him begging silently with his hands. *I won't hurt you,* she said in her mind, in exactly the same way she had talked to Adam.

There was a flash of movement before her, then another, this one more clear. Then he was standing there again. She threw her arms around him and lifted him to her. Her mind and his mind seemed to swirl together, and it was sheer pleasure and joy, like counting every number to the highest number, and knowing that there would be ever more perfect numbers ahead.

Katelyn came out of the woods.

As Conner went to his mother, Lauren asked him, "Where are the other shooters? Can you tell?"

"Close your eyes," he said.

She saw an image of a man lying at the bottom of a ravine with his shoulder bleeding, a woman bending over him. They were huddled together, obviously desperate, trying to keep warm. John and Mrs. Kelton had given up the fight and moved to safety.

Conner asked Lauren, "What's happening?"

"It's going to end, honey. Very soon, it's going to end."

His face turned red, he grabbed her shoulders. *"What is it? Why do they hate me?"*

"Conner, it's going to end, it has to end."

He pushed back from her, his eyes rolling back into his head. "Dad needs us."

They began running, then, all three of them coming out of the shock of the moment, realizing that lives still depended on them.

They found both Rob and Dan, and Terry Kelton nearby huddled in the snow. As it turned out, Lauren had missed and he wasn't even wounded, just in shock. His eyes were glazed with fear and he kept shaking his head. "What—what," he whispered, "what?"

He'd come out of it, whatever Mike had done to him, whatever evil, evil thing.

Dan was still alive and conscious, and as they lifted him Conner took off his own jacket and tucked it around his father.

Lauren hurried to Rob. The moment she looked at him, she began to weep. She reached out and touched his graying face. The eyes stared, the lips lay open as if amazed by a death that had been, also, a discovery. With trembling fingers, she closed the eyes. Then she doubled over, gasped, and began to grieve.

Conner came. "He's not dead," he said, as if that was the strangest idea in the world. He laid a hand on his forehead, and Rob's eyes flickered open. "See?"

Rob gazed up at her, silent. She looked to him, then to Conner, then back to Rob.

"Help us," Conner said. Katelyn was trying to get Dan to his feet.

"Let me look," Lauren said. She'd had standard survival and first-aid training, and she saw that he had a bullet-pierced shoulder. The bones were intact. The shoulder, while dislocated, had not been shattered by the bullet. There was blood, though, a lot of it. "You need a hospital," she said. "Right now."

On the way to the car, she saw more movement in the woods beside them. She whirled—but there was nothing there. To her horror, she realized that she had left the pistol behind. That had been stupid but it was also a warning that she was in shock. She had to be careful, now, force herself to stay rational for them all. Survival, always, was in the details.

The movement came again.

Dan saw it, too. "A deer," he gasped.

"Conner?" she asked.

He waved her to silence.

They continued to the car, the five of them, following the tracks that had been laid in madness and terror. Dan cried out in pain, but they managed to help him across the Niederdorfers' fence.

Once on the other side, he leaned on it. "Give me a second . . . a second . . ."

"We need an ambulance," Katelyn said.

Lauren opened her cell phone. Fortunately, they were close enough to the town for a signal. She called Alfred, got through to Rob's adjutant, and reported Rob as severely wounded and the pilot as a KIA to a very saddened young man. Then she arranged for air evac. Because of the trouble in the town, it might be delayed, but there was nothing more they could do.

The Air Force would come and gather its dead pilot and take him home in a box, where he would lie in honored earth and the memories of those who loved him. But maybe Rob would live to fight another fight.

Are you gonna marry him?

She actually laughed a little. "If I can."

Katelyn gave her a questioning look.

"Terry," Conner said, "your mom and dad are okay." He looked at Lauren. "There's another one out there."

"I know, Rob."

"No, alive. Near Rob. He's crawling. He's trying to get to me."

"Can he, Conner?"

Conner shook his head.

"What are you talking about?" Dan asked

"Nothing," Conner said quickly.

Lauren heard in her mind, *Don't tell them I can hear their thoughts.*

No, Conner, I won't.

Dan touched the implant in his ear. It almost seemed as if he had heard Conner talking again, his voice curiously gentled, coming from the center of his own head. He would have to understand this, but not now. Now he had to save his family. He leaned on Katelyn as they walked, and she whispered, "I love you, Dan, I've remembered it all, and I love you."

He turned to her. As much as he hurt, those words filled him with a torrent of swirling, strengthening relief. He raised his arms and held her, felt her against him and felt in his depths the love that defined his soul, for his Katelyn.

She raised her face to his and kissed him, and the kiss seemed to give him new life—until a wrong movement sent a firebrand of agony through his shoulder.

Tears in his eyes, he managed a smile as he went toward the car. "The spare," he said. "I'll change the tire."

"We'll change it," Lauren said.

The light was almost gone, now, but they weren't but two hundred feet away from the car.

"We'll drive straight out Wilton Road," Katelyn said, "and take you to the hospital in Berryville. Unless this insanity is all over the place? Is it, Lauren, do you know?"

"Hold it." Lauren could not believe what she was seeing. "Don't move."

An enormous dog had jumped onto the roof of the Callaghans' car.

THIRTY-FOUR

THE DOG STARED STRAIGHT AT Conner, a long string of drool sliding out of his panting jaws.

"Jesus," Dan said.

"That's Manrico," Katelyn said. "That's the Keltons' dog."

"Conner, what's happening?" Lauren asked.

Conner took a step back.

The dog jumped off the roof, came toward him.

"Don't look in his eyes," Conner said.

Manrico started toward them.

As he had with the people who had gotten like this, Conner tried to send Manrico calming thoughts, but the dog kept leaping through the snow, coming right toward him.

At that moment, a deer—a graceful, careful doe—came out of the woods. Her appearance was so unexpected, her form so exquisite, that even the onrushing Manrico paused and turned.

She had great, soft eyes and long lashes, and a face like a deep song. She walked forward, her narrow legs pushing aside snow that gleamed gold in the sun's long, final rays. Then she sounded, the vaporous whistling that signals alarm in that peaceable race.

Manrico's ears pointed toward her. She came closer, her delicate nose questing in the air, her eyes as calm and dark as midnight lakes.

The Two felt sure that the dog could be drawn away, now that the transmitter was no longer broadcasting its order to kill. He did not understand that the animal's savagery would not end. While he knew he could not control the dog's mind, he could distract him the way he was doing, by appearing to be a succulent deer. He went closer, projecting every single detail of a female deer that he could recall.

Conner's voice said, *Be careful.*

The Two went closer yet.

"Is that really a deer?" Lauren asked.

"Of course it is," Terry said.

Conner took Lauren's hand.

The deer came closer. Manrico looked from her back to Conner. He growled softly, a deadly sound. The deer sounded again, then began limping as a mother deer will when her fawn is threatened.

She was close now, just beyond the fence. Manrico's haunches stiffened, his ears pricked forward, he whined a little. She sounded again and limped, lurching in the snow. That did it: he leaped the fence, barking and howling as he reached her and tore into her throat.

She screamed, then, and suddenly she was not a deer at all, she was a gray and in terrible trouble, being torn apart by the maddened dog. The gray leaped away from Manrico, one arm dangling, his head wobbling horribly.

Conner screamed and ran for the fence, but Lauren tackled him. "No!"

Sparks like fluid began spewing out of the gray. As the dog screamed and twisted against himself, the gray whirled faster and faster, until he became a dervish of sparks and flying fire.

Then he was gone, nothing left but a melted area of snow, some smoking earth, and the seared body of Manrico.

"Get in the car!" Lauren shouted.

They did, but they could go nowhere. "We have to change that tire," Lauren said from the backseat, where she'd gotten in with Conner. "You three stay here, I'll do it."

"I'll help," Conner said.

"No," Lauren said.

"I'll *help!*"

Lauren responded: *No, it's too dangerous.*

Why are you so good at this?

I've been in training for years to be your teacher.

He looked up at her and frowned. "I find teachers extremely boring."

I won't be.

Mike was still out there somewhere, maybe incapacitated but maybe not. She could not expose Conner to the long, clear sightlines that led back to that concealing wood.

Overhead, a dark helicopter appeared, a red cross on its belly. Katelyn and Lauren got out and waved and shouted, but it set down behind the trees, in the clearing where Rob and dead Jimbo Kelton lay.

Terry Kelton, who had refused to get in the car, began to cry, standing on the roadside, holding his head in agony.

Another car appeared, coming from town.

"Careful," Katelyn said.

"Conner," Lauren whispered. "Can you tell?"

"How can he possibly tell?" Katelyn snapped.

Conner closed his eyes and found that he could go racing down the snowy road and look into the car. *It's Paulie. They're okay.*

Thank God.

The grays made me like this?

Yes, they did.

It's never gonna end, is it?

She smiled at him. "Do you want it to?"

He met her eyes, and she found it hard, very hard to look at him. She missed Adam.

Conner suddenly got out of the car.

"Conner!"

"It's okay, Lauren."

The Warners pulled up behind them.

Conner started to walk toward their minivan.

"No," Lauren said, coming up to him, putting her hand on his shoulder. "No."

"Listen," he said, "it's okay. They're not—not affected." He whispered to her. "Let me go."

She released him.

He got into the van.

"You missed it, didn't you?" Paulie asked.

"I got a picture on my phone."

"Mom! Dad! I told you and told you, they missed the riot!" He regarded Conner, his face alight. "There was a whole huge riot in the town and the National Guard's there in Humvees, and it's gonna be on the network news. It was totally incredible, and *you* missed it, lil' fella. Momma had to take you home."

Katelyn leaned in the window. "Dan needs a hospital, we've got to take him to Berryville right now."

FAR ABOVE, A SMALL SILVER dot glittered in the rising light of evening. The worn space inside the little craft where the Three Thieves had lived through so many long ages now was empty. The iron bedsteads where Katelyn and Dan had had their souls mingled, where Marcie had been laid, and Conner, and so many thousands of others over the centuries, stood still and silent.

As if it was alive—which it might be—the little vehicle turned round and round, looking for some place to go. The collective, at a loss, tried to understand how to replace the last triad. But who could do the work of another without training? Their minds were not flexible enough.

There was no place for the little machine, nobody to replace its triad. It hung there, left empty in the sky.

CONNER SAT QUIETLY BETWEEN PAULIE and Amy in the van's third row of seats. In front of them, Mom and Lauren helped his dad.

He could feel his dad suffering, could hear whispers of fear coming from the implant that connected the two of them, but he intended to be very, very careful in listening to what it broadcast, to use it only if it was absolutely necessary. He wanted his dad's love, not his fear.

As he listened to the humming of the tires and the soft voices of the adults, and Terry's miserable sobs, he kept feeling an absence in him, and the more he felt it, the more he came to understand that it was the absence of the collective. For a little while, being part of it had felt like a kind of music in him, and he knew that he could conduct that music, could make it bright and great and true.

One day, perhaps, he would be strong enough to reach the collective on his own, to join it to his mind. Until he could, though, he would be in the most profound sense blind.

He needed the Three Thieves, they were woven into his being, part of him. Without them, he could feel the vague, distant presence of the collective calling to him, *Conner, Conner,* but he could not answer, not without the mind of the Three Thieves to amplify and relay his response.

Conner swept out of his body and through the snowy woods, following a glowing silver wire that connected him to a burned place near the Niederdorfers' fence, where lay a pitiful little mess of rags and sticks and empty black eyes.

Wake up, he said in the secret air of the mind, *come back to me.*

There was stirring in the snow, but only a little, for the damage the Two had endured was very great.

A sentence came to Conner, *Or ever the silver cord be loosed, or the golden bowl be broken . . .* and he knew that it was the love written in the bible, a secret code for those who know.

"Behold," he murmured, "he comes leaping on the mountains . . ."

And in the field, broken flesh fluttered in the night wind.

In the seat in front of him, Terry Kelton sobbed, his head hanging low on his chest.

Conner thought, *I can help him.* He did not know how it was or why it was that he could leave his body so easily. He knew all about out-of-body travel, of course, he'd experimented with it, as he had with remote viewing and all such things, because he understood the physics of superposition, and how it was that the electrons in the brain, during meditation, would become ambiguous, no longer in any one place, and you could use that to prowl in hidden pathways.

He slipped upward and outward, and saw, in his mind's eye, four Air Force guys with two aluminum gurneys in the snow. He looked at the faces of the victims, and saw that John and Mrs. Kelton were alive. "Your mom and dad made it," he told Terry. "You lost your brother and Manrico."

Terry turned around. "How do *you*—"

Conner met his eyes. *Your soul knows,* he said inside himself. Terry blinked, then looked away and was silent for a time. Finally, a whisper: "Thanks for telling me."

Conner had work to do. He brought to mind the Three Thieves as they had appeared last night, dumpy and scared, hiding behind the trees and terrified of making a mistake. He imagined them bobbing along in the night the way they had, so upset about scaring him, so unable to understand how not to.

I need you, he said in his mind.

His thought was met by silence.

They pulled into the Berryville Hospital emergency room. Medical personnel in green oversuits ran up, their portable stretcher rattling on the concrete driveway.

The Air Force helicopter roared into view, dropping down onto the hospital's rooftop helipad.

Can you see who's in it? Lauren asked in his head.

Conner went out of his body again, traveling up to the ceiling . . . and found that he could go through it . . . he saw up the legs of people, then went higher, up through the next ceiling. He was on the roof now, and he could see the Keltons lying strapped to their stretchers.

There was another man there, Lauren's friend, the handsome officer with the mangled hand and the burns.

Then they brought out a fourth man. He had a narrow, careful face and rusty gray hair. He was in agony, his teeth bared, his head turning from side to side as he forced himself not to scream.

He raced back into his body. "It's him," he said, "he's up there."

"Who?" Lauren asked.

Conner knew what she wanted to know. *Your friend.*

Lauren burst into tears.

"Conner, what's the matter with her?" Amy asked.

He shook his head. How could he explain?

"Conner," Lauren whispered. Then, between their minds, *You healed him, didn't you?*

I don't know.

Amy's hand slipped toward his—hesitant, trembling a

little. He took it. She closed her eyes and leaned her head against his shoulder.

Paulie shook his head. "My sis is a piece of work, buddy."

They sat side by side on blue plastic seats in the emergency waiting room. She smiled a little, and he saw one of the silver threads running between the two of them. He looked down at it where it disappeared under his shirt. With his free hand, he tried to touch it, but his hand went through it.

He met her eyes, and saw there a sparkle of love and hope. She closed them, and he saw her face change. She threw back her head and laughed, and he put his arm around her.

"Oh, boy," Paulie said.

"Shut up, little boy," Amy snapped. She kissed Conner on the cheek and giggled.

Mom and a doctor came out of a double door across the room. The doctor said, "Your dad's going to be fine."

Terry went to his feet. Behind the doctor, his parents had also come out. He ran to them, and the family embraced.

Mom sat down beside Conner, and put her arm around him. As he felt the comfort of the two women, his eyes closed.

"He sure goes to sleep fast," Amy said.

"He's your little boyfriend," Paulie said.

"He's been through a lot," Katelyn responded, "he's real tired."

Behind them, a group of uniformed Air Force personnel ran into the emergency room.

"Who are they?" Paulie asked.

As they hurried through the double doors into the emergency room proper, Lauren saw Rob on his stretcher. Uttering a little cry, she went running to him. She held his face in her hands. He opened his eyes. A weak smile came. "You're a hell of a sight," he said, his voice a bare whisper.

She tried to smile. "Is that good or bad?"

"Good, lady. Real good."

She kissed him then.

"Sir?"

Rob turned his head away from her. "Yes, Major?"

"We're detailed to detain Colonel Wilkes."

Lauren said, "Was he in the evac?"

"Yeah," Rob said faintly. "Oh, yeah."

AT THAT MOMENT, CHARLES GUNN was half pulling, half carrying Mike down a hallway. He heard voices behind them and went faster, pushing through an alarmed exit door, setting off a steady beeping behind them.

Charles's TR was there, its hatch glowing with amber light from within. Otherwise it was invisible.

He helped Mike up the ladder, then drew it in behind them. The Air Force officers swarmed out of the hospital exit and began fighting to get into the TR. Charles mercilessly shot one of them, and they all fell back. Leaving Mike in the access tunnel, he slid into the cockpit and hit the stick, causing the fans to whine for a moment as they revved.

Below him, the officers were drawing their guns. He knew how vulnerable the TR was to gunfire, and twisted the flight controls, slamming the power switches all the way down as he did so. The world outside whirled wildly and critical maneuver alarms sounded.

But the hospital spun away below, and the shots that were being fired did no damage. He headed the nose of the craft toward the dark, and was off into the night.

SLEEPING BETWEEN AMY AND HIS mom, Conner dreamed of when the bluets would rise out of the ground along the roadsides and the warblers would come back to Kentucky, and he saw his own backyard going green again, and his dad filling the pool with the garden hose. He dreamed then of the days of summer peace. He woke up a little and murmured, "We're going to be free, all of us."

"We are free," Amy said. "Sort of. Aren't we?"

"Sort of," he said. "But there's a lot more to come."

But in his heart, he despaired, calling, *Come back to me.* Silence continued to be the only response.

"Look here, Conner Callaghan, if you're gonna be my boyfriend, you have to pretend not to be totally geeky. Can you do that?"

He smiled a little. "I'll give it a shot." His eyes fluttered closed and he tried again to find the mind of the collective.

The snow, dark now, slowly covered the body of the Two, and in the ashes of the grain elevator, the curious metal bones of his brothers, also, were dusted with it, deep in the black ruins.

EPILOGUE
LATE AT NIGHT, WHEN THE
DEMONS COME

THEY'D COME HOME, HE AND Mom. Dad had to stay at the hospital for a few days. Lauren was with them, and Conner knew that she was going to live here, she had to, he needed her here.

Late that night, Conner lay wide awake, letting his silent tears flow. He was down in his basement room. Mom was in her bedroom upstairs, and in his mind's eye, he could see her sleeping. Lauren was awake.

He went upstairs. She sat in the living room, sipping from a tall glass.

"Conner!"

"Hi."

"Can't sleep?"

"I'm wide awake."

"Me, too." She held up her drink. "Want a sip?"

He shook his head. "They make me drink wine at dinner. One of Dad's many theories. Every time you do that, did you know that you kill about six thousand neurons?"

"I've heard that."

"I need all my neurons."

"Come sit beside me." She patted the couch and he came close to her. "Are you scared, Conner?"

"Oh, yes." He looked out the dark glass doors that opened onto the deck. It was bright outside now, a low moon making the snow shine softly.

Conner.

"I want to just talk, okay? I don't like to do that mind stuff."

"I didn't."

"Yeah, you did, you said my name."

Conner.

"I heard that, too, but it's not me."

Could it be? But no. He sighed. "My friends are dead."

"Your friends? The Kelton boy?"

"Yeah, him too. But I mean—you know—the ones we're not supposed to talk about. I need them, Lauren. I'm lost without them."

"I feel that way about my friend. He was a gray, but they're not really monsters at all, they're full of need and hope, and—" She stopped, looked down at him. He was so small, just an ordinary little kid, narrow shoulders, soft, unfinished face, all promise and potential.

"You miss him, then?"

"Earlier, I could feel him in you, sort of, and that was nice. It was like being home again, a little bit."

He thought about that. "Boy, if people heard us talking about this stuff, they would think we were weird."

She sensed that he didn't want to address the matter of Adam. And why would he? Adam had died for him, and that would be very hard to face. "I'm in the military," she said. "My friend, he was in his military, sort of. The grays' military of the spirit. I mean, they have no actual army, as such. In the military, though, we always know that death is part of it. Oh, you don't think about it, you think about life. But death is part of it."

She had to stop. She did not want him to hear the tears in her voice.

Conner?

He blinked, sat up straighter, stared toward the deck. That wasn't Lauren, she was leaning over with her eyes closed and full of tears, almost about to spill her drink.

He got up.

"Going back to bed?"

He hardly heard her. He went out on the deck.

"Conner?"

The night was huge and hollow, the sky aflame with

stars. It was cutting cold, but it felt good, somehow, as if
the winter night belonged to his grief.

She came out behind him, and then Mom did, too.
Mom brought his coat. He had big lamb's wool slippers
on already. "What are we doing at three A.M.? May I
know?"

Then, through the skeletal trees, there came a glow. It
flickered and was gone.

"Is that a flashlight?" his mother asked.

But Conner was off, racing down the deck stairs and
across the hard frozen yard. "You guys," he yelled, his
voice slapping the deep silence.

He plunged through the woods, pushing twigs aside,
getting scratched by branches. Then he stumbled into
the stubbly field and saw hanging there just a hundred
yards away, the little ship that had started the whole
thing.

It wasn't glowing much now. In fact, there was just this
flickering blue light playing across its skin. As he approached it, he saw that it was bigger than it looked.

"Conner! Conner, be careful!"

Take care of her, Lauren. Tell her I'm okay.

Are you?

I have no idea.

He went closer to the thing. It was making a sort of rattling sound, like ball bearings clicking together in something that was turning slowly, just ticking over. There was a
round opening, not a hatch, just an opening. Inside, he
could see the wooden framework that held the thin outer
skin. He pushed at it, and it wobbled slightly in the air.

He peered in.

Then his mother was there. "No," she said in a voice
harsh with terror, "we have to get away!"

"Mom, hey."

"Conner, Conner run!" She pulled at him, she started to
drag him away.

"NO!" He shook her off. He lifted himself inside, and
saw, sitting on a little bench, three very tattered and
bedraggled grays.

"You guys?"

They stirred, backing away.

You guys.

Thank you, came a nervous reply in that innocent, mechanical-sounding voice of theirs. *Thank you for our lives.*

I brought you back to life?

Conner, we're part of you.

"Conner! Oh, God, Conner!" Mom came pushing and crashing in. Her eyes were filmed with tears, glaring, her face pouring with sweat despite the cold. She bared her teeth like the wild animal Conner knew she had become. "I remember this thing," she hissed, "and it's terrible, Conner, it's *evil.*"

The Three Thieves had backed against the wall. Inside his mind, they moaned and cried.

Stay calm, Conner projected to them. Then he said aloud, "Mom, I want you to sit down."

There were two narrow black gurneys against the far wall.

When she saw them, she went practically rigid. The hands of the grays went up to their cheeks, the mouths opened. They pressed themselves against the wall as hard as they could.

"Conner, this place—this is where—" She looked at the narrow iron gurneys. "Oh my God." Then her face changed. "It was always a sort of nightmare. I didn't think it was . . . this." She went to the gurneys, touched one of them. "I remember," she said in a suddenly loud voice. "I remember it all."

Conner saw her change and become a girl again, just as Amy had become a woman before his eyes a few hours ago. She was a beautiful, blond girl, freckled, in a white summer nightgown.

And then there were stars all around her, and he saw a boy on the gurney beside her, and the stars surrounded them both.

When the vision ended, Mom was sitting on the edge of one of the gurneys, stroking the ugly black metal. "Conner," she whispered, "this is where your dad and I were brought together. Right here."

He went beside her, put an arm around her shoulders.

"If they hadn't done this, then my whole life . . . I never would have found Dad." She shook her head. "Conner, they made us, they made our family." She looked at him, and now her eyes were soft mother's eyes. She hugged him to her.

Slowly, carefully, or rather, as carefully as the clumsy Thieves could manage, they came out of their hiding place and drew closer.

Conner heard the one say, *Let's touch her.*

The Two replied, *We can't do that!*

The Three asked, *What do we do?*

"Mom, put out your hand."

She tried to, but it was shaking too much. Conner took it in his hand, and together they reached out to the Three, and their hands touched.

Mom snatched her hand back. "It shocked me!"

Don't do that!

We're scared!

"They won't do it again," Conner told her.

This time, she reached out and touched the face of the Three, and he, with his own hand shaking like a leaf, touched her face, and the One and the Two came close, and the five of them formed a circle.

A sound rose in Conner's mind, the great humming song he had heard before, the voice of the collective raised in hope and joy.

Then there came ringing. The Three Thieves rushed to the far wall. The voice of the collective faded.

What's going on in there? Lauren asked.

"Mom, answer your phone."

The Thieves looked at each other. Katelyn fumbled out her cell phone, listened for a moment. "We'll be there," she said. She closed her phone. "Dad's awake and he wants us." She started for the hatch—and looked out on a field racing away, houses spinning in the starlight, then darkness. "Conner, they've kidnapped us!"

Then there was a thud outside, and light came in the opening. Another thud, and more light. Conner joined his mother at the edge of the opening. "You know what this is?"

"No, Conner! Is it another planet, because your poor father—"

"Come on, Mother."

He helped her down onto the hospital helipad, which had been flooded by automatic lighting as soon as the Thieves' craft landed on it. The thuds had been the switches turning on the floodlamps.

They had not gone two steps before the body of the craft blazed bright and the Thieves shot off into the night.

Conner heard faintly in his head, *Where are you? Conner! They took us to the hospital, Lauren.*

An orderly came out of a door and trotted across the helipad toward them. "Where is your emergency?" he shouted. He looked around. "Excuse me, but what's going on here?"

"We're here to see a patient," Katelyn announced. "Dan Callaghan."

"But what? Uh, oh, okay. Did you come by medevac? Where's the chopper?"

"He was in a hurry," Katelyn said. "And so are we."

They went down then, along a green-tiled corridor and into a room filled with equipment, and there in the bed was Dad.

Conner let Katelyn go to him. She bent and gingerly kissed him. His eyes met hers, and they kissed more. Then Conner went close, and the family was whole again.

High above, three others—people also, but of a very different shape—came together, also, arm in arm.

Lauren drove like a madwoman along snowy roads, skidding into the hospital emergency entrance. She left her car where it happened to stop against a curb and sprinted into the building.

She ran down a hallway, vaulted stairs, then turned a corner and burst into Dan Callaghan's room breathing hard.

She stopped, stunned by what she saw.

The Callaghan family had come to the end of something. Instead of huddling together, perhaps weeping, cursing God and their fate, they were all asleep. On the bed, Conner lay beside his father, who snored softly. Katelyn sat in a chair beside the bed, her head back, her mouth open. Her hand lay along the sheets, her fingers touching her husband's bandaged arm. His good arm was around his son.

As she stood in the doorway, she thought how very innocent they still were, even after all they had done and seen.
And that boy, with his dusting of beard just barely visible
along his lip, what dreams must he be dreaming in the
ocean of thought that he now contained?

She came into the room, went to the bedside, looked
down at them. How extraordinarily resilient people were.
Had she been asked before this, she would have said that
they'd have needed sedatives or even straitjackets, but that
underestimated the power of the human heart and the simple, central thing that is the family.

She bent over and kissed Conner's downy cheek. He
made no move, no sigh of awareness. She tried to make
herself quiet in her mind. The Callaghans might be at
peace, but in her mind there lived demons, the demon of
fear-of-future, the demon of distrust, the demon of
danger-of-deceit.

She got the one chair that was not in use and stepped
across to the doorway. She sat down, angling the chair so
that she could see both the Callaghans, the dark window
behind them, and the gleaming, silent hallway.

"May I help you?" a passing nurse asked.

"No, no, I'm fine."

"His vitals are good."

"I know."

The nurse smiled slightly, then walked off, her footsteps
clicking on the gray floor. Lauren watched, methodically,
first the hall, then the window, then the Callaghans. For
what, she was not sure. Perhaps for nothing. Perhaps the
fight was truly ended, and Conner would be able to enter
his training.

But where would it lead? What was she to do?

She laughed a little to herself. How absurd that question
was. It would lead beyond imagination, past the edge of the
known world.

Three o'clock, an alarm beeped in another room, and
nurses hurried past. Half past, the wind came, rattling the window. Conner sighed and muttered words that brought to Lauren's mind the tone of prayer. She prayed, then, to Conner's
favorite god—that is to say, whatever one happens to be real.

The spirit of man had triumphed this day. Ignition had been achieved. Now, the ascent.

She watched through the deeper hours, watched and waited for the dawn.

2012

WHITLEY STRIEBER

THE WAR FOR SOULS BEGINS!

SEPTEMBER 2007

Every 26,000 years, Earth lines up with the exact center of our galaxy. On December 21, 2012, it will happen again. Ancient Maya calculated that this event would mark the end, not only of this age, but of human consciousness as we know it. But what will actually happen? Whitley Strieber presents a frightening End Days scenario: three parallel universes collide, igniting a terrifying war for possession of every human soul!

Hardcover • 0-7653-1896-2 • www.tor.com

Visit the author's official website at www.unknowncountry.com